P9-BJA-279

COLLECTED WORKS OF A.M. KLEIN

SHORT STORIES

EDITED BY M.W. STEINBERG

A.M. Klein's reputation as a writer rests on his poetry and to a lesser extent on his remarkable poetic novel *The Second Scroll*. But he also wrote short stories over a period of more than a quarter of a century. Until now few people have been aware of these; many exist only in manuscript form, and most of those that were published appeared in magazines not readily accessible to the general reading public. This volume brings them together.

Klein's range of themes and styles in his short fiction, as in his poetry and in his journalistic writing, is broad. He draws on his Jewish experience, focusing on legends, festivals, and ceremonies, well-known character types, and familiar aspects of Jewish life – in the synagogue, in the home, and on the streets. Klein was not limited, however, by his Jewish concerns. He also wrote social and political satire and parodies of the detective story and of literary debates. His pervasive sense of humour is often closely associated with his feeling for the macabre, producing a quality of black comedy that is distinctively Kleinian.

The stories in this volume are an invaluable addition to the canon of Klein's works and their publication will extend and reinforce his already considerable reputation.

M.W. STEINBERG is Professor of English at the University of British Columbia and co-editor with Usher Caplan of *Beyond Sambation: Selected Essays and Editorials 1928–1955.*

A.M. KLEIN

Short Stories

EDITED BY
M.W. STEINBERG

UNIVERSITY OF TORONTO PRESS
Toronto Buffalo London

© University of Toronto Press 1983
Toronto Buffalo London
Printed in Canada

ISBN 0-8020-5598-2 (cloth)
ISBN 0-8020-6469-8 (paper)

Canadian Cataloguing in Publication Data

Klein, A.M. (Abraham Moses), 1909–1972.
Short stories
(Collected works of A.M. Klein; v. 2)
ISBN 0-8020-5598-2 (bound). – ISBN 0-8020-6469-8 (pbk.)
I. Steinberg, M.W. (Moses Wolfe), 1918–   II. Title.
III. Series: Klein, A.M. (Abraham Moses), 1909–1972.
Collected works; v. 2.
PS8521.L45A159 1983   c813'.54   c82-095347-4
PR9199.3.K588A15 1983

40, 231

FRONTISPIECE: Klein in the mid-1940s.
Public Archives Canada, PA 125749

This book has been published with the help of grants from the Canadian
Federation for the Humanities, using funds provided by the Social
Sciences and Humanities Research Council of Canada, and from the
Canada Council and the Ontario Arts Council under their block grant
programs.

Contents

INTRODUCTION vii

Epistle Theological 3
Prophet in Our Midst: A Story for Passover 14
By the Profit of a Beard 18
The Lost Twins 24
The Triumph of Zalman Tiktiner 30
The Parliament of Fowles: A Short Story 35
The Chanukah Dreidel 43
The Meed of the Minnesinger: A Vivid Short Story Based on
    the Life of a Great Thirteenth-Century Poet 49
Master of the Horn 62
The Parrot and the Goat 68
The Bald-Headed Monarch 73
Too Many Princes 78
Once upon a Time ... 83
Shmelka 89
The Seventh Scroll 97
Blood and Iron: A Satire on Modern German Ideology 111
Friends, Romans, Hungrymen 116
Beggars I Have Known 121
A Myriad-Minded Man 125
Whom God Hath Joined 154
Yclept a Pip 175
No Traveller Returns ... 185
Portrait of an Executioner 191

vi   Contents

The Tale of the Marvellous Parrot 201
Memoirs of a Campaigner 205
Detective Story, or A Likely Story 210
We Who Are About to Be Born: A Parable 213
One More Utopia 217
The Trail of 'Clupea Harengus': The Scientific Detective
    Story and How She Is Writ for Summer Reading 224
Kapusitchka 232
... And It Shall Come to Pass 236
And the Mome Raths Outgrabe 240
Letter from Afar 255
A Fable 272
The Bells of Sobor Spasitula 275

TEXTUAL NOTES AND EMENDATIONS 309
NOTES 319

Introduction

A.M. Klein's reputation as a writer rests on his poetry and to a lesser extent on his remarkable poetic novel *The Second Scroll*. Rarely, if ever, is mention made of his short stories, although he wrote many over a span of more than a quarter of a century. The reason for this neglect lies primarily in a general unawareness of their existence. Many of the stories are in manuscript form only and very many of those that were published appeared in a relatively small magazine, *The Judaean*, a monthly paper of the Young Judaea movement in Canada, and in a weekly Anglo-Jewish paper, *The Canadian Jewish Chronicle*. Neither of these papers was widely read by the general public and copies are not readily accessible. Furthermore, the published stories, for the most part, appeared well before Klein's first volume of poetry drew attention to him as a writer.

Abraham Moses Klein, born in 1909, lived virtually his entire life in Montreal, where the Jewish community existed in most respects as a self-contained ethnic entity. His immigrant parents were poor – his father was a presser in a clothing factory – but Klein's recollections of his early life are happy ones. His parents were pious Jews who carefully observed the Sabbath and religious holidays and followed the prescribed laws and customs of orthodox Judaism. Klein's father, a learned man himself, valued learning. He not only sent his son to a Hebrew school, as most Jewish parents did, but also provided him with a series of private tutors. Abe Klein, an excellent pupil in both his secular and Hebrew religious education, for a time seriously considered studying for the rabbinate. His first published story, 'Epistle Theological,' in part reflects an inner debate regarding his vocation, a characteristically logical yet humorous analysis of the problem, which he resolved by opting for a career in a secular profession, law. In the fall of 1926 he enrolled in the arts program at McGill University.

While at McGill, Klein became very active in the Zionist youth movement, Canadian Young Judaea. He served as national education director and edited its monthly magazine, *The Judaean*, from 1928 to 1932 and shortly after was for a term national president. In addition to the editorials and articles that he wrote for *The Judaean*, he contributed many poems and short stories. Nine of the thirteen stories that he wrote during this period appeared first in *The Judaean*. To some extent the kind of stories that he wrote was influenced by his readership – Jewish youths ranging from approximately twelve to eighteen years of age – and by his purpose to heighten through literature their Jewish awareness. In an article called 'Jewish Folk Songs,' published in *The Judaean* in 1932, Klein wrote that the quality and flavour of Jewish life in eastern Europe are epitomized in folk songs, which provide 'sufficient material wherewith to conjure up, as by incantation, the phantom of that picturesque past.' What he says here of the folk songs applies as well to the folk tales and other fictional accounts which convey essential characteristics of a way of life. Klein's stories at this time were very much in the tradition of the great Jewish short story writers such as I.L. Peretz, Chaim Nachman Bialik, Sholom Aleichem, and S.J. Agnon. These stories often centred about Jewish holidays and ceremonies – the Sabbath, Chanukah, Purim, Passover, Yom Kippur – and frequently involved goats, demons, mystical or saintly visitants, and Solomonic legends. The characters, aside from the occasional otherworldly intruders, include the half-wit, the 'shlimazl,' and a wide range of well-known community figures such as the scribe, the scholar, the 'baal tekiah' (master of the horn). Like many of the stories of his predecessors, some of Klein's such as 'By the Profit of a Beard,' 'Master of the Horn,' and 'The Seventh Scroll' realistically depict aspects of Jewish life: activities in the school and the synagogue, in the home and on the street; domestic and social relationships; the presence of anti-semitism and the yearning for Zion. But Klein also, like his predecessors, often went beyond the realistic. In early 1931 he criticized Lion Feuchtwanger's book *Success* not only because it was too long and complicated but because of its ultra-realism, 'where no detail is omitted and all is recorded with mathematical precision.'[1] In the following year Klein wrote scornfully of the rationalists who denigrate mysticism and leave no room outside of natural law and scientific hypotheses or syllogisms. 'Immune to parable and impervious to metaphor' they condemn that which they cannot understand – the mystic's poetic way of speaking truth and reality.[2] Klein's animal stories and fairy-tales, which stem from his romantic imagination working within and beyond the framework of ordinary experience, express the poetic way.

Clearly Klein's mind and imagination, as seen in his early stories, were shaped by his experiences in his predominantly Jewish world and by the Yiddish and Hebrew literature with which he was familiar. The subject-matter of these stories parallels in many respects that of his poems written during the same period, particularly those in the poem sequences 'Portraits of a Minyan,' 'Of Sundry Folk,' 'Of Kings and Beggars,' and 'Of Holy Vessels' in *Hath Not a Jew*. The tone is also comparable: in both we find a similar blending of wit and whimsy, and a somewhat irreverent, half-teasing affection for his people and their ways. There is a similar tendency towards a characteristic blending of sentimentality – tenderness or pathos – and wry humour, the humour reflecting a delight in the human comedy, and at the same time the need to hold in check the sentimentality – to keep at some distance the situations that stirred the story-teller's own deep feelings, or his strong inclination towards the rhetorical, or the lyrical and lovely. This ambivalence in tone, seen clearly, for example, in the abrupt reversal at the conclusion of 'The Parliament of Fowles,' is characteristic of Klein's stories.

Although Klein was undoubtedly aware of his connection with the traditional Jewish short story writers, and conscious, even as W.B. Yeats was, of the importance of literature in arousing and heightening cultural sensitivity, he did not write as an apologist, propagandist, or educator. His primary purpose was not didactic. He was a story-teller who sought to entertain and loved to entertain. He took delight in the exercise of his imagination and fancy, in his witty handling of words and situations, and in his presentation of people with their rich variety of follies, virtues, and yearnings.

Even in these early stories, written largely within the tradition of the Jewish writers, dealing with similar situations and characters, in somewhat the same tone and within more or less the same framework of values, Klein was no mere imitator. He imposed on his material his own idiosyncratic impress. The setting for many of these stories is the Canadian urban scene and the situations that develop grow out of a Canadian-Jewish context, not a middle or eastern European ghetto. There is far less emphasis on poverty and the physical deprivations and suffering that follow from it, and more on the stresses that come from blows to one's dignity or self-esteem, such as occur in 'By the Profit of a Beard,' 'Master of the Horn,' and to some extent 'Shmelka.' Although there is in such stories the familiar setting of the ghetto environment, and the situations involve familiar ceremonies, religious and folk practices, and easily recognizable Jewish character-types, the themes such as the awareness of encroaching and enfeebling old age transcend the parochial atmosphere and setting.

The romanticism that underlies most of Klein's early stories, whether it derives from the play of fantasy in a faery or animal world, the exotic settings of the Middle East or of the medieval world, or the affectionate relationship between children or husband and wife, is often held in check or undercut by Klein's sense of play. It is also altered at times by his acute realism, which prevented him from simply acquiescing in a lovely end to a tender tale, and provoked rather a pathetic, even bitterly ironic conclusion. The use of heightened antithetical tones, often unexpectedly introduced, reverses and deflates our expectations, producing at times an effect that is merely comic but on occasion the suggestion of the presence of a malignant fate. The rather sardonic ending to 'The Seventh Scroll' reflects an aspect of Klein's developing dark vision of life that recurs frequently in his later stories. A comparison between Klein's story and Agnon's 'The Tale of a Scribe,' based on a very similar initial situation and pattern of events, clearly reveals the individuality of Klein's handling of his material. In both stories a poor but very skilled and pious scribe and his gentle wife live an almost exemplary life of tender love and devotion to each other and to his work. In both, the couples are childless, a source of abiding grief to them, but a condition that deepens their love for one another. In both stories the wife dies young and the scribe determines to write and dedicate a Scroll in her name which would serve in lieu of a son as a memorial and as a supplicant, a substitute sayer of Kaddish for the repose of the wife's soul in Heaven. The Agnon story, lyrically and lovingly told, ends with the joyous reunion of the couple in Heaven; the Klein story drastically reverses this outcome. The scribe in 'The Seventh Scroll' is persuaded to remarry so that he can more easily accomplish his task, but his second wife is a harsh shrew who makes his life bitter. Klein describes with realistic detail the degradation and defeat of the scribe. The vision of life that emerges here is one in which evil, social and metaphysical, and frustration, defeat, and suffering, make the worthwhileness of life questionable.

While at McGill (1926–30) and later at the University of Montreal, from where he graduated in law in 1933, Klein broadened the scope of his interests and his circle of friends. He became identified with the literary circle that included A.J.M. Smith, Frank Scott, and Leon Edel, and was influenced by Smith's emphasis on the seventeenth-century metaphysical poets and on such contemporary poets as T.S. Eliot and W.B. Yeats. Klein wrote a semi-humorous column for The McGill Daily, and for a short time in 1930 edited a literary magazine, The McGilliad, in which 'The Parliament of Fowles' appeared. For the most part, however, during his university years the time and energy that he could spare from his studies were devoted to his Jewish interests, particularly his Zionist work through Young Judaea. In 1932 he spoke of his years in Young Judaea as 'the most felicitous and the most constructive years of my life.'[3]

Klein's position vis-à-vis the Jewish and the non-Jewish communities was, however, increasingly ambivalent. In what is in some respects his most important early short story, 'The Meed of the Minnesinger,' Klein explores the question of the artist and his relation to his work and his society – a concern that continued throughout his career and deepened towards the end of his creative period in the 1950s. Susskind von Trimberg, an accomplished thirteenth-century poet passionately dedicated to his art, is unwilling to work within the limits of his own culture, feeling that his obligation to his art and to the creative impulse within himself transcends his obligation to his own society. Despite his father's pleading he turns away from the traditional Jewish ways and values to find freer expression for his art and what he believes will be a larger and fitter audience. But he discovers to his sorrow that this audience is crass and unappreciative. Prompted by jealousy and prejudice, they taunt him because of his Jewishness and humiliate him. For Klein himself, the problem did not present itself in quite these terms. Unlike Susskind, he was profoundly loyal to his people, its culture and its fate, and indeed he was inclined to subordinate or to use his creative literary talents when necessary to champion the Jewish cause. Nor is there any evidence that he suffered directly and personally from anti-semitism in his literary career. He did object, however, to being labelled a Jewish poet, and he resented the slighting criticism and neglect of his first volume of poetry, *Hath Not a Jew*, on the grounds that his subject-matter was limited and parochial. His aim was to create a worthy literature out of the amalgam within himself of the two cultures, Jewish and English, and he believed that he succeeded, but his view, for much of his literary life, was not widely shared.

In the mid-thirties Klein continued his efforts within the Jewish community: he became president of Canadian Young Judaea in 1934 and for a short while was editor of *The Canadian*

Zionist. Other forces, however, were directing his attention to issues and conditions outside these central and specifically Jewish interests. His initial experiences as a lawyer during the period of the Great Depression not only left him with much idle time on his hands, but also presented him with some serious financial worries. In the opening of 'Whom God Hath Joined,' a story written at this time, he conveys briefly the anxiety of a young lawyer dimly hoping for clients. The dismal economic conditions and the political unrest accompanying the Depression – the rise of fascism and the civil war in Spain – became an increasing concern that found expression not only in such poems as 'Diary of Abraham Segal, Poet' and 'Barricade Smith – His Speeches,' but also in Klein's fiction. His grimly absurd story of the rise of a Nazi dictator, 'Blood and Iron,' was published in 1936 and followed by two 'Depression' stories – 'Friends, Romans, Hungrymen' and 'Beggars I Have Known,' published in left-liberal magazines. In the latter two stories, Klein experimented somewhat with surrealistic effects, achieving a quality of strangeness, or even madness, a pattern of responses outside what we regard as our rational norms, a quality rather reminiscent of some of Kafka's stories. These stories present an absurd, chaotic world that attaches no value to the lives of people and is unresponsive to their needs. The disintegration of the narrator in 'Friends, Romans, Hungrymen' reflects a disintegrating society. Klein's interest in the bizarre took on a ghoulish aspect in his grippingly told story 'No Traveller Returns ...' and to a slighter extent in 'Portrait of an Executioner.' In the longest, most complex story written during this period, 'A Myriad-Minded Man,' Klein presents as his central characters a strange pair of egotistical adventurers – Godfrey Somers, sadistically arrogant, and Isaiah Ellenbogen, whose ego-directed and compulsive intellectuality leads him into dangerously perverse ideologies. Klein's view of his world floundering futilely in an economic morass and increasingly beset by evil doctrines and violent political forces, was obviously darkening.

From the early 1930s on, Klein was a frequent contributor to *The Canadian Jewish Chronicle,* a weekly Anglo-Jewish newspaper published in Montreal. In 1938, after he returned to Montreal from Rouyn, where he briefly practised law, he was appointed editor of the paper. For the next seventeen years he contributed editorials, articles, reviews, poems, stories, and commentaries on current events – a remarkable performance that effectively chronicled the times and revealed many facets of Klein's character and personality, his learning and literary skill. Usher Caplan sums up well Klein's journalistic achievement:

> Quite by chance, Klein's term of editorship coincided with the most terrible and most glorious years in modern Jewish history. In his empathic sensitivity to the events of those years, Klein spoke personally for a nation, thereby revealing the complete range of his own emotions – his fears, his pain and despair, his quixotic outrage in the face of injustice, his sardonic wittiness, even his sometimes ghoulish attraction to the humorous side of tragedy, and his rare moments of jubilation.[4]

Klein's responsibility for weekly editorials and comments on the news, his role as spokesman for his people to the general public, championing their causes, compelled him to immerse himself deeply and constantly in contemporary affairs. He had continually to respond to the evil evident in the world around him – fascism and its attendant anti-semitism, increasing violence and treachery by individual leaders and governments, the plight of refugees driven out by dictators and turned away by democracies, the horror of the Holocaust. While in his editorials and other public statements Klein maintained a brave, defiant front, voicing courage and optimism, we see further signs of a darkening vision in his short stories and in such poems as 'Psalm vi,' where he gives voice to his anger and despair.

In an unpublished story, 'Detective Story, or A Likely Story,' probably written in 1943, Klein pictures the creation of the world, its existence, and its end as one vast master criminal joke. In 'We Who Are About to Be Born' he depicts our world as an abhorrent place from which an unborn soul destined to sojourn here recoils, desperately pleading to be spared such a fate. 'One More Utopia,' an anti-Utopian science fantasy, is presented as a parable for our times. Stability and order are seemingly achieved through creating a 'mass man' population, a society in which all differences are eliminated – a totalitarian vision carried to its logical extreme. Even though Klein shows confidence in human nature in that beyond a certain point the people subjected to this process of de-individuation rebel, asserting their individuality as the precious essence of their being, the final scene in the story is one of upheaval and destruction.

Not all of Klein's stories in the 1940s strike so sombre a note. Klein was an avid reader of detective stories, and his fascination with this sub-genre and with the world of criminals, crimes, trials, and executions is not only evident in 'Whom God Hath Joined,' 'No Traveller Returns ... ,' 'Portrait of an Executioner,' and in his poem 'Sleuth,' but also in an unfinished story, 'Hapaxlegomenon,' in which the central character, whose background parallels Klein's closely, after becoming a somewhat unsuccessful and bored lawyer abandons that profession to become a detective. Klein, with his yearning for the romantic and the dramatic and his keen analytic mind, was fascinated by the detective's role. In real life he probably never seriously entertained the notion of becoming one, but he liked to let his mind play with the notion. In 'The Trail of "Clupea Harengus"' he playfully parodies the genre.

A light-hearted parody of a different sort, reflecting another area of Klein's experience and interest, is the literary satire 'And the Mome Raths Outgrabe.' At least from the time of his involvement with the McGill poets in the late 1920s, Klein evinced an interest in literary criticism. In many articles and reviews he made his own values and opinions clear.[5] In 1945 he was appointed for a three-year term to a Visiting Lectureship in Poetry at McGill University. It was a very pleasant and for a while exciting experience for him, but though he enjoyed his work, he did not feel deeply committed to teaching or to the scholarly profession. This daily involvement with literary criticism and his semi-detached attitude towards it enabled him to regard with an amused eye the deadly seriousness of the professional critics, and in 'And the Mome Raths Outgrabe' he parodied zestfully the debate at a supposed meeting of the Modern Languages Association in which the critics project with increasing clamour and fierceness their own personalities and pet theories.

The end of World War II saw a sharp diminishing of Klein's anxiety over anti-semitism and the fate of the Western democracies, and of the Jewish people in particular. He allowed himself to be drawn, reluctantly, into politics, probably through the persuasion of his old friend from high school and McGill days, David Lewis, who was already then one of the national leaders of the CCF party. He permitted his name to stand as candidate for the CCF in the Cartier riding in Montreal, but withdrew it before the election. In 1949 he was again persuaded to stand, and this time he was badly defeated – a rather embittering experience, for Klein felt he deserved better from a constituency that was largely Jewish. In a tone of self-disgust he recorded in his diary his regret at this venture into party politics. His distaste for the political game probably reinforced his awareness, developed in the 1930s and 1940s, of the general dearth of principled, enlightened political leaders. In his satire 'A Fable,' which appeared as an editorial in *The Canadian Jewish Chronicle* in 1952, Klein returned to his earlier animal tales, but, perhaps prompted by George Orwell's *Animal Farm*, he used the fable to express his own political concerns as he mocked the hypocritical stances of the great powers debating peace and disarmament in the United Nations.

All was clearly not well in the world as Klein presented it in his short stories. The existence of the atomic bomb with its threat of world annihilation was for Klein, as for most concerned people, a nightmarish fact, as he makes clear in his story '... And It Shall Come to Pass.' The rapid cooling of relations between the Soviet Union and the Western powers by 1950 resulted in the beginning of the cold war. Klein's dislike for the totalitarian aspect of Soviet communism and his fear of the regimentation of mind and body involved in the attempt to establish a monolithic society, attitudes that were frequently reiterated from his earliest writings on, found renewed expression in the post-war era not only in editorials but in his fiction as well. The Soviet purges in the late 1930s appalled Klein because of their harshness and the outrageousness of the procedures, but they fascinated him because the victims seemed so willing, even eager, to confess and convict themselves. His frequent allusions to these events in his journalism attest to his continuing interest in this political and psychological phenomenon. The spy ring investigation and the ensuing trials in Ottawa following Igor Gouzenko's defection in 1945 sharpened this interest in the world of intrigue and manipulation. Klein wrote a quasi-historical novel, 'That Walks Like a Man,' still unpublished, dealing with this dramatic episode, and a short story, 'Letter from Afar,' also unpublished, in which he imaginatively explores what he conjectures to be the basis of the strange confessions of guilt, seemingly unforced, in obviously staged and most unjudicial performances.

One of the most hateful and disastrous consequences of the totalitarian mentality, for Klein, particularly as it found expression under Joseph Stalin, was the way it viewed art and the artist. In 1932 he protested against the opinion voiced by communists that literature must serve the party purpose, the class revolution, or support the communist state, an attitude that perverts art into propaganda and squeezes life, which in its fullness is the province of the artist whose work belongs to all ages and people, into 'a preordained ideological mould.'[6] Plato banished poets from his republic, Klein remarks, but Stalin uses them. In 1930 he praised the poet J.I. Segal for avoiding in his descriptions of the sorrows of penury any didactic note which would exhort the reader to become class-conscious. 'Our carmine comrades, votaries of proletarian literature, may look askance at such taciturnity – they would prefer to see his poem end with propaganda writ in red italics, they would be pleased, if it not only adorned a penurious tale, but also if it pointed a Marxian moral.'[7]

Inseparable from the problem of the perversion of art into propaganda is the question of censorship. For those who would not let themselves be used as ideological tools, there was enforced silence. In a review of Isaak Babel's volume of short stories, *Benya Krik, the Gangster*, Klein laments the unexplained silence of this 'extremely talented Russian-Jewish writer' and he agrees with those who explain it on the grounds that under Stalin's rule 'only Stalin can be ambivalent; the rest must speak out (in one sense) or shut up (in all senses).'[8] Somewhat earlier in the same year (1948), Klein wrote an editorial entitled 'Sha! Sha! Shostakovich!' in which he criticized the Soviet effort to exercise political control over the Russian composers Prokofiev and Shostakovich, and to dictate what was suitable music.[9] This topic, handled rather mockingly in the editorial, became the subject of Klein's last and in many respects his best story, 'The Bells of Sobor Spasitula.' The probable date of the typescript is 1955. The Soviet artist in this story is silenced by the authorities.

The artist, however, in Klein's view, suffered not only in totalitarian countries. In the late 1940s and 1950s Klein was increasingly preoccupied with the role of the artist in Western societies as well. Here the pressure was on the artist to sell his talent through the media and cater to the mass taste, or turn his talent into more directly rewarding commercial channels. In an unfinished story, 'The Inverted Tree,' Klein, through his central character who in many respects resembles himself, describes the forces that compel a gifted writer to abandon his craft and become a huckster, a writer of slick advertisements. To some extent Klein himself engaged in such a practice in the 1940s and early 1950s, regarding his speech-writing for the philanthropist-distiller Samuel Bronfman and his public relations work for Seagrams as a surrender of his artistic integrity. If the artist, however, is to maintain his integrity, Klein felt, he must pay a high price: he incurs the neglect or hostility of his community. The dedicated artist is isolated and though in his response he 'makes of his status as zero a rich garland, / a halo of his anonymity,' he, sadly, '... lives alone, and in his secret shines / like phosphorus. At the bottom of the sea' ('Portrait of the Poet as Landscape,' *The Rocking Chair and Other Poems*).

In one of his very late writings, an exegetical essay on Joseph, 'The Bible's Archetypical Poet,' Klein presented Joseph as the artist rejected by his brothers, condemned, and sold into slavery.[10] Klein's retreat into his long silence, which began about 1955, when he was just reaching the height of his powers, at least as a fiction writer, may well have been in part his response to a society that he believed did not listen – or if it paid attention, it did so only to pervert art into propaganda or commercialism.

A.M. Klein died in August 1972, after almost seventeen years of silence.

NOTES

1 *The McGilliad*, January 1931
2 'White Magic,' *The Canadian Jewish Chronicle*, 7 October 1932
3 *The Judaean*, June 1932
4 Usher Caplan, *Like One That Dreamed* (Toronto: McGraw-Hill Ryerson, Ltd 1982) 81
5 For a discussion of some of Klein's views on the aims and values of literature, see my article 'The Conscience of Art: A.M. Klein on Poets and Poetry,' in *A Political Art: Essays and Images in Honour of George Woodcock*, ed. William H. New (Vancouver: University of British Columbia Press 1978) 82–94.
6 'Proletarian Poetry,' *The Canadian Jewish Chronicle*, 5 August 1932
7 'Baal Shem in Modern Dress,' *ibid.*, 14 November 1930
8 'Isaak Babel,' *ibid.*, 10 September 1948
9 'Sha! Sha! Shostakovich!,' *ibid.*, 20 February 1948
10 'The Bible's Archetypical Poet,' *ibid.*, 6, 13, 20 March 1953

Acknowledgments

I am grateful to all fellow members of the A.M. Klein Research and Publication Committee (Usher Caplan, Mark Finkelstein, Gretl Fischer, Noreen Golfman, Colman Klein, Sandor Klein, Tom Marshall, Seymour Mayne, Zailig Pollock, and Robert Taylor) for their guidance in the preparation of this book. I am particularly indebted to Usher Caplan for his valuable suggestions and criticism at every stage in the editing of the stories, and to Professor Zailig Pollock for his very helpful detailed comments. Others who contributed in various ways to the completion of this book include Rabbi William Altschul, Ruth Huberman, Irene Rebrin, Dr J. Rothschild, and Esther Steinberg, and to them, for their generous and unfailing assistance, I am deeply obliged.

The Public Archives of Canada was most helpful in making available its A.M. Klein Collection and in providing special use of its facilities. Other institutions whose research collections were used during preparation of the manuscript included the Jewish Public Library of Montreal, the University of British Columbia Library (Vancouver), the University of Western Washington Library (Bellingham), Jews' College Library (London, England), and the Hebrew University Library (Jerusalem).

The financial assistance provided to the A.M. Klein Research and Publication Committee by the Social Sciences and Humanities Research Council was invaluable in furthering the work of the Committee and the making of this book, and is very much appreciated.

Biographical Chronology

1909
born to Kalman and Yetta Klein, Orthodox Jews, in Ratno, a small town in the Ukraine, and brought to Montreal, Canada, with his family probably the following year (officially claimed to have been born in Montreal, 14 February 1909).

1915–22
attended Mt Royal School. Received Jewish education from private tutors and at Talmud Torah.

1922–6
attended Baron Byng High School.

1926–30
attended McGill University, majoring in classics and political science and economics. Active in Debating Society with close friend David Lewis. Founded literary magazine, *The McGilliad*, with Lewis in 1930. Associated with 'Montreal Group' of poets and writers, including A.J.M. Smith, F.R. Scott, Leo Kennedy, and Leon Edel. Began publishing poems in *The Menorah Journal*, *The Canadian Forum*, *Poetry* (Chicago), and elsewhere.

1928–32
served as educational director of Canadian Young Judaea, a Zionist youth organization, and edited its monthly magazine, *The Judaean*, in which many of his early poems and stories appeared.

1930–3
studied law at the Université de Montréal.

1934
established law firm in partnership with Max Garmaise, and struggled to earn a living during the Depression. Served as national president of Canadian Young Judaea.

1935
married Bessie Kozlov, his high school sweetheart.

1936
active in publicity and educational work, and on speaking tours, for the Zionist Organization of Canada, and editor of its monthly, *The Canadian Zionist.*

1937
moved to Rouyn, a small mining town in northern Quebec, to join Garmaise in law practice there.

1938
returned to Montreal, and re-established law practice in association with Samuel Chait. Assumed editorship of *The Canadian Jewish Chronicle*, to which he contributed numerous editorials, essays, book reviews, poems, and stories.

1939
began his long association with Samuel Bronfman, noted distiller and philanthropist and president of the Canadian Jewish Congress, working as a speechwriter and public relations consultant.

1940
first volume of poems, *Hath Not a Jew ...* , published by Behrman's in New York.

1942–7
associated with the *Preview* group of poets – F.R. Scott, Patrick Anderson, P.K. Page, and others – and with the *First Statement* group, in particular Irving Layton.

1944
The Hitleriad published by New Directions in New York. *Poems* published by the Jewish Publication Society in Philadelphia. Nominated as CCF candidate in federal riding of Montreal-Cartier, but withdrew before the election of 1945.

1945–8
visiting lecturer in poetry at McGill University.

1946–7
wrote his first novel, an unpublished spy thriller, 'Comes the Revolution' (later retitled 'That Walks Like a Man'), based on the Igor Gouzenko affair.

1948
The Rocking Chair and Other Poems published by Ryerson in Toronto.

1949
published the first of several articles on James Joyce's *Ulysses*. Ran unsuccessfully as CCF candidate in the federal election of June 1949. Awarded the Governor-General's Medal for *The Rocking Chair*. Journeyed to Israel, Europe, and North Africa in July and August, sponsored by the Canadian Jewish Congress, and published his 'Notebook of a Journey' in *The Canadian Jewish Chronicle*.

1949–52
travelled widely in Canada and the United States, addressing Jewish audiences, principally concerning the State of Israel.

1951
The Second Scroll published by Knopf in New York.

1952–4
increasing signs of mental illness. Hospitalized for several weeks in the summer of 1954 after a thwarted suicide attempt.

1955
resigned from editorship of *The Canadian Jewish Chronicle*. Ceased writing and began to withdraw from public life.

1956
resigned from law practice and became increasingly reclusive. Awarded the Lorne Pierce Medal by the Royal Society of Canada.

1971
death of Bessie Klein, 26 February.

1972
died in his sleep, 20 August.

SHORT STORIES

Epistle Theological

You have exceedingly flattered me in presuming an omniscience on my part concerning the comparative advantages, spiritual and temporal, of the degreed professions. With gracious genuflexion I acknowledge the compliment; as for its reply, it is only hesitantly and with a sense of duty incumbent that I prepare to make answer to your interrogations. I say duty, for before our father (may his soul be bound in the bond of the Eternally Living) died, he left you his money and me, your care. That I have since acted as a good brother and a better guardian, you will not deny; at this juncture therefore, it does not behoove me to refuse my thrice-ruminated counsel. From the various digressions, excursi, circumlocutions and irrelevancies of your letter I gather that your volubility inquires briefly this: Shall you enter the Rabbinate?

You do not, forsooth, put your query as pertly as I have stated it; that would be breaking the respectable tradition of our ancestresses, who held that out of a multitude of words at length cometh wisdom. No. You first suffer yourself to undergo the self-inflicted *Cheshbon Hanefesh*, the introspective purgatory, the soliloquy of reminiscence, the summation of the soul so typical of our cautious mentality, and then after much autobiography and braggadocio discover yourself on the verge of making a decision. You are weighing careers; you are balancing possibilities. Many roads are open to you; few lead home ... You frankly confess, and I admire your frankness if not your confession, that you have your heart set on comfort and fainéantism, and your eyes on life, leisure, and lucre. Let me remind you that such l's are paved with good intentions ... and that our father, may peace be his eternity, continually held up before us the example of the prophet who, though fed by ravens, was privy to the secrets of God. However, I judge from the general tone of your communication that asceticism holds no charms for you. *Laudas divitias, sequeris inertiam.* You are seeking a paradise of idleness in an Eldorado of riches, and you seek it via the professions. So be it then; my fraternal affection forbids me even at the outset to wrap your ardour in asbestos and tell you that you are doomed to discomfiture.

You have, for the end that you may eliminate them, enumerated the callings with an inducement. All of them, it seems, have yet to attain the attractions of the irresistible. With a peculiar mental reaction you first turn your calculations to law, and law, you assert with the wistfulness of the disillusioned, is overcrowded and undernourished ... Every Moishele, Shloimele, and Berele of the bourgeois immigrant aspires to a forensic career. Nincompoops, mediocrities and Litvaks, so runs your Sephardic facetia, vie with each other in the soliciting of trade. The roll-calls of colleges rhyme monotonously with bergs and vitches. All of them, sooner or later, hear the call of justice, the intellectual subpoena. Only enigmatic examinations and birth control can remedy the situation ... As a result the Law is being rewarded with cynical jests aggravated by penury. The cadaverous lawyer, hunger-smitten and penniless, who stalks the country in search of clients and food, according to your hyperbole, has become proverbial; and the affluent one, masticating a fat cigar, and heralded by paunchy avoirdupois, is the anomaly spoken of with envy as one dwelling on the blissful banks of Sambation. Sheisters and ambulance-chasers multiply and fill the earth, and prolific colleges let loose hordes of lawyers, inspired with the will to uphold the law and hold up the public. You, artistocrat and intellectual, therefore refuse to rush into a profession where angels fear to tread; you have loftier ambitions and more prosperous hopes. You are to be praised; I commend you for not bringing the fair name of our family down to the dust by such a step.

The sequential alternative, of course, is medicine. I remember one of the favorite attitudes of your youth. You then expressed displeasure by closing your nostrils between thumb and fore-finger. I can almost imagine you making the same indecorous gesture in your consideration of therapeutics. With subtle dialectic you declare that you are too human to profess the humane art; you can not suffer the sight of blood nor can you endure the groans and grimaces of agony. Furthermore you are nauseated by the prospect of deft obstetrics, and disgusted with the idea of treating anaemic spinsters, hypochondriac millionaires, and patients hali-totically garrulous. In conclusion, you maintain, the honorarium is negligible.

As for dentistry, the third of the professional trilogy, that, you assert, is no profession but a labor. In addition, it too is oversupplied; with statistical accuracy you declare that there is about one dentist for every human set of molars, and finally you opine that this is a sustenance earned by the skin of the teeth ...

The professorial too repels you. You do not wish to gain a living through the dead languages. Fastidiousness teaches you to shudder at the thought of addressing freshettes on the prosody of Catullus, or millionaires' sons on the theories of Karl Marx. You climax your intention by quoting Ludwig Lewisohn on the difficulty of you, a Jew, being granted a professorial rostrum in these our halls of learning.

It is strange, then, that after such sifting and choosing, you should stand wavering on the threshold of the seminary. The odour of sanctity has wrapped you about, and the spirit of the Lord, it seems, has shaken you mightily. You heard the still small voice, and you ask, How much is there in it for me? You want information on the assets and liabilities of the Rabbinate: Attend.

Allow me to dissuade you from such a course. You are trifling with the angels, and like a hook-nosed Prometheus are stealing fire that is not yours. You will no doubt refer me to many Rabbis who have been distinguished; I will point out to you packed Pantheons with no Rabbi. Do not, moreover, suspect me of heresy, and of a soul that scoffs; on the contrary, I have God and the Fathers on my side. Let me remind you of the dicta of so eminent an authority as Hillel, who declared: He who makes a worldly use of the Torah shall waste away; whence thou mayest infer, that whosoever derives a profit unto himself from its use, maketh his own soul to perish. I strengthen this assertion when I invoke Rabbi Zadok, whose very name testifies to his piety. He enjoined: Make not of the Torah a crown wherewith to aggrandize thyself, nor a spade to dig. The image of the digging spade is particularly to be noted; it is reminiscent of the poet royal: He made a pit and digged it, and is fallen into the ditch he made. But I fear I am on the verge of a labyrinthine *pilpul*. Shemayah, the famous colleague of Abtalyon, left no room for ambiguity on the matter when he in definite imperative bade: Eschew the Rabbinate.

But you, *mon frère et mon semblable*, belong to the race of the stiff-necked. Such objections will therefore not alter your determination to take the Ivory Gates by storm. Seeing that there is no commandment to the contrary you will persist in coveting that which is God's. How then will you approach the upper *Pamalyah*? Will it be in the modern dress of Reform, or in the skull cap and caftan of Orthodoxy?

Knowing well the proclivities of your youth, I am of the opinion that the burden of the six hundred and thirteen injunctions, plus the minor prohibitions intended to safeguard the aforementioned six hundred and thirteen, will lie all too heavily upon your Americanized vertebra. You will be forced to forsake the levities of your past, and the anticipations of your future must needs be forgotten. Your all-embracing amours will have to be left as a symbol of a terrible fate which you escaped by the light of the Lord, even as Saint Augustine his fate at Carthage. You would do well, therefore, to read, before you are ordained, the seventh chapter of Proverbs so that you may know the distance that lies between the worship of Venus and the service of the Lord.

You will don the strait jacket of Orthodoxy; a paragon of piety, you will observe every jot and tittle of the Law. The dietary injunctions, I know, will be indigestible to you; you will hunger after the flesh-pot of Egypt and the ham-sandwiches of the

Gentiles, but you will deprive yourself of the delicacies, none the less. *Kashruth* will be under your especial surveillance; and as for answering *shealith* upon the religious edibility of a mutilated and gut-swollen chicken, your duty will compel you to straighten the betraying curves of your sensitive nostrils. In addition, you will be called upon to cultivate the pious hirsuteness, sidecurls and beard, with which the Oxford cut of your clothes will be somewhat incongruous. In the course of time you may even recall those inimitable gestures which you have forgotten, the Talmudic twist of the thumb, and the casuistical turn of the voice. In fact it pleases me to imagine you sitting over a ponderous tome, your sparse beard clutched in your skinny hand, your eye twisted with the convolutions of logic, and your nostrils emitting the pleasant hum of an intricate ratiocination. For the sake of a further sanctity, you may even acquire both the phylacteries of Rashi and of Rabbenu Tam. Cause a sudden atavism to possess you; medievalize your thought, antiquate your spirit; rabbinize your soul.

It will fall upon your shoulders, too, that your congregation be equipped with a *Mikvah*, in which the sins particularized in *Nidah* may be writ in water. This is a cleanliness which is more than gnomically akin to godliness. If your synagogue is located in some far-flung village where our brethren the children of Israel number the essential *minyan*, you may be asked to perform other duties, such as that of executioner of fowls, and occasionally (see Malthus) that of *Mohel*, thus using the sacred blade for the purpose of introducing the feathered into the felicity of the deceased, and the young Hebrew to that of the quick. Having initiated the sucklings into the original rite, surely you will not leave them abandoned to ignorance, even as Hagar her Ishmael. You will follow up the covenant of Abraham with the law of Moses. These incumbencies will not be heavy; teach them a little Yiddish and less Hebrew. Ground them in the inflectional notation for the purpose of Bar-Mitzvah. A weekly sermon replete with Midrashic quotations and didactic anecdotes, to stir the laggards in your community in the devotion of the Lord, will be delivered by way of avocation. If there happens to be no Cantor or Reader in the congregation, you will do justice to your high calling if you read the Scroll yourself. In your spare time, after disposing of these amanuenses, you may apply yourself to the study of the great Commentaries, and to the writing of complicated *Responsa*.

Do not await luxuries from such a life; you may perhaps find yourself the recipient of a salary not characterized by regularity of payment; despair not. The operation of religious nativity may profit you somewhat; a union in marriage may support your tottering finances; and a bill of divorcement may have the same pecuniary advantage. An interment, be it said upon the heathen, may also resurrect your dying financial ambitions. A blessing at the Law, in favor of some opulent bourgeois, may net you a weekly allowance. Gifts at Purim may come in handy, and a fee for the sale of *Chometz* is not utterly despicable. *Kaddish* for the deceased without offspring has been known to be quite lucrative, if in sufficient numbers. And even if poverty is your sole reward, and hardship your only honorarium, remember the words of Rabbi Joshua the son of Levi, who said: This is the way that is becoming to the Torah – a morsel of bread with salt thou must eat, and water by measure thou must drink; thou must sleep upon the ground, and live a life of trouble the while thou toilest in the Law. If thou doest thus, happy shalt thou be, and it shall be well with thee (Psalms 128:2). Happy shalt thou be in this world, and it shall be well with thee in the world to come.

If these words are not sufficiently convincing I offer you for emulation the example of Rabbi Akiva, who being a mere *am ha'araz*, laboured in the law for twenty years, poverty and the love of Rachel his sole encouragement. I could, if I knew that enumeration carried conviction, continue the catalogue of the righteous who lived a good life the while their purses were lined with silken cobwebs, but I already am aware of your impatience. You are no doubt telepathically reminding me that you stipulated as your prime condition a position of affluence. It is the Reform Rabbinate which you are now greeting as the pious do greet Queen Sabbath.

Here indeed you have struck, if not the wisdom, at any rate the Mines of Solomon. There is in sooth great booty to be found in the temple. The wealthy Jews, your congregationalists-to-be, are proverbially lavish with their gifts to the footstools of the Almighty; having no worthier object upon which to bestow the overflow of their cornucopiae, they will, in an effort to atone for the questionable methods of its amassing, distribute munificently of their riches to the Temple which dispenses Judaism, Liberalism, and forgiveness. You, as Rabbinical treasurer, and financial intermediary between Providence and the providers, will be in for some lucrative oversupply yourself. But to insure your keeping of the position a certain line of behavior will be advisable. You are well aware, I hope, of what qualities are expected of you in the event of considering this as a career. If not, these words may be deemed advisory.

Your appearance is to bespeak piety married to modernism. Your jowls must be meticulously clean; if you insist on a beard, let it be the triangular tuft which indicates intellectuality. Your congregation should be granted ample opportunity to draw complimentary contrasts between your refined exterior and that of the benighted Rabbis of the East Side; your very clothes, though conscientiously subdued, should be an index to the mental emancipation of which you are to be the embodiment. As a crowning touch you may arrange your hair in careful disorder, in the manner of the European intelligentsia, so as to lead some to suspect that there is something beneath them.

Having made yourself presentable, present yourself to the pillars of the Temple. See that you find favor in the eyes of the President and his Executive – this is of paramount importance; your very existence depends upon the goodwill of these who have been so divinely chosen. You may achieve this by studying the good qualities and virtues of these gentlemen, and showing your appreciation in no whisper. I admit that such a study might often require microscopic investigation and hardy perseverance, but none the less I assure you such research receives its adequate reward. Mistake me not; I am not inciting you to flattery, but to a just recognition of the worth, no matter in what modicum, of your fellows.

Learn, therefore, to cultivate a loud appreciation of the almost imperceptible abilities of your superiors (chafe not beneath the word, custom will inure you); learn to develop an acute perception of all that is even fractionally good in them, and let not your discoveries suffer the languishment of taciturnity. Address them in paeans; apostrophise them in eulogies. As for their peccadillos, is there not somewhere a proverb which declares that the blind may on occasion walk with even more than visual safety?

If, however, some of these honorables are unusually immune to a retelling of their worth, it may profit you to approach their wives. Inspire the bejewelled dames of the Sisterhood with your personality; they will be enamoured of you. Speak to them about ideals; they love it. Your youth and your beatific compliments ought to reconcile any aversion they might have to an impecunious newcomer. Certain respectable intimacies would solidify their good graces. Influence them that they may even think of you and their marriageable daughters in a single reflection. Win an alcove in their hearts; they will remember you favorably to their husbands.

To preserve such congenial amicalities only the most acrobatic diplomacy can suffice. Petty jealousies may sometimes break up your congregation; like Aaron, pursue peace. It would not do to have your members broken into clans; keep then, if nothing else, a superficial unity.

So that these bonds of genial relationship may continue to exist you must adopt two methods. The first is for those aristocratic families whose pedigrees are carefully recorded in the encyclopedia. They, like glass, must be handled with care. There is a certain brittleness about their temper which warrants anxious manipulation. Gross flattery commends not itself to them; unlike most thick things it is all too transparent. Let then your affabilities seem incidental, your sycophancy opaque, your adulation disguised in casualness. You may soothe their egos by verbal concoctions whose contents elude analysis. And instil in your conversation imperceptible opiates of flattery; they will slumber cherubically in your arms.

There will on the other hand no doubt be some in your congregation whose aristocracy has been purchased through affluence, and whose pedigree has been created as an afterthought; the newly rich whose arrogance is in direct proportion to the misery of their past. These will present but small difficulties in your way. One requires little technique and less discretion in the buttering of their conceit. They desire it thick. Do not scruple about exaggerations, your audience will recognize in them merely a modified truth. Emphasis in this exigency is a virtue much to be commended. If your nouveaux riches are not fully impressed with their own success, unlikely as it may seem, repetition from your lips will be accepted as a graceful memorandum. Let your appreciation work itself up to a pure white lather, in your epithets be effusive, in your compliments, ooze.

If you would have your popularity not merely ephemeral, fortify your reputation in your sermon. The gullible on all occasions succumb to the glib. Mouth your platitudes with that prophetic air which will lead your audience to dote on your aphorisms. A fit subject, and one which troubles your good Jews not a little, is the conception of the Deity. Set yourself up as an iconoclast by asserting in true radical fashion that God is not a bearded patriarch; this will titillate the conscience of the modernist. Assert rather that to you God is a growing Being, accommodating Himself to the inventions of science, and hobbling along to keep up with the progress of civilization. This pronouncement will surely find supporters among the mildly sceptical.

Apart from the subject of divinity, you may occasionally relieve yourself of a political prejudice. Any attack upon the Socialist economists is sure to evoke the admiration and win you the affection of your Temple; they will rejoice if you point with alarm; they will revel if you view with disgust – wherefore, it matters not. Instead of violent abolition of property, advise benevolent philanthropy. Tell them that charity is the purgative of sin and the emetic of wickedness, and that all the behests of the Bible and of Humanity indicate the duty of lending a helping hand to our less fortunate brethren. Let your idealism seek sanctuary in exhortations to good deeds. Pry open their hearts with promises of heaven. That their employees are overworked and exploited leave unmentioned; attribute rather the poverty of these to lack of initiative and executive ability, and the divine will. Inform them that the poor were created for the express purpose of furnishing them with the means of a redemptive *mitzvah*.

Occasionally you may expatiate on sin, but then let your discourse have the entertaining vagueness of the abstract. Though your congregation, I am sure, are seldom infatuated with metaphysics, this will be a time when they will appreciate the purely philosophical. If, however, this is a field too narrow for your oratory, inveigh against vice, vice I say, and not the vicious. The former is a target that retaliates not. And of the deadly sins, those inspired by avarice and materialism are to be attacked, if at all, by ignoring them. A random shot inspired by an onslaught on unscrupulous business is likely to find a victim in your audience. Let your vocabulary be harmlessly harsh, carefully unpointed. If you wish to inject humour into your declarations, insert some Jewish phrases; the very foreignness of the jargon is certain to evoke a supercilious smile. Moreover, and this too is important, if ever you make a hasty and too potent generality, temper it by alleging that there are exceptions to the rule aforementioned; your pews will forthwith be filled with self-imagined exceptions. Even when your curbed indignation breaks loose at the sight of some flagrant injustice, let your expletives have the charm of innocuous impersonality.

Your duty, I must say, does not end with the delivery of commonplace moralities and the magic solution of the hydra-headed Jewish problem; there is a Sunday-school, there is a Young People's Society which have claims upon your inspiration. Demonstrate to the world at large that your interest is not merely with the petrified fogies of the moribund generation; show also that you have marked sympathies with the young people upon whose shoulders will fall the duty of taking their place in the world's activity. Young people, I admit, are quite difficult to attract to a place of worship; institute dances, community affairs, teas, socials ... Entice them to the Word of the Lord by anticipations of a fox-trot; let them be attracted to your spiritual lectures by the prospect of post-oratorical tête-à-têtes. Bear it always in mind that the young people will in the course of time become the supports of your Temple and the consolation of your old age. The sucklings on the other hand are to be nurtured in your Sunday-school, where you are to adopt that paternal camaraderie so pleasant to the recipient and so entrancing to the spectator, especially if she be the mother of the precocious child.

In your spare time, and with shrewd delegation of duties, you will have it in plenty, you may dedicate yourself to the writing of religious treatises with modern interpretations. But before you justly undertake any such opus, collect a library. Let the walls of your study be ominous with book-backs; see to it, however, that these books have their pages cut and that the dust of ignominy settle not upon the covers of erudition. Let your visitors mistake the bibliophile for the scholar. Magazines of sophistication and religion, too, should be strewn upon your desks; as for your reading, outlines, concordances, and books of familiar quotations could give the necessary impression of book-browsing.

About your remuneration, have no concern. Your salary will give you every comfort; your diplomacy will win you every luxury. In fact, I have even known that some of your colleagues bet on the stock market, obtaining their tips from men in the financial world.

This then is the foretelling of your destiny, and this your way of life in the days to come. If you would be a Rabbi, let me say to you in a word pregnant with twin-meanings: reform ... for such is the kingdom of heaven ... If, however, you have by this time developed an aversion to the celestial vice-presidency, may I say in the words of the President Himself: It is good ... But then again, perhaps there are greater things than are dreamed of in my philosophy ...

Prophet in Our Midst: A Story for Passover

About six weeks before Passover we began to study the *Haggadah*. The ordinary curriculum of the *Cheder* was abandoned; the class-room was full of the talk of miracles, and out of the Four Questions a million others bristled. Our days were spent in the calculation of plagues; the Rebbe proved that if the ten plagues were a finger of God, fifty plagues must have been inflicted on the Egyptians when He lifted His right hand, which, explained Leibel, the bright boy of the class, had five fingers; our nights, too, were glorious with dreams of angels and heavenly ministers. At recess periods, while pampered Pee-Wee, the richest pupil in the *Cheder*, could afford to crack nuts as early as three weeks before Passover and while Jeshurun (the Rebbe gave Fatty that nickname because it is written 'And Jeshurun grew fat and kicked') – while Jeshurun already nibbled matzoh, we discussed the Egyptian afflictions, and it is a strange thing that all of us agreed that the slaying of the first-born was the least, and the plague of lice the most terrible of all. I remember very vividly that it was only Mottele the orphan who held the opposite view.

But more fascinating than these arguments about frogs skipping in *Mizraim* and about Moses waving his magic wand over a land of blood, were the tales of Elijah the prophet. When the Rabbi dwelt with glowing picturesqueness and biblical quotation upon the piety and poverty of the man of God, I felt that he was describing my father. It was only when he appended to the description of the prophet a long and flowing beard, that the similarity failed, for my father's beard, alas, has always been shorter in America than in Europe. But even if Elijah did not look like my father, I could still evince an interest in him, so engrossing a character was he ... Elijah, wandering from town to town, and from village to village, performing miracles here and doing wonders there. Elijah, saving Jews forever hard beset by Jew-gluttons, Elijah bringing splendour to the house of the pauper, and imparting high secrets to the heart of the pious Rabbi, – how we loved him, how gladly, had he appeared in our midst, we would have hailed him! Such a just man was he, we might even have made him referee over all our games!

What intrigued us most, however, was the story that on Passover night Elijah wanders from house to Hebrew house, sipping some wine from the goblet designedly left for him. First of all, we questioned, how could he go to so many places in one night, for, as the Rebbe himself told us, the Jews were scattered in all parts of the world? A little astronomy came to the Rebbe's salvation. He explained that while it was night here, it was day in Palestine, and so Elijah had really two days wherein to do his sipping. But if the wine was sour, how could Elijah drink it? Ready for all occasions, the Rebbe answered, first, that Elijah only sipped a little from each goblet, and second that in the mouth of the prophet all things turn sweet. I always wanted to ask how he kept himself from becoming drunk, after putting his lips to so many cups and after, in going from *Seder* to *Seder*, mixing his drinks. But I was afraid. The Rebbe might become angry at this impertinence and call me '*Shagitz*.' The figure of a long-bearded Jew, staggering through ghetto streets, his coat-tails flying behind him in the spring wind, and his silhouette lit up by Passover moonlight, has haunted me ever since.

II

If Simeon the half-wit would have failed to appear on our street about Passover time, the ghetto gossips would have talked about a belated spring. He showed his bearded countenance as regularly as the three maple trees of our ward burgeoned their buds. All winter he retired into a mystical seclusion; he hibernated; but at the earliest twittering of the sparrows, he took up his position at the synagogue doorstep, and dressed in a heavy hat and tattered coat, he dozed away his days. He never worked; he lived upon the compassion and charity of his neighbours ... 'a screw was loose somewhere,' men said, as they put a finger to their temples. Simeon, for one thing, was obsessed by a mortal fear of blueberries. If you ever wanted to get rid of him, all you had to do was to show him a blueberry. Had he looked at the face of the Angel of Death himself, he would not have been more terrified. He also had the habit of tying his sleeves to his wrist – he feared that devils would creep into his clothes, and seek shelter in his hairy bosom. And he liked a little drink on any and all occasions. Practical jokers, possessed by a cruel ingenuity, would sometimes treat him to a glass of schnapps but would throw into the red liquid a blueberry. 'Poison! Poison of death,' Simeon would shout, and spit mightily, leaving his benefactors a reward of choice curses.

But he was not dangerous. He was merely a half-wit; doctors said, however, that a great shock at any moment might deprive him even of the last vestiges of sanity. They spoke about chronic alcoholism, and prophesied that his brain would weaken. But he was not dangerous; so, while on a hot summer day, wrapped in a mass of rags, his beard falling over a collarless neck and his mouth open for the exit and entrance of flies, Simeon slumbered away his mad life, Jews passed him by with a shake of the head and a recollection of blueberries.

III

I had finished asking the Four Questions. We were all reading the *Haggadah*; my uncle outsang my father, my mother outsang them both; amidst the sound of the prayers, I skipped several passages. I could not keep my mind on the Hebrew; either I looked at the pictures in the *Haggadah* trying to distinguish the different plagues as they were represented in the blurred woodcuts, or I kept a vigilant eye upon the cup of Elijah, to see that its contents did not diminish.

The moment came – my father told me to open the door as he announced the prayer 'Spill Thy wrath upon the heathen, O Lord.' I opened it. The moon was visible, shining over the roofs. On the other side of the street, a shadow stalked. It made its way towards our door. As it approached we could distinguish the tatters, the beard, the rheumy eyes of Simeon; as he entered we heard his adenoidal breathing. 'Elijah, the prophet, as I am a Jew,' laughed my uncle: 'Come in! Sit down! Take a glass of wine, Reb Simeon. "Let all who need, come and eat",' he quoted the *Haggadah*.

IV

My head was turned at that particular moment so I don't know whether it was really the goblet of Elijah that my uncle gave him. At any rate, Simeon drank. He drank for a legion of Elijahs. My uncle and father insisted, moreover, on calling him Elijahu *Hanavi*. They spoke with him, they argued with him, they convinced him that he was the prophet himself. In the state in which Simeon found himself at the end of the *Seder*, before the eating of the *Afikomen*, you could have made him believe anything. But the idea that he was Elijah the prophet tickled him particularly ... Even on that very night, he felt insulted when my mother, forgetting the play for a moment, called him Simeon. 'I am Elijah the Prophet,' he shouted, 'I am Elijah.' And truth to tell, since that night, he has changed his name to Elijah, and as the spirit moves him he indulges in petty prophecies.

When he left our house, I looked through the windows, and in the Passover moonlight I saw the figure of a long-bearded Jew staggering down the street, his tatters playing behind him in the spring wind.

By the Profit of a Beard

It was the pride of patriarchs that kept Reb Zalman's backbone unbent beneath the burden of sorrow and age. Not that the blood of Rabbis flowed in his veins, not that he boasted even a remote descent from the great ones in Israel – his family tree indeed struck roots in soil most unaristocratic – but that he felt himself by reason of signal distinction to be an especial protégé of God. He was not a learned man, it is true; his erudition exhausted itself in a knowledge of the Psalms, and of anecdotes about Chassidic Rabbis. He was not a particularly pious man; he abode by all of the six hundred and thirteen injunctions of the Pentateuch, and the subordinate behests of the Talmud; but that assuredly did not exalt one to sainthood. It was his beard. Conjure up the countenance of ubiquitous Jewry: study the portraits of the orthodox sons of Jacob, past and present: imagine cheek and jowl weighted with the fertility of Eden itself, and perhaps you may receive an intimation of the proportion of Reb Zalman's beard. It began in religious spirals curling down his cheekbones; it spread itself luxuriously on his jowl and jaw; like the gardens of Babylon, it hung from his upper lip; it flowed from his capacious chin, hiding his neck in a cool and hairy arbour; it covered his chest with a white splendour.

Reb Zalman gloried in the impressiveness of his beard. When he went forth into the street, tall, erect, straight as a violin string, he was the surprise and wonder of every little boy in the neighbourhood. They thought him Moses descended from Heaven. The women, too, pointed to him as a Jew of the old type, the kind that one no longer sees in America, a Jew a saint, a *Zaddik*. The *Shechinah*, they said, rested on his beard. Reb Zalman did not let a single flattery go astray; he cherished every word of praise, he preserved every worshipful look, every gesture of adulation, and in his spare moments he gloated over his hoard of compliments.

In the synagogue, too, his patriarchal beard won him admiration, respect, and summons to the Torah. He would sit over a snuff-stained psalter, reiterating the sacred words, and if during his incantation a hair fell out of his beard, he would preserve it piously among the pages of the Holy Book. He looked far more dignified than even the blear-eyed Rabbi, and he knew it. During the recitation of the Eighteen Prayers, standing at attention before the Divine Presence, he was a marvel to behold, a palm tree of the Lord. His clear blue eyes, the slight colour in his cheeks, and his beard, his omnipresent beard, threw a sanctity over the synagogue. People came there to pray, to pray and to behold Reb Zalman.

What if he was a pauper? What if he did have to live on the crumbs that his unprodigal sons flung him? These things were as naught; the Lord had blessed him with a consolation that grew daily ... Bitterness it was to feed upon the begrudged bread of one's sons, and sorrow to be compelled to ask for money from the offspring of one's loins. Reb Zalman never had a coin in his pocket. What does the old man need money for? He has where to sleep? He has where to eat and drink? What more does he want? With impeccable logic his sons argued him into pennilessness. What of it? Let the *goyim* be content with their wealth, and again, let us not fool ourselves: were these really sons? Would they say *Kaddish* for him after a hundred and twenty years? No, they would bury him, and put a heavy stone over his grave to make sure he would remain there ... Reb Zalman stroked his beard, – that was his *Kaddish*, that was the offspring that would intercede on his behalf at the Heavenly gate.

His grandchildren, however, atoned for the sins of their fathers. They would climb upon his chair and toy with his beard.

The little ones would tug at the hair and laugh gleefully. 'Antisemite,' Reb Zalman would cry, 'Heathen blood! So young and already it knows how to pull Jewish beards.' But he was happy when they passed their fingers through the labyrinth of his hair, he felt that he was imparting Judaism to them through the sense of touch.

Yes, he might be a poor man, and an old man, and a man cast upon the goodwill of his sons, but he was a proud man. God had lavished upon him the multitudinous benediction of a beard, the like of which Judah hath never known.

When he went to bed, he rested his beard on the coverlet. This procedure was always the same: to undress; fix the skull-cap on his head; get into bed; arrange his beard and say the *Krias Shma*. With Gabriel at the head of his couch, angels at both sides, and a beard on top, what impudent demon would dare disturb his slumbers?

II

It seems that the passing of days saw a beard develop even at the back of Reb Zalman's head. His hair hung over his collar in shaggy edges, and from the rear he looked like a Hebrew poet. It seems also that Reb Zalman refused to go to his sons to ask them for the fee of a barber – they would give him the money he knew, but they would look skeptically at the baldpate (the crown of his head was bare) who lavished cash on a fractional haircut. So unconcernedly he let his hair grow, before and aft, crowned with the halo of a natural tonsure.

But God does not forsake his wards. He sends salvation to those that serve Him, and His message is borne even on the lips of the lowliest. It was almost a divine coincidence therefore, when Reb Zalman met Mr. Katz, newsvendor on Main Street.

'How are you Reb Zalman, how do you like something America?' He had been in the country for years, but people still insisted on inquiring after his reaction to the golden land. They could not help but regard him as a transplanted European.

'What is there to like in America? America today, America tomorrow, it's one black year. One lives and one struggles. But let us not blaspheme, if the Heavenly One decrees, no doubt He knows what He decrees. It's their America. Empty synagogues and full moving-picture houses ... and Jews – may they be sown thickly to sprout sparsely – *goyim*, apostates, defilers of the Sabbath in public. A beard among them you can't buy for a treasure.' He stroked his own with paternal approval.

'Nu, what could you do? Could you make over the world? Ai, Reb Zalman, it could be, *taki*, that a beard lends grace to a Jewish countenance, but a haircut one must take also. There is nothing in the Torah against cutting the hair on the back of the head. On the contrary, I am told that the Belzer Rebbe used to spend hours on end combing his hair before the morning service. He used to say: "If you had to appear before the Czar wouldn't you comb yourself, dress yourself, even perfume yourself like Esther in the house of Haggai, how much more so when you appear before the Czar of Czars, the Holy One Himself, in dignity and in person, blessed be He".'

'Yes, you are right but,' – there was helpless apology in Reb Zalman's voice, he hesitated, he stuttered, he sought refuge in his beard. He lifted it as one who calls it into council and looked insinuatingly from the corner of his eye. Mr. Katz surmised his meaning.

'Money? money, shmoney. Here money is mud! In America you can get a haircut free. I mean without joking. There's a place downtown where Frenchmen, *goyishe kepp*, will give you a haircut for nothing. Not a cent will it cost you, as I am a Jew.'

Mr. Katz gave him the directions to the free barbershop.

III

Reb Zalman hesitated before he entered the barbershop. At first he walked up and down the street looking through the window of the shop. He saw young men busily engaged in shaving plebeian faces, and in cutting the hair from unpedigreed heads. Over the door was printed in black letters, 'Montreal Training School for Barbers, Haircuts free,' but Reb Zalman could not read English. Innocently he entered the academy of hairsplitters.

His appearance immediately evoked a suppressed mirth. The barbers tittered at the sight of a Rip Van Winkle, and a Jewish one at that. There walks a whole course on the tonsorial art, they reflected, and winked significantly to one another. Reb Zalman felt uncomfortable at these inhospitable manifestations, but did not have it in him to leave. What do you expect, Reb Zalman – he was addressing his inner self – they should embrace you? One is here in exile. Let them laugh, the *goyim*, let them laugh. When I will eat roast leviathan, them I will give a good disease.

Suddenly they beckoned to him; it was his turn. He sat down in the chair, took off his hat, and doffed the *yarmalke* that he always wore beneath it. At the sight of the concealed skullcap, the apprentice barbers and the laborers and navvies in the barber shop could hardly contain their laughter. Reb Zalman looked at them with superior scorn, as if he were regarding lunatics; he combed his beard with his fingers, and gestured to the boy who was at his side that he desired only a haircut. He passed his hand over his beard, and looking severe disapproval, shook his head emphatically, as much as to say that this was forbidden territory. He described a circle about his head, and nodded a smiling and benign permission for the youth to proceed. The youth proceeded.

He must needs have a heart of stone who would describe with gruesome detail the vandal performance of the student of the Montreal Training School. He shaved the head of his victim until it looked like a convict's, he left not a hair standing on his crown. But that was not all. In passing, his clumsy scissors had wrought piteous havoc upon the beauty of Reb Zalman's beard; an indentation here, an unsymmetrical angle there, had changed a thing of glory into a miserable tuft, unworthy even of a goat chin. The shears had snipped wisp after wisp of beard; they had made devastating incursions everywhere.

While these ravages were being perpetrated upon his chin, he was utterly unaware of them. His original amazement had befuddled his brain, he had thought that the barber was merely brushing his beard. He rose from his chair. He beheld his face in the wall mirrors. His face?

Had he not leaned against a nearby chair the gusts of laughter that greeted his introspection would have thrown him over. He could not recognize himself; a lump gathered in his throat, he gulped his anguish down. He shouted in Yiddish, knowing well that they would not understand him, but seeking momentary relief from the fingers that seemed to be clutching at his throat.

'You bandits you! May a cholera smother you! May a devil possess your father's father! For every hair you cut, may an abscess afflict your muzzle! I'll show you yet you bandits, you murderers! You'll cut my beard, my pride, my glory you'll cut!' He was shaking his finger at them. 'I'll take you to Court! You'll pay! Like a father you'll pay! You'll cry and you'll pay!'

He was weeping. His tears trickled from his eyes and settled on his scrawny beard, glittering like sharp mementos of sorrow. His whole body quivered with a sense of encompassing tragedy. He felt himself hard beset by foes. His last consolation had been snatched from him. The strings connecting him with vivid life had been snapped. He broke forth again, shaking his fist, gesticulating madly, speaking in a voice saturated with tears. He changed his attitude, he pleaded.

'What did I do to you, what? Have I harmed you? Have I stolen something from you? What have you got to me?' His audience answered his gesticulations with grins. He grew more and more enraged as he became aware of the futility of his arguments.

'May a strange death overtake you, you murderers, may the grave reject you, and may the dogs lick your bones.'

The barbers were getting tired of his performance. They showed him the door. Abashed and discomfited, he left. As he feebly closed the door he raised the collar of his coat and concealed his maimed beard behind large lapels. No one would see him in this plight. He hurried away, a salty taste in his mouth. His back was bent, an unknown burden heavy upon it. After that he was not seen in public for weeks. He sat forlorn, as one who mourns the bereavement of his kin.

The Lost Twins

On a time in a land which is not charted on any map, there lived a town full of Jews. This ubiquitous folk, tradition has it, has penetrated by the grace of God, and expulsion by their persecutors, even to those domains upon which no geographer has set peripatetic foot. Old textbooks in which even the Latin is outmoded contain sketches of this unknown land. A vast open space, dotted here and there by miniature double triangles to represent cities and hamlets, has writ across it in sprawling characters, 'Hic Sunt Judaei – Here are Jews'; to the south where is the sea, there swim letters announcing 'Hic Sunt Pisces – Here are Fish'; to the east and west the legend reads, amid a density of woods and forests, 'Hic Sunt Gigantes and Hic Sunt Nani – Here are Giants and Dwarfs'; and to the north where high mountains darken the plain, there twinkle glittering words, 'Hic Sunt Astrae – Here are Stars.'

In one of the double-triangles which is to be taken for a village there dwelt a penurious widow, whose husband had left her, as legacy, Velvela and Esterkah, obstreperous twins. Let no bright child here ask how we know these intimate facts about unknown people in an undiscovered land; he who reads between the lines is privy to all manner of irrefutable secrets, and the wise man who told us this tale spends his library hours perusing blank pages, made up wholly of 'between the lines.' This widow was a very pious woman, and though she was poor, she still contrived, by some economy, ingeniously feminine, to prepare for the feast after the Yom Kippur fast a tender chicken, which served, as a *Kaporah* (scape-goat), for the souls of her little ones, and which furnished them with meat and broth.

The day before Yom Kippur, as she was cutting up the unfeathered fowl, which was to honor God's day with its delicious morsels, she suddenly stopped short, dropped her knife and cried out, 'Ah woe is me. There is a blemish in the bird! It may be *traifa*. Thus money is thrown to waste, the feast is spoiled and a living creature has died to no one's profit or good use.' She clasped together her fingers in despair and groaned four times – 'What shall I do,' emphasizing a different word at each groan. After she had put herself the query in all the varied tones of its agony she found an answer, and calling into the garden where Esterkah and Velvela, washed and clean in their holiday clothes, were playing with mud pies, she said to them, 'I want you to go to the Rabbi and ask him a *shalah* about the chicken; tell him I found a bruise upon it and that he should look into his holy books and find out whether it is Kosher. Tell him also that your mother is poor; perhaps the law of bruised chickens is more lenient in the case of the poor.'

So the twins wrapped up the chicken and began walking in the direction of the Rabbi's house, which was on the outskirts of the city; for the Rabbi was a very holy man and spent a great deal of his spare time going for walks with angels in the fields. And presently Esterkah was tired and thirsty and sat down near a cold clear stream. She cupped her hands and drank. Velvela sat down beside her and began playing with the fine smooth pebbles in the water.

'Why are there so many pebbles by the water side?' Esterkah asked her brother who knew everything. 'Because,' sagely he replied, 'this is the cemetery of the fishes and these are their little tombstones.' 'Yes, and the water lapping against them are fishes' tears,' Esterkah added, looking into her brother's eyes to see whether her explanation found favor in them. His face showed no expression, like a wise man, who knows that women are not to be encouraged. There they sat for a long time talking about fishes, and of their happiness at not having to take a bath before the High Holidays, and how they could play about in the water without wetting their clothes, and how there were no orphans among them. Suddenly Velvela recalled the holy mission upon which they were bent, and he exclaimed 'but this is fish, and we are concerned with fowl, let us on our way before night will be upon us.'

They rose from the rock on which they were sitting and Esterkah, who was carrying the holy mission under her arm, said, 'I wish this chicken would turn back into an egg, until we get to the Rabbi, it is so heavy.' Her brother Velvela, who was very clever for his age, understood what she meant and took the fowl from her.

They trudged along for another while and then stopped beneath an oak tree to rest. They looked up into the multitudinous leaves, and Velvela remembering that he had learned on the previous day that God had called the stars by name, thought that it was unfair to discriminate in that manner neglecting, for example, the leaves of such a noble tree as the oak. He therefore began counting the leaves, giving them fantastic names, each name beginning with a different letter until he had several times exhausted the alphabet. Meanwhile Esterkah was watching the clouds twist themselves into the most torturesome shapes, now forming flocks of sheep, now herds of cattle, and now companies of unicorns. When they wearied, Velvela, of his original nomenclature and Esterkah, of her nebular zoology, they were aware by a darkening of the sky and the hollowness of their stomachs that the afternoon was far gone. And when they made to go to the Rabbi's, they wandered hither and thither, to and fro, until they were lost and did not know which was hither and which thither, which to and which fro.

So they kept on walking and Esterkah was already weeping. It grew very dark and her tears shone like bright stars. But Velvela who was a brave lad did not weep; to lighten his spirits, he whistled Kol Nidre instead. Esterkah, however, was very much afraid, because her mother had told her that at night goblins with four mouths prowled about the field, and demons who like only soft child flesh, hid themselves in dark corners, and bears who were not particular whether the flesh were soft or no, stalked through the woods. Also they were very hungry, and thought of the boiled chicken, which they would be eating, and of the marrow which they would have sucked from the bones. Now, they gloomily reflected, it was already Yom Kippur and they would have to fast another day.

Of a sudden they noticed before them a small humped-back dwarf who was standing in their way, naked, but with a long beard, which flowed down to his middle, and which he wrapped around himself several times, like a garment of hair-cloth. 'What do you want little children?' he asked in a voice that trickled slowly and sweetly like poured jam. 'We have lost our way, and we are hungry.'

'Pooh,' he said lifting his arm in an explanatory gesture, 'lost your way? God is everywhere, you need not fear, as long as you are on earth you cannot lose your way. If you fell off the planet, for instance, then you could call it losing your way! But as it is – Pooh!'

When he had poohed away this argument, he lifted his other arm to consider their hunger. 'You are hungry?' he said, 'for shame such little stomachs like yours should crave so regularly for food. Look into the sky and there you will find a message of the Messiah. May He come in our days! The clouds will be a heavenly *Chala*, the dotted heavens an ambrosial *matzah*. Even the waters of the ocean will taste like wine, and the moon will be a slice out of the palatable Leviathan, which is millennial meat. With such a pantry, wine cellar, butcher shop, bakery and refectory about you you still say you are hungry! Childishness, my children!'

Velvela was about to tell the dwarf that they were famished indeed, and might, before the Messiah prepared this appetizing table, presently be dead; but remembering that when the Messiah would come he would be alive anyway, and having respect for the dwarf's gigantic beard he was silent. While he hesitated the dwarf poohed himself into thin air, and all that remained in his place was an echo.

'He was a very strange man,' Esterkah flung from her chattering teeth. 'Oh,' Velvela answered with an air of one who was accustomed to these visitations, 'That was a miracle!'

'What is a miracle?'

'A miracle is when it happens what doesn't happen.'

It was now very cold, and Esterkah was shivering with chill fear. Autumn it was, and the leaves came falling down from the trees, making dry noises, like the sound in the throat of their father when he died. Things brushed velvety against their faces; their hair stood on end as they thought of foul bats alighting on their heads. Esterkah held Velvela's hand so tightly he began to think it was his own. When one is frozen and famished and alone, prayer, Velvela remembered, is known to have its advantages. He said in a voice tinctured with tears.

'God, you are not busy now. You have just listened to your Jews sing out their Kol Nidre, and it will be quite a while before they resume their prayers. In your spare time you may hearken to a little boy's plea. Direct me home or to a shelter for the night.' When he had concluded his speech in which he had stuttered not even once, he looked boastingly towards his sister, as one who is on talking terms with Divinity.

They pushed their little bodies ahead and had now passed from the midget dominion of the dwarf to the vast territory of the giant. As they stumbled over a natural milestone they suddenly beheld before them a huge building whose windows were glazed with strange glass representing biblical episodes, and upon whose top there rose resplendent a golden *Mogen Dovid*. Over the lintel of the door there swung a heavy *Mazuzah* in which the word 'Shaddai' shone like a constellation. The door was locked. But its key-hole was so large that they climbed up to it and walked into the room. Here they were confronted by a man who looked like Og, King of Bashan, so tall was he, and so evil-looking. He bent down over them, squinted his lunar eye to see them the better, and in a thunder-clapped voice roared, 'This is a synagogue, the Jews here have cast a spell over me, and I am their *Shabbos Goy*.'

With a wicked look in his eye he said to them, curtly, 'Follow me.' He led them to the huge furnace which heated the synagogue, and in which the giant threw fuel for every holiday. As he opened the door the twins saw before them a veritable Gehenna. Velvela divined the *Shabbos Goy's* intentions. In the home town, the *Shabbos Goy* was a kindly old soul, but here it seemed he was intending to throw them into the flames.

As they approached the furnace and were already standing over the threshold of its glowing door, Velvela quickly climbed over the back of the giant and, sliding along his neck, drew himself up to his chin and poked his foot into his nostril, just long enough to make him want to sneeze. As the giant drew his head back to sneeze, Velvela slid down his foot again. The giant sneezed, and so powerful was the force of it that he stumbled right into the furnace.

On the next day the children met all the Jews of that synagogue, and when they came home they told their mother how warm it was in the house of worship since the giant furnished such excellent fuel for the furnace. May his carcass be a right clean *Kaporah* and atonement for us and *Kol Yisroel*!

The Triumph of Zalman Tiktiner

Zalman Tiktiner was as indispensable to a Zionist meeting as a blue and white flag. No assembly which gathered to discuss the much laughed-at and wept-over Jewish problem was complete without him. Not that he took a part in the vociferous or the furious orations; he was, on the contrary, a singularly quiet man, who at an assembly shuffled unostentatiously to a coign of auricular vantage, and seated there, his head, by reason of partial deafness, twisted on a side, he lent the speaker of the occasion a devouring ear, nodding from paragraph to paragraph in utter agreement with his eloquent perorations. He was the kind of lecture-goer, you would imagine, who if ever he came late to a meeting, would tip-toe forward with a billowy motion to an empty chair, his shoes creaking out weak and humble apologies. Only Zalman never came late. He would be there hours ahead, even of the committee, and would spend his time listening in to conversations, gathering an economic slice here, picking up a political crumb there. Zionism was an ideal that moved him; it was moving him from Canada to Palestine now for a period of about thirty years; and this is the story of how Zalman Tiktiner outstripped the categories of time and space, laughed at difficulties physical and spiritual, fooled an administration and its closed-door immigration policy, and how, after a great longing for the land did finally embrace it.

Ever since the early days of his youth he had heard of the episodes which had so romantically transpired in Palestine and a compelling nostalgia had possessed him. The smoke of the Temple destroyed by the abominable Titus was still in his nostrils and worked upon him like a drug evoking epic memories. He felt himself to be a vicarious native of Erez Israel and now an unwarranted expatriate. Before his eyes Jerusalem ever shone with her hundred glistening domes, and Hebron murmured with a holy murmuring, and Safed was bright with its terraces. Though he would go wandering in foreign lands it was before an implacable wailing wall that he continually arrived. The Tomb of Rachel on the road to Bethlehem (house of bread, indeed) and the guarded sepulchre nigh unto Hebron, these sent to him voices, still and small, that outshouted the turbulence of oceans, and were heard above the din of dynamos. Such were the visions and voices that came to him in the early days of his sojourn in America, after he had at the age of about twenty left Warsaw, when his religion still shone resplendent upon his young beard, and when he thought of Palestine as a territorial *Yeshivah*, an antechamber to the Palace Celestial.

In due time he changed his opinions. Before he had left Europe in 1903 he had listened to Herzl himself; he still remembered how that man who looked like a Messiah, had concluded those words that rang like prophecies, and how the tears stood in his eyes, and how he saw through their nebulous blur fields of golden grain, and cities rising from sand.

He began also to read of students who came to work in Palestine as farmers, bearing towards their labour medals and scholarships; and of Chassidim who forsook caftan for overalls, and water-carriers who laboured a labour of love in the wine-cellars of Rishon-le-Zion. So Palestine was not merely a refuge for greybeards and scholars, but was a land *mit leiten gleich*, which would once more release from its soil its secret bounties, and drop from its heavens its beatific dews.

When at the termination of the *Seder*-service, he cried with a lusty cry, 'Next year in Jerusalem!' – how much longing and yearning there was in his words! If he could catch hold of Elijah by the hem of his ancestral coat as he fluttered in through the door to sip of his very own goblet, assuredly he would implore him to take him back to the land from which he had through many generations been uprooted. But miracles are rare, and cash for transportation still rarer. Zalman decided, in view of the fact that he had not the power of *psiyas ha-derech*, to save his pennies for the purchase of a steamship ticket, third class.

In those years he would not work on the Sabbath. Accordingly he got himself a job in a Jewish printing establishment. Even this pious work demanded of him a religious compromise. Gutenberg's invention has always been unkind to religion, and in this case it was cruel. As Zalman was bending over his machine, his beard, now of manly proportions, was caught, and tugged with a vicious vehemence worthy of a battalion of cossacks. Zalman had to abbreviate his beard. People afterwards said that he looked like a Russian *maskel*, with that short tuft of a beard, or like a member of a French artist colony; such are the indignities that *parnassah* imposes on one.

When the war broke out, Zalman lost for a time all hope of returning (I say returning, though never in the flesh had he really been there) to Palestine. Then a ray of hope. The Jewish legion was being organized, and although it was merely a Zion Mule Corps, were not thy wild asses upon the mountains, O Galilee, worthier than the thoroughbreds in the stables of Pharaoh? And did not tradition say that Messiah would come riding, if not on a mule, at least upon a related donkey? Zalman was thirty-three years of age; he applied as a recruit. He was rejected. Reason; flat feet. But, expostulated Zalman, if it's going to be a mule corps, a second-grade cavalry, what difference does it make if I have flat feet? There was no appeal.

Zalman cursed the printing business to which he now attributed not only the loss of his beard, but also the flattening of his feet. Throughout all the years of the war he lived in utter misery, reading carefully all the reports of Allenby's activities and Jabotinsky's speeches. All this time moreover, he was saving his money for that blissful voyage to Palestine.

When the Armistice was signed, and when on November 2, 1917, the Balfour Declaration was issued, Zalman went wild. He gave a modest banquet, at which speeches were made in Hebrew, and the wine that was drunk, and copiously, was Palestinian. Zalman danced, yea, even upon his flat feet.

He now had quite a sum in the Home Bank. In 1921 he was prepared to leave. The land was calling him, he must go. But after the riots of the previous year, immigration was temporarily stopped. That meant another delay. The path of love (and what man knew a greater love than this?) never did run smooth.

This delay cost Zalman the circumvention of his hope. He waited until the edict would be recalled. It was. He had some further preliminary arrangements to make. Hence another delay. Then came the failure of the Home Bank, settling with its depositors at 25 per cent.

Zalman went grey over night. The hope of his lifetime was lost, gone forever. He was now approaching his fiftieth year. Surely he could not go now to a colonization agency and ask them to do what pride in his earlier days had forbidden him to ask. Furthermore they did not want *Chalutzim* who were old enough to be grandfathers. His tragedy preyed upon him. He grew decades older from day to day. To think of it – already was he approaching the land of his fathers, not stealing through the back door of Jericho as did Joshua, but advancing straight towards the harbour of Haifa, and midway to be halted!

There is no purpose in lingering over the misery and the disappointment of Zalman's last days. He was like a man who had lived a whole lifetime for a taste of heaven, and then found it beyond his reach. In 1929 he died.

But he was not buried before he had, by a posthumous ruse, achieved his purpose. Solomon Dickstein, reputed a wit, declared, with that poker face which he put on when he was being funny, that Zalman had adopted underground methods.

For in his will, Zalman Tiktiner, of sound body and mind, dedicated the 25 per cent which he had saved from the Home Bank, now in bankruptcy, for the purchase of earth in Palestine, which holy soil was to be placed beneath the head of the aforementioned Zalman Tiktiner, when deceased, and interred in the cemetery on Mount Royal.

A war, immigration laws, army restrictions, and a bank failure could not and did not keep Zalman from the land of his fathers.

The Parliament of Fowles: A Short Story

King Solomon was wearied of his thousand concubines. He thought of the long line of international beds in his royal dormitory; and shuddered. The spirit was willing, but the flesh was weak. As a venture in diplomacy his harem was an overwhelming success: his collection of women of all shades and temperatures, the prettiest of their tribes, into one palace, explained to no small degree the world peace that prevailed throughout his reign. But as an enterprise in matrimony – Solomon sighed. The Lord had endowed him with wisdom, but not with strength ... He was no Samson to be equal to all the demands put upon his time and energy. There was an age, indeed, when his royal bedchamber was besieged every night, and his sleep invariably wrested from him. This would have continued, no doubt, and would have brought his black hairs to an early grave, had he not taken measures against their passionate sallies. His method is immortalized in Scripture: Behold his bed, which is Solomon's; three-score valiant men are about it, of the valiant of Israel. They all hold swords, being expert in war; every man hath his sword upon his thigh because of fear in the night.

Howbeit, the fact remained that women were an affliction, and useful to him only as material for the great thesis on vanity which he was at the moment considering. The interest of domestic peace, however, counselled him to hide behind his pseudonym Koheleth.

Women, moreover, were not the only annoyance in the monarch's life. This late afternoon in spring he was equally peeved by another elusive pest. He had invited some eastern mages to a private banquet, and the bald-headed greybeards had insisted on discussing theology. He had attempted to keep their mouths occupied by ordering additional courses, but these wise men forsook even the pleasures of food for the ecstasies of dialectic. For three hours they had considered divinity and, to use Solomon's favourite phrase, the conclusion of the matter was a headache. After he had dismissed them with ambiguous compliments, King Solomon sighed a sigh of relief, and strolled forth into his garden. Even to wisdom and knowledge there was a surfeiting, and out of much talk came little profit. All that remained to him of his conferences with the sages was a pain at the back of his head and a desire to use vile words. Imperiously, he doffed his crown, upon which full beads of sweat shone like diademal jewels; he tossed it among thornbushes. He had no niggardly worries about it. A slave eager to vindicate his honesty, he thought, would no doubt return it to him. And even if he didn't, gold was cheap, and styles in coronets were fickle.

The subject of crowns brought his mind to the subject of politics. Inspired by some unspoken reflection he thumbed his nose at no one in particular; and then looked around to see whether anyone had noticed his departure from monarchical dignity. Indeed, no one. The garden was as that garden inclosed which in a poem of his youth he had compared to his sister, his spouse ... Politics, fie! There was no contemporary prince worthy his mettle. Hiram, King of Tyre, woodcutter on a grand scale; the spinster Queen of Sheba travelling presumably in search of wisdom; and a cripple on the throne of Mizraim ... They were simpletons and dolts; and politics with these was a weariness to the flesh.

He was tired. Boredom had been sent to him as ambassador from God knows what court; and in his head one thought pursued itself like a monkey in a cage: All was vanity ... For the third time in the course of an hour the king had sighed. A philosophic asthma possessed him. He sat down and leaned his back against a tree, and murmured: All is vanity. Was he becoming a dotard, forever drivelling one sentence?

In the west the sun was setting. It daubed the sky with a multitude of colours, and tinted the horizon like a master's palette. Purple melted into carmine, carmine faded into scarlet, scarlet waned into crimson, and crimson disappeared into pink – the variations of a theme, – Red. The doomed day stalked to its pyre in the west; from the east hurried the dusk, rendering the green grass greener, and the blue sky more blue. King Solomon regarded the sky and suffered in his brain a torment, and in his heart an ecstasy ... The sunset was too beautiful even for Hebrew words, crisp words baked in the desert. The sun was a rose upon the bosom of the sky. He thought of the Shunamite, and of the sunset, and of this glory about him, and he knew that all was not vanity. There remained a truth eternal; – and it was beauty.

Because the day was at its end the garrulities of the birds grew louder and louder with the imminence of dusk. Their chatterings were sharp with argument, and there was a haste in their words that smacked of the laws of closure. It was evident that some matter of great import was being bandied across the branches of the trees. Song rebutted song, twitter refuted twitter, and the little wood was full of a forensic chirping. Polished beaks uttered melodious syllogisms, and birds' eyes twinkled with the light of novel ratiocinations. The leaves rustled, the twigs quivered with the vigour of debate.

Solomon, who knew the language of the birds, eavesdropped on these their squabblings and gathered that the tiny feathered aesthetes were discussing the beauties of a sunset sky as compared with those of a noonday one. Here indeed behind these plumaged ribs, reflected the monarch, there was an understanding that surpassed his, a knowledge of the things that had true and weighty import. These creatures were obsessed by no sense of vanity, and overcome by no emptiness; they lived as neighbours to Heaven. Chafed by no worldly concerns, they balanced beauty on a feather ... This thing endured.

The discussion, as the falcon who was the local sage on heraldry expressed it, turned on the relative merits of azure and gules, noon and sundown.

'I am pleased by a sunset,' chirped the robin, swelling his

breast with sleek self-admiration, 'solely because of a high and selfish conceit. Imprimis: my spouse yonder becomes singularly amorous towards nightfall; accordingly I have, as you will understand, a pardonable partiality for the drawer of the red blinds. Secundo, in the rays of the setting sun, choice tidbits in the stubble appear even choicer, curdled, as it were, with strawberry-cream; and tertio, the ruddy horizon makes a perfect match to my vest. Ergo, as libertine, as epicure, and as dandy, I must perforce be sun-worshipper.'

'But,' interrupted the canary in timid monosyllables, 'for like cause I should dote on the moon; the blue bird should go mad with the love of the sky; the black bird praise the mid of night; and the grey hawk laud the clouds – which things are not so.'

(King Solomon leaned back against the tree and smiled benignly. He was regaining his good humour).

'Are you sure of that?' queried the robin, his arrogance expanding along his waist, 'are you sure of that? Where did you learn your scientific knowledge? Do you not know that it profits the blue bird greatly to find himself in an azure environment? Do you not know that precisely that is the reason he eludes the hunters, the vultures, and the poets? The same truth applies to the hawk, and as for you, it would benefit you enormously if the world were amber, or if at least, you nested in daffodil fields.'

(King Solomon admired this ornithological elucidation of a scientific theory. He pricked his ears; he would miss not even a comma from out their conversation).

'That is true, that is true,' meekly assented the canary, thinking of his compeers behind gilded wires.

'That is true? You should have known that before you opened your beak to let out folly. You now concede what you never should have questioned. You have not the courage of your convictions. You are yellow.' And the parabola of his breast swelled into a semi-circle. The canary was silent. He hopped three steps along the twig, and regarded the sunset, admiring beauties hitherto not admired.

(King Solomon gloated over the zeal with which these birds

fought for the principles of science and art. Beauty wedded to knowledge! Admiringly he shook his head, pursed his lips, and let out a smack of approbation).

'The truculence of the robin,' cawed the crow from behind his ministerial sable, 'is unwarranted, unjustified, and unbirdlike. Such bellicosity is fitting for the biped moulted birds of the Greek philosopher, but not for birds of our respectable feather. What difference does it make whether the sunset or the noonday sky has the most ravishments? Are they not both the handiwork of God?'

(King Solomon groaned).

'Do you therefore cast hallelujahs on both? It is sinful to admire such superficial charms; and as a servant of my God, and as one who is concerned not only with form but also with content, I feel that –'

'Get you to your carrion. Listen to him,' bubbled the thrush, quoting his parody of a well-known author to whom he owed a debt of gratitude for publicities rendered, 'listen to him:

God's in his heaven,
To hell with the world!'

He was pleased with this antithesis; and lest you should think that he never could recapture the first fine careless rapture, he repeated it.

The crow cawed at the profanity, and flapping his wings flew away.

(King Solomon sighed the fourth sigh of the afternoon, but this time he enjoyed it).

The rooster seemed highly indignant. His comb was of a furious red. He wanted to direct the argument through its proper channels.

'The purpose of this debate is entirely misconstrued,' he interrupted. 'There should be no talk here of the respective attractions of noon and sundown, but of noon and sunrise. There,' – he raised an emphatic claw, – 'there is a beauty for the true aesthetic soul. It is not only for the purpose of catching fat worms that the right-thinking bird should early rise, but also that he might behold the sun in its birth. Feast your gizzards upon earthworms, if you will; I have loftier tastes. I feast my eyes upon the rising sun. When the early dawn appears, there am I, already strutting in my courtyard. I climb to the thatch of some hut, or I settle on an open barn-door. Monarch of all I survey am I. I hold the sun in fee. The beauties of dying Lucifer I judge; upon the lightening of the sky I look with favour. I behold the sun, rising, like a silver cymbal in the east; I approve; I cast the gravel of my voice at it in complete appreciation.'

And the rooster crowed over his opponents, as in victory. He felt that he had pecked a million holes in their contentions.

(King Solomon now understood why the pious offer a benediction upon hearing the crow of a rooster at sun-up).

'You have spoken with less than your usual cacophony,' commented the woodpecker, who was also a logic-chopper. 'Nonetheless, your contribution to this discussion is utterly irrelevant. As for me, I only break the silence to indicate a point of order. My own opinions on art are considered philistinish. I am a materialist and my criticism, when given, is invariably destructive. Besides, I am not a brilliant conversationalist. I frankly admit it. I bore. *C'est mon métier.* Hence I desist.'

A twitter of applause greeted his silence, and commended it. The parliament was tired of sophistry and procedure. It was longing for something lyrical.

Sang the nightingale, compounding rhythm and reason, 'Blue is the sky, like lapis-lazuli, and like milk whiteness is the welkin white. Veined marble pumiced to a dome, – such are the heavens; footstool of the Lord, where skylarks rise to fall, low at His feet. The sky at noon is beautiful, a flower of white and pale-blue petals, beautiful; but far more beautiful the sun at dusk. O crimson arras dropping down the sky, O target of the west, O torch of fire that fulminates thin lightning in the brain, alembic of the day, curfew of birds, precursor of the moonlight tryst, O heart bursting into the starry song of night!'

All the birds were silent before the song of the nightingale.

Up piped the linnet: 'Although professional jealousy may with justice be imputed to me, still will I persist in the face of antagonizing criticism to say that the last lyric of the nightingale, in which I smell a sonnet, does not warrant that dumbness with which you have all been smitten. The form, I will admit, is admirable; it has a series of fine but classical images, and a good many mixed metaphors. But for context, profundity of thought — the croakings of the raven hold more matter than his. The nightingale supports the sunset because it is the herald of moonrise, but is not the noon-day sky the herald of sunset? Is the sire to be rated above the grandsire? Mere fallacy! Sophistry of song!' And the linnet warbled a composition of remarkable ingenuousness.

(King Solomon was pleased. He brought forth from a concealment in his royal robes, a length of parchment, and began taking notes. He had solved a great riddle; he had found that to which there was no cloying).

The peacock had hitherto held his peace. He had vaunted his tail, but had kept his silence. He now paraded his fan, and pompously approached the arboreal pulpit. All expected to hear some beautiful phrases, some elaborate dictions. The peacock had only a simile to offer. In a voice which had been better preserved behind the sternum of a corbel, he opined:

'The sky at noon is a banner of Cathay.'

'Or,' added the eagle whose nose was evidently Semitic, 'a flag of the Jews.'

Throughout the whole argument, the doves had been as peaceful as their reputations. Perched on some leafy branch, romantically they cooed. At intervals an especially amorous pigeon would push his beak into that of his enamoured one, and recite,

'Roses are red;
Violets are blue;
God loves me,
And I love you.'

(King Solomon was elated. The event had reached its climax. He had discovered on this afternoon's excursion, not only bird-talk, but also beauty, and science, and art, and love. Here he beheld life in its open sincerity. The whole chirruping conversation was unsullied by anything vulgar, nothing had entered to mar the perfection of this seance with the birds. After all, all was not vanity. With a dash of inspiration, he wrote on his parchment, 'The flowers appear on the earth, the time of the singing of birds is come, and the voice of the turtle is heard in our land.' As he completed the last word with a calligraphic flourish something fell from the branch of the tree under which he was sitting. It splashed on the parchment, and blotted his verse with greenish-white substance. King Solomon crumpled the parchment and threw it away. He rose from beneath the tree. He spat royally. 'Vanity,' he said, – 'that isn't the word for it! Perfect beauty, indeed! ...')

The Chanukah Dreidel

Even to this day the Chassidic disciples of Reb Itzik'l Podebosher, with much raising of the pious eyes towards heaven, and much shaking of the side-curled head, narrate the exploits of the Master, may his name be a blessing upon Israel. The memory of him still dangles in their brain like *tzitzith*. Especially when the Chassidim speak words of Torah or serve the Lord with many benedictions upon wine, especially then does his spirit hover about them. Thus on Passover nights when they make an end to the Seder with many an ecstatic ditty and devoutly see the *afikomen* hid in the capacious folds of a Chassid's caftan, they regale one another with stories of how Reb Itzik'l did on a time hold converse with Elijah the prophet, and at the Purim banquet they inevitably make mention of the day when the Rebbe to the end that he might bring more felicity to this dismal vale of tears, disguised himself together with other Purim spieler as Mordecai and tripped it from house to Hebrew house caroling joyous catches. The Chassidim invariably add that this constituted no diminution of the *Zaddik*'s dignity, for did not the Baal Shem himself maintain that even he who brings joy upon earth by hopping for the mob's delectation in the market-place, that even such a one is serving the Lord right properly? Such tales they tell; and on the Feast of the Maccabees they repeat the miracle of the Rebbe's Chanukah *dreidel*.

One gathers from the parentheses with which they break the sequence of this marvel, that had not an accident happened at the parlous moment, Satan, may his name and his memory go down to oblivion, might have forever become the vassal and slave of Reb

Itzik'l. Ah, what bliss would have then descended upon an earth untroubled by Satan's tale-bearing, and unmolested by his goings to and fro, and unmortified by his devilish pleadings before the *Pamalyah shel Ma'ola*! In such case the sky would have been as a big-bellied samovar from which the rain would have come down as acceptable as Sabbath tea, the birds would have sung *zmiros* in the branches of the trees, and with roast Leviathan the Chassidim would have gorged themselves. The sons of man would have honored Reb Itzik'l and marvelled to see him, little man that he was, ordering Satan about, a humble and whipped Satan with his tail between his legs.

But the time was not yet ripe for such a miracle. The Holy One, blessed be He, saw that it would be premature to visit such good fortune upon a world so steeped in sin and wickedness that it would not even know to make itself worthy of the disappearance of Satan. It might even mourn his departure. And so Reb Itzik'l almost vanquished the unhallowed one, almost, but not quite.

In his consideration of religion Reb Itzik'l was especially original. He interpreted life with a joke-book. To him a loud and hearty laugh was better than a hosanna, a well-placed witticism more gratifying to deity than a hallelujah. He preferred a bon mot to a heavy piece of Tosfoth; and an uproarious song full of joy and gusto, he felt sure, rang more musical in the ears of God than the pious cantillation of the Psalms. God, he maintained, gave the world with its birds and flowers and stars as a gift to his Jews, and it was insult to shut one's eyes to the Lord's proffer. Wherefore it was not surprising that Reb Itzik'l expressed more love for the Chanukah *dreidel* than for the Chanukah *Menorah*; not that he scorned the eight-branched candelabra which brought back memory of the Maccabeans and their valiant opposition to the knave Antiochus but rather that as a matter of preference he was more attached to the *dreidel* which furnished pastime to him and his Chassidim.

Thus on the Chanukah nights, when the candles lit up the room with their living blossoms, and the Chassidim sang melodiously-nasal songs in praise of Mattathias, Reb Itzik'l, his furred *shtreimel* on his head, his caftan descending to the floor, and hiding the spotless white stockings, Reb Itzik'l would sit at the table, nibbling a *latke*, and turn his *dreidel* solicitously watching its fall.

He cherished the *dreidel* (it was an heirloom from his great-grandfather, and once, tradition had it, had been twirled by the fingers of the Baal Shem himself). From year to year he hid it as carefully as he hid the edition of the Zohar. For Reb Itzik'l saw in this thingumbob a significance apart from the excitement which it afforded. There was also in it a mystical meaning.

The vulgar, Reb Itzik'l maintained, interpreted the Nun, Gimmel, Hai and Sheen, embossed in lead upon the sides of the *dreidel* as the initials of the phrase *Nes Godol Hoyoh Shom*: there, there chanced a wondrous miracle; but he, Reb Itzik'l was privy to profounder secrets. He had studied *gematria*; he had pored over Cabbala. Was not the Hai the symbol of God's name, Jehovah? Did not the Nun signify the number fifty, a number of marvellous implications? Was not the Gimmel, alphabetical substitute for three, a side-glance at the idea of trinity? And the Sheen – what ignoramus did not know that that stood for Shaddai, the Almighty? So the Rebbe turned the *trendel* and watched trinity fall as *Shaddai* rose, and as the Nun fell the Hai shine forth.

It is told that on one Chanukah night when all had gone home to dream of a jolly Messiah and his lusty *Shofar*, Reb Itzik'l sat alone in his study, twisting the *dreidel*, and watching the blur of the letters. He was computing the value of the letters which fell, intending later, when the spirit of the Lord would settle upon him, to deduce from the total some esoteric meaning. Outside snow was falling and wind whistled through the trees like a robber calling his henchmen. Suddenly the Rebbe heard a knocking on his door. If it had been Passover he might have thought that it was a ritual blood-pogrom. It was Chanukah, and surely no one could harbour evil in his heart this rollicking night. He unbarred the door. A tall man with a goat-beard filled the threshold.

'Good *Yomtov*.'

'Good Year.'

'I passed by. I was cold. I saw your candles through the window-pane. I thought I would drop in and warm up.'

'You are ever welcome,' replied Reb Itzik'l. 'Sit down, take off your overcoat.'

'I won't bother. If I take off my coat I won't be warm ...'

Reb Itzik'l did not see the logic of this last remark, inasmuch as a stove in the centre of the room was crackling with the ecstatic accents of warmth. He bade the stranger have some *latkes*, which the Chassidim, in an inexplicable oversight, had forgotten to devour. The stranger helped himself. Between munches he talked about the weather, he talked about miracles, he talked about everything. An exceptionally garrulous stranger. Finally he came to a consideration of souls. Reb Itzik'l became suspicious. One did not discuss one's soul with a stranger. Affably he suggested a little turn of the *dreidel*. The stranger was willing.

Reb Itzik'l proudly twirled the mystical family heirloom. He had singularly good luck. He almost invariably foretold upon what letter it would fall. The *dreidel* was made of lead and was fashioned about a little central spoke on which hung four miniature blocks inscribed each with its letter. The stranger was soon aware that the reason the letters fell on Sheen and Hai was that there was more lead in these blocks, and thus the force of gravity achieved what the powers of mysticism claimed. As he meditated on this phenomenon abstractedly he raised his hat to scratch his head. Reb Itzik'l let forth a loud cry. Beneath the stranger's *yarmulkah*, for he wore one beneath his fur cap, bulged forth two horns. Reb Itzik'l was so excited that he stamped his foot. This time the stranger yelled. Reb Itzik'l had stepped on his tail.

'I may as well introduce myself,' said the stranger, 'a mere formality I admit, but a necessary one. For the most part I travel incognito, or sheltered behind a nom de guerre; I am, yours truly, Mephistopheles Satanas. I said yours truly: that is precisely the mission upon which I came here – whether I will be truly yours or you truly mine. In fine I wish to gamble my soul against yours. Whosoever guesses two successive turns of the *dreidel*, he is victor. Imagine, Reb Itzik'l, the glory which will be yours when it is given to you to redeem the world from my machinations and when I, who am dedicated to evil, will be the servant of good. Imagine not so much the honor and the glory, but the knowledge that you have rid the world of what the world calls a pest.'

'And if I lose?'

'If you lose, then you are merely another of those who have fallen by the wayside, you are another feather in my already much be-plumed cap.'

After much argumentating to and fro (it must be admitted that Satan was a debater more convincing than Reb Itzik'l), they set to playing.

(When *misnagdim*, who spurn God and reject his *Zaddikim*, tell this story, they conclude it by saying that the Rebbe got the better of the bargain; he lost the game. But Satan had been cheated; the Rebbe had no soul. We mention this merely to draw out how ingenious can be the minds of wickedness in devising calumnies against the saintly.)

They set to playing. The Rebbe twisted the *dreidel* and cried, 'Hai'; on Hai it fell. Satan twisted it and squealed 'Nun', on Nun it fell. The explanation was simple. Satan, who had studied physics, had noted that the weight of the lead had much to do with the falling of the *dreidel*, and accordingly he had chipped off with his long nail part of the lead on the Hai, thus giving Nun a preponderance. But Reb Itzik'l had been watching the fingers of Mephistopheles. In his heart he justified himself before God and scraped with his finger nail a shaving out of the Nun. Now the Hai carried weight. Thus they tossed the *dreidel* back and forth, scraping and scratching at it until it became almost a shadow of its former self. Neither had won two successive victories. Suddenly an idea occurred to Reb Itzik'l. He scratched a thin shaving from the Nun, and with a deft movement of his finger stuck it firmly to the Hai, so that if Satan would scratch the Hai it would still retain its former weight. Satan was inwardly gloating about his most recent capture. He failed to note the Rebbe's ruse. The Rebbe had one victory to his credit. The *trendel* turned on the table performing mystical revolutions. He would win and Satan would be vanquished. Suddenly Mephisto realized what was happening. The *dreidel* was now very small indeed, but still it could bring confusion even to the mighty Satanas. Satan inhaled deeply, and with a sudden effort breathed upon the *dreidel* while it was still in motion. His breath was a fire. The lead *dreidel* melted before his exhalation ...

To this day no one has seen the famous *dreidel* of Reb Itzik'l Podebosher, but the Chassidim still maintain that, had not at the parlous moment an accident happened, a mere wind of breath, Satan, may his name and his memory go down to oblivion, might have forever become the vassal and slave of the good Rebbe of Podebosh.

The Meed of the Minnesinger:
A Vivid Short Story Based on the Life of a Great
Thirteenth-Century Poet

Arya Leib von Trimberg had sown in joy, and was reaping in sorrow. He had brought a son upon the world, and in him he was sorely grieved; for he had awaited a consolation in his old age, and had found but a hastener of gray hairs. Daily his son, Susskind, withdrew himself more and more from his fold; and if ever he had had a Jewish heart, he now hid its cubits beneath his ribs. Had Arya Leib not been assured of the piety of his spouse, he would most certainly have taken oath that she had consorted with Satan, and that of such a diabolic union was Susskind begotten. But Judith was as vexed as her husband by the waywardness of their son, meandering through the devil's estate, aping the manners of the Gentiles, and even lauding Edom the while he spat scorn upon his own people.

Susskind screwed a wry face and curled wrinkled nostrils when he spoke about the meanness of his tribe. Sickened he was by the wretchedness and the utter abasements of his people; the lewd indignities that were heaped upon them; the envenomed words that were slung at them; the scapegoat tomfooleries. If his people had fallen valiantly in battle, and by the sword had perished out of the memory of man, then it would have been well; but that they should ignominiously survive and stealthily look to the left and to the right of them that none might behold them breathe, that they should by night be in terror of the cabals of the wicked in high places, and by day fear the mud pelletted by baptized urchins, this was disgrace, and infamy beyond sufferance. He cursed the day whereon an infant's blood was shed to seal the Covenant of

Abraham, a covenant with misery, a pact with pain. He felt in his heart an estrangement from those who had suckled him; he grew to hate their penury; he knew, and in his own congregation he had encountered them, Jews who rotted in gold, and who still attired themselves in the tatters a Christian beggar would disgustedly doff. Stubbornly he interpreted this as national stinginess, and as a knavish insensibility to beauty, and showed grinning and incredulous teeth when he was told that thus unostentatiously did his people elect to sojourn in the land, lest with their riches and noble deportment they bring down upon themselves the biting envy and the devouring wrath of Christians unable to endure in their midst the infidel, waxing fat and prosperous.

Too, Susskind felt himself unmoved by the tribulations of his kin; they were, he considered, too meek, too long-suffering, a people with souls fashioned of stuff more malleable than putty. Surely this was not the stiff-necked race, he said, that issued from Mizraim, proud even against its God – surely these were not they, but rather a degenerate and dwarfed posterity, a breed of homunculi, shrunken by sandal-licking and flattery. Howsoever he worshipped God according to the law of Moses and of Israel and felt that he could never barter Jehovah for a trinity or multiplicity of lesser godlings, still he could not find it in him, despite rabbinic injunction and the behests of his elders, to shed tears over his forlorn lot, nor hasten the coming of the Messiah with contrite breast-pounding and great crying of *peccavi*. So might act the Jews of the hamlet of Trimberg, their eyes mirroring the spectral reflections of sorrow, and their faces masks of tragedy, whereon a melancholy beard was stuck askew; a community of Jeremiahs.

The poet Susskind was in wonder whether these gloomy shadows ever in their hunted shiftings to and fro upon the earth beheld the moon in glory, the stars in splendor. A sour smile he smiled, as he reflected that Jews ushered in the day not by a benediction upon sunrise, but by a benediction upon the rooster whose crowing announced the call to synagogue. The sun had faded from their thoughts. Even when they lifted heels in dance before the full moon, they were as scarecrows troubled by a mysterious wind.

Yet to him these things were of the very quintessence of life. Daily his heart grew big with gratitude to the unerring Alchemist who in the crucible of earth, using sun as cauldron, and the planets as varied flames, and the moon as drawer of water, with such fine craftsmanship produced the deep dyes of the flowers of the field, and their honeyed fumes, and out of all created the elusive elixir. The waters of Saale, upon whose banks he had so thriftily wasted many afternoons, rippled joy within him. The green meadowland in which pastured contented cattle; the fields quivering with standing sheaves of gold; the forest, dark and sombre, an army of knights with sable banners; all of these shaped themselves into song in his brain. The castle of the lord, dentellating the sky with its turrets, in the light of day of solid yet delicate stone, in sunset as if of burnished brass, showed him beauty and strength wedded. While birds bubbled music from their throats, while flowers lavished upon the land their lordly largess, and while even the serf hummed some quaint ditty behind his wooden ploughshare, no regret, assuredly, would make parchment of his face, and no sorrow would inscribe its dismal legend thereon.

And he, Susskind, was troubadour, minnesinger to their lordships, welcome at any baronial board where viands were tasteless and wine watery unless spiced and strengthened by song; an eastern turtle-dove he was, fearless of falcons. Though a Jew, he knew chivalry, his rhymings exalted virtue and honor, courage and hardihood they made immortal. In the cage of his verse he captured nightingales.

For he was enamored of all beautiful things, even they be the possession of the Gentile and thus profaned in the sight of the Lord. Comely to him was the sight of plumed knights upon their steeds caparisoned, comely though marked with the cross; in his marvelling he forgot Crusaders burning synagogues on the Rhine, forgot pillage, and sanguine massacre, and blood-quenching fire. From between his teeth the imprecatory spittle might dart, and upon his lips the curse of desolation might tarry, yet standing before a cathedral he was all wonder at the miracle of its stained-glass and at the exquisiteness of its sculpturing. He knew the body to be corrupt, and the soul clawed by the devil, yet how soothing to the eye were the rich and noble, arrayed in the white caresses of ermine, and glorious in their satins and silks. And though they wasted breath upon a haunting ghost, the young choir-boys, singing in their milk-and-honey voices, most certainly made a joyful noise, and it was pleasant by chance to hear their chanting hymns. It was not the content that Susskind worshipped, for that, indeed, he did heartily revile, but the vessel that had cast its spell upon him.

High-born ladies flattered him at his juggling of words; other troubadours saw in him a rival whose musical throat they would gladly have slit; and count and noble, as meed for his song, sometimes threw him a jingling purse. Accordingly, Susskind could discover no reason wherefore, the sun shining, the river flowing, and birds singing, he should mortify the flesh by fasting, and weep out his eyes in lamentation.

As he sat on the bank of the Saale, lazily he fingered his lute, musing on the welcome that he was to receive at the castle of Duke Berthold von Saale. He recalled how the duke's daughter, the lovely Eloise, had favored him with a short but pedigreed smile. Perhaps fancy brewed strange potions in his brain, perhaps he might conjure up into his life that high romance that so frequently leaped through his song, the love of the Jew for the princess, the moth for the purple; and, – was it ever dreamed of in Franconia? – Susskind to the ghetto born, might be lord of the manor.

He seemed pleased at the thought of besieging a castle with ballads, making the grand assault in heroic verse, winning it to the clarion of a happy conceit. Susskind's fingers tripped lightly upon his lute in joyous measure.

'Strumming heathen melodies again?' Arya Leib on his way to the synagogue addressed the rebellious scion of his family. 'In exile, and in a strange land, you dare lift up your voice to utter words other than the praises of the Lord?'

'Not a song, but song is pleasant to Him above. Why should I hush my heart when it trembles with joy? Why should I place a muzzle on my mouth when happiness clamors to issue therefrom? Were the Jews smitten with dumbness when they crossed the Great Sea?'

'In exile we dare not sing. It is blasphemy to chant on soil unholy and in words profane.

"*By the rivers of Babylon there we sat down, yea, we wept, when we remembered Zion.*

"*We hanged our harps upon the willow in the midst thereof.*

"*For there they that carried us away captive required of us a song, and they that wasted us, required of us mirth, saying, Sing us one of the songs of Zion.*

"*How shall we sing the Lord's song in a strange land?*"'

Reb Arya Leib's voice quivered with tragedy. In the darkening twilight he seemed like a phantom, a hawker come from nowhere to peddle tribulation.

Susskind implacably replied, 'These are arguments of old Babylonian vintage. It is enough that the *goyim* impose upon us all the strictures of their devising, without that we ourselves should add to them, jot or tittle. You are your own mortal enemy, for he who makes joy to perish hath already murdered life ... Moreover, matters have not all those bar sinisters your gloomy heraldry marks upon them. We are given liberties and even privileges in trade; our religion is seldom molested; and I, your son, am accepted in the duke's halls.'

Arya Leib was angered; he uttered harsh words.

'When a dog slinks into the refectory beneath von Saale's ducal legs, a munificent bone is thrown him. When Susskind von Trimberg lilts a tune, shall they put wool in their ears? No, Susskind has a good voice, a voice that could be put to worthier uses in *Chazanuth*, but he prefers to waste it on profane songs, and surely no duke will shoo away the singing bird from his casement; Susskind has a good conceit, but one which could be better used in writing liturgy; howbeit stiff-neckedly he creates epics that are not his folk's. And concerning your privileges of trade; we are battened so that we be tastier. They let us amass our ducats, then come their tax-gatherers and their papal legates and cut bleeding holes in our pouches. They are as mice continually in our cellars, waiting for a rich smell. And religion unmolested? Fie, my son, that you should be so blind! Why, they keep our synagogues by papal edict no higher than anthills; and lest the heathen rage we must perforce talk to God in whispers. Give over these pursuits of the un-Jewish and make an end to them. You have been instructed in medicine; make of that your livelihood.'

'Yes, and fix dirty bandages, and dispense laxatives, and meddle in midwifery? To which I make answer with a mouth-filling nay.'

Arya Leib bit a tuft of his beard sullenly; Susskind was silent, his arguments lying in ambush on his tongue's tip. Arya Leib thought to smoke them out with brands of sarcasm.

'Tell me, Susskind, are you truly intent on becoming one of these vagabond troubadours who come to our fairs and market-places, the grimaces of their mugs and the nimbleness of their limbs their sole merchandise? Have you already acquired scholar-ship in the prestidigitating arts? Can you catch apples featly with two knives so that you may find favor in the eyes of a bored potentate? Can you produce snails from jugglers' cups and make puppies leap through hoops? Can you mimic the cry of the peacock, or repeat the rooster's cock-a-doodle-doo, or for the greater delectation of the vulgar rabble, evoke the nice echo of an ass's bray? For these accomplishments, as you, destined suppli-cator for my soul's salvation, most certainly know, are the especial masteries of your jongleurs, not to mention the red plastered beard and the horsehair wig.'

Susskind swallowed his wrath, a bitter brew. He would not wag an unruly tongue against the honor of his father. He said, 'I do none of these things; I am the duke's minnesinger, not the mob's buffoon. I leave the somersaultings and the acrobatics, the nose-thumbing and rib-tickling to the clownish mountebanks who earn their sweated bread therefrom. I am a maker of songs; the viol and flute, the gigue and salteire, the chifonie and harp, these are my instruments. I am a member of Berthold's court.'

'So is the concubine who satisfies his gadfly desires; so is the spaniel whom, to keep in your sodality, he has christened Ezekiel.'

'And when the lord desires to reward, he will doff his cloak with vair or with miniver, and though he come from paying twenty mark for it, it is mine for a ditty that pleases him.'

'There are gifts; and there are gifts.' Arya Leib's voice took on the sententious; he spoke in parables. 'When Esau greeted his brother Jacob, it is written that he kissed him, but over the script the scribe of the scroll has made flourishes that look like fangs, to imply that even in his buss there was a bite. For the wise it is sufficient to wink an eyelash.'

'But I sing of love ...' Susskind spoke as simply as a peasant-boy.

'Love you sing? Fiddlesticks and kettledrums. You may teach a bear to dance, or an ape to strut like a cavalier, but love you cannot teach your oppressors. They will turn you the other cheek, provided it wear a visor.'

'Father, you misunderstand me. It is the love between lord and lady that I make immortal in my songs.'

'Further abomination! It is the consecrated lecheries of erected beasts that you pass on to posterity as a thing of beauty; the clandestine sins of the mighty, the evil lusting after the flesh.'

Susskind's mind went fleeting through the scriptures. 'Yet did not Solomon sing of his well-beloved, and of love better than wine, and of that fire which many waters can not quench, nor the floods drown? And did not Halevi pen verses for his darling, and did not likewise many another?'

'I have instructed you in the lore of your people, and in vain. You will glean the chaff and leave the wheat. Did not your teacher inform that Solomon's Song was the love-song of Israel towards the Holy, if you will, or of the week-days towards the Sabbath? Evidently his leather-thong was thin-worn and his instruction feeble.'

The sun was setting. Susskind regarded it and thought of gules and or upon fields of argent and azure. 'The time for the *Maariv* service is at hand,' confided Arya Leib into his beard.

II

Count Berthold smacked his lips, delicately wrung his gravied moustaches, and sucking loudly betook himself to the marrow of a juicy bone. 'A hound and a cook will make excellent venison out of cornered deer.' He spluttered his words. 'How we sweated at the hunt this afternoon! A rust must have grown upon the metal of my clothes. And we nearly lost our quarry. Suddenly I was overtaken by a belly-ache, and what with the bounding of the horse, and the stumbling over hidden tree-trunks, I thought my innards would out. I had to dismount and take my ease; no simple process, I tell you, with tunic and jerkin and hose, and seven changes of apparel worn at once.'

The lovely Eloise made a noise with her knife upon her plate. The guests and the clergy hid their noses in their dish; such talk did not whet one's appetite. Behind Berthold capered the clown Eiselkopf, haw-hawing uproariously at his master's tale, the while with his bauble he tickled himself beneath the armpits. From time to time the servers trotted in, holding dishes above their heads. At the door two armoured retainers stood motionless, engrossingly watching the erratic journey of a fly upon the hanging tapestry. Hard by at the door, seated upon a stool, was Susskind, whom dietary laws did not permit to partake of the Gentile repast.

Berthold gluttonously continued his gobbling. He quaffed down his food with foaming beer straight from the spigot, and made a noise as if he was rinsing his mouth. He clicked his palate, patted his paunch, and belched, 'Begin the fiddling.'

Susskind lifted his stool and brought it nearer to the duke's seat. The duke kicked Ezekiel out of the way; the dog limped into a corner, yelping. A bone was thrown at him; it struck him in the nozzle, but the spaniel, without much to-do, bit and licked from it the last lingering tastes of flesh. Susskind, his young beard cocked dreamily, began his strumming on the lute, singing.

He sang of a person of low estate whose heart was enamoured of a lovely lady. With many figures of speech he painted this adorable one, she whose hair was as ripe flax, and whose eyes were like two blue flames stolen from an alembic, and whose lips were petals of heavenly flower, the only likeness of which upon earth was the rose. Her cheeks were beautiful without paint, and her neck was as a swan's for comeliness and grace. She was utterly a flame to kindle the hearts of men. The while he sang, Susskind looked at the lovely Eloise, as if he were pointing at the meaning of his parable. She regarded him, and her eyes were full of pity. Berthold had no taste for such sentimental singsongs, and guffawed loudly at its conclusion, opining that firstly there were no such ravishing beauties and he who had his bedful of wenches ought to know, and secondly that the servile knave was a knave indeed, and too docile and chary to be worthy of hot flesh. The bishop, Theophilus, scrawny and cadaverous, upon whom his sacred robes flapped loosely, curled a thin lip at the Jew, daring in his presence to sing of love, and thus bringing Berthold, whose soul was under his especial care, to blasphemy, and nigh to perdition. Howbeit an unknown thought appeased him, and smiling beatifically, he slid his finger caressingly along the dell between his cheek and his jaw. Eiselkopf whispered stertorially to a serving man that the Jew's music would issue much more mellifluously if his gullet were greased with lard. He went on audibly to wonder whether the strings of Susskind's lute were torn from the entrails of a ritually-slaughtered animal.

'Sing us,' cried Berthold, slapping a fat hand upon the table, 'of my father Arnaud, and of his valor.'

Susskind's finger once more drew and twanged at the strings. His voice was loud and martial. He told of Arnaud's jousts and tournaments, of his single-handed exploits, his chivalrous enterprise, his clanging combats, how he had charred the fair-haired Saxons with fire, and chalked the swarthy Provençals with fear, how he had discomfited Huon the Braggart, and bearded Conrad the Lion. As he sang these high matters, the armored retainers gave over spying the fly errant, and hearkened to Susskind's song. Susskind, spell-bound by the verse of his own making, stared at the stiff retainers. Their heads seemed perched upon their shoulders, like little castles upon a high rock. Their ears in the blur of his gaze seemed small turrets, their eyelids curtained casements, their teeth a portcullis of ivory staves. Into his song he put the fury and red renown of war. Waving musical banners, his song made truce.

'That was done masterly.' Squeamishly Berthold praised; Susskind had forgotten to mention among his father's assaults the victory over that innermost donjon whence he himself had sallied. The lean Theophilus was spilling some ticklish joke into a brother bishop's ear. The latter laughed so much that tears came to his eyes, and with the shaking of his paunch the cross upon it dangled merrily … Eloise looked forlorn, in mind still wandering through the episodes of her grandsire's exploits. Eiselkopf mimicked a hoarse snoring, and suddenly waking from his snooze, shook his cap and bells, rubbed his eyes, saying that he had been dreaming.

'The purport of your dream?' Berthold's voice was shrill with a sot's inquisitiveness.

'I dreamed that a Jew was singing war songs.' Slyly Eiselkopf caught in the palm of his hand a titter squeezing through his teeth. Through the brambles of his laugh he continued, 'I knew a deaf man who eavesdropped, a blind who spied, a fingerless who labored in a scriptorium, and a Jew who mouthed martial words. Why, they are a people of peace who would use a sword the wherewithal to slice bread, and a helmet in which to drop their coins, and a shield whereon to mark their accounts … Better suited are they for their books and parchment, growing blind over holy script, and through getting by rote their usurious debtor-bills. Imagine Walther von der Vogelweide in prayer-shawl and phylactery; fluting his song through such a labyrinthine nose.' Eiselkopf spoke in a low tone for the especial edification of his cronies; from his gestures, his supplicatory hand-waving, his

Hebraic nutations, his caressing of a non-existent beard, Susskind gathered that he was the subject of the buffoon's parody.

Meekly he said, as if answering a question pendulous in the air, 'Only the vanquished can truly know the exultings of the victorious ...'

The count made no comment. In his eyes a jest seemed to frolic. The bishop, too, was apparently initiate in the joke; his lean face looked jollified. Berthold called the other minnesingers to give their performance.

They came, with a pride in their gait that was absent in Susskind's. Eble was there, and Colin of Speyer and Hermann of Salzburg. The one told with much humor, and to the great and thigh-slapping amusement of Berthold, of the cunning manoeuvres of Reynard the Fox in the realm of beasts, and concluded with barbed allusions to crafty Jewry. He was rewarded with scarlet slippers and a furred tippet.

Then another took up the lute, and he sang of the hard fortune of the troubadour, how he gets himself hoarse singing for the somnolence of the high-born, how he catches a chill journeying in foul weather to castle whose ramparts were clouds, and how as remedy for torn throat and frozen humor of the blood, he receives much applause which flatters the ear, yet leaves in their old pangs the gullet in shreds, the aching fingers, the stomach agonized by a great void. The duke took the broad hint, and threw him a weighty purse, the jingling of which woke the spaniel from his music-lulled slumbers.

The third piously sang of the young Christian lad of Worms who had been spirited away by bearded men at Eastertide, and how the bishop, discovering the abomination that had been done in their midst, rooted out from the city every unbelieving carcass of a Jew, and how, the wistful ending came, up within this Jew-town they sprouted again, like wild grass upon a field of dung. There was a great deal of professional venom in his composition, as he made pregnant pause to let his innuendoes bear fruit. Him the count gave a rich cloak, embroidered with crosses; and the bishop promised a jawbone, the relic of St. Chrysostom.

In the interim, Susskind was waiting at the door for his gift. As an afterthought the duke of a sudden recalled that the Jew had received no honorarium for his efforts. Nonetheless he took from his stool at his side a small casket, which was evidently prepared beforehand. His eyes twinkling amusingly, he offered it, bidding him not to open it before he returned to his home. Upon the casket was written in well-fashioned characters, *Qui rejecit accipiat.* Theophilus grinned and nudged the fat prelate at his right hand. Towards Susskind then hopped the courtjester, and with many mock obeisances, offered him another casket, repeating and paraphrasing with sly variation the injunction of his master.

In the light of a lopsided moon, Susskind walked by the banks of the Saale, on the way to his home. Curiosity sent an itching to his fingers. He opened the box upon which was written the Latin legend; his eyes grew to the size of dove's eggs at what he saw therein. A crucifix. The letters I.N.R.I. Jesus of Nazareth, King of the Jews. Berthold hung no seven veils over his meaning.

He opened the clown's proffering. Anger daubed his face with crimson blotches. The buffoon had given a small pig carved of wood; in its cleft snout a piece of parchment was rolled. It was the chapter of *Deuteronomy* preserved in *mezuzahs,* evidently spared from some compassionate or neglectful hangman's fire. Susskind, hitherto as patient as a wether, was enraged. This then was the purport of their gigglings, of Hermann's song, and of Eiselkopf's sporadic gaieties. They were ramming swineflesh and Christianity into his mouth. Violently he threw the wooden image into the waters of the Saale; it floated down the river. He regarded the crucifix again, and for an instant thought to foil his tormentors by preserving its metal to be molten into coin, but reconsidered. He would have no traffic in images; he flung it into the river, a Christ rebaptized.

The drunkard staggering to his home from a tavern hard-by might have beheld that night a candle burning in the window of Arya Leib's house. Had he stumbled through the rutted and muddy lane he would have seen through the window Susskind holding up to the candle a manuscript inscribed with irregular lines like those of verse, the parchment burning with a slow flame; Susskind watching the fire industriously efface the script, to make of the parchment a black and fragile shroud of ash.

Master of the Horn

Reb Mayer felt old age come upon him. It caught him by the beard, and left it like white ash; it smote him on the cheeks, and rendered them hollow; it touched him on the head, and brought him baldness; it dug its finger-nails into his brow, and inscribed the wrinkled script of doom ... Yet age set upon him imperceptibly, it approached him, stealthily approached him from the rear, clapped its hands upon his eyes, and to all his queries retorted, 'Guess!' ... Only when Reb Mayer stood before the mirror, when he beheld the rings that were like pendulous brown blots beneath his eyes, the lines that elongated his face into gauntness, and the white ghost of a beard that once was jet black, only then did he suspect that he was no longer young.

These reflective introspections invariably ended with a wistful shake of the head, a commentary on the yesteryears. Yet not utterly forlorn was he; he convinced himself into rejuvenescence – he attributed all his physical changes to a scapegoat called 'Tsoros,' and diagnosed himself, not as an old man longing for lost youth, but as a stripling prematurely ancient. Mentally he tabulated a series of the indices of youth; only on rare occasions did his voice thicken itself into a cough; only at infrequent intervals did his breath fail him when he climbed his flight of stairs, long as the Jewish exile though it was; only to a small extent did his scale of production in the shop become minimized; and it was only four years ago that his wife had brought him a son to console his old age. His old age – he spat ...

Tsoros – the afflictions of this world: daily bread, monthly rent, and perennial disease. These were vampires sucking the blood, gluttons of the heart. They robbed strength, they stole energy.

What was the meaning of life, this antechamber of the Palace Celestial? To run every morning to the first *minyan*; rush home, where Sarah had prepared the food parcel, invariably forgetting the salt; sift ashes; heat the stove, hurry down-town to shop; spend the day dancing before the blue light of a press-machine hopping a profane *Kedusha* before the American seraphim; listen to the deafening din of the machines, the repeated borborugmus of industry; suffer the aesthetic criticisms of Motke the boor, with reference to the brilliance of coat-lapels; steal away from the machine towards dusk on pretext of physical urgency to whisper in some dark corner the twilight service; trudge home for thrift of a car ticket; home, receive reports of the misdemeanors and damages caused by Yankel and Sammie; confer with Sarah on the economies of the pantry, and the necessities of the Sabbath; read the pre-somnal prayers; and to bed, not unmolested by those whom Reb Mayer called 'the Landsleit' ...

Was it a wonder that he was growing old in this benighted land of toil and turmoil? One squandered one's strength for these bosses and blood-suckers – this was his plaint during the week. But on the Sabbath he was a new man. Youth and strength returned to him with the singing of the Song of Songs, which ushered in the Day of Rest.

On the Sabbath he was a new man. Because of his learning he was regarded with respect by his synagogue brethren. On Sabbath afternoons he would expound chapters of *Haggada*, in a voice entirely out of proportion to the necessities of the five grey beards who formed his audience. Reb Mayer was proud of the strength of his voice; whenever he was summoned to the Torah, he sang out the Benediction in clear metallic notes, mindful of every inflection, and meticulous in his diction. Even at the business meetings of the Anshe Volhynia his tenor stood him in good stead. He spoke loudly, emphasizing every sentence equally, so that no word of his might perish through weakness; he gesticulated; he pounded his asseverations, he was eloquently militant. He gained a reputation as an orator, he was acknowledged a 'strong speaker.'

Reb Mayer gloried in his strength. This was a subject on which he was especially reminiscent. Besides being the genius of the town, he had been, you had his own word for it, the champion wrestler of Ratno. The peasants had quaked in his presence.

'If I landed anybody a dig in the ribs or a punch beneath the heart, he had to hold and to remember! I had a pair of shoulders – a terror they were!' That was his own testimony. His pugilistic endeavours, moreover, covered two continents. In Montreal, too, he had engaged in a fracas with some Frenchmen.

'It was like this. I was going down-town to work – a little job by Davidovitch the contractor, somewhere in all the black years in the east end. Frenchmen there – like locusts! And Antisemites – what means Antisemites – Jew-gourmands. A Jew is by them like an ache in the eye. So I go on quickly down St. Denis street. All of a sudden my shoulder brushes against a young Frenchman – unintentionally. I say, "excuse please." What can you do in a strange land? He, however, he turns around, he sees my beard – aha – "un Maudit Juif." He begins to make with his hands, anger burns him up, he calls me "Meester mit the wheeskies" – he pushes. I see that it's such a story. I lift up my hand, and frask! in the muzzle. Nu, so it began a fight.' –

Whereupon he proceeds with his description. The Jews, being a persecuted race, have about twenty synonyms for the word 'blow'; Reb Mayer uses all of them in his autobiographical report. It is quite evident from the narrative that he did not abide by all the rules of the ring, in fact, it seems that foot work, literal foot work, played a prominent part as a factor in his victory. And he concludes the story with the envoi – 'But that was twenty years ago.'

At entertainments, more pacific than the aforementioned, entertainments such as the celebration for the Covenant of Abraham, or the sanctification of marriage, he manifested his eternal vigour by drinking copiously. The benediction made over a glass of good wine, he said, was both pleasing to God, and refreshing to man. He pleased a family of gods. He guzzled one cup after the other; he smacked his lips; he shook his head in supreme approbation; proudly he lifted a finger, and said, 'Ah, *that* is good wine,' with the inflection of one who has sampled others in an eternal and ever-futile search for the perfect brand of the vintner, and at last has found it. And may the Lord forfend, it was not that he was a drunkard; he drank to fulfil the injunction of the Lord's commandments.

Moreover, he facetiously justified his practices with subtle dialectic. 'If you take a truly strong *schnapps*,' he averred, 'you are a new man – and being that, is not a new man entitled to a drink?' And so, ad infinitum. From his ability to out-swill any other Jew of the same age he gained a feeling of power, a confidence of strength, an assurance of youth.

At weddings he dances, Cossack dances, exhibition dances. He takes a central position on the floor; the invited gather about him; he shouts to the grinning musicians, *'A Frelichs!'* They hit up some catchy tune. Reb Mayer lifts his right hand to his earlocks, describes a circle, and begins action. His feet stamp out emphatic rhythm; his face becomes contorted with ecstatic world-oblivion; the coat-tails of his hybrid garment flutter like black wings; as the music increases in tempo, he, too, accelerates his pedal pistons; he rotates; he lifts himself from the floor, landing on alternate legs, higher, higher; the audience keeps time; Reb Mayer becomes a human crescendo; and as he rises to a climax he strikes a consummate attitude. Finis. Applause.

Out of these things Reb Mayer eked a consolation of youth and might. It is true that after a feast and drinking bout, he suffered for a day from headaches, and lived on a diet of Bromo-seltzers and aspirins; it is true that after the dance his limbs ached, and Sarah had to apply liniment at night, but what were these things compared to the joy of strength, the confidence of power, the assurance of youth? He wasn't merely a Jew, a scholar; he was a man of guts.

The High Holydays approached. St. Lawrence Boulevard was placarded with signs announcing the world-renowned qualities of foreign cantors. The chicken stores plied a cackling trade; the fish markets were full of bargaining and gossiping women. Theatres and halls were being transformed into pseudo-synagogues. Almost every Jewish street was disturbed by the practices of improvised choirs – and Reb Mayer was made this year, as in former years, the Master of the Horn.

Throughout the whole month of *Ellul*, during the morning services, he blew the *Shofar*, mightily. His success was not always assured, but the congregation being a small one, it sufficed. He considered these performances merely as a prologue to the swelling theme, practices for the first day of Rosh Hashanah.

Rosh Hashanah. All morning Reb Mayer sat on pins. Would he be able to undergo the ordeal? Would the blowing of the *Shofar* pass without error? His thoughts punctuated his prayers – his thoughts became prayers.

After the morning service some Charity worker harangued the congregation on matters philanthropic. He played up the sanctity of the day, the future of our American children, and the flowing of Jewish blood. By the time the sounding of the ram's horn arrived the synagogue was crowded. The girls and children who had stayed home up to this hour, began to appear to listen to the curious sounds emanating from the quaint instrument.

Reb Mayer ascended the almemar. The cantor uttered the preliminary prayers, invoking all good angels to issue from the mouth of the horn and to act as defending advocates before the heavenly throne. The prompter who stood by the side of Reb Mayer instructed him in the length of the blasts.

The whole congregation rose. The women made an end to their interliturgic gossip. Little boys stood up on the benches to attain a better view of the rustic instrument. A whisper passed over the synagogue, every one hushing every other one. The *Gabbai* slammed his hand on the table, enjoining silence. Reb Mayer cleared his throat. The prompter in a Cabalistic voice intoned, '*Tekiah-ah.*'

Reb Mayer lifts his *Shofar* to his lips, fixes it in a position to assure success, and puffs his hollow cheeks to their pristine proportions. Anticipation. Cacophony ... Shattered sound ...

Splintered music ... Reminiscence of slaughtered cattle, emitting the ultimate low ... Mutilated melody ...

Reb Mayer's face, red with the effort of the horn, became pale again as he listened to the noises which afflicted his ear.

Once more he tried. With consummate precision he glued his lips to the horn at an angle known only to the initiate. He blew.

Not angels sallied from the *Shofar*, but demons, hordes of midgets, battalions of dwarfed witches, legions of imps ... Hideous and weird sounds. Labials of inarticulate beasts ... Wailing of afflicted souls ... Discord of Gehenna ...

The whole synagogue was full of a hushed whispering. Young men grinned at Reb Mayer's efforts; old men shook their heads, a gesture eloquent of the ways of life. From behind the curtains where the women prayed, commiserating gossip issued. Agony scurried down the wrinkles of the cantor's grimaces. The prompter looked stolid. The *Mizrach* wall where sat the synagogue officers, was confusion – as Master of the Horn, Reb Mayer was a bad choice. The scene should have been avoided.

As for Reb Mayer, his hands quivered like palm leaves on the Feast of Tabernacles. Bewilderment pounded at his temples. His legs were weak as if after a long fast. The saliva in his mouth was glutinous; he licked his lips. A film of despair glazed his eyes. Out of his bewilderment and despair he realized one thing – age. He felt himself encompassed on all sides. Age was a strait-jacket.

Should he try again? Should he humiliate himself before the congregation once more, proclaiming his impotence from a bugle? Should he feel once more the floating amusement of the young men, and the nodding commiseration of the elders? It was of no use.

He conferred with the cantor. He whispered to the *Gabbai*. Reluctantly they agreed. Reb Mayer put down the *Shofar*, rushed from the almemar, bewildered, weak, old ...

Towards the conclusion of the service, when the cantor lifting his eyes towards the Ark of the Covenant, and spreading his *tallis*-draped arms in appeal, sang out in sobbing voice – *And cast us not aside in the days of our age, at the ebb of our strength leave us not* – the weeping in the synagogue was bitter and long.

The Parrot and the Goat

Chad Gadyah, a kidling, for two zuzim bought, a kidling, Chad Gadyah!

When Abba bought the egregious Chad Gadyah for paltry two *zuzim*, it was a bargain so cheap that the contemporary rhymesters did forthwith immortalize him in a rondel. Yet they forgot, these poets in their enthusiasm over a price, they forgot the reason for his depreciation, and did liefer concern themselves with the sundry and divers retributions that were visited upon his persecutors. They did not see fit to make clear why so sleek and fat a goat as Chad Gadyah, whose polished horns shone like horns of light, and whose beard endowed him at once with beauty and dignity, should suddenly fall from his high estimation in dinars to the low one in *zuzim*. Either in their proverbial short-sightedness they overlooked this fact, or in their proverbial compassion they of purpose omitted that which would make out of a tripping rondel a heavy and tragic ode. Or they did not know that Chad Gadyah had had a past.

It is only in the light of this period in the life of Chad Gadyah, who at that time was nothing more than an ill-groomed kidling, effervescent with animal spirits, that one can understand the evil that came upon him in the days of his old age, when he of noble goat-pedigree was chaffered away for two cheap coins.

It appears that Chad Gadyah was a romping goat cavorting about on the farm of Plauni who owned a few hundred acres, barns, poultry and domestic animals. There were fat chickens that went cackling about the farmyard, scratching up worms as dainties choice for their palates; geese waddling on their webbed toes with the preposterous air of swans; pigeons preening themselves in their pigeon-house, making brilliant rainbows of their necks; a turkey blowing itself into a gobbling pride. In the stables and in the barns there were cows, stupidly ruminating on their past and future food, – horses neighing over their oats, – in the fields sheep gamboling like so many clouds driven by a frivolous wind, and a dog vigilant that the play went not beyond the limits of decorum or of the farm.

But among creatures, feathered or furred, there was not one that was of so exotic and foreign a character as Popygai the Parrot. She hung in a green cage which was suspended from a hook on the balcony, and all day long she would imitate the sounds about her until her throat became a barnyard symphony.

What beautiful sounds there were to mimick from early dawn to dusk! The cock-a-doodle-doo of the rooster as he sang his greetings to the sun; the monosyllabic quacking of ducks; and the minced twittering of birds supplied the altos to the choir in which the lowing of cows and the whinnying of horses furnished the bass. And to this general music Chad Gadyah occasionally added the falsetto of his lugubrious maa-aa.

Chad Gadyah, it must be admitted, was something of an aristocrat; after all it was from his kind that sacrifices were made at the temple. Accordingly he kept himself aloof from the common rabble that infested the barnyard. He scoffed at the plebeian nature of the horse who laboured from sun-up to sun-down for the somewhat negligible reward of a bin of oats and a manger of hay; he laughed in his beard at the docility of a cow who allowed herself to be milked, her only remonstrance being the switching of her tail. The ducks' waddle, too, amused him greatly, and filled him with a feeling of superiority; and as for the chickens he felt infinitely above them on general principles. It is true that the rooster vaunted a ruddy comb which was no mean beauty, but it grew pale before the glory of his horn. He was, indeed, Chad Gadyah reflected, a very splendid fellow.

Moreover, even apart from his ordinary outward appearance, he was different from the general run of the barnyard in the new spiritual ecstasies that were his. No animal breast, he felt, had ever pattered to those emotions which were now making of his heart a very resonant gong. Chad Gadyah was in love.

In love, yet not with an ordinary passion for an ordinary fellow-goat. A much more exalted affection sprung daily in his heart, one that sundered him from the commonality of goatdom. He was infatuated, hoof over horns, with the exotic beauty of Popygai the Parrot.

For many days he had watched her from his green pasture as she hung in her green cage. She had for him a peculiar fascination. When he looked at her he thought of strange lands and the romance of distant jungles. The colours that shone in her, the green and the red with a touch of yellow, cast brilliancies in his brain. Willingly would he have sacrificed himself for one of her slightest feathers. And her flirtations! Her coquettishness! The way she imitated in her own inimitable manner every sound that issued from a barnyard throat, adding in her own version a commentary of satire, and teasing the mind to find the secret of it all – this was an accomplishment than which he knew none greater. Even when she imitated his sorrowful maa he considered it at once a flattery and a declaration of love.

At first he seemed to have a rival. Chathul the cat used to sleep on the balcony with too unconcerned an air to be entirely indifferent to her charms. Occasionally he would open his eyes, blink at the sun, look up at Popygai, lick his lips with his small red tongue, wipe his whiskers with his paw, and doze off again. 'Probably to dream about her,' muttered Chad Gadyah under his breath, – 'the sly puss!'

Well, he would win favour in her eyes by his own achieve-ments, and every rival would slink away discomfited, and he would be acceptable to her. Chad Gadyah had heard rumours in the barnyard that there was about him an odour which was not entirely conducive to conversation, let alone love-making. He would change all this. Accordingly he would seek out every clear crystal stream in the vicinity, and would bathe in it until his shaggy hair drooped smoothly over his ankles and made a sleek vesture to his skin. He would then roll about in fields of clover, until there came from him such a perfume that he could hardly recognize himself. His beard too he combed with the needles of pine cones, and his horns he polished against thick green grass. He would then regard himself in the mirror of a pool, and he was comely to behold.

His toilet accomplished, he returned to the fence that enclosed the farmhouse, and would stare pitiably at the green cage in which sat his beloved Popygai. Oh, if he could only speak as she, if he could only reveal the secrets of his heart, and tell her of how he spent restless days and wakeful nights, touching neither fodder nor food. But he was dumb. His emotions were summed up in a syllable – maa.

And even this declaration, inadequate as it was, divided him and the object of his devotions; and yet that infernal cat was near him all the day. He dared not overleap the fence. He might have had a secret rendezvous with her at night, but his master, alas, took the parrot into the house every evening and shut him up in his stable, leaving him to his dolorous meditations.

It was when Plauni his master had forgotten one night in Abib, to take the parrot into the farmhouse that occurred the incident that was to have remarkable consequences in the career of Chad Gadyah. He was shut up in the stable for the night, but through his window he could see the cage swinging in a slight breeze. He even noticed the green of Popygai's eyes when she looked up at the moon that shone upon the earth. In his heart there grew an overwhelming love and his bones became suddenly light. A strange feeling possessed him. He regarded her again through the window, hanging his head over the wooden sill, sniffing at the air, and dishevelling his beard. In the light of the moon her feathers green and red became most romantically beautiful. Before he was aware of it, his horns had butted through the stable door. His thin legs danced over the green sward, a dapper goat performing some heathen rite, he made for the fence. He leapt over it, fell on his knobby knees, but in a moment was on his legs again, standing before the cage on the balcony.

Suddenly he found that at last when he was alone with her, he had nothing to say, yet his heart overflowed with love. He would show her with actions how much his soul longed for her, and how his heart languished. He stood up on his hind legs and pranced about in a wild ecstasy regardless of the din and of the broken glass and of the smashed boards. While he was thus performing his antics the moon looked down at him sedately, and Popygai blinked at him unmoved and untouched. But in no such calm mood did Plauni appear on the door, aroused from his sleep by the unearthly noises on the balcony. As soon as Chad Gadyah beheld the wrathful face beneath his master's nightcap he took to his heels.

It was not until the next morning when the moon was still in the skies that the shepherd discovered Chad Gadyah forlorn and sad, his beard raised on high, gaping at the moon and sighing again a melancholy maa.

The rumour of the escapade spread far and wide along the countryside. Chad Gadyah achieved the reputation of being a dangerous goat. No one would purchase him from Plauni who was already eager to sell him. His price went down day by day until Abba who chanced to pass by the village, bought him for the historical two *zuzim*.

Chad Gadyah, a kidling, for two zuzim bought, a kidling, Chad Gadyah.

The Bald-Headed Monarch

The barber was clipping the beard of the philosopher Suleiman the Wise. The latter had gained a reputation for sagacity by a long life of silence, broken only by his most favourite proverb, 'I doubt it.' Towards all things he maintained a sceptical attitude, and all things he regarded with a quizzical expression. Especially critical was he of theology and priest-craft. He continually asseverated that the Koran was unnecessary and that Mohammed was superfluous. Even Allah himself was nothing more than a phrase in the mouth of the muezzin. The barber of Bagdad, ever eager for an argument, and seeking some preoccupation while he cut the philosophic hairs from Suleiman's metaphysic beard, was attempting to prove to the cynical Suleiman that the ways of Allah are mysterious to mere mortals, and that not by syllogisms alone can man live.

'Reason is sufficient to carry men through the ordinary business of life,' he asserted between the interruptions of his scissors, 'but for a knowledge of the deeper secrets, the profounder verities one must have divine revelation. The eyes of man are sealed, even as a kitten's in its first days, until the brilliance of the Koran reveals the splendours unknown.'

The philosopher was about to offer an objection, but the barber held on tightly to Suleiman's beard. Under such conditions debate was difficult, and so he allowed the barber to continue to split his hairs, capillary and philosophic.

'The fountain-head of the Koran waters the rose-tree of knowledge. The bird of divine revelation sings in the garden of science. The perfume of religion anoints the head of the thinker.

The spices of belief season the viands of philosophy.' At great pains to his chin, Suleiman added to the already complicated metaphors, 'And the lullaby of faith cradles the infant of thought.'

'Suleiman, you may scoff, but some day you will learn that the knowledge of astrologers, and the discussions of sages, and the pronouncements of all the wise men of the East are as nothing against the enigmas of existence. Understand me; I do not spit upon the garments of reason, nor do I throw stones at the broad brows of logic. But I do declare that he who offers to man, reason, alone, is as he who gives false coins to the beggar at the gates, or as he who serves wine which is but coloured water. He is like the bald-headed monarch.'

The barber lifted his arms for a space, to stretch them. In the fortunate interval Suleiman took the opportunity of freeing himself of a few criticisms. 'You are a barber,' he said, 'and I can take your words only for their face value. You know your trade, you sprinkle the lotion of creed upon the beard of reason. You seek to establish the House of God upon a foundation of metaphors. With your bird on the rose-tree and your rose-tree near the fountain you think that you have found a solution to the higher knowledge. You have only painted the wall of mystery, you have not torn it down. And besides, who was this bald-headed king you invoke as a witness to your case?'

The barber cleared his throat, as if he was preparing for an unusually lengthy monologue.

'Well, it appears that once upon a time there lived a happy king. All happy kings lived in that golden age known as once upon a time. He reigned over two hundred and thirty and a half provinces, sharing his four hundred and sixty-one states with his chief concubine. He possessed several hundred wives, the acknowledged beauties of the eastern world. His treasures were untold. In his coffers there was the wealth of India, and the largess of Cathay. In his diadem were set the most priceless of jewels, his crown shone like a halo about his head. Diamonds buttoned his purple robes and from the buckles of his royal shoes rubies and emeralds cast their brilliant rays. The diamonds in the hilt of his sword dazzled his foes into helplessness. His gardens were like the symbol of Paradise upon earth; three hundred gardeners tended a single one. The catalogue of the fragrant flowers filled tomes. His stables were filled with the proudest chargers of Arabia, and the most mettlesome steeds out of Egypt. His library contained all the wisdom of the East, including manuscripts in Solomon's very handwriting.

'Everything that the king desired, he had. Moreover, he was comely to behold. Tall and well-featured, he was the handsomest man in his realm, a king among men, even if he were deprived of his throne. Especially proud was he of his long golden locks which seemed the very fingers of Allah in benediction upon his head.

'And so the dove of contentment rested upon the wrist of royalty. But not for long, for soon it flew away and in the heart of the king there nested the vulture of vexation. Because of his riches the monarch was much disturbed in spirit, and could find no ease for his soul. By day he feared the foe at his gates and by night the conspirator in his halls. In his brightest wines he seemed to see the shadow of poison and in the rays of the sun he saw rebellious daggers. The countenance of the monarch lost its beauty. The scribe of time wrote on his brow the verses of doom. But misfortune of misfortunes! His hair began to fall from his head, even as the gold leaves in autumn.

'Now the king was not a little vain of his personal comeliness. Seeing that the ravages of age and worry left their signet-mark upon him, he henceforward eschewed mirrors, and quiet pools, and all bright surfaces, lest he behold the terrifying reflection of himself. But the truth had to be faced. His head was now as bald as an egg; it shone like the sun at noon time. When the king pushed his head through his casement of nights, the moon-worshippers raised their prayers. His crown was now two sizes too large for him. The poets who used to describe his beauty in detail, discreetly did not allow their descriptions to go beyond his forehead. If for a moment the king forgot about his misfortune, the very flies would buzz it into his ear, after sliding off the slippery surface of his head.

'The king looked about for a remedy. His baldness was a

continual source of embarrassment. In his harem his calamity was a daily witticism. Even his scullery maids laughed into their pots and pans at the thought of the dignified king with the babe's head. Among his fellow-kings, too, he lost respect. His baldness was complicating international relations.

'So he called together his sages and wizards and ordered them to find a hair-restorer. His academy of thirty-seven wise men spent weeks on the project. They crushed the oils out of aromatic herbs; they washed his head with the milk of goats; they bathed him in pure rain-water. Powders and pomades rendered the skull of the king even thicker than it was by nature. But all to no avail. The king was as bald as marble. The astrologers, too, regarded the stars but saw in them no omen. Courtiers of the king tried to solace him by telling him that grass did not grow on busy streets. But the king was not comforted. Uneasy lies the head that has no hair.

'While the wizards were delving into mystical lore to find some miraculous seed to plant upon the kingly skull their own hair grew longer and longer, and the king stayed as bald as before. At last he became exasperated and ordered their execution. On the following day thirty-seven heads were displayed in the market-place. Tradition says that the president of the academy had declared as a final taunt before his death that it was impossible to grow grass on a stone, or as he phrased it: "A royal stone gathers no moss."

'The king then decided to send couriers throughout his realm to proclaim that whosoever would deliver the monarch out of his predicament would be given authority over a quarter of his dominions. In the market-place of every hamlet, announcements were made, and even from the minarets the royal proclamation was issued.

'For weeks the king languished in expectation. The baldness of his head almost went to his brain. At last there presented himself at the gates of the palace a poor barber, attired in flowing tatters. He wished to have an audience with His Most Terrible Majesty. The audience was granted; a long conversation ensued, and when the barber left the palace he was a Grand Vizier of forty provinces.

'But the king made no official appearance for weeks. He was living in seclusion behind the latticed windows of his castle – at last he showed himself to his subjects. He had regained his former beauty; his face shone, and from his head, – marvel of marvels! – there hung long luxuriant locks.

'Well, Suleiman, I can see that you are drowsing off. Happily my story and my operation are at an end. You are wondering, I presume, how this sudden miracle of growth on a bald-headed man was achieved, and also what is the moral to be derived from the tale. Understand therefore, that there was no miracle. The luxuriant locks on the crown of his majesty were but part of a cunningly-devised wig. When the natural availed not, the supernatural, or rather the artificial prevailed.

'The Koran, if I may be permitted to utter an unintentional blasphemy, is even as the aforementioned wig. Without it man is a poor bald-headed creature, his brain ends where his bone begins. But alas the head is not complete merely with what is below the skull, there must also be an extraneous embellishment. If need be, it is a wig. In things spiritual, too, the mind of man is not complete only with an apparatus of logic and reasoning; a beauty must be bestowed from above. Such is divine revelation. This is my parable; harken therefore, to the meaning thereof.

'I may say, too,' – the barber was wiping his scissors with an air of finality, – 'that when the wig was glued on to his royal dome, he lived happily ever after.'

Suleiman the Wise rose from his cushions, and in that scoffing manner which was his, muttered, – 'I doubt it.'

Too Many Princes

Let him who seeks to prove this tale journey to the Mediterranean, and there upon the shore lift up a sea-shell to his ear. At first he will be hearkening to the wordless voice of the deep which in time will grow clearer, and speak to him, saying:

Upon a time there reigned over an isle in the Great Sea the monarch Suleiman, during whose reign though he ruled not with a rod of iron, but with a wand of willow, there was peace in the land. And all his loyal subjects lived happily, each man going to his labour and returning to his goat's milk and pressed dates. And though they lived on this frugal fare the land was rich in gold, and in harvests, and in the cloths and wares which the men who go down to the sea in ships brought back to their shores.

From Carthage there came Punic mariners bringing much corn and grain, and from farthest Ind came swarthy sailors, with cargo of gems and precious metals. Upon the rose-tree of content there sang the nightingale of happiness.

But this was not to last long. There sailed into the harbour, borne by some ill-wind, the ship which flaunted from its mast a flag bearing a horrific device: a skull and cross-bones. From one end of the island to the other the cry went up: Pirates! Pirates! The inhabitants did not wait long to verify the rumour, for hardly had they become aware of the fatal craft which had anchored near their shore but the pirates, whooping some barbaric whoops, were upon them with scarlet firebrand and crimson scimitar.

When the pirates left the island, a lighthouse of fire in the Mediterranean, they bore beneath their hatches much booty and many captives. Ingots of gold, and bars of silver, bales of purple and whole granaries of corn, and many black-haired beauties to be sold in distant slave markets, such was the cargo of their ship as it disappeared beyond the horizon while the gloating pirates could in the distance see the vultures flying over the domain of Suleiman, eager for carrion.

But as they sang some hilarious chanty, their joy was disturbed by the fact that King Suleiman and his small sons were not among the captives. And neither were they among the dead. For as soon as the monarch had seen his castle in ruins, and his subjects corpses, and his kingdom a cemetery, he boarded his small ship, and taking with him his sons and some holy books, he had escaped from the chains of the sea-robbers.

It was then that he who was once mighty upon a throne realized to the full the bitterness of life. At first he went from palace to palace through the islands of the Mediterranean proclaiming that he was a king. But the princes and potentates looked upon his tatters, and laughed. From some courts he was even buffeted and cuffed as a presumptuous impostor. He who had known the powders of the apothecary was now to touch the dust of affliction. Who was the beggar who sat at the gates of Bagdad, and lifted a palsied hand for alms? Suleiman, once king. Who was the hunched pedlar who trudged through the back lanes of Paris, hawking old clothes? It was the voice of a monarch, no longer imperial. Who was the disconsolate wretch who had for his home a hovel so low that even the hunched had to stoop in it? Suleiman, through whose palace-halls and ruined porticoes there stalked the jackal by day, and by night there screeched the screech-owl.

So did he wander about from land to land occasionally lifting a vain cry: I am King Suleiman, I am King Suleiman. Sometimes the street gamins would pelt him with stones as a half-wit. It was no wonder then that when the Angel of Death tapped him on the shoulder, he turned round with a smile. As he lay upon his death-bed he called to himself his four sons and gave them each a holy book. He lifted his weak hands and blessed them, saying: 'You are the heirs of my kingdom, bright pearl in the Mediterranean. Sell not your heritage for a mess of pottage. Until your dying day seek to convince the scoffer and the sceptic that yours is the gem, and that palace your habitation. Take you each a holy book, read in it, and read in it. Carry it from where the sun rises to where the sun sets, in every clime and in every land. And after years you shall deduce from these scriptures where your titles to the land are hidden.' And as he breathed his last breath the candle on the bare table flickered, and through the window one could see a falling star.

And so the four sons set out on their travels. The first, Abdullah, who was held to be a saint, journeyed all over the world and frequented many places of worship. He knelt in Chinese joss-houses and frequented synagogues and cathedrals. One day the voice of God came to him and urged him to go to a certain place and there dig in the earth. He did so, and from a deep pit he uncovered a charm which the kings of the Mediterranean used to wear upon their necks and which everyone knew was a symbol of royalty.

The other son, Achmed, who loved justice, travelled all over the world and sat in many court houses. He learned equity and fairness from the tribunals of the world. And one day as he was passing from a court house in Germany through a dingy market place, a man offered him for a few gulden a miniature scales of justice. Out of curiosity he bought it. Imagine his astonishment when he saw after he had scrubbed the dirt and dust from it, the signature of his father at its base.

The other son, Mahound, who was a mighty man, earned a living by joining armies as a mercenary soldier. He served in many legions; in his home he had a whole arsenal of war-like weapons, but most treasured of all was a sword which he had acquired in the Orient and which he called Cheiruth, (Liberty). It was with this instrument that he hoped to prove his title to the throne of his father.

The fourth son, Kalba, who was a shrewd man, decided that in view of the fact that all his brothers were travelling he would stay at home. He calculated that if his brothers obtained the title to the throne his right to the realm was assured by the fact that he was their brother.

Needless to say that with three such powerful arguments as a miraculous charm, an authentic scale of justice, an irrefutable sword and a verifying brother their claim to the island was immediately recognized.

Alas, it was then that their troubles began. Not that they quarreled as to who should be king. They all agreed to have a praesidium in which all would be invested with the dignity of royalty and yet would have equal authority. It must be remembered that throughout these years while the sons were away journeying over the face of the earth their little island had gone from bad to worse, and was now in a deplorable condition. The question arose: how was one to bring back this desert isle to its pristine prosperity?

Abdullah, the saint, suggested that the land should be dedicated to the culture of citrons so that they could supply the whole world of Jews with this article of worship; they were also to establish factories in which they were to manufacture idols and crucifixes so that from this island would come the word of God.

Achmed, on the other hand, wanted to make the island a model place to live in. Here, he said, they were to cultivate beautiful flowers, and they were to make it a paradise on earth. This island would be such a strange appearance in the world that even if the home industry of flowers would not be so profitable, it was worth while: such a strange sight as a blessed isle, he maintained, would attract the tourist trade.

Mahound, with a scornful gesture of his hand, dismissed both of the suggestions. What this island needed, he said, was a strong army so that the accident which happened to their father would not be repeated again. Furthermore, his island provided with a strong garrison would be able to control the trade-route of the Mediterranean. To prove his arguments he held a fiery speech which he concluded by waving his sword in the air.

At all of these discussions Kalba merely shrugged his shoulders. As far as he was concerned, he said, the best plan would be to have a part of the island dedicated to flower-beds, another part to citron groves, another to ammunition factories, and the rest to sensible undertakings.

But the brothers were obstinate. None of them would surrender. 'What,' said Abdullah, 'I ask for a citron-state, you give me a lemon.' 'Do you think,' cried Achmed, 'that you will bury my theories beneath a flower bed.' 'Never shall my ammunition factories,' shouted Mahound, 'go up in smoke.'

And so they argued and argued. Debate followed debate, discussion followed discussion, and soon the island was full of plot and intrigue. A generation passed and the sons of Mahound, Achmed, Abdullah and Kalba were still arguing. Upon the whole island there was not a single farmer nor a citron culturist nor a soldier: the arguments had made lawyers out of all of them. Meanwhile the island was going from bad to worse, the land was uncultivated, the ruins of their father, King Suleiman, were still ruins. The Mediterranean ate up more and more of the shore.

At this juncture the sea-shell to which you have been listening will suddenly sob and go silent. You will hearken for a moment and you will wonder how the argument ended. The sea-shell will continue.

There is nothing more to tell. While the brothers were so busy in their arguments and in their theories and in their plans, the Mediterranean which knows not these things gradually crept up on the shore, and in the course of time the island was completely inundated. The domain of King Suleiman and that of his sons lies beneath water, and there where the monarch once issued his royal decrees and where later the jackal roamed and his sons debated, there now swim little fishes in among its lofty pillars.

Once upon a Time ...

The sly moon blinked down upon the fairy ring below, a pale green cirque in the centre of the glade. Superciliously, she regarded the bustling elves, importantly flitting hither and thither in the moonlight; she twisted her lips into a lunar smile. Cunningly, to the million mischievous stars who filled the sky with stifled glee at the impending farce, she winked. For they all knew what the conclusion of the matter would be; the parliament of pygmies, after much chatter and small talk, would, as on past occasion, end in a hurried adjournment. In the interim, however, it was amusing, and perhaps instructive, to watch the pranks and antics of the wee folk.

This was, as one may read in the elfin Hansard, written in moss upon stone, the thirteen-thousandth session of the federation of fairies. Already had Titania Queen tripped through the countryside, leaving everywhere the fragrance of her blossoming dress. In the bright moonlit glade, the singing of distant nightingales could be heard, fluting the ode of welcome to the lightly-dancing fairy-delegates. Midnight it was; the minster-clock of the village hard by struck twelve sonorous strokes, so clear-sounding in the spring air, mortals might have said an unseen hand had made of the bronze moon a cymbal ... Somewhere crickets impatiently scraped their fiddles. The parliament must to business.

With a willow-wand as mace, the president, a fat faun, seated on a high sun-flower, called the meeting to order. Stroking his trim goat-beard, he looked about him at the motley assembly:

stout Dutch pygmies, wearing tulips for hats; African dwarfs, shaking large beads of frozen dew from the dark lobes of their ears; outlandish djinns of Arabia; British brownies, sniffing snuff from Jack-in-the-pulpit boxes; Irish fays; Turkish goblins, decked with cockle-shells for fezzes; pixies; gnomes; elves; midgets, an international crew. Officiously he asked for credentials; there was a rustling of bark in the air. Good; the registrar, a bespectacled sprite, would take note of the attendance of all the tiny delegates; using the stump of a tree as desk, a reed as pen, and the juice of blood-root as ink. The registrar carefully inscribed the names of all present upon a crisp sheet of oak-leaf.

The fairies sat upon mushroom stools, the djinns and goblins plunked themselves down on the grass, their skimpy legs beneath them. There was silence, broken only by the rude intrusion of an owl's screech. Busily, the pixie-secretaries, using a luminous will-o-the-wisp as desk-lamp, scratched away. The president began:

'Fays and fairies, from the greenwoods of all parts of a verdurous world are we gathered here this midnight. Upon the shins of yonder pixie there clings the perfumed alfalfa of the south; this goblin comes redolent of eastern musk; that dwarf bears the sweet message of our brethren of the west. Truly, we are a representative body, and no small clique usurping the fairy rites. And indeed we must be. Since our last session, our troubles and trials have grown like mildew upon wheat, like moss on stone, like the canker in the rose. Little did our ancestors, those worthy spirits, think in the heyday of their glory that their progeny would come to discuss their very existence which is now being so ruthlessly attacked. But such has come to pass. Not from the beasts of the field whom we have in the past time goaded with our baggage of tricks; not from the birds of the air whom we have in days gone by driven into insane song by our malicious – we admit it – our malicious pranks, but from man, whom ever we have befriended, whose children we have nurtured upon the sweet honey of fancy – from these our threat, from these our peril! Had we dropped poisonous herbs into the porridges of the son of man, had we settled malevolent Pucks drilling nonsense in his all too-eager ears, had we changed, by our magic lore, their faces into muzzles, their hands into paws, and their feet into hooves, we would have done better by ourselves, and would not have to come to this dismal lot, nor fallen upon these our evil days.'

His eyes shone with the glowing jewels of tears. His voice was choked, as if his throat were being held tightly by a noose of vine-trailer. His audience sighed numerous sighs, which froze on the air into mystic and vaporous circles. A wise old gnome scratched his head with a wisp of straw; a sentimental elf wiped away some approaching tears with a lily-petal handkerchief. He continued:

'Persecuted, we are being driven out of our ancient strong-holds! Outlawed, we have to seek sanctuary in caves, and in forests find refuge. (Peeping cries of "shame.") We cannot cry our out-rage to the world; our voices are too weak to reach up to God in His heavens; and the ears of man are stuffed with cotton. Only the rose-bush can be our confidant. (Sighs.) Only the babbling brook will receive our tears, too frequently interrupting us with her own mean gossip. (Relief, at the sally of elfin humour.) Time was when babes and sucklings called us by name, when our dynasty found loyal service in the innocent hearts of children, when our family sat upon a throne secure in the nursery. Today we have been banished from that same nursery! (Microscopic groans.) The attack of the philistines began on old Mother Hubbard, a well-meaning but cheap imitator of our fairy-lore. She, man said, was immoral; she kept her children in a shoe. She was unman-nerly; she taught little Jack Horner to stick his fingers in pies. She was perverted, she made a hero out of a simple pieman. Now after they had done with poor old Mother Hubbard they betook themselves to the fairies, arguing that the minds of children should not be befuddled with such silly tales as those which fairies wove. Our literature, they termed nonsense; they even began to doubt our existence.

'In America, we have been deleted from the text-book, and banished from the playground. Little ones are taught to play with trains, and all manner of mechanical contrivances, scorning the simplicity of our folk. Once their children fell asleep to the sagas of our heroes; today a radio lilts their unseemly lullaby. And, as for us, our wings are racked upon their dynamos.

'In Russia, we are not even admitted. We cannot pass the frontiers. We can show no marxian visas. We are said to interfere with the five-year plan. Stalin fears sabotage from fairies and pixies.

'This, then is our problem: How are we to get back into our own? How are we to lead a counter-revolution in Russia, a romantic revival in America? In the name of Robin Goodfellow, in the name of Peaseblossom, Mustardseed, Cobweb and Moth, our great national heroes, I invoke you to consider the destiny of our folk.'

There were sagacious frowns wrinkled upon the foreheads of the spirits. They were thinking. In a shaded corner, beneath some copsewood, a few gesticulating gnomes were holding a caucus meeting for the purpose of presenting a common plan. Seated on a swinging branch, an obviously-recalcitrant elf was preparing a minority-report. A dwarf, a little hunchback, rose up on a stool, and asked for the green.

'It is my opinion, sir, that our plan of attack should be centered chiefly against the elders. The methods which we once adopted against animals, can be profitably turned against men. They must be tortured into an uncomfortable realization of our existence. A pixie can be sent to make his home in the nostril of the president of the United States, – a brownie may nestle in Von Hindenburg's mustachios, and direct matters of policy from that high point of vantage. A goblin might spread an experimental pestilence through Stalin's domain, and afflict the dictator himself with boils and blisters.'

'Not practicable,' vetoed the chairman. 'No one would ever attribute such plagues and pests to us. Modern civilization would in all likelihood blame either the microbes or the millionaires.'

A goblin, cleaning his pipe of acorn-bowl and dandelion-stem, with a rush, was clamorous for his say. As he spoke a braying of asses in a neighboring meadow interrupted him, but he continued undismayed. He declared that their concern was with the youngsters, and not with the forlorn greybeards; he urged a careful propaganda amongst the youth. Fairies should slide down chimneys, and secretly whisper to urchins playing with their toys. Sprites should sneak in through key-holes, and develop fanciful dreams in the minds of sleeping babes. Gnomes would turn the hearts of youth against their prosaic elders. He completed his peroration to the accompaniment of the braying asses.

His speech made some impression, until an Arabian djinn rose to his feet, delicately he fixed his turban of rose-petals, adjusted his robes, and scratched himself a stance with his sandalwood sandals. – 'Let us leave mankind to its own tribulations. Let us found an international republic of sprites, where we will dedicate our efforts to ourselves, and leave brutish man to his own designs.' He was a man of few words; amidst a meditative silence he sat down, while his servant elves fanned him with fig-leaves.

Suddenly there was heard a thumping on the grass, and a breaking of twigs. Into the moonlight there appeared a small hunched figure, heralded by a long white beard. The delegates recognized him. Elijah, the only Hebrew elf known in history. The fairies clapped their wings in faint applause.

Elijah was a trifle tipsy. He had just come from sipping at many wine-cups in Jewish homes. He staggered a little.

'Tell us, Elijah, what to do in our dilemma. Tell us; you have a Hebrew head, Elijah!'

Elijah coughed, and then spake: 'It seems to me that the best that we can do under these fell circumstances is nothing. Nothing at all. Let machinery bring its own ruin. We will wait. Let the skyscrapers collapse out of their own weight. Let the youth grow up bored and disillusioned. Let them feed, not on manna, but on tabloid pills. Let them drink, not nectar, but gasoline. The time will come when they will of themselves revolt against the dry dust of their windy cities, the hard touch of their hard grassless streets. Then will they come hopping back to us; then will ten men lay hold of an eleventh, and say to him: Art thou a sprite? Then save us.'

The applause which greeted this oration was disturbed only by the neighing of animals approaching nearer and nearer. The note of optimism relieved the fairies, but it was not enough. What would they do in the long meanwhile? Should they continue idly to gambol about the greenwood, toy around with nymphs, and snooze away their days in the hammocks of buttercups?

No, said Elijah, a roving commission should be appointed to ferret out the Jewish fairies who had become assimilated among other folk. He was not the only Hebrew sprite. He was only, so to speak, the last of the Mohicohens. His smile apologized for the atrocious pun. When the Hebrew fairies had been discovered, Elijah prophesied, they could be co-opted into a committee to discuss ways and means for immediate measures. In the meantime watchful waiting was the policy.

Hardly had he finished his last syllable, when on the meeting there burst a wild stampede of donkeys, braying and neighing and whinnying, and making other unfairylike noises. The fairies scurried to cover. The gnomes scampered away; the dwarfs hobbled out of sight; the sprites danced into the air; the elves leaped into rose-buds; the djinns vanished. Only the fat faun seated on the sunflower could be heard, triumphantly announcing to the stupid asses and invisible elves: Next meeting in Jerusalem!

Elijah, too, had disappeared. In the fairy ring, the asses were nibbling grass. The moon smiled down from above. So silent it was, one could have heard the music of the spheres; the stars chuckled.

Shmelka

When Mr. Sender Neugewirtz brought his brother Shmelka to Mrs. Finklestein as a boarder, the latter, striking the posture of a female Colossus, her plump arms akimbo, her not-uncomely head implacably set, scanned the diminutive Shmelka from top to toe, from corn to crown, sniffed audibly at his surrounding atmosphere, and issued her categorical negative.

No, it was absolutely impossible, it was utterly unthinkable. Such a room for eight dollars a month! Such a room, with a window opening into the backyard and a lilac tree before the window! And clean – clean was a slovenly word for it – pure, spotless. And snug, and cosy, and warm – warm as a burning earlobe. One might, saving Mr. Neugewirtz's grace, go about naked in it and not feel cold. The linen, she could bring the Chinese laundryman in to testify, laundered every week it was – King Solomon in his palaces slept on none whiter. Now Mr. Neugewirtz who was a business man could himself bear witness to the high cost of living. Bills, Mrs. Finklestein averred with a dogmatic inflection in her voice, had to be paid. She was not going to truckle with lawyers who flay the skins of the poor. There was coal, there was electric, there was the landlord – in these computations Mrs. Finklestein brought in the help of her round little fingers – and there were eighteen other little expenses that she could not mention at the moment. No, eight dollars – that was ridiculous. Let Mr. Neugewirtz not render himself foolish in her eyes.

Again too, one had to consider – and in bargainings one must be blunt – that Mr. Neugewirtz's brother was not exactly all there.

Mr. Neugewirtz himself admitted that Shmelka was queer and that there was a screw loose somewhere. A man like that – may the Lord forfend such a visitation from her household (here she spat thrice, – before her once, and once on either side) – a man like that was like a babe, he needed a mother's care. And Mrs. Finklestein, believe you her, was known for her maternal and unprofessional solicitudes. He could ask Mr. Abramowitz, who was leaving for Palestine, and who had been for two years her boarder; in fact ever since her husband, might he have an illuminated paradise, died. And to mention Mr. Abramowitz in the same breath as a man slightly off, was, she did not mean it as an insult, sacrilege. Mr. Abramowitz, here was a man! She showed the whites of her eyes to the ceiling and made a pious twittering with her lips. Mrs. Finklestein wasn't pious and all that, but she knew how to esteem a Man of God. And even he, Mr. Abramowitz, paid twelve dollars a month. Now that he was gone the room was empty, but she would rather let the mice scamper there, the roaches parade in it, than let it out for eight measly dollars. Of course there were no mice and cockroaches. Mrs. Finklestein's teeth grinned the apologetics of an afterthought, – that was merely a social phrasing, a folk saying. No, eight dollars compared to the true value of such a room was a spittle to the ocean. She would not hear of it.

Mr. Neugewirtz, portly and dignified, with a pudgy hand laid hold of his beard which was in the way of being a compromise between the injunctions of the Bible and the exigencies of business, and contemplated reconsiderations. Mrs. Finklestein, aware that Mr. Neugewirtz was undergoing a change of mental outlook, suddenly dammed her flow of eloquence, and in silence climaxed her arguments by regarding Mr. Neugewirtz's brother with feigned nausea and amusement unfeigned.

Slowly she took in the details of Shmelka's appearance, and at every discovery she gave Mr. Neugewirtz a reportorial glance. Throughout the whole conversation Shmelka had stood by dumbly, his mouth gaping as he stupidly watched the bargaining. Humble he seemed beyond humiliation as he stood there, helpless as a slave at a slave-market, as impersonal as a chattel on an auction-board. Mrs. Finklestein took note of every inch of

Shmelka's pitiful five foot two: she made mental memorandum of the glutinous and mucous stains on his coat, transcriptions of his daily menu in hieroglyphs of grease: she stared impertinently at elbows shamelessly showing their nakedness through their threadbare investment, and trousers baggy and distorted by the genuflections of bony knobs. For a long and uncomfortable time she let her gaze rest on his cracked and soleworn boots, covered with the geologic strata of a week's journeyings. His face would have wrung tears from a heart of adamant. Peaked it was, and thin, pitiful to behold, his jaw drooping stupidly, his eyes rheumy and lustreless staring at nothingness as if gouged by inquiry, and two long lines running down his face, like a circumflex about his nose. He was evidently short-sighted, and he stared so continuedly, and so fixedly, that his whole appearance suggested desire and hunger. He looked like a starved dull animal. Mrs. Finklestein concluded her appraisal with loud olfactory noises, to which Mr. Neugewirtz senior was not entirely oblivious. He took his hand from his beard; from the innermost depths of his paunch he sighed, and said, 'All right. I'm not the kind that haggles. I'll pay twelve a month.'

Thus Shmelka became Mrs. Finklestein's boarder on a par with a Man of God. He was, the landlady began to affirm even more loudly than before, a queer customer. He did not talk to anyone. He would go out for walks early in the morning and came back late in the afternoon to make himself some tea. He drank it hot to the boiling point, gulping it stupidly. Like an ox at a water-trough. His sense of taste, touch and smell seemed to be dead. And he was terribly myopic. After his tea he would retire to his room, and without undressing, even without putting on the light, he would go to bed. Mrs. Finklestein was disturbed by the thought of him lying on her bed, on her clean linen sheets, staring with those two heartrending eyes of his, for hours at a dark ceiling. Her lilac-tree too was not much appreciated. Shmelka never opened a window; the room began to smell like a stable.

But twelve dollars a month was one hundred and forty-four dollars a year.

After a while Mrs. Finklestein began to notice that Shmelka regarded her over his teacup with a dull and hungry look. Mrs.

Finklestein who was still buxom and sprightly felt tickled at the idea that Shmelka cast towards her, if not admiring, at any rate amorous, glances. She did not, be it said in vindication of her good taste, for a moment consider him as a possible substitute for her late husband, may he rest in peace, but she was pleased that a trousered person still found her beauty fascinating and torturesome. She would purposely bend down to pick up some knickknack or other, thus lowering her bosom to show the enticing suggestion of fulsome breasts, and she would from the corner of a self-satisfied eye watch his Adam's apple struggle with the tea. She would accidentally raise her skirt, displaying the fleshly swell of a leg, and derive a titillation at the sight of Shmelka's fingers unconsciously twitching. The consciousness that he was following every move of her hamlike arm, every ambulatory jactitation of her buttocks, with that docile and desirous look, filled her with a sense of pride not unadulterated by amusement.

But Shmelka of course would not dare to make advances to her. He was too meek, and too conscious of his uncleanliness. After regarding her with eyes almost voracious his jaw dropped, his tongue lolling over his lips. A normal lecher would have licked his lips lasciviously; Shmelka just stared short-sightedly. When he would suddenly grow aware of his all too manifest attitude he would retire to his room. Mrs. Finklestein would giggle self-flatteringly as she continued with her work in the kitchen.

The thought of his absolute filthiness and of his dumb stupidity would suddenly invoke in her a nausea. She considered that choice room of hers. Now it had become a stable. She remembered how in changing the sheets of his bed she would invariably find incriminating stains, and she giggled again, flattered in her healthy and robust superiority by the miserableness of a man lying on a single bed, longing and unappeased.

II

On Saturday night Mrs. Finklestein's children would come to visit her. They were a cheerful and good-natured litter, full of animal spirits, the kind of children one would expect such a one as Mrs. Finklestein to spawn. The most jovial of her offsprings was Yankel, a husky boy of twenty, with a juvenile relish for practical jokes and discomfiting pranks. In his younger days he had teased his teachers to distraction; his rebbe had ever complained, but most especially after Yankel had tied the pendules of his prayer shawl to those of another synagogue worthy, thus bringing indignity to both, that he was unruly enough to make a soldier consumptive. Even now after he had attained the years of his majority he was ever on the lookout for a right-rollicking lark.

The conversation had turned to the idiosyncrasies of the new boarder. Mrs. Finklestein was describing them with gusto and hyperbole; she punctuated her sentences with muffled snickers as she dwelt with a widow's emphasis upon the details of his suppressed desires. She did not mention her ingenious tantaliza-tion. 'Perhaps,' she concluded with a smirk, 'we ought to find a match for this lonesome man. After all it's a God's pity; here a *shadchan* would be better than a medical specialist.'

Amused, Yankel was listening attentively, as a grin expanded across his face and as his eyes began to lighten with forecasts of witticism, the Finklesteins awaiting some brilliant suggestion. 'Pardon me for a while,' he said, 'I'll be back in a second. Where is your coat, Sarah?' He was addressing his sister. He hurried out, chuckling; his merriment was so great that it could not all find egress through his mouth, and one could also hear it snorting through his nose.

In a few moments he returned; he was greeted with the applause of a family's laughter. In the brief interval since he had left the room, he had donned his sister's coat tight-fittingly, padded his shirt with two pillows in the shape of pectoral protuberances, daubed his lips with unsymmetrical smears, rouged his cheeks, powdered his nose clownishly, wound his mother's false switch of hair about his head, and crowned it with an old and much-beflowered hat. Tightening his coat about him so as to show all the contours of the temporary feminine, winking his eyes with flirtatious enticements and pursing his lips to a diminutive pout, he had come in with mincing steps, displaying to advantage his fascinating form and his improvised bosom. 'How will I do for a woman?' he queried in a falsetto voice. Pointing his finger to Shmelka's bedroom he added in the tone of a Jazz Singer, 'I wanna man. You, Ben, you can be the matrimonial agent, you fix it up for me.'

The family was so amused in watching his serpentine gliding and his elfin trotting that for a space they could hardly begin to consider plans. When the cachinnations of the Finklesteins were reaching their diminuendoes, Ben, pressing down the lapels of his coat, ruffled by the laughing palpitations of his breast, took hold of his chin in one hand and caressed it as if it was a beard, and with the other grasped an umbrella, adopting the attitude of a *shadchan*. He scrutinized his brother from head to toe, lingering lovingly over the padded undulations of his torso. He smacked his lips appraisingly. 'A tasty virgin,' he said, 'she needs no dowry.' At the compliment Yankel stuck a finger in his mouth, turned on the ball of his foot with the posturing of a demure maiden.

The *shadchan* took him by the hand and led him to Shmelka's room, which was adjacent to the kitchen where all were congregated. He knocked on the door. He heard a grunting from within. He opened the door and switched on the light. There was Shmelka on his bed, blinking stupidly on the newcomers.

'Your brother,' Mrs. Finklestein explained, 'told us that you would like to get married. So we brought you a girl, not young it is true, but she will make you a good wife.'

Yankel advanced forward and was introduced as the bride-to-be. With a delicate gesture he extended his thick butcher fingers. Shmelka charily accepted; he was so immune to sense of touch and so short-sighted that he failed to see or feel that these were very masculine digits that he was holding. But even then Shmelka continued protestations. He was not properly dressed he said, and he was not contemplating matrimony. His hungry looks at Yankel's manufactured contours betrayed the joy and the expectation that were his. With awkward movements designed for the purpose he sought to preen himself in Yankel's maidenly eyes.

'We had better leave the couple alone,' suggested Mrs. Finklestein, with a wink of her eye. 'Oh, no,' Yankel lowered his eyelashes shyly, and deliberately sat down on the bed next to Shmelka. They were left alone. The members of the Finklestein family were taking turns in peeping through the keyhole at the impromptu amour of the boarder. Their laughter was stifled; every now and then one of them would go away to another corner of the house to let loose undisturbed all the muffled laughter in him.

As they each in turn kept their eyes glued to the keyhole they saw Yankel making passionate advances to Shmelka. The latter was bewildered by the sudden outburst of kindness on the part of humanity, felt his heart grow bigger and in his uncouth manner he returned the caresses. He even made so bold as to embrace Yankel and seek to kiss him. But Yankel, remembering that he was virginal and naif, winked to the eye behind the keyhole, and adopted a frigid aloofness. Shmelka was pleased at the maidenly virtue of his bride-to-be. He took hold of his hand and patted it lovingly. He rested his head upon Yankel's rotund breast; wearily he sighed. Yankel mimicked a transport of bliss.

In the other room Mrs. Finklestein was laughing so much that she nearly rolled off her chair. Her sons and daughters, too, were struggling at the keyhole for a glimpse of the comedy. Their eyes twinkled; smugly they grinned; their bellies quivered with merriment. Oh, it was good to laugh, good to let oneself go in uncontrolled joy; laughter was so cleansing, so purifying, it made the heart fresh and the head clear. They were having a jolly time. Blessed be the Lord, Creator of funny things.

Yankel was already tiring of the tomfoolery; moreover, he wanted to get out and receive the plaudits of the family on his histrionic hermaphroditism. He waited for an opportune moment to leave. Shmelka in the half-witted manner of his was making a love-speech to him; he was promising to be a good husband, and was prophesying eternal happiness for them together. Suddenly Yankel rose; he doffed his hat – his luxuriant locks fell to the floor; he undid his coat – down went his feathered breasts as if by a miraculous amputation; he wiped his face – he was Yankel the butcher again.

Shmelka watched the process, dumbly. Dumbly he saw Yankel leave the room. He lowered his head to the pillow.

Yankel had felt somewhat ashamed when he beheld Shmelka's countenance miserable and dumbfounded at his departure, but as soon as he came into the kitchen he was greeted by loud and flattering gusts of laughter. He had done wonderfully; his brother Ben would be more than content with a wife who had as much sex-appeal as he had displayed. It had been a perfect show. Yankel expatiated on the nuances of his acting, of his psychologic tricks, on his subtle and delicate suggestions of his passion.

They laughed. They could not get over the joke, it was so excruciatingly funny. Laughter was like a fountain, rising higher and higher from the throaty Finklestein spouts. Every chuckle, every giggle was like a sparkling spray, shot into the air, spreading out joyously.

Suddenly there was a lull. From the next room there came a sound. A man was sobbing, bitterly; one could almost hear his tears roll down his face. From the dark room there came the sound of quiet weeping. A red ugliness which was shame suffused the faces of the Finklestein family. The fountain of laughter went lower and lower. Silently they looked at one another.

The Seventh Scroll

His back curved in ghetto hump, and winged with two bony shoulderblades, Reb Yekuthiel Geller sat on his hard chair, and stared at the square Hebrew letters arrayed like legions of black dwarfs on a field of parchment. For a dizzying moment, its hooked characters, he thought, brandished their glossy flourishes and lustrous curves before his eyes, wearied and as if enmeshed in cobwebs. Impulsively shaking his head, he broke the spell which drowsiness and fatigue had cast upon him; and now saw, as through a dissolving haze, the symbols of the ancient alphabet, at Sinai granted to his ancestors, engraved with God's chisel on tablets of stone. A great love possessed him, a sacred passion for these twenty-two seals of Deity, in Holy Writ variously arranged, to declare the Lord's intent. His eyes fondled the tricornate *Shein*, and the right-angled *Dalid*, and the ominous iota; he was enamoured of the thin strokes terminating in thick shapely blots; mysterious weapons from the arsenal of *Shaddai*.

It was now fifteen years since he had begun his meddling with parchments, inks, quills. In that period of time, and at the behest of rich patrons, he had written six scrolls of the Pentateuch, an untold number of talismans for phylacteries, and he knew not how many *mezuzahs*: he had mastered the art. And the art of the scribe was no copyist's perfunctory scrawling. It required hours of excruciating care, and meticulous precision, and a native genius for calligraphy. Every letter had to be shaped by hand; the lines were to be measured, traced and squared; certain characters must be crowned with flourishes, others diademed with dots. An error in orthography, especially if it occurred in the spelling of the Lord's name, the erasure of which was sacrilege, rendered the entire scroll useless for synagogal purposes. It had then to be sealed in an earthen vessel, and buried in the coffin of a saint. Never in the decade and a half in which he had been articled to the ghost of Moses, had this happened to Reb Yekuthiel Geller. He had not, it is true, that skill of ben-Kamzar, who was wont to manipulate four pens between his five fingers, and write a four-lettered word at one stroke; but his eye had accuracy, and his right hand was sleeved in sanctity. Punctiliously did he approach his labours, and with reverence. Unlike the Alexandrian scribes, he gilded not heathenishly the name of Jehovah; simply he wrote it, in bold black characters, but how devoutly he lingered over the contours of the tetragrammaton! How scrupulously he shaped each letter, while in piety he brooded over the drying ink! And always before he would take pen in hand to inscribe the *Yud-Hai-Vav-Hai*, he would lave his hands, meditate the arcana of Torah, and, following the prophet Ezekiel's injunction, circumcise his heart.

Not that Yekuthiel, labouring in piety, was aloof to art. He was no mere scrivener. No Jew ever beheld a more beautiful parchment roll than that on which his hand had inked the Song of Moses, with its verses metrically arranged, like bricks in stone wall, no battering ram of Pharaoh could breach open; and no Jew ever set eyes on an arrangement more symmetrical than that in which Chapter Thirty-two of Deuteronomy shaped itself beneath his pen. But Yekuthiel, exalting intention over deed, prized the strict letter in sanctity born above the fancy curlicues fashioned by the hand, facile and mechanic.

Yet, despite his talent, he was poor, pitiably poor. The profession of scribe is, beyond doubt, the most niggardly rewarded profession in Israel. Honour, Judah seems to proclaim, to the Torah; but no honorarium to its scribe. Keenly Yekuthiel suffered the cruelty of this never enunciated principle. With borrowed money he had to buy his own parchment, treated with gallnut and lime, his own indelible ink, and dried tendons to sew the sheets together, and rollers of ivory, from which to unfold the convoluted manuscript, – and then, after a year of labour at the multitudinous verses of the Pentateuch, perchance sell it for a few hundred dollars. But he accepted his poverty as an ordinance from on high. Did not the Great Assembly, as Rabbi Joshua ben Levi reports, observe twenty-four fast-days so that the scribes might not wax wealthy, and throw ink and pen aside?

Now, wearing skull-cap and silken threadbare jacket, upon a hard chair he sat, staring at the first completed chapter of his seventh scroll. His eyes, wreathed in crow's feet, like two iotas with embellishing traceries, scrupulously examined the script. As he bent over the goatskin manuscript, his small tuft of a beard poised, like an oriental brush, above the writing. His jowls were covered with patches of hair, which were neither beard nor down, but a set of black smudges, curiously grained; contrasting with black dot-like eyes, and fine hirsute nap, there shone from his face the white splendour of a broad brow, and the red glory of two full lips. Despite his venerable thirty-five years these features gave him an appearance of femininity – a slip of a girl masquerading in beard and moustache – an appearance accentuated by his frail scarecrow form, composite of taut skin and small bones.

Of the many scrolls which he had copied, and which now reposed in various Arks of the Covenant, this, his seventh, was to be his masterpiece, the consummation of all his skill, the object of his entire devotion. At the last flourish of the last letter of the last word, *Chazak! Chazak!* he would cry, and would donate the scroll to his synagogue in commemoration of the soul of his deceased wife, now in paradise. It would be for her a monument eternal; unlike stone slab over charnel plot, no conspiracy of rain and wind would destroy it. Raised aloft on High Holidays, all would behold her name knitted in gold braid on the mantle of the scroll, and the *Pamalyah shel Ma'Ala*, the Heavenly Court itself would be mindful of her, seeing what mementos of her virtue were left upon earth.

Certainly this was the least that he could do to render her name immortal. For fifteen years Miriam, on her memory, peace – had been his wife, faithful, devoted, loyal. The Lord had cursed her womb that it was barren, and out of their wedlock no child had been born, but out of her humiliation she had loved him the more. She had revered him, like a lesser god. Her heart had been bruised at the thought of her sterility, and always had she reproached herself for that which was not of her doing. In her shame before womankind, she had with her own lips brought down upon herself the epithets of abasement. She was a hard and unfruitful stone; a well dried up; an unfertile furrow. She was not worthy to wash his feet; she was meaner than the fingernail of his little finger. He had consoled her, laughing at her protestations. But despite his solace, she had walked about, pregnant only with guilt. Her heart, he knew, had swelled with gratitude because of his lovingkindness. A duller wit and a harder man would have used his Talmudic prerogative to throw her a bill of divorcement long before this. But he had been kind and forgiving, and of a magnanimous soul. She had repaid him, therefore, in the minor domesticities of everyday, those petty solicitudes which manifested her continual desire to please him, to show him how her whole being was absorbed in his worship and adoration. After prayers, his tea had always stood cooling on the table; and in the evening she had brought him his *Mishnaioth*, to hand, watching him proudly while he intoned its mysterious content. She had preserved him — she always heated the stove herself — from the inclemencies of chill winter and of torrid summer. She had studied his every propensity and aversion. He, in turn, had been grateful, and had spoken of her as of that virtuous woman lauded by King Lemuel, whose price was far above rubies.

And suddenly The Angel of Death had fluttered his wings over her bedchamber, and the glow had vanished from the ruby, leaving a gray, dead stone ...

She would not go down, unremembered, to the dust. He had decided it, even as the clods callously knocked a farewell on her coffin-boards. This would be his token. Upon parchment and in ink, indelible, he would raise to the halidom of her name a sacred mausoleum. The thrift of his past years would be well dedicated, indeed, towards a monument of the Law, and virtue. Already he was beginning to neglect the other duties of his calling. He no longer experienced an ecstatic thrill when he caressed the blue and white silk of prayer-shawls; no longer fingered the smooth thongs of phylacteries, and their talismanic cubes; the threading of *tzitzith* with their eight pendules and five knots, was now merely a procedure to him; he sold his brass candlesticks, his silver wine-goblets, and his yellowed tractates, as if they were no more than profane wares. Even the citrons and the palm-leaves, which he distributed for use at the Feast of Tabernacles, left him now with no nostalgia for fragrant groves. His mind was in the House of God, and his heart trickled in inkdrops upon a scroll.

He took his pen in hand and began to shape the square block-like letters, copied from an exemplar before him. Such divine transcription was not to be done from memory. Before every word he paused, meditating its deep significance, so that it might be said that the very ink itself had been mixed with the fine powder of his brain. Presently he grew weary; his eyes could no longer distinguish the *Hai* from the *Ches*. His head seemed to be flailed by a whirl of letter strokes.

In his fantasy he saw his work finished, completed down to the final implacable verse: *the great terror which Moses showed in the sight of all Israel*. The scroll was ready to be lodged in its sacred dwelling-place, the mahogany Ark of the Covenant. He beheld before him many Jews, shouting youngsters released from *cheder* and old men, stumbling along with canes, quietly jubilant, all following him, beneath a scarlet canopy held by four pious post-bearers, and himself bearing the Torah scroll, in velvet mantle, braided with gold, and covered with a silver breastplate, against which flowerlike bells tintinnabulated a quiet liturgy. Behind him a fiddler and a bugler played Hebrew melodies. On the sidewalk old women in perruques looked on and nodded one to the other, marvelling at the honour shown to the Law by a poor man. Windows were flung open; and wondering heads looked out. And among the crowd there rises a great questioning. Who gives the *Sefer Torah* to the synagogue? And the answer goes from lip to lip: Reb Yekuthiel, in the name of his wife, Miriam-bath-Rachel!

II

Yekuthiel, in greasy apron, stood before a stove, and stirred the flaky rice, boiling in an aluminum pot. Sighing, he added some salt to the bubbling mixture, and wondered whether the brew would taste as horrible as it did yesterday. Sweat hung on his beard like dewdrops on grass. A long spoon, he reflected, was certainly no stylus in a scribe's fingers. It was all a cruel joke – his wife a corpse, himself a cook.

Suddenly the doorbell rang, and the tall gaunt form of Reb Jonah Kalimeyer, insurance agent and matchmaker, appeared in the doorway. That quivering *lulav* of a man had swept his caftan across his threshold frequently of late; and he was evidently come again upon his matrimonial mission. Quickly doffing his apron, and wiping his beard, Yekuthiel led him into the study. He hoped that Jonah had not caught him at his culinary occupation; it would be formidable evidence in the hands of that merciless debater. But Kalimeyer was as observant a detective as he was a polemist irrefutable. His profession – the marrying, as the Yiddish proverb has it, of two diametrically opposite walls – demanded such aptitudes.

'Nu, Reb Yekuthiel,' – he smiled a gat-toothed smile – 'isn't it a shame that a *Talmid Chacham*, a student of the Law, a scholar, should so descend from his high estate as to piddle with pots and pans? Say yourself, isn't that a woman's work? It is written: I rejoice in my house; whereat the Rabbis explained, "my house" that is to say "my wife".'

For a moment Yekuthiel's face clouded; he thought of his household now domestic in a grave; and hated the crude Jonah for his brutal reference. Kalimeyer noted the melancholy that brooded on his countenance, and added:

'Of course, I would not even speak of these matters had I not Talmudic sanction.'

Kalimeyer always spoke with Talmudic sanction. His whole vocabulary was composed of a series of quotations from the sages.

In every argument he hauled the Rabbis and sometimes even Divinity Itself to testify in his behalf.

'Three High Holydays have already elapsed since your wife, may she rest in peace, has been taken from you, and it is time that you took your mind off sepulchres, even if it is only to place it on stoves ... Who would have thought it – Reb Yekuthiel a chef!'

'There is no disgrace in that. The great Rabbi Meyer used to insist on chopping his fish himself on Fridays.'

'Granted.' The glow of victory shone on the face of Kalimeyer. Yekuthiel had walked into a Talmudic blind alley. 'Granted. But Reb Meyer used to fritter about his oven only on Fridays, and that, naturally, so as to show respect for the approaching Sabbath; but here I find you, Reb Yekuthiel, writer of scrolls, garbed like a maid, and perspiring over pots, when? In the middle of Wednesday ... No, you are not a *mensch*, if you will pardon my saying so. Even the Patriarchs did not mourn so endlessly. I ask you: did Jacob stay unconsoled when his Rachel died?'

'He had other wives.'

'And Abraham, our Father, who only had Sarah. Did he begin cooking for himself when she departed? No: without fancy solemnities he went right away to the sons of Heth, and talked business. A burying place he wanted; and there was an end.'

'Yes, but Sarah was one hundred and twenty-seven years old when she died. My Miriam was only thirty-three.'

Kalimeyer was about to refute with the statement that people lived longer in those days anyways, when he noticed tears, like pale mourners, creeping from the eyes of Yekuthiel. He did not wish to have these sentimental intruders bias his line of argument. He adopted the tone sympathetic.

'You are right. What's true is true. But after all, there's a measure to all things. Even Moses was mourned for only thirty days. And believe me, your wife Miriam is happier now than you are. Why, you're only half a man; for is it not written: *Male and female created he them, and called his name Adam, a man.* When did he call him Adam, a man?' His voice quivered with the tremolos of logic and his eyes stared interrogatives. 'When? When He had created him, male and female.'

'Well, I have already been created, male and female. The female was lost. That was God's doing, not mine. I at least fulfilled the behest of the Rabbis: The son of eighteen years must to the wedding canopy go.'

'And now that you are thirty-six the behest applies doubly. Besides you did not fulfil the biblical command –'

Jonah did not continue. He saw the pitiable look on the scribe's face; and could not bring even his ruthless tongue to utter the cutting: *fructify and multiply.*

'And more than that, Reb Yekuthiel. Why, the old sages used to wonder, does a man court a woman, and not a woman a man? Because he who loses something goes to look for it. Man in his slumbers lost a rib; therefore he wanders through life seeking that rib. You, Reb Yekuthiel have lost it twice.'

'I admit that.' Yekuthiel grew meek before the onslaught of so many authorities. 'But I have my scroll to finish, even before I can consider canopies and wives.'

'Not necessarily.' Yekuthiel saw another quotation emerging from Jonah's learned sleeves; he prepared himself for it. 'The Rabbis of yore discussed that very same problem. Does the duty of study precede that of marriage? The consensus of opinion was, marry first and study afterwards.'

'But what does Rabbi Jochanan say? "You hang millstones on his neck – and expect him to pore over books?"'

'Reb Yekuthiel, I am only doing my duty. I see a man, young, no children, a scholar, taken from his holy work by reason of his bachelorhood. I say to myself: It would be a *mitzvah* to find him a spouse. After all, that is God's work. A Roman matron once asked a *Tauna*, what God did to occupy his time since He completed the work of creation. And the *Tauna* answered: He sits up in heaven and arranges marriages. But is God going to go down from His high altitudes, in His might and majesty, and Himself say to Yekuthiel, I have a good match for you, upon my word, an excellent match, Reb Yekuthiel? No. He sends His Jews instead, His Kalimeyers, His minions like me to do His command. And for a *mitzvah* I walk a mile.

'And that is precisely what I came here about. When I talk, I don't talk just in the world. No, it's like this. I know a widow, a modest, quiet Jewish woman, about your age, maybe a little older, who is looking for a husband. She has a grocery on the Main Street; makes a nice neat living out of it. The neighbours even say that she has a handsome knot hidden away in her stocking. But that I won't guarantee. What I will say is that she wears a perruque; she goes to synagogue every Sabbath; she observes the dietary laws. A kosher soul, as I am a Jew.

'Nu, I think that such a match will just be perfect for you. She could be in the store, and you could move into the double-parlour, and do your copying. You would save money; you would have your meals; and if the Lord would wish, maybe a child, a *kaddish*. But of course if a Jew is obstinate, go scream *Chai V'kayom*! Last year's snow hears you? That's the way he hears you. I am not your father; I can't compel you. As a good Jew, I can only advise you. But if you say no, it's no.'

Kalimeyer looked at the scribe who seemed to be weighing some plan in his brain. He considered it the psychological moment to desist from persuasion. He rose to go.

'Anyway, think it over. I may be passing here tomorrow – Reb Itzik is having his son circumcised – and I will drop in on the way.'

III

Reb Yekuthiel Geller was utterly miserable in his new environment, among the barrels of briny herring, the boxes of dried pears, the pyramids of sardine-cans. He longed for the cool repose of his study, with its fragrance of phylactery-leather, its aroma of citron in cotton wool. Here in the narrow grocery of his new wife, where he could not take a step but he bumped into a crate of cubed sugar, or tripped over a clattering pail, or awkwardly elbowed down from the shelf a ketchup bottle, he was veritably in exile. The sounds, the smells, the very taste of the atmosphere in the grocery nauseated him. Those days when he had fingered the tassels of a prayer-shawl, or crooned over a holy book, or written his scrolls of divine dictation now belonged to a remote and enviable past.

For the marriage had not prospered as well as the ebullient Kalimeyer had prophesied. The grocerylady – that was what the neighbours called her – had, he soon discovered, an indomitable will beneath that pious perruque of hers. She did faithfully observe the Sabbath, it is true, but that, Yekuthiel maintained, was religion well directed. A shrew of her kind needed some liturgy to mellow her. She was finicky, indeed, in her fulfilment of the dietary injunctions, but that was no difficult matter for a wife who fed her mate on a diet of ill-prepared meals, and of menus of monotonous identity. Even the consolation prize of her merits had been delicately exaggerated; she did not have, Yekuthiel soon found out, a handsome savings account hidden in her stocking, or in her bosom, or in any other of the concealments which womanhood has invented.

At first she had treated him with respect. A scholar and a man of saintly ancestry was no common catch for a widow. She had even boasted of her recent acquisition to her neighbours. She had allowed him, moreover, to continue his work while she wrapped her parcels, and hopped about the store like a live broomstick. But when she discovered that he was dedicating his Torah scroll to his late wife, jealousy made her sharp bones glow like embers. The gall of the man! Her husband, and offering a Torah in the name of his first wife. It was like adultery, she swore. She began to complain about the arduousness of her duties in the grocery; it was a shame that a man should sit at home, waste his time in writing scrolls which nobody would buy, because they were not even offered for sale, while she sweated and worked herself to the bone to provide his bread. At length he consented to help her out in the store. When Mrs. Geller considered the aid and succour which he gave her, it turned out, in her depreciating phrase, that he was no more than a message-boy. It was a ludicrous sight, indeed, to behold him, his little beard pointed forward like a goat's, his fragile body bent, and his eyes, dreamy and nostalgic, – drawing by a long handle a little cart, laden with wrapped kippers, wax-papered loaves, jars of preserves, and bags of fruit. When he was not running errands – leading his cart and tramping through the street, on the road and not on the sidewalk, like a pony, his plight was even worse. He had to stay in the store, serving Mrs. Itkovitch with a half-pound of sugar, or Mrs. Cohen with two pickles, of those that are three for five, please. His slightest error was visited with condign punishment by the vigilant and fastidious Mrs. Geller. She would let loose her vixen tongue upon him, and flog him with insults, in the sight of no matter how many customers. And all day long it was: Wrap those loaves! What, are you standing there like a *golem*? Weigh those onions! Are you going? for today or for tomorrow? Come, trundle yourself! She no longer called him Yekuthiel, only plain, imperious Yukel.

At home in the double-parlour she would pounce upon his slightest gaucherie, his most innocent comment as an excuse for prolonged harangues, characterized mainly by the fact that they consisted of her own refutations of her own objections, and subsiding only when she realized that she was carrying on a marathon monologue. A scold among the scolds in Israel, her full-mouthed, spicy maledictions, had they any potency, would have thrown blight and bane upon an entire seraglio of husbands, let alone the poor, hunched, humble, self-effacing Yukel. For to her the process of cursing was a ritual, a sort of witch's incantation. Her ingenious oaths, moreover, tripped featly from her tongue in rhyme: did he gently suggest that the tea was cold, quick came the answering echo: May you soon grow old. Did he faintly remonstrate that the meat lacked pepper, out of her mouth it leaped, – May you become a leper. These, however, were merely conversational couplets, extemporaneously uttered to express mild displeasure; it was when she observed him in the dining-room at his seventh scroll, that an avalanche of maladies, a torrent of afflictions, a tornado of calamities, rushed, streamed, and whirled from her termagant lips. But Yekuthiel, long-suffering and adept at volitional deafness, persisted in his labours, and was now completing the Book of Numbers.

Kalimeyer, conscious of having been a contributing agent to Geller's misfortune, now sedulously avoided him. It was an accident when they did meet on the Main Street, as Yekuthiel was picking up from the gutter some bundles which had slipped off his cart. It was his turn, now, to open the conversation.

'Nu, Reb Jonah, how does it look for a scholar to be an errand-boy?'

'There's no disgrace in that. Reb Jochanan was a shoemaker, Resh Lakish was a gladiator; many renowned scholars had ordinary professions. As a matter of fact, they cultivated their vocations of purpose, and not out of necessity. They did not want to make of the Torah either a crown with which to honour themselves, or an axe with which to earn themselves sustenance.'

Yekuthiel, realizing the number of precedents which Kalimeyer always had on hand, immediately surrendered.

'I suppose you are right. I suppose there is an answer in the holy writings for every complaint. Our love is a treasury of many coins, and every coin has two faces. For example. You remember you spoke about wedlock and ribs? Why did the Lord create woman out of a rib? You had an answer. Well, listen to this one. Because He feared that if He fashioned her from Adam's foot, she would be a gadabout; if from his mouth, a prattler; if from his ear, an eavesdropper; but in the end Divinity was foiled. Created from a rib she still was gadabout, prattler, eavesdropper. A wink is sufficient to the wise ...'

Delivering himself in this manner, Yekuthiel gave his cart a violent tug, and hurried on his way. Almost regretting his marriage-commission, Kalimeyer shrugged his shoulders, and bore himself off, meditating insurance policies.

Sometime later the y.j.a.a. — the Young Jewish Amateur Athletic Association, composed mainly of ambitious urchins, played their daily baseball game in the lane skirting from the Main Street. The ground was so arranged that left field included the territory covered by the Geller grocery. At the ninth inning a left-handed pinch-hitter swatted the ball right into the show-window of Geller's Family Grocery. Mrs. Geller rushed out of the store, waved her hands, clutched her perruque, and cried calamity. But the gang received her imprecations *in absentia*. They had scurried away, running into doorways, and hiding behind sheltered porches, leaving the doleful Mrs. Geller clasping her palms, and performing all the antics of anguish and despair. The street was deserted; the plate-glass window yawned lugubriously at a self-commiserating Mrs. Geller, picking a smeared ball from the ruins of a jam-jar.

There was nothing to be done. Curses, even she realized, could not mend the glass; a glazier was needed for that; and it was too late to call one. But the store could not be left unprotected during the night. It was decided that Yekuthiel sleep in the grocery and act as watchman.

That night it rained continually, a chill, insistent drizzle, from midnight until dawn, when Yekuthiel awoke with pains in his back, a sore throat, and a maddening headache. He went home, and into bed. During the day his pains grew worse. When the doctor was called, he had developed pneumonia.

The invalid, moreover, was not heartened by the number of evil-smelling bottles, and bitter powders, and pills like nuggets, that made his bedroom an apothecary's paradise. He was filled with misgivings, and premonitions; from his fever he seemed to hear a command, like the voice from Moses' burning bush. That night he rose from his bed and opened the scroll at the last chapters of Deuteronomy. From *give ear O you heavens, and I will speak* until the ultimate syllable of the fifth Book he wrote furiously, stopping only when he came to write of the demise of Moses in the land of Moab, where no man knoweth his sepulchre. He shed hot tears.

When he returned to his quilts and pillows he burned with the seven fires of Gehenna. Mrs. Geller stood at his bedside, sorrowful, crestfallen, oppressed with a sense of guilt. She called the doctor again; he looked at him once, and said that never should he have left his bed. But ten horses could not have kept him back.

Mrs. Geller was now personally sensitive to every remark made by the physician. The doctor shook his head.

Yekuthiel now seemed to be delirious. In a weak voice he kept muttering only about his scroll. Occasionally one could distinguish from his feeble undertones a few words, a phrase, sometimes a sentence. He kept repeating, Miriam-bath-Rachel! Miriam-bath-Rachel! He wanted his scroll dedicated in his name, and in the name of his wife, Miriam-bath-Rachel. It would be his *kaddish*, a real *kaddish*, a holy intercessor on his behalf before the Judgment Seat ... For a long time he mumbled strange incoherencies, made lucid only by the refrain of Miriam-bath-Rachel! a *kaddish*! a *Sefer Torah*! At last, as if returning from his transcendent delirium to the urgencies of the moment, he made an effort, lifted his head from the pillow, and ordered almost in a loud voice that a Rabbi be sent for immediately to examine the scroll. Then he relapsed into a sleep broken only by his wheezy breathing, and his inarticulate moans.

When the Rabbi came, he marvelled at the neatness and the accuracy of the work. Genesis, Exodus, and Leviticus had been done with the pen of a master. But Numbers and Deuteronomy – he sighed and was silent. He pointed to a *Yud, Hai, Vav, Hai* in Deuteronomy. An error in the name of God. The scroll was –. The Rabbi shut his lips firmly; nullifying adjectives were not to be applied to a work once intended for sacred purposes.

On the next day the body of Reb Yekuthiel was led to its last resting-place. A scroll was buried in an earthen vessel in his coffin.

Blood and Iron
A Satire on Modern German Ideology

After the dukes and princelings were banished, the state bugler bugled out an empire. After the emperor was banished, the state bugler bugled out a republic. After the president was banished, the state bugler was out of breath.

No citizen then knew to what rule he was subject. Diplomats, however, referred to the government as a republican-imperioligarchy, and to its cabinet ministers as having forthright leftist leanings.

The permanent civil servants, bewildered but still bureaucrats, called upon the people to sign oaths of allegiance in triplicate, one to the emperor, one to the republic, and one to a blank space.

These documents were kept on file, so that upon a change of government, any burgher might be proved, as necessity dictated, either patriot or traitor.

It was then that an obscure label-paster in a patent medicine factory inserted an advertisement in the leading national journal, offering to become dictator upon being given a two dollar per week raise over his then salary. This increase, he said, was requested not because he sought to make profit out of patriotism, but because he would have to work longer hours. The fact that the new job would entail a lesser responsibility, he wisely concealed.

But the ad was mistakenly inserted in the Lost and Found column; and the dog-fanciers who usually read it were then more interested in thoroughbreds than in politicians.

Little did they suspect that they had passed up on one of the finest bloodhounds who ever coursed through history.

Accordingly, the label-paster, seeing that he was forever doomed to rub away this tongue at stickers, decided that he could with the same amount and the same kind of energy, become an orator.

He trained his voice in the best taverns. In gymnasiums he studied gesture. But he realized as he rummaged in the vacuum of his mind, he had no philosophy of life. And a savior, he had been told, must have such a philosophy. At first he thought of dropping in on a neighbour, and borrowing one; but after several attempts, he understood that people will not readily part with their sole and only possession. Suddenly, as he regarded a patent-medicine bottle which he had forgotten to return to his employer, an inspiration struck him. He ordered another quart of beer, on credit, stood upon a table, and shouted: 'What this country needs is more and better blood.'

Then, having waved his iron tonic bottle, to describe astronomical curves in the air, he put it down, lifted his beer mug to his lips, and drank wassail to the arterial system.

In the tavern, he gathered about him some well-known topers, and assigned them their respective tasks in the national renascence. One, an expelled schoolmaster, wrote a thesis on *The Teleology of the Corpuscle*; another, an economist, prepared a brochure on *Colonial Expansion via the Venous Stream*; and still another, an adventurous and gallant pyromaniac, planned a set of lectures on *Fire in the Blood*. The label-paster himself, went to see his employer about royalties on the sale of iron tonic.

Soon the whole country was agog with the new philosophy. Upon every street corner, disciples of the label-paster orated about the metaphysics of gore; and crowds of anaemic citizens stood by, shouting applause through megaphones. Their voices were weak from hunger.

Shortly thereafter, an election took place. The people turned out en masse to vote for the blood-and-thunder ticket. The opposition was almost completely swamped, and what was left of it was disposed of by a highly scientific form of blood-letting.

The label-paster then attracted towards him an aristocracy of men with rich red blood and dubbed them the elect. Some, indeed, were of so sanguinary a humour that the richness of their blood burst forth and budded upon their faces in numerous pimples. Those with the greatest number of pimples qualified for cabinet office.

Several changes were then introduced into the social life of the country, all by proclamation.

The old flag of the empire was prohibited. In its stead, there flew from the flag-poles of all public buildings, banners bearing as their symbolic device, a leech rampant against a background of gules.

Old-fashioned music, too, was abolished, as being too mellifluous for a race inoculated with superior blood. Henceforward the national music was to be played by Big Bertha, a prima donna whose monotonous iteration of a single note was inspirative of purposefulness.

Certain areas in the land were, by dictatorial command, dedicated to a study of philosophy. These lyceums were very wisely bounded by barbed-wire fences, so as to keep out trespassers. Armed guards too, were stationed at important points. The dictator knew if an alien were to stumble in upon these academic precincts he might overhear the secret of the renascence.

Upon festive occasions, the label-paster would arrange for grandiose banquets at which a luscious fare of liver and blood-pie would be served. After the repast, the guests would repair to the execution grounds to behold how the enemies of the state were liquidated by hemorrhage.

Scientists, too, were enlisted in the service of the national ideal. Day and night, they laboured, perfecting a new machine. Finally, it was completed, and upon strategic points at the frontier, one could see tall cylindrical tubes, like gasoline tanks, whose function it was to attract and suck in blood from the inhabitants of contiguous countries. The inventors of these Exsanguinators were rewarded with a recently created Order of the Mosquito.

The support and maintenance of the blue-blooded aristocracy swelled the national expenditure. An economist, taking a com-

pulsory course at one of the above-mentioned lyceums estimated –
without the help of a tutor – that the cost of keeping the dictator's
aide-de-camp in medals and mufti – this worthy even took a bath
in a uniform – was sufficient to clothe the metropolis. This
drainage of the state's resources soon came to a dismal pass: the
people at large began to suffer from pernicious anaemia.

As the blood ran thin through the veins of the citizens, they
endured bitter cold. Even the plan of the country's leading scientist
– the manufacture of a substitute for cloth, whereby the populace
would be fitted with neatly sewn, well-styled suits of cellophane –
availed not. The people froze.

Upon the advice of the most pullulating of his council, the
label-paster ordered all books in the realm to be burned in public
places for the greater warmth of the populace.

Soon there were no books in the land.

Someone suggested the writing of new books-to-be-burned;
but a census revealed that all the good writers had fled to parts
unknown, with the exception of one whose fingers had been
chopped off in an unfortunate testing of his blood.

The tax-payer, paying through the nose, continued to be
subject to nasal haemophilia; and was cold.

A special cabinet meeting having been called, a proclamation
was issued ordering every citizen upon meeting another, to wave,
by way of greeting, his right arm furiously. Thus heat would be
generated. The cabinet then went for a rest to a southern climate,
content that now the citizens would be warm.

They shivered.

In the meantime, the label-paster felt his blood grow richer
and richer. When he clipped his mustache, even the hairs bled.

Rumblings were heard throughout the land, and they were
not the belches of surfeiting. The basso coughs of the consumptive, the pizzicato death-rattles of the dying, the minor-keyed
cries of the agonized, swelled into orchestral music for a *danse
macabre*. The anaemic blood of the folk boiled, frigidly.

The aide-de-camp of the dictator trembled in his greatcoat.
The knights of the Order of the Mosquito shook as in a malaria

fever. The dictator himself was mentally bewildered as fear clutched him in the pit of his stomach.

Nobody knows what really happened thereafter. It is known only that when an autopsy was performed upon the cadaver of the label-paster, the doctors discovered a clot in the brain.

The history-books do record, however, that when the news of the dictator's demise was announced, the state bugler bugled out a song without words.

Friends, Romans, Hungrymen

So one day, way back in the time of the fairytales, the boss called me into his cave and said that he was sorry but he was going to lay me off. He said it nicely, like an ogre elocuting fee-fi-fo-fum. He grabbed me, wrapped me up in a little package, and laid me down upon a dusty shelf. Then he stuck out a long tongue, licked the gluey side of a strip of paper, pasted it on me, and read it over: Unemployed.

At night, when I heard no more belches in the cave, I knew the boss had gone home for a refill of his belching stuff. He is a sick man, he always eats. I wriggled out of the package, and went to the park. I applied for membership in the zoo.

I have been there ever since.

Sometimes I am very hungry. Things in my stomach toy about with my intestines, pulling them out like elastic, and letting them go snap.

At those times, I go through the lanes of the city. I lift the haloes from off the garbage-cans, and always find a tid-bit. Manna. It tastes like whatever one wishes it to taste. I only want it to taste like food.

Once I realized that it would be a long time before I would get a real meal. So I took out my false teeth, polished them off on my cuff and wrapped them in a piece of cellophane that I picked up in the street on a cigarette box. Soon I put the teeth back into my mouth. The better to smile with, my child.

I smile to the dames that pass through the park. They look good, and when they are gone, a sweet smell still floats in the air.

But they never give me a tumble. I think I am too skinny. They don't like ethereal guys.

It is terrible not to have a roof over your head. All day, white molten lead is poured over me from a big cauldron which somebody on purpose hangs up in the sky.

At night I sleep on a bench in the park. A lot of other bums do the same. Before I fall asleep, I always watch the shadowy cobras, and the prowling leopards coming towards me. In the morning I wake up, and my shoes and cap are wet from the licking of the beasts.

My head is getting duller and duller. It feels like a cage in which mice are scampering about looking for cheese that isn't there. It is because I am getting so stupid that I was nearly run over by Ezekiel's chariot which came rushing at me, stinking like a field of over-ripe radishes, and screaming with the voice of a dinosaur. I was picked up from the gutter, sugared with dust like a Turkish delight.

As I turned a street corner, I met God. I asked Him for a dime for a cup of coffee. He told me He had no small change, but recommended to me a swell flophouse on the Milky Way. Then, as an afterthought He put His hand in His pocket, and took out a couple of cheap comets. Because my pockets are torn, I tied one up in my shirt, lit the other, and strolled down the boulevard, puffing like a plutocrat.

There is nothing like a bit of self-confidence. I went back to the boss who was swathed in many rolls of pork-loins. I asked him for my job. He said: Can't you see that you are lying on a shelf? Go away from here, you are a ghost. I pushed my fingers between my ribs and pulled out my heart, and said: Look, it is going. It's a fake, he answered, you just wound it up.

After that I had to take a drink. I drank at a public fountain. But I did not enjoy it. A creature, with two arms, two legs, a wooden fang, and growing blue wool all over him, kept watching me. And when I stopped to wipe my lips with my sleeve, he said – in English – Move on.

The best is to sit on a bench in the park. There are all kinds of papers lying around, and if you are not tired, you can read them, for nothing. I like to read the menus. Yesterday, I picked up a nifty, and the birds who were looking over my shoulder sang, *Fricassee! Fricassee! Pâté de foie gras!*

But you get rubbed out sitting too much. Some day I will have to sit on my sixteenth vertebra. I look around. There is a sign which says KEEP OFF THE GRASS, but the sign itself breaks the rule. So I lie down on my belly, and watch the ant-hills. I have nothing to do. I give every ant a name, names of fellows who used to work with me in the office. The fat ant is Bill the accountant, the skinny one is the office boy Fred, and the one with the shaking head is Old Man Harris, the Credit manager. I envy the ants. They all have jobs.

Did you ever come to think that birds and beasts are always employed? They all have jobs. They are always doing something. They are laid off only when they are dead. That's civilization for you.

And the birds that work all summer go to Miami for the winter. Even the squirrels save up their nuts for a snowy day. Perhaps the boss kept something for me, to give me when he laid me off. I went to him, and asked him for my ten kegs of sweat which he was keeping back. The boss pulled up his lips, and showed me his teeth. I heard noises going on in his throat.

That night I dreamed I was up in the sky. I picked bright blueberries out of its floor, and ate them. Then I washed it all down by drinking a bucketful that I pulled up from a well of golden soup.

But in the morning my mouth was dry. A kind lady gave me a sandwich. I took it to the park and ate it. All the bums pointed their fingers at me, singing: Shame! Shame! He's ea-ting! He's ea-ting!

The benchers of the park say that the trouble with the system is that there are not enough coins in circulation. They are going to issue some of their own. They had a fight about whose map to put on the ducats. Big Tom wants his face there, but Sam says he looks nicer. Somebody suggested an Indian's head. Naw, we don't want no foreigners.

Then somebody said that it would be better to have a symbol.

No, a face. No, a symbol. Alright, a face and a symbol. So it was decided that we put a skull, anybody's skull, on the coin. Now we have to find the metal.

I have no faith in their plans. I would like to be a sweeper in the mint.

On the park bench I found a newspaper. I noticed one page on which the printer had forgotten to set any type; then in the corner I observed a number of bugs arrayed in a funny combination on the blank paper. They weren't bugs: it said Man Wanted. I went to the place. The man at the door said: You have a late edition, buddy, that was a month ago.

I scrammed. On the way I met my cousin Gerald. He stopped his car, and undid the top buttons of his pants. It's tough, he said, and caught his breath. I said yes. Why don't you go into business for yourself, he said. That's a good idea, I said. I am going to get a sky-rocket and shoot up to the moon. I will take the moon off its hinges, and hide it somewhere. I will say: You want moonlight, pay. Then I will rent the moon out at so much per night. Cut rates for sweethearts. Then I will organize a company and sell moon-beam shares. Yes, I will go into business for myself. Anyway, give me your paper.

In the paper there was a headline, with a big fat exclamation mark: There is a job! When it came my turn to see the guy who was looking over the candidates, I said: Gotta job? It must have sounded foolish, after me waiting in line for so long. Gotta job? How much am I offered, he said.

I went back to the park. I threw my soul into a thimble which a nursemaid had lost under a bench. I planted the thing in the earth. I spat upon it; I said: Let it grow.

And now, now I want to die. The bums in the park had a long talk about suicide. They said to me: If you want to die so much, why don't you throw yourself from a sky-scraper?

I haven't enough weight to hurt myself, I said.

How about poison?

I *have* eaten in relief joints, I said.

Ah, they said, shooting?

That's to kill healthy men with.

Then they got sore. Go and hang yourself, they said.

I got sore, too. You dumb clucks, I said, can't you see my neck's too thin not to slip out of any knot?

Somebody said, Have you tried starving, when a guy who was eavesdropping on us, jumped on a bench and shouted: Friends, Romans, hungrymen, lend me your tears. Then he threw his arms up in the air, and pushed out his chest, on which his arms landed when they fell. Then he craned his neck this way and that, and asked a lot of questions, and didn't wait for an answer. We lent him our tears, and he wept.

Suddenly there appeared a herd of those same creatures that once moved me away from the fountain. They were grabbing the boys by their manes, and pushing them into a waggon. One of them bit me over the head with a wooden fang, and dragged me to a station. That is the name of the lair of these creatures.

Then I was stood before a head which was lying on an open code, and the head said that somebody had overheard me talking about suicide. This was a crime, the head said, and screamed numbers at me. My life belonged to the state. I felt very proud because they were making a fuss about me killing myself.

Then the head said that I would be charged in due course with attempt at suicide and disturbing the peace. In the meantime, if I wanted to make a statement, I didn't have to, and if I didn't want to make a statement, I might. Or something like that. Then somebody gave me pen and ink.

That's how I come to write down everything that I have written down. I am very happy because they tell me that I am going to jail. I hear that they have meals there, regular.

And I hear too that they have work. They even make you work. Imagine! Nobody says how much am I offered?

I hope I stay there forever and forever, amen. This is my statement.

Beggars I Have Known

I get along very well with beggars. Perhaps it is because they feel that I shall soon be one of them.

Whenever I pass a panhandler on the street he buttonholes me. Even when I say, No, I can't spare a dime, he never feels resentful. He knows I am telling the truth, even if I am wearing a new suit.

But when I have the change I give it to them. I am not one of those who go around making nasty remarks about beggars just because their mouths smell of beer. I know that when a fellow has only a nickel to his name he would rather, and it's much wiser, too, spend it on a glass of beer, than on a cup of dishwater. Coffee just washes your insides and keeps you awake, whereas beer fills you, tickles your guts and makes you drowsy. It's easier to sleep on hard benches that way, and besides, if your mouth smells of beer the flies don't fly into it when you're asleep with it open.

I remember once when I had a dime between myself and hunger, I thought of how to spend it. If I bought something to eat, I figured, I would be hungry again in no time and would have to walk the streets with an aching belly. So I went into a cheap movie and for four hours forgot all about my hunger, except now and again when I saw on the screen how the rich eat.

There is a man on our street, an old Jew, who lives in the Home for the Aged. Every day, except Saturday, you can see him walking around the block with his eyes glued to the sidewalk looking for cigarette butts. He keeps the butts in regular cigarette boxes which he picks up in the gutter. Whenever I see him nosing around for his butts, I always give him a brand-new cigarette; sometimes I don't notice him until he turns the corner, and then I run after him to give him his smoke. He always takes my cigarette and then blesses me. I should live to an old age: I should be rich: I should have pleasure from my children. I always feel good when I leave him, because he blesses with so much heart, caressing my shoulder at each blessing, as if he was loading them on my back.

I told him he could pick up a lot of butts outside the Arena on wrestling nights, because the fans go out to have a smoke between bouts and always at midnight there are hundreds of butts on the sidewalk. As a matter of fact, once when I was coming home from a show downtown at twelve o'clock, and walked up by way of Fletcher's Field, a beggar walked up with us and stopped at the Arena to pick up these butts. But the old Jew tells me he can't get out of the Home for the Aged after eight o'clock.

There is a beggar who rings our door-bell on Mondays. To tell the truth I never saw him ring it and I often wonder how he does it because the fingers of both his hands are all chopped off. My mother gives him a nickel – we're poor, too – and he grabs it off with his palms and with the stubs that are left of his fingers. When my brother, who is eating dinner, asks my mother who it was at the door, she always tells him, and begins to describe the buttons of flesh where the fingers should be, and my brother says, Can't you see I'm eating?

I know all the beggars of our city personally. Most of them are real beggars, but some of them are fakes. There are a couple of guys, for example, who patrol Peel and St. Catherine Street, who are nothing more than racketeers and who, if they are ever found out, will give begging a bad name. These fellows get themselves a pair of returned soldier buttons, and every time they nab a customer they flash the badge and say something about a country fit for heroes to live in. But Tommy Kinsella, on Place d'Armes Square, who is a real returned soldier, lost his badge and all he can show are two sawed-off legs. Everybody pities him, however, when he tries to get on a street car.

He's a funny case, too, this Tommy. He doesn't seem to mind his stumps so very much, but he's always complaining about getting T.B. because his nose is so near the ground. I suppose you get that way, from trouble.

Then take Steve Szopik. He is the fellow who hangs around our factory and runs messages. Occasionally he gets a sandwich and a Coca Cola. Now he's been trying to break into the beggar game for years. But he can't do it. He just can't get a license. No pull. Everything is politics.

On the other hand, a snob like Burke – the violinist in front of Christ Church Cathedral – has all kinds of pull, and gets a license, and one of the best spots in town. Stuck-up! That's not the word for it. He calls himself a mendicant.

It's the blind beggars who are really handicapped. When you're blind and a beggar you can't run after your clientele; it just passes you by. It doesn't even feel embarrassed. You're blind.

And they can throw into your box whatever they feel like throwing. You can't ever know.

I just can't see old man Rosenbloom. He is blind and is led around by his little boy. He wears dark glasses and carries pencils in his hand. It's the idea of the pencils that I can't get. I imagine that if you are blind you are entitled to charity without giving away presents. Apart from the expense, it's foolish. What does he want, his patrons to write him a letter?

So, as I am saying, I get along swell with beggars. They remember that when I had money I was no piker. They tell me all their secrets: Why the doorstep of some churches are more profitable than others; what restaurants throw you out, and which ones give you a hand; how to approach elderly ladies and how to tackle young slickers; where the book-makers are, and what time the barbutte finishes, and the winners come out; how to feel the denomination of coins; what words to open up your plea with, and what phrases to leave out when the giver doesn't seem to pay any attention; when to talk clearly, and when to mumble; when to be bold and when to be humble; what districts have dogs in their porches; how to shake a coin-cup so that it should make the greatest amount of noise with the least danger of the coins falling out; and numberless other tricks of the trade.

As a matter of fact, they have often asked me to become one of them. They don't mind a little extra competition if it comes from a decent fellow, and they lead me to believe that I am such a fellow. They tell me, too, that it is a very happy profession, that you are out in the open all day, that you have no overhead expense, and that you can never be laid off because you are working for yourself. They've planned a union for beggars, but have found it impossible. It's a capitalistic society, they say. But even without a union, one can make a nice living. You can't strike in your trade, I said. People would be happy if you quit work. Would they, though? they said. A rich man can't live without a beggar. He needs him to protect his conscience.

So they were trying to persuade me to join their ranks. My wife wouldn't stand for it, I said. She always talks about beggars in a sad voice, and gets herself weepy about armless sleeves and folded trouser legs and empty sockets and men with dumb, pitiable expressions.

That's nothing, they said. For us to be blind or crippled is only a school degree, like a doctor's or a lawyer's. That's the way we hang out our shingle. Our superiority over those who give us money is this: They still pity us, but we have stopped pitying ourselves.

Anyway, I said, I'll think about it.

I have been thinking about it. But I am afraid to broach the subject to my wife. I know that she will begin to cry. She is too proud. And I, too, am afraid that I can't afford to take this step – I have no ailments, I am not blind, I am not crippled, I am perfectly healthy. Only I am poor; and that's like being blind and crippled. Worse, because you feel helpless without any excuse. But I can't become a beggar; I can't learn to stop pitying myself.

A Myriad-Minded Man

In the whole period of our somewhat casual acquaintanceship, I received but a single letter from him, and spoke to him but once. Everything else that I know of his life, and that I surmise of the struggle which tormented his many-tentacled mind, I gathered only by rumour and report. Yet so strong was his effortless influence upon me, and so mysterious and complex the personality which he brought within my ken, that often, when routine diurnalities which earn me my bread are over, – when, for a space, I abandon my daily labours to go pondering in fields which I suddenly recognize as metaphysical, the enigmatic parable of his existence, with its implications and its ambiguities, haunts me, a shadow over my brain. Alone, sometimes, in the solitude of my office, as I purposelessly look through my files, marvelling at the moral conflicts that are so flatly compressed between two manila covers, legal size; or again, when upon my brief vacation, I find myself alone upon a peak in the Laurentians, with nothing to think about except space, time, man, God and the next meal, the curious and absurd figure of Isaiah Ellenbogen will rise before me, to puzzle and bewilder me with the mysticism which emanated from him and from the thought of him. Was he knave or fool? Sane or mad? Was he sincere in his idiosyncrasies or only an exhibitionist flaunting lunacies in the hope that true genius is to madness close allied? Was he really a spiritual man, or only one making a great to-do about seeking out divinity, so that he might himself be regarded as something more than human? I do not even now know the answer; I have myself been torn by doubts, sometimes passing judgment upon him as an unspeakable faker, and sometimes, – attributing to my juristic and pedestrian mind an innate incapacity to understand such men as Ellenbogen, – thinking that had he lived in another time and age, he might have founded a new sect, and have been remembered as a prophet and seer.

I first met him about a decade ago, when I was at law school. As a matter of fact, it was a chance encounter. Godfrey Somers and I were at the McGill Library, doing some hectic pre-examination cramming. At about five o'clock in the afternoon, we were both very tired, our eyes red, and our heads whirling in a merry-go-round of doctrines and principles. Somers suggested a walk. I expected that we would take a leisurely stroll along Sherbrooke Street beneath the elms and the maples, there to amuse ourselves with watching and estimating the girls in their pied spring dresses. It was a game we played. The girls would pass by, and both of us would mentally record whether, given the opportunity, we would or we wouldn't; then we would compare notes, and discuss aesthetic standards. Instead Somers insistently directed me ghettowards, – for quiet peripateticism, – as he phrased it.

I know my ghetto and I smiled. For had he been a Jew, and familiar with the ghetto which forgetting the other six hundred and twelve biblical injunctions still piously and industriously remembered the *Be fruitful and multiply*, he would never have attempted to hurry down Main Street on a Saturday night. We found it almost impossible to make any headway. Pushed this way and that, elbowed hither and thither, the progress that we did make on our way we achieved by walking on our toes, holding our breath so as to elongate ourselves into slimness, reducing ourselves to profiles and thus stealing through the clefts that remained between body and serried body. Hundredweights of avoirdupois impeded our way. Corpulent tubs. Fleshpots of Egypt. The pavement was crowded with Jews and Jewesses doing their weekly shopping, some actually entering the welcoming stores, most making their purchases vicariously. There were many, and much of them. Here and there an old and bearded Jew, a rabbi (even the enlightened Godfrey Somers, though his best friends were Jews, was still under the impression that all the bearded were rabbis, and that Hebrew piety was measured by hirsuteness) shuffled from the synagogue, his prayer-shawl wrapped in a Yiddish newspaper, held beneath his arm. Bulky sausage-armed Jewesses pushed carriages holding at least two sons of the Covenant, while their husbands, in most cases diminutive and cadaverous-looking homunculi, walked by their sides. The delicatessen stalls sent out appetizing and spicy odors from their ever-open doors; the butcher shops were loud with the sound of bone-chopping, and bargaining. From a gramophone-store shrill spangles of song fluttered over the air, as a falsetto-voiced singer pronounced to a listening world, oi, the virtues of her boarder ...

When these women walked on the side-walk Godfrey had to get off on the road to advance ahead of them. Jewesses were terribly fat, he remarked, rolls of fat; unctuous double chins; exuberant bosoms. He recalled the couplet that he had heard in the smoking-room of the University:

Sadistic Saxons have a pedal use
For pendulous buttocks of the Jews ...

'Strange,' he continued, 'how sloppy Jewish women become after their *nuit de noce*. Just fall apart, droop and drip ... Melting pot, indeed – everyone a melting pot, organic grease thawing with the heat of motion. See them! Vertical barrels! And the puny pizzicato the fathers of these mice beget mountains. There,' he pointed his little finger, '*mirabile visu* a dwarf pushing the perambulator, a dwarf underfed and overworked, and his wife at his side, gigantic, circular, flesh-padded.'

We continued along our way; we moved with difficulty, but Somers was having a good time. He elbowed my ribs.

'She doesn't look half-bad, does she? Did you notice her? Also fat. Pleasantly plump, she would probably say, with a smile that created three chins. Looks quite comfortable too, – mark her up. Fat men, overflowing with carbohydrates, boasting dewlaps, instead of necks, – disgusting; but the girls don't look half-bad at all, not half-bad. And after all, aesthetically they may not be so pleasant, but connubially, eh? Western standards of beauty are all wrong. The "she-was-tall-and-she-was-fair" idea, the slender willow, posh, a skeleton in the closet. Algerian standards heap much better. Fatten your wives before marriage, like cannibals before a feast.'

To all of Somers' rhetorical questions, I made no answer. In the first place, I felt some kind of inward resentment at the character of his remarks, and in the second place, I was too far behind him to shout my reactions over half-a-dozen heads. He, however, valiantly pushed forward, relaying to me his comments. At last I was at his side.

'And the gibbering! How your Jews can talk! Born Demostheneses. Their gesticulations – a new geometry of conversation. Flip their words off their fingers, hurl their phrases, slap down their dicta, index-finger their innuendos. The discobuli of words.' He tried to illustrate his speech with his arms; and in the process almost got into a fight. 'Your people are the true masters of pantomime, only they overdo it. They add verbal speech. To them the arm is as important as the larynx in conversation. No wonder the psalmist combined in one verse as a condign punishment for the forgetting of Jerusalem the cleaving of the tongue to the roof of the mouth, and the loss of the right hand's cunning. A sort of "strike me dumb" exclamation.'

By this time we had reached Ontario Street. We stopped before the electric sign which announced in intermittent gasps 'Kupchik's Restaurant,' and looked in through the windows. For a while Godfrey hesitated. Slowly he entered, I following, and gazed inquiringly about the dining room. Evidently they had not yet arrived. We sat down in a corner, away from the general crowd where his Anglo-Saxon features would not be stared at by Semites curious to know how this goy had wandered into a Jewish restaurant.

Godfrey, then, like one solving a mystery, explained to me that he had come here to meet Sam Jacobson, whom I knew, and who was to bring with him a 'character.' He wanted me in on this experience. Sam Jacobson was a free-lance impresario of freaks, a hunter-up of human curiosities, a fosterer of pseudo-geniuses, a fisher of men. For a time he had taken to his bosom one Louis Lazarovitch, self-crowned king of the hoboes. On another occasion he had protected and advertised Abdullah, the Negro, who could talk Yiddish, and who was a professor of gymnastronomy, a science invented by Abdullah, which was a curious combination of calisthenics and star-gazing. He had even cultivated the acquaintance of Moses Mozen, homosexualist and father of seven children. And now he had discovered Isaiah Ellenbogen.

Although Somers did not know it, he too during the period of his early friendship had been but an addition to Jacobson's collection for his empirical museum. He had been introduced to him at a college tavern, and there while Jeffries, classical scholar, after drinking well but not wisely, had begun to recite whole passages from Theocritus, he had heard Somers, prize scholar in Hebrew, and son of the Reverend Aloysius Somers, quote with an accent somewhat goyish the first few Hebrew verses of the *Canticum Canticorum*. He later discovered that Godfrey was quite familiar with Jewish legend and custom and that he had read widely on Jewish ethnography. Somers moreover was somewhat of a philo-Semite. It was not that he was terribly enamoured of Jews as persons, – one could very easily see that from his attitude, – but that he respected them for their culture and tradition. Agnostic, he even forgave them their monotheism. He loved Moses, and Joshua and Mordecai with an epic love; these were symbols of history; but for Mr. Cohen and Mr. Levy he had an abhorrence which he admitted not even to himself. While he could work himself up into raptures about the famous Sanhedrin, which inflicted the sentence of death but once in seventy years, while he could exhaust his hyperboles on Jewish institutions and Semitic contributions to civilization, still he did not hesitate to indulge from time to time in witticisms illustrating the proverbial and uncomplimentary Hebrew traits. He revelled in distinguishing the nation of prophets from the nation of profiteers; he liked to speak knowingly about the People of the Bankbook; he glibly wisecracked about the Jews and money-theism. For Somers the admirable Jew, despite his contributions to culture, was still a biblical and Talmudic character. Godfrey disliked the immigrant, but he saw a wistful beauty in the nomad; the shepherd by the waters of En-gedi was a character of romance, assuredly no kin to the pot-bellied cigar-belching, diamond-studded cloak-and-suit manufacturer of our day.

But this he conceded, that while a good number of the Jews were unprepossessing in appearance and unsociable in manner, they certainly were endowed with extraordinary intelligence and made interesting company. They were, he further admitted, excellent characters for novels, and Godfrey Somers in his spare moments when he was not writing poetry, sought relief from his leisure by working on what was to be, he fancied, the first Canadian novel – and, as Jacobson said, all about the Jews.

Sitting at his table he scanned the faces of the people in the restaurant. There was, when you came to think of it, – he was confiding in me – no real Semitic type. These Jews, especially when they wore their hair in pompadours, looked like Russian anarchists; some of them, the swarthy ones, might in costume pass for Spanish hidalgos. The shape of the nose was absolutely irrelevant – as a matter of fact he had read that only about twenty-five percent of them had hooked noses. Among the faces here there was a preponderance of platyrrhine noses, Ethiopic. Atavism of Mizraim. Certainly red-headed Jews were not a pure breed, although Judas was reputed to have been of that colour. It was Graetz, was it not, who spoke about an onslaught of the Nordic tribes upon a Jewish community, the result of which was a sprouting of blond bastards? So after all the Jews were Nordic. A touch of war makes the whole world kin. The purity of the Jewish family was a myth. A Jew's ancestors would form a League of Nations in themselves. This would be a good subject for a novel. He took out his note book, and wrote: A young Jew throws himself heart and soul into the Zionist movement. Works for the Hebrew Renascence, re-establishment of a nation, regeneration of a culture. Attains high office in Zionist Organization. Falls in love with Christian girl. Chapter on intermarriage. Does not marry her – must preserve purity of Jewish race. Last chapter discloses him to be a war-child of the massacre of Kishineff.

Hebrew culture, however, – this was a concession to me, made with a sensitive regard to my national feelings, – must be continued. Even though the purity of the race wasn't much to speak of, a recompense might be found in the situation. The New Man; amalgam of Occidental and Oriental, of course, the present type of Jew must be eradicated. These were merely exile specimens, parasites; at best saprophytes. And yet in them too there was an echo of old unhappy far-off things.

As I settled down to read an evening journal, he took a menu-card and on the unprinted side began a sonnet. The whole scene that he had witnessed on his way down appeared in a new light, and despite its sordidness and malodour, there was something inspiring and elevating in it. It was strange how thought crystallized itself when one took pen in hand, and how in the passing of time a rose-bush would flourish even upon a dung-heap. He wrote:

It being no longer Sabbath, angels scrawl
The stars upon the sky; and Main Street thrives,
The butcher-shops are as so many hives,
And full is every delicatessen stall.
Obese Jewesses, wheeling triplets, crawl
Along the crowded thoroughfare. Fat wives
Lead little husbands, while their progeny dives
Between fat legs in a ubiquitous sprawl ...
The whole street quivers with a million hums,
And Jewish arms tell jokes that are not funny;
Upon the corners stand the pool-room bums;
Most valiantly girl-taggers smile for money;
From out a gramophone loud-speaker comes:
'O, Eli, Eli, lama, zabachtani.'

Emending his scrawl until it appeared almost like a palimpsest, he read the sonnet over again. He read it to me. 'Fine conceit,' I said, 'this making the angels endorse the sky with their initials. Critics speak of the artificiality of the sonnet, why, here you are able to pack into fourteen lines more than you could ever put into that number of paragraphs. The thing's compact. Very good.'

'Yes,' Somers added, helping me praise him, 'and the last line too, as in all good sonnets, is the real raison d'être of the whole poem. Of course Jeffries would reprimand me for bringing God into the poem, by the horns, as it were. But then one does not have to be religious to speak of Providence. After all, God is merely a pronoun ... '

At this juncture Jacobson entered together with the illustrious incognito. Godfrey hastily hid the menu-card in his pocket; he did not wish them to think that he was seeking a sensational method of bringing to the newcomer's attention the fact that he was a poet.

'Meet Mr. Ellenbogen, Isaiah Ellenbogen, chemical engineer of the University of Berlin. Mr. Godfrey Somers of McGill.'

I too was introduced.

The first impression that Ellenbogen gave was that of a theme for a vorticist drawing. He seemed to be made on a geometrical design, a Euclidian man. His short fat legs were inverted cones, suffering a gradual widening of the diameter as they approached to support the corpulent torso, a somewhat lopsided cylinder. At the top the cylinder sprouted two pistons, one on either side; what anatomists would call a neck was nothing more than a glandular band, attaching a huge cerebral globe to the cylinder of his body. On being introduced to Somers, Isaiah extended his piston, nodded his globe, and somewhat inclined his cylinder.

Upon second impression, after the mechanistic illusion had faded, one saw a short squat Jew, shabbily attired, his suit unpressed, his cuffs frayed, and his cravat askew. His head was enormous: Ellenbogen was top-heavy. He looked like an embryo in its fourth month, an embryo which had prematurely escaped from the womb. His face was pale and colourless, except where here and there it was dotted with little red pimples. A pastry adorned with berries. His flat nose which seemed to disintegrate into his cheeks made his wide face appear even wider. It was his brow that impressed one particularly. High and pale, an intellectual cliff of Dover. Looking at his forehead I recalled the line of a sonnet by MacDonald, a poetaster who ended his sonnets after the first line: Broad-nosed, broad-browed, broad-minded Socrates ...

We sat down to eat; there were seven courses to the meal. Jacobson, Ellenbogen, Somers and myself were examining the menus making our choice of the food. A gourmet's bout in seven rounds, I thought, and by the look on Somer's face I saw that he thought so too. He said, 'I've eaten chop-suey with sticks in a Chinese restaurant, I've twirled spaghetti with a dexterous fork in Italian joints, and I've swallowed the poetically-named dishes of the French cuisine, but all my vast experience as an epicure stands confounded before this card. But, I'll try anything once. I'll let Jacobson choose my courses for me. If I don't eat it however, don't take it amiss.'

The Socratic countenance of Ellenbogen raised itself. From the cylinder as from a hollow there came oracular tones discussing the cuisine.

'If you have eaten as many cosmopolitan dishes as that, Mr. Somers' – his accent was heavily European; for a space Godfrey was so fascinated by the transatlantic bouquet of his diction, that he hardly heard his words – 'you will find no difficulty whatsoever in this menu. If your alimentary canal has welcomed within its gates all the foreigners that you have just mentioned, surely it will establish no quota law for these immigrants, too ... The first thing that I would have you understand is that there is no national Jewish cookery. That disappeared when Titus burned the greatest of Hebrew kitchens, the Tample at Jerusalem.' Something in the cylinder rattled; Somers took this for a giggle – he counter-grinned politely. Jacobson looked from one to the other; they were getting along fine. 'I don't want you to misconstrue my last statement as blasphemous; I am deeply religious; but the fact remains that the Diaspora destroyed the Jewish culinary art, which was mainly a religious one. The order to go into exile eliminated the Hebrew chef, just as the second commandment killed the Hebrew sculptor. On Sinai we received ethics instead of aesthetics, the Golden Rule instead of the Golden Calf ...

'In Palestine the staple foods were the seven famous fruits of the Holy Land, and the products of the dairy. The Exile changed all that. The vine and the fig-tree became metaphors, not meals. Travelling from country to country, the Jews acquired, together with their new cultures, new courses for their tables. They began, naturally enough, on very modest beginnings. Juvenal throws some light on the Jews of his day whose basket and hay was their furniture ... *Judaei quorum cophinus faenumque supellex.* We became keepers of the vineyards, but our vineyard we kept not ... You may object that even in Palestine the Jew showed a partiality for leeks and for fish, but I would remind you that this was a taste acquired in Egypt, whence, as you will discover in Scripture, came the recipe for these dainties. The Palestinian diet was purely a pastoral one. Our ancestors, I will wager, most certainly did not eat *gefilte fish* by the waters of the Jordan. That was a taste developed by the waters of the Don, the Dnieper, the Rhine, the Vistula. Yes, the story of this art reads like the martyrology of the palate. At present the Jewish cuisine is a *pot-pourri*, in the literal sense of the word. Take, for example, the proverbial smoked meat sandwich, well, that is, I have no doubt, a relic of the Middle Ages. The supply of meats had to be kept fresh for a whole winter; until the time of the Crusades they were merely salted ... After the Crusades Europe received a spiciness not only in its architecture and literature but also on its food. And sausages, too, their origin is as noble as that of the Rothschilds of Frankfort ... *Mamaluge'* – here Ellenbogen turned his head towards Jacobson who was born in Bucharest – 'our sojourn in Roumania inflicted that golden pastiche upon us. Towards the sustenance of the Jews Lithuania contributed the herring and the unpeeled potato. As for the *kugel*, although there be some who declare its origin as of Poland, I am inclined to believe that the *lokshen kugel* is a perversion of Italian macaroni, – macaroni under an auto-da-fé, as it were. The conclusion of the matter is that the Jews haven't been home long enough to develop an autochthonous meal ... '

Somers was very much interested in this discourse. He felt, however, that Ellenbogen was monopolizing the conversation: the man spoke in essays. He was not accustomed to remain a mere auditor. He said:

'It's a pity, – that alone is a good argument for the Zionist cause. A nation born in a pot. The old dictum works in the general as well as in the particular; the way to win a man's heart is through his victuals. A very interesting treatise could be written on the relation between a national diet and a national genius. A culture, as well as an army, if we may believe Napoleon in a non-diplomatic utterance of his, walks on its belly. It is the roast beef of England that makes the British constitution ... '

Somers looked from face to face to see whether his pun had struck fertile soil. Jacobson was grinning, but that he knew was not necessarily a sign of intelligence ... he always grinned when he watched the meeting of his protégés. Ellenbogen seemed to have a good grasp of the English language: a giggle was revolving in the cylinder.

Somers continued: 'German Kultur no doubt rose, like Venus, from an ocean of lager dotted with an archipelago of pretzels. No man familiar with the human larynx would dare to deny the effect of the agglutination of involutionary spaghetti on the operatic tremolos of the Italian voice. Dieticians, I will venture to say, could easily have prophesied the Russian Revolution when they beheld the Russian peasant feeding on black bread, vodka, and borsht. It is only with the Chinese that I am somewhat puzzled – a people that is supposed to draw its sustenance from rats, and that writes poetry about peach-blossoms and chrysanthemums.'

The speech was interrupted by the aproned waiter who brought the soup, a chicken soup so rich that it appeared golden, dotted with shimmering haloes. Ellenbogen bent his head over it, and seeing an opportunity to take the conversation from Somers, remarked:

'My old Talmud rabbi used to tell me that a good soup is like the devil: it has a thousand eyes.' A smile began to crawl over Somers' lip, stealing from one end of his mouth to the other. Then Ellenbogen added, 'And he meant it in all seriousness. He believed in demons.' Somers' precipitous smile made a hurried retreat. 'The Talmud and the Cabbala informed him as to how many bones, muscles, horns, hooves, wings, each particular demon had. One can compare with these disquisitions the preoccupations of the Schoolmen with the problem as to how many angels could make a needle a dancing-pavilion. And yet despite the fact that I received a scientific training in European universities, and despite the fact that I am not religious in the orthodox sense, I am myself inclined to believe that there are such things as demons, presiding genii, djinns. Their name, even as their existence is universal. You may, if you will, associate me with Sir Oliver Lodge and Conan Doyle and Spiritualism, that last infirmity of noble minds ... I repudiate all connections with the like ... Nonetheless I feel these spirits and demons hovering about me; they are in the air; they seep into the brain. It is this very consciousness of angels and heavenly ministers everywhere present that makes religion anthropomorphic. Perhaps I am an anachronism, the last of the pagans believing in the sylvan gods, the last of the fanatics credulous of the omnipresent lesser deities. Perhaps even in devouring this soup I am cannibalistic in tendency, for as you may readily surmise, demonology is kin to hylozoism.

'I said that despite my university education I had a faith, no, not a faith – that word is of the evangelists, – consciousness, that's better, it suits the modern psychology, of spirits beyond and before ... I should have said because ... Somehow I feel that Boyle's law of gases is really a theological dogma. Gases, of course, can be rendered as a supernatural fluid ... and the law that these expand under heat could very well be considered as a fundamental principle on the workings of inferno. Newton's principle, too, may be adapted to this phenomenon. Every body remains in a state of rest or continuous motion in a straight line unless impelled by some other body to change that state – What is that but an innuendo that spirits must be propitiated, that is to say, forced to change their condition, by prayer; and *orare est laborare*. The third law that every action has an equal and opposite reaction is nothing more than the scientific formula for the principle of retribution, the physicist's nemesis. How do these spirits exist? Where do they find their resting-place? A clear understanding of Einstein's fourth dimension will answer that.'

Somers did not know what to make of all this abracadabra. He felt that he was being mesmerised by gesticulations, hocus-pocused by great names. He wanted to interrupt, to ask questions, to demand commentary to all those cryptic utterances; but Ellenbogen continued. There was no stopping him.

'It is not only physics but also what the Elizabethans called physic, you know what Shakespear bids you throw to the dogs, that points index-fingers towards the supernatural. Medicine, too, may furnish the scent to the hounds of God. Some may call it demon, *shaid*, and others may call it microbe. German professors, avenging themselves upon the Latins, give these demons classical names. A rod wherewith to chasten the wicked – bacillus ... Would I be stretching metaphors too far if I called the tetanus germ the demon which smiteth one dumb ... Take the Black Plague, for example, whose origin the doctors do not hesitate to ascribe to evil germs. I am not surprised that the mediaeval man thought it the express visitation of an evil spirit. *Ruach* – spirit – wind – breath – animus – virus – the transition is more than a glib philological one.

'Then, of course, there is the classic division between good and evil which has some enlightening features. Angel and demon, Ahriman and Ormuzd, toxin and antitoxin, – the manichaeism of medicine.

'An erudite professor has discovered that there are several thousand bacilli to which the flesh is heir. Rabbi Jochanan knew three hundred different kind of *shaidim* living near the town of Shittim. Is there really any great difference between both of these assertions? I do not think so.

'Rabbi Abba Jose of Zaintor waved his town from harm when

informed that a water demon had made his dwelling there by causing the townspeople to go down to the water's edge at dawn equipped with spits and iron rods. Intimation of sterilization. Evidently the bacilli had settled in the water. The going down at dawn and the rods wherewith to flog, after the manner of Xerxes, the intractable water is merely the classic touch.

'What is commonly regarded as the antithesis between science and religion becomes, through an Hegelian evolution, the fundamental synthesis. Personally I am against ceremonial and ritual, the wafer or the matzoh. It is the prompting of the inner spirit that I would consider, the intuitive knowledge of God. The magnifying glass in the hand of the astronomer, or the microscope in that of the biologist do not modify the greatness of God. They only reveal it.'

Jacobson was still grinning. He could hardly refrain from comment. He glanced with pride at his new specimen, a modern who believed in deity, God arising from a test-tube. Somers was silent, too. He thought of his father, the reverend, and the new arguments that he was missing.

'You, Mr. Somers, look at me in that quizzical manner which seems to say, if I may use your vernacular: How do you get that way? Well, the question of ultimate cause has always puzzled me. No matter what logic I employed, no matter what probings of science I used, the Prima Causa was always a *cul-de-sac*. It was an infinite retrogression. About ten years ago, I was witness to an incident that pointed a way. It was a divine innuendo, a celestial insinuation. It didn't prove anything; it didn't solve anything; and God remained in the same *camera obscura* whence He made His exodus, – but it was a suggestion.

'I was living in a small town in Russia before the Revolution, employed as a Hebrew teacher in the homes of the wealthier Jews. The village was just awaking to the blessings of civilization. A railway station had been built, and I still remember how two of my pupils on seeing the iron horse, puffing its smoke, glaring with its headlights, and racing like a dragon on wheels, I remember how they had fled in terror to the synagogue, to the horns of the altar, as it were. The richer homes boasted even a plumbing system. And the synagogue had fitted its Eternal Lamp with an electric light. It is true that there were some fanatics who looked askance at these innovations, and deplored the passing of the wax candle. Nonetheless, the electric candelabra were introduced with a great deal of ceremony, and the Rabbi preached on the text, *Fiat Lux*. I will admit that the mechanics of the lighting system were not what they might have been. The switch went on of itself, and of itself as frequently went out. The lamps weren't perfect, and the sockets sometimes didn't fit.

'Well, a rumour was spread that the synagogue was haunted. Tradition has it, of course, that at midnight the souls of the departed leave their graves, and robed in their cerements, as in prayer shawls, dance on the floor of the synagogue, singing the Lord's hallelujahs. The townspeople were certain that this was happening to their place of worship. The *Shamas* even asserted that he had heard noises and seen lightning-flashes in the synagogue. Between *Mincha* and *Maariv*, the old Jews would sit in a corner of the synagogue near the bookcases and tell in hushed whispers of similar occurrences that had happened in the days of their grandfathers. The serious-minded would quote Scripture on the necessity of appeasing these spirits and finding for them their merited rest in the Eternal Home. Facetious *batlanim* laid the blame on the cantor's deplorable Hebrew pronunciation, which, in supplicating the Lord on behalf of the deceased, had evidently used such barbarisms that even God couldn't understand His own language. The little town wondered: Through whom had this visitation come upon us? The women of the village are beyond reproach; the erudition of its Rabbi would take him to Heaven even through its keyhole; the water of the *Mikvah* was pure; the ritual *shechita* was carried out meticulously according to the injunctions of the Talmud; and there were no apostates in the town. Why then was the city troubled? Perhaps this was but the forewarning of things more unusual?

One day, the *Shamas* was groping about in the old attic of the synagogue when he found the floor littered with torn papers bearing Hebrew script, ancient and holy books, snuffmarked, moth-eaten, and covered with wax from dripping candles. This was the *genizah*. Here, all the shreds of holy books, scrolls of the Torah, which had in them some error of the scribe, an error beyond emendation, such as the misspelled name of God (for it was ominous to erase that Word) were kept until a sufficient amount accumulated for it to be disposed of in the ordinary manner. They were not thrown away, for fear that they be put to a profane use; they were not burned, for that was too much like the work of the Christian hangmen; they were buried beneath the heads of pious Jews, together with a little sack of earth from the Holy Land. In this attic, the *Shamas* found enough to make a pillow for all the dead saints buried in the local cemetery. That was it, then; the souls of the departed were restless for want of the Sacred Word; they asked their due.

'Accordingly, the thumbed pages, the loose excerpts, the holy *shemoth*, were buried in the Jewish cemetery. But it did not help. One still saw, rumour said, torches and lights in the synagogue, and moving shadows.

'Especially on autumn nights, when an eeriness pervaded everywhere, and when the leaves of the trees in the synagogue-court kept falling monotonously, and when the wind beat against the loose boards and the rattling eaves of the house of worship, were these phenomena visible.

'I must point out now that no one ever saw these ghosts, no one ever came skull to skull with these skeletons.

'At last, Itzik the blacksmith, a strong broad-shouldered, big-bearded and brave-hearted Jew, prompted by piety and the desire for renown, decided that he would venture into the synagogue at midnight. When he staggered out, he was as one smitten with palsy; he quivered from head to toe, and from his frightened gasps one gathered that as soon as he came before the Ark of the Covenant a great flash of light hit him between the eyes, and a moment after, he found himself in darkness. In his haste to escape from the spirits encompassing him, he had fallen over benches and bruised himself severely.

'This incident strengthened the legend. People began to believe even more firmly than before that the synagogue was haunted. No one ventured to repeat the blacksmith's experiment until Chatzkel, a listless sort of fellow, who seemed to hold a conference with himself before every step that he took, decided that he would investigate. Without being irreligious, he was something of a sceptic. He did not believe in those old wives' tales about ghosts and haunted synagogues.

'Chatzkel did not decide upon this in a moment. He contemplated it for days on end. Everything that he did, he did after meditation and reflection. He had a lot of time. When he said his prayers, he took twice as long as the most pious of rabbis; he stopped at each word, he weighed its meaning; he considered its interpretations, and then, after a lengthy counsel with himself, he offered it as a gift to God. When he ate his scanty meal, he prolonged it into a banquet. Every one of his actions, from the handling of the fork to the moving of his jaws, seemed premeditated. And when he walked, no matter how short a distance, the villagers would remark: Chatzkel is crawling; he will arrive at his destination the day after to-morrow. The synagogue wags would swear that Chatzkel would be late even for his own funeral.

'So, one midnight found Chatzkel on his way to the synagogue. Carefully he opened the door, put his right foot forward as is the custom according to the *Shulchan Aruch*, then brought forward his left foot, and thus, step by step, he moved, a slow shadow stalking into the synagogue. He was still in darkness; but as he approached the Ark of the Covenant which was near to the pulpit, and stepped on a creaking board, a ray of light suddenly illuminated the house of worship. Instead of immediately turning around, to see who was behind him, as the ordinary and natural impulse of man would impel him to do, Chatzkel stood stock still. He was as if paralyzed. But his inertness was not brought about by astonishment; he was considering his next step.

'Meantime, the light was still on. It was not a flash, as Itzik had said. It was an illumination. Slowly Chatzkel turned about. As he did so, his foot slipped from one board onto an adjacent one. He heard a snap as of a loose board which has risen after it has been released from a weight. He was in darkness again.

'Chatzkel considered his next move. Slowly, like an automaton, he turned back to his original position. A board creaked. The light was on again.

'Well, you may perceive by now what was haunting the synagogue. Nothing more than the faulty mechanics of the lighting system of the place. The wire ran under the floor of the synagogue, and in certain places, the boards were loose, and when one stepped on them, one established an electrical contact. So slight a pressure was necessary, that even a gust of wind could cause the momentary illumination of the synagogue.

'Thus Chatzkel brought enlightenment to our town ... Itzik of course was the laughing-stock for some time; he was too quick for science, and as for me, that incident, although, as I said before, it did not prove anything, nor establish anything, still it suggested to me that there might be some relationship between Science and Demonology.'

'Yes,' said Somers, 'between faulty Science and Demonology.'

The meal was over. Somers felt that he had spent, if not an edifying, at any rate, an interesting evening with Ellenbogen. On the way out of Kupchik's he asked, 'When can I see you again, Mr. Ellenbogen? Are you very busy? We may spend another evening together.'

'Any night will do – just give me a call. I am not so very occupied at present. Life, as you know, is mostly thought and conversation; conversation, at any rate ...'

II

I never did have an occasion to take advantage of his offer of 'thought and conversation.' Two years passed and I did not see him, nor hear of him. He may have been in Montreal all that time; I don't know, our circles never crossed. I really think that he was something of an introvert. He never, at this time, went to any public gatherings; I never saw him at any social affairs, and I do not recall anyone ever associating a woman's name with his.

Strangely enough, the first reminder that I had of his existence, was, of all places, in a law report, in the case of The County of Meadows-vs-United Iron Smelters Inc. It appears that the farmers of the County of Meadows, in one of the Western provinces, were complaining bitterly, and in about seventy allegations, against the havoc that was being wrought to their crops by the great clouds of smoke that issued from the chimneys of the smelting plant. The smoke, it was declared, had in it all manner of noisome ingredient, and settling as it did upon field and farm, brought blight and bane to local agriculture. An injunction was requested, and damages demanded. Appearing as expert for plaintiff was Isaiah Ellenbogen, whose testimony at the trial in the lower court, was extensively quoted by the learned judges of the superior one.

Ellenbogen had spent months upon his investigations. His evidence showed that he had approached his task with an ebullient zeal, a zeal not so much to uncover facts that would be favorable to his employers, but a zeal to study, impartially and scientifically, the effects of these frequently invisible fumes upon the lives and destinies of the farmers. This much I gathered from the judges' comments. Out of sheer curiosity – my own practice, I felt sure, would never encounter a similar case, – I wrote to the clerk of the court for a copy of Ellenbogen's depositions.

In it, he described his work in detail. There was something uncanny about the manner in which he phrased his conclusions. The judges winnowed out the fact and figures from the metaphors; but it was the metaphors that were of interest to me. I could see that Isaiah regarded himself as a sort of prince, come to rescue the farmers from the ogre hiding in the chimneys, hiding his funest head, but sending out, now and again, the flame-tongues of his wrath. He imagined himself, from the innuendoes of his replies to the cross-examiner's questions, there was no doubt about it – an oriental magician, seeking to bottle up again in their reeking and fatal tube, the evil djinns that industry conjured up. No, upon second thought, I revise my impression. It was not as here that he pictured himself; it was mystic that he desired to be. He strung off his percentages, averages, statistics, experimental conclusions with the air of one who had raked the clouds for a rain-drop of truth, who had scoured the skies for starry secrets, who had snatched from the very air the precious arcana of science. He described, to the satisfaction of the judge, how he had gone forth with his charts and his instruments and had trapped that phantom wraith of smoke that passed over the towers and steeples of the County of Meadows, pierced through its wire fences, trod upon its flowers and its grass, thwarted the alchemy by rain, and spat its black spittle into the crucibles of the sun. He had performed an autopsy upon this smoke cadaver. He had climbed up to this Mohammed's coffin hanging in mid-air, and had pried open its lid, there to find corruption and that miasma which had blighted the countryside.

Then, his depositions grew less interesting to me. There followed long paragraphs of incomprehensible jargon about carbon and chlorophyl and nitrogen and plant-cells. He spoke of that unseen conflict which is continually going on in nature, where one element has its arm lifted up against the other, how in the natural state this strife paradoxically resolves itself into an ineffable harmony, but how, when the many inventions of man obtrude upon the picture, there is confusion worse confounded.

Then as I sped over this desert of scientific sand, I came upon the conclusion of his testimony. It was this which gave me an insight into the joys he must have had during these weeks of investigation, an appreciation of that feeling of superiority which strengthened and fortified him, that privy knowledge which set him upon Olympian heights, looking down upon the midgets who were his contemporaries. A subtle scorn, an elusive sarcasm at the expense of those for whose enlightenment he was expounding, ran through the current of his phrases. It was as if he were muttering, in an antiphonic undertone to his dry-as-dust experimental revelations; that they little knew what spirits and phantoms were concealed in the, to them, inscrutable labyrinths of the earth.

What did they know of death floating in a hundred forms in a drop of water? What did they understand of the secret poisons that they inhaled with every breath of air? They did not even grasp that daily they jostled against the insubstantial shoulder of pestilence, that hourly they clasped the moist finger of the ubiquitous visitant. And certainly they knew less than little of how to circumvent and thwart and outwit the conspiracy which the very earth and sky and air were conspiring against their intruders.

All of this, of course, was not written into the depositions. But it was there; it was there; written between the lines, hiding behind a semicolon; circling about a period – it was there.

III

It was some time later that I heard of him again, and this time not from a printed page, but from the very lips of his herald, Sam Jacobson, whose custom it was always to maintain an interest in his human *objets d'art* even long after they had been safely catalogued away, and had become mere memories, evocative of anecdote. Jacobson rushed into my office one morning, and after the usual small-talk – he was a sort of *liaison-officer* to our firm, giving us the inside dope about everything and everyone in town – and after having read my morning journal, probably to see whether the newspaper had received its information correctly, he suddenly queried, as if he was starting a game with me:

'Guess who I saw yesterday?'

He might have seen a thousand people; I was not going to begin a roll-call. I said:

'I bite! Who?'

'Ellenbogen, Isaiah Ellenbogen. Remember? The fellow we met at Kupchik's, you know, with the pimples on his face and the bees in his bonnet?'

'Yes, yes,' I was eager to hear more. The man had been haunting me, imposing himself upon me, – and Jacobson was asking whether I remembered him. I was impatient.

'Where did you see him?'

'At the circus!'

'The circus! Come, come, what's the catch?' I was incredulous. Isaiah Ellenbogen wasting his precious moments by going to a circus, like a kid on Sunday. I suspected one of Jacobson's gags.

'Did he bring peanuts for the elephants?'

'Works at the circus!' Jacobson answered. 'Works there!' Then as a footnote, he added, 'A barker!'

How have the mighty fallen, I thought. The theosophical Isaiah hawking the wonders of Barnum and Bailey! Ellenbogen, the peddler of freaks! Ellenbogen!

'You should have heard him,' said Jacobson, preparing himself with my newspaper rolled into a megaphone, for illustration, ' "Ladies and gentle-men, right this way, please, this way, only ten cents, one dime! Come and see the wonders of creation! Behold the marvels of the world! For one dime, step right into Fairyland".'

Fairyland! Can you imagine how that word sounded issuing from the antarctic circle of that cranial globe of his!

' "Come and see them ... Tom Thumb, the littlest creature on the face of the earth, the world's greatest midget." '

Greatest midget! Colossal!

' "And see Rumpelstiltskin, the man with three legs, the wonder of locomotion, who hops with one, steps with the other, and jumps with the third! See her, the half-breed princess, half white and half Indian, the left side pure Caucasian, and the right pedigreed Iroquois, the renowned, the glorious, the wonderful Princess Rose-Red-and-Snow-White!"

'He went on like that or with some similar balderdash, for about fifteen minutes, a steady flow of exaggerations. And he seemed to enjoy it!'

'Did you speak to him?' I asked.

'Sure, I got all the lowdown on him, and directly from the horse's mouth. He's had some tough luck, it appears. Lost his job as engineer; laid off. Couldn't find a thing for months. Finally ended up in Toronto, good and sick. Almost dying, in fact. Somers – edits a paper in the Holy City – suffered a blood transfusion for him. Hung around the place for a while, sort of factotum to Somers, and then landed this job with the circus. Loves it. Even the pimples have gone from his face.'

I still couldn't understand it. Ellenbogen, the barker! The sophisticated one dangling freaks before the hoi polloi! Jacobson saw the query in my eyes. He continued.

'You know Ellenbogen, he develops philosophies about his jobs. I really can't guess whether he took up barking because the spirit moved him, or whether the spirit moved him after he began his spiel. But whatever it is, he has woven metaphysics about this – what does he call it now? – his *modus vivendi*. Since his western adventure, he says, he has never been so much in his element. He talks as if he were the advertising agent for God. You see, he has a notion that these freaks are the only real authentic manifestations of divine creativeness. To him a pinhead is a heavenly miracle; a woman with four tongues, the Creator's masterpiece. The Siamese twins are the celestial gemini on earth. Yes, I made the natural and obvious objection – these people are not normal, therefore, they are queer, intriguing, fascinating. He seemed annoyed. How did I know they were not normal? Because the majority were like me? And what is normality? Perhaps, he argued, perhaps these freaks are the true and real cast and die of humanity, and my two-pronged forks, as the Chinese say, are the abnormal. Simply because there are a great number, running around, all looking like so many peas in a pod, does not yet set a value upon standardized goods. He imagined that on the contrary, it would be to the unique, what I would call the freakish, he said, that merit should be attached.

'We don't applaud an actor when he repeats an old trick. We applaud him when he deviates from it, when he adds some new quirk, some new curlicue to his performance. Otherwise, it's like seeing the same show twice.

'Well, – that's his argument, not mine, – Divinity works in the same way. Creation did not end upon that biblic Sabbath – Creation continues every day. Genesis is being consummated always and ever. But it is not in the normal that one sees the Lord's creativeness – He would so repeat Himself – but in freaks, that which the prosaic and dull of mankind confine to circuses, whom they should house in churches and synagogues. There should be a special ceremonial at the birth of every freak, a legal and religious holiday should be declared. And the State should keep and preserve them, in thanksgiving that the Lord saw fit to bless their soil with the novelty of His works.

'Did Nature create snowflakes of monotonous identity? No, they all have some different geometrical design. So, too, midgets, and men with webbed feet, and two-headed bipeds, were all examples of his experimentations, his exercises in the novel.

'That's the way Ellenbogen expatiated. I'm not kidding – he was in dead earnest. What better environment could he choose for himself than the museum of God's masterpieces? What was more conducive towards an exaltation of the human soul than beholding daily these new works of deity. In most mysterious ways, he maintained, is splendour revealed: a man-child, born with paws, he whispered to me, had intimations in it.

'I tried to meet him on his own ground. I asked how about men being created in God's image. Wasn't his theory sacrilege? He pooh-poohed the suggestion. A mere quibble. I didn't understand Holy Writ, he said. *In His own image* was not to be taken literally. Even as conservative an authority as Maimonides indicated that these anthropomorphic phrases were only metaphors, used, as he said, *l'shabair eth ha-ozen* – to break the ear, to render the words comprehensible to minds unaccustomed to thinking in the abstract.

'So that's the theory, and that's the job. I can't possibly figure him out. Probably building up these theories about himself to bolster up an inferiority complex at having to yap out those wild men of Borneo. Or, probably just plain crazy; a little knowledge, you know –'

I expressed a desire to see him and speak to him myself. We motored over to the circus-grounds. They were deserted. The tabernacles of the freaks had been removed; the tents of the Lord were gone. Isaiah Ellenbogen had journeyed on to the next town to spread the gospel according to St. Barnum.

IV

All this time, I was convinced that Ellenbogen was a queer egg, simple in his very complexity; queer, but no more. It was in the summer of 1933 that I began to suspect that he was really a scoundrel, a careerist, a man who would sell his soul for a salary. For it was during those hot July days that there began to appear on the news stands in Toronto, an antisemitic journal, which revived all the ancient bugaboos about Jews, beginning with the ritual blood accusation, and ending with the *fetor Judaicus*. Upon the masthead of the paper appeared the name of Godfrey Somers.

Such a journal in the hands of Somers was particularly dangerous. He knew just enough of Hebrew to misquote; his columns bristled with garbled quotations from the Talmud, distorted references to the Bible. The cartoons which he allowed to decorate his sheet paraded Jews with angular and bulbous noses, stuck onto dark stubble-covered faces of a strange and diabolic ferocity. They read like counts in an indictment, the captions to his articles, and the articles themselves invariably ended with a vituperative and exclamatory *Hierosolyma est delenda*. The Jews are thieves, the Jews are rascals; buggery, arson, rape and murder – Jewish professions all! By toning down the screeching demagogic editorials, there appeared subdued academic treatises upon the superiority of the Nordic over the Semite, treatises replete with quotations from Chamberlain and paragraphs from Drumont, essays full of much writing about long heads and short heads, blue eyes and black eyes, blond beasts and brunette barbarians. To all who read, there was no doubt about it: the paper was soaked in acid, and inked with venom.

Sedulously the Yiddish press of the country followed the libels of *The Viking*, always with a view to refutation, and did indeed carry on a kind of shadow-boxing with the Jew-baiting journalists. Futile, of course; they were preaching to the converted. Jews did not require lengthy discourses by their literary men to convince themselves that they did not devour babes for Passover nourishment. The readers of *The Viking*, needless to say, in like manner never read the Jewish press.

But soon it was discovered that somebody in *The Viking* office did read the Jewish papers, and more than that, translated into English the juicy epithets of opprobrium, the blunt attacks upon Somers. It was suspected, moreover, that the person who wrote those tedious disquisitions upon the effect of blood upon culture, pedigree upon civilization, the genius who signed himself Hahbaz, was — the proof lay in textual comparisons — the same who did the translating, and who inserted the italicized and supercilious *sic-sic's* in the translations. It was clear, too, that the chromosome expert was a Jew.

The community was full of the outrage. A Jew maliciously slandering his own, at so much per column! Meetings were held, rabbis delivered sermons, taking as their text the verse from Isaiah: *And from thine own loins will come thy destroyers*; editorials were written; Christian philosemites were appealed to; and committees were formed. I found myself upon such a committee.

I did not believe it when I was informed that the author of the shameless scribblings was one Isaiah Ellenbogen, a German-Jew. But the fact that my authority was usually reliable, that Somers, Ellenbogen's friend — and my friend, too, once — was sponsor of the vile thing, that the dummy body of Ellenbogen was often seen stalking into *The Viking* office, and that the articles bore the unmistakable imprint of his style — all of these facts militated towards the dispelling of the doubts favouring the accused.

I decided to write to Ellenbogen. I expected no reply. I received one. It was the words in which the answer was couched that led me to believe that the whole business, dark as it seemed on the face of it, was not entirely an instance of intentional evil-doing. The man was simply the dupe of his own fancies; he was a fetish-worshipper whose fetishes were varied in form, but identical in principle — now it was chemical formulae, now throw-backs and freaks, and now, now blood.

What followed after this epistolary exchange is not particularly important in this account, save that as a result Ellenbogen again found himself without a congenial element, a *modus vivendi*. We appealed to the courts of the land, and in a judgment since become famous, both because of the principles it enunciated, and the classical style in which these were phrased, the publishers of *The Viking* were restrained from continuing their calumnies, in any shape or form, and under any name whatsoever, the whole subject to specific penalties thereinabove indicated. *The Viking* went down with all hands on board.

I still have in my possession the notorious epistle of Isaiah to the Hebrews, which if I have not exactly treasured, I have to this day preserved. I can still picture him now, the robot with the versatile soul, as, setting his many-hinged torso before his desk, he plied his lever to write:

'I am surprised that you, a lawyer, seem to be ignorant of the fact that passion is not conducive towards reason. Anger is the least elucidatory of emotions; no one has yet rushed into the truth in a tornado of wrath. Had you read my articles with more concentration and less fury, you might have adopted an entirely different attitude to our mutual problem.

'My contention is, Sir, that there are superior races and inferior ones. You, no doubt, consider yourself miles above Lo the poor Indian, or the African Kaffir. You will agree that a decade of Europe is to be prized above a cycle of Cathay. Nothing odious do you see in such comparisons. Why, then, are you so full of resentment and rage when you are subjected to a comparison which leaves you somewhat lustreless?

'Me, an examination and study of history convinces that the palm must be accorded to the Nordic. It is all a question of blood. When certain people declare that they think with their blood, take it from me, this is no empty phrase, no chauvinistic fancy. It is truth, efflorescent.

'I do not intend here to enter into a panegyric of the northern races; my paeans can add but little to the largess which has been by nature bestowed upon them. Their moral outlook, their bright-eyed gaze upon all things, has moulded, influenced, created Western civilization. To blame and censure me for enunciating scientific truths is to grant me an undeserved martyrdom. You make me one with Galilee.

'It may be true that Mr. Somers makes certain deductions concerning our race that he believes based upon these ethnological premises. I am not responsible for them; my duty is merely to search and seek. I am bound by my conscience to reveal what I find. I find that, as our Bible has declared it, the blood is the life.

'Where the blood is corrupt, there also is the thought. Where the blood is distilled purity, the *sangre azul*, the science and the arts flourish. It is written in the tractate Baba Bathra: *At the head of death stand I, the blood.* Yea, and at the head of life, too.

'You impertinently ask me how I, a Jew, can by such theorizing, spit in my own countenance? I ignore, moreover, your references to the spawn of Galicia. My answer is: Truth is truth, no matter whom it injures. Your indulging in personalities is a mere fallacious *argumentum ad hominem*. It can avail nothing. I regret that I have discovered that all people are not born equal. I can do nothing about it. But, I must say, that next to being oneself of pure and noble blood is to appreciate it in others.

'I may add, finally, that if I was not born with Nordic blood, I have acquired it.'

I do not know whether he was being hyperbolical, or whether he was referring to his blood transfusion.

v

I never saw him nor corresponded with him again. I was about to say that I forgot him entirely, but this was not exactly the case; at times I would find myself wondering about the vicissitudes of his life, wondering about what he was doing, and what new fad or fancy had captured his mind. It seemed to me that if only he had persisted in a single one of his interests, he might have won himself at least two inches in the Britannica; as it was he had frittered away his madnesses, and instead of concentrating them into something inspiring, had allowed time and circumstance to dissipate them in the form of sulphureous mental sparks, throwing a faint and momentary glow and leaving behind a sickly odour. It was quite easy to dismiss him as a lunatic; but misgivings always followed such a facile gesture. And to dub him impostor and faker, was, it seemed to me, entirely unjust. And it was quite clear that with the genius which he possessed for salesmanship of ideas he could have made himself a fortune in some other and more congenial walk of life.

But I was not yet to hear the end of the fellow. For when he was about to depart, he sent me his second and last letter, a communication that was half apology and half auld lang syne.

He is not on our continent any longer. When Trebitsch Lincoln, calling himself Ming-Qao or Qua-Ming – I forget his exact appellation – recently travelled thousands of miles from his oriental seclusion, where he had founded some Buddhist sect to snare whatever Western converts came his way, the newspapers reported that the said Lincoln had been dismally unsuccessful.

Indeed, it seemed so, when Trebitsch, with his half-dozen disciples, disconsolately boarded ship – sans converts, sans acclaim, sans everything – to return to their monastery, there to meditate upon how prophets and seers of all time must meet the scorn and scoffing of the populace. But he did not know, as the word of Isaiah informed me, that in the next boat there followed after him, one, full of contrition in his heart and a strange amaze in his eyes, eager for revelations, jubilant with apocalypse. Isaiah Ellenbogen had decided to renounce the pleasures and vanities of our world, and give himself over in that distant clime to the study of the subtle and profound innuendoes of existence.

Whom God Hath Joined

Salvaged from the jettison of legal small-talk, this record of a *cause* which in the Province of Quebec in the last decade of the nineteenth century disturbed for a space the ideological serenity of judicial circles, and, for a space, confounded the codifiers and their codes, is presently and here set down for the sole and only reason that no elsewhere does it appear. There is not living any local Blackstone nor provincial Coke who can to-day narrate in articulated sequence the full details of that *cause célèbre* which so set at naught both the vast erudition of bespectacled judge and the juristic subtlety of gowned advocate; but occasionally, when lawyers do congregate in the stuffy corridors of the *Palais de Justice*, and jubilant with judgment or downcast with dismissal, they discuss *la glorieuse incertitude de la loi*, someone, probably one learned in the law as of yore, will facetiously break in with the case of the Siamese twins, whereupon others, veterans too, of the legal confraternity will contribute each his casual remembrance, while hard by, the fledglings of the bar, listening to the sapience of their elders, will grin pleasantly at the intellectual acrobatics of days gone by.

For not otherwise can the full and complete narrative be gleaned; no tome of jurisprudence makes reference to this eminently leading case; the lawyer for the defence has these many years pleaded before a court higher than the Privy Council; and the files of the Crown Prosecutor's office are accessible to none but the initiate. The newspapers of the day, too, were not then as thorough in their court reports as they have since become, and reference to their bound copies will avail but little in shedding light upon this unjustly forgotten joust in the tournaments of law. Were it not, therefore, for the technical quips and the disjointed reminiscences of the ancients of the profession, the case dubbed *Regina vs Gemini* would still to-day remain a secret and an enigma.

It may be stated, by way of *obiter dictum*, as the judges say, that there are some of a more cynical and sophisticated generation who, esteeming it but the result of some do-nothing solicitor's day-dreaming, do hold in doubt the authenticity of this record, to put the whole matter and mystery down in the category of legal fictions. Howbeit …

II

As he leaned back in his swivel-chair, his hands behind his neck, and his feet, like two leather-bound codes reposing upon his desk, the mind of Timothy P. Thorne contemplated his clientèle, and the mind of Timothy P. Thorne was a blank. For days now not a soul had entered his office, not a one, save the landlord, and to a tenant a landlord was technically not a soul. Neither plaintiff insistent on redress, nor debtor imploring delays beyond delays, had this many a week, set foot beyond the threshold of his door. Such unwelcome and compulsory leisure had not been utterly a loss; militating toward his greater knowledge, enforced idleness had compelled him to read over and over again the score of books of his meagre library – his codes in English and in French, the recent commentaries of Mignault, the bound volume of the *Revue Légale*, and the few copies of Canadian Criminal Cases, issued to date. But such erudition, no matter how elevating to the mind, was alas, not acceptable, according to the law of the land, as legal tender in payment of bills. Disconsolately, therefore, he leaned back in his chair, and regarded the cracks in the ceiling.

Suddenly there swam into the emptiness of his thoughts, the sound of a persistent buzzing. A big fat fly was beating itself with small thin clamor against the window pane, zooming about in a vortex of discomfiture, at every sally astounded that that which was transparent was not also permeable. Thorne recalled the burden of the daily threnody of Mtre. Chenevert, with whom he had been indentured: A troubled conscience is a buzzing fly.

He rose from his chair, and raising the window, said 'Phht! Beelzebub! vamoose! Conscience for a lawyer without a practice! Phht!'

He looked down upon the cobblestones of the Rue St. Paul. The street was littered with papers, broken ice-cream cones, corks, bottle-stoppers, the debris of wooden boxes used as seats, and pamphlets advertising the circus come to town. Only a half-hour earlier, he had himself watched the passing bands, with their bombastic drums and fustian flutes, leading the parade, followed by dominoed clowns, somersaulting, cartwheeling, performing with antic and grimace, before the hundreds who lined the sidewalks. The elephants bowing acknowledgement with their trunks; the drum major tossing his arms in all directions, like a prestidigitating octopus; the tattooed princess and the sword-swallowing prince; the little homunculus of a midget walking beside the ankle of Goliath the giant; the vans filled with cages of lions and of leopards; the beautiful lady cuddling a cobra; and bands, and more bands, all richly dight, with serge of the bluest and buttons of the brassiest, all of them had passed between the gauntlet of the populace, to the accompaniment of shouting, and hurrahing, and clapping of hands.

'Go join the circus!' Mr. Thorne said, lowering the window, as the fly buzzed away for parts unknown.

Back to his chair, he picked up, for the fourth time, the morning newspaper. Who, if anybody, he wondered, was doing any legal business? From the journal he gathered no clues; all he saw in the columns were business advertisements. He sighed as he realized that the city was to him fatally law-abiding and its citizens dangerously unlitigious.

Another dust-gathering day, Thorne reflected as he wiped his desk with a rag. His eyes wandered in the direction of the hatrack. It would be best to close up shop, call it a day, and go to the circus.

Then there was heard that knock on the door. It startled him, like a short burst of unaccustomed music. It caught Thorne unawares. Hastily he shoved his dusty rag into a drawer, opened a ponderous volume, heaped some legal documents in impressive disorder upon his desk, and with his head bent over his tome, said 'Come in.'

Between the lintel and the open door, there appeared a head. Ah, Thorne glowed, a client! He smiled. The head advanced forward. Behind it there suddenly sprang up before his eyes, as if from nowhere, another, a similar, an identical head. Two clients! It didn't rain but it poured. He said: 'Good day, what can I ———'

It was then that he really noticed the monstrosity that stood before him. Siamese twins! Only they weren't Siamese. Their swarthy complexions, the lustrous eyes and dazzling teeth that shone in the darkness of their faces like stolen gems in some sombre cache, their many-coloured raiment, the gold ear-rings piercing their lobes, these proclaimed them definitely as belonging to that same type of gypsy that was so frequently haled before the courts charged with vagrancy and fortune-telling. The motley of their vestment was startling enough – balloony trousers of a vernal green that at the knees snuggled into purple woollen stockings, terminating in cowhide boots that covered a fraction of the shins – blouses crimson and embroidered with black and gold lace, and hats each sporting a triumphant feather – startling enough this pied array, but positively amazing was the abnormal and monstrous juxtaposition of the twins. Their heads, as like as two peas in a pod, gazed, like a tzigane Janus, in opposite directions. Separate and distinct from the head to the middle, they were joined in inseparable union at the pelvis, dividing off again at the lower extremities in such manner that when the one walked forward, the other followed by walking backward. In his amazement, Thorne had not noticed the girl who had escorted them. As the doubled creature ambulated towards him, with its unnatural gait, the gold-coins on its necks tintinnabulated a suborning jingle. Another fortune-telling case, he thought, and the girl come with them to act as interpreter.

'What can I do for you?' he asked. Would they try to prognosticate that his path of life would be crossed by two dark gentlemen? 'The shingle outside says that you are a lawyer.' The English of the speaker was irreproachable, though accented; and the girl was not an interpreter.

'The shingle outside does not exaggerate,' Thorne replied. 'I am.' He pointed to the diploma on the wall announcing *Omnibus has literas inspecturis salutem in Domino*. The gypsy looked at it, and understood the gesture, if not the Latin.

'My name,' he said, 'is Petru Romano. This is my brother,' he pointed his thumb over his shoulders, 'Demetru. We are with the circus; you've heard of us, no doubt, the Tzigane Twins.'

'If Mohammed won't come to the circus ... ' reflected Thorne, and said encouragingly, 'Yes?'

'And this,' said the gypsy, grasping the hand of the girl, a short buxom parcel, standing offishly with a sheepish grin on her face, 'is Gretchen Metzinger.'

Thorne nodded his head in acknowledgement. He still didn't see how he was going to make bread out of circuses. He was troubled, too, by the suspiciously open manner of the gypsy; he seemed to catch now and again, a faint phantom of guile lurking in the eyes of this Romano whose frankness was to him but the reverse side of cunning, and whose candour but the cloak of deceit.

'We want to get married.'

Married? Thorne could barely conceal his astonishment. He looked incredulously from one to the other; he didn't appear to understand who wanted to be bound with whom in holy wedlock.

Coyly Petru added, 'Gretchen and I have been in love for a long time. Now we want to get married. We are strangers in these parts. We didn't know exactly what formalities are required; so here we are.'

As he spoke, his teeth flashed joyously, and his eyes took on a vague romantic look. His brother, Demetru, didn't seem elated at the matrimonial plan; a scowl corrugated his swarthy profile.

'This isn't a publicity stunt?' Thorne adopted, at least for the moment, a moral tone. In reply Petru pursed his lips, and threw up his hands. Far was it from him.

'Well, I must tell you, sir,' – should he have said *gentlemen* – 'that I am only a member of the bar and a commissioner of the Superior Court. I can perform no marriage ceremony. In the Province of Quebec, marriage is not only a civil contract, it is also a sacred sacrament, and must be performed by a minister. What country do you come from?'

'Hungary.'

'Roman Catholics?' He nodded. 'I would advise you to go and see the priest.' He tore a sheet from his pad, and wrote down the priest's address. 'Here, l'Abbé Gauthier will look after your spiritual needs, and if he says that it's alright in the sight of the Lord, you come back to me and I will take you to Notary Labelle for the drawing up of your marriage contract. There may be some gifts that you desire to give your wife' – Fraulein Metzinger looked triumphantly at her future brother-in-law, – 'you will give them in this contract. Without it no person can make substantial gifts – real gifts, I mean, not Easter presents – to his wife after marriage. That's the law; it was Napoleon's idea, not mine.

'I think it only fair to tell you that even if there are no impediments to your marriage from a religious viewpoint, the meddling law may nevertheless seek to play a little game with you. You see, it suggests itself to me that some crown prosecutor, seeking to justify his salary, may begin studying the definitions of bigamy.'

'I told you so! I told you!' The first words Demetru had uttered throughout the entire interview, he threw them viciously over his shoulder. 'I was always against it! I still am! Looking for unnecessary trouble, head of a cabbage! You don't need a wife, Petru, and all *that* one wants' – he pointed at the Dutch girl – 'is your money. If you knew you'd want to get married, we could have – '

'Shut up, Demetru!' The groom was losing his temper. 'If

you want to get married, you may do so, too. I have no objection. Come, darling, let us go to the priest. Thank you very much, Mr. Thorne. We will come back to you, when we need you again. In the meantime, will this do? I have no money with me.'

He took off the necklace of gold coins from his throat, and like a seigneur distributing largess, threw it on the desk.

Timothy P. Thorne was loath to accept that kind of a fee, but not very loath. In days to come, he was to remember that gesture – a string taken off a throat.

'Good luck!' he said, as he led them to the door. The tzigane twins ambled out, and Gretchen waddled away at their side.

He returned to his desk. A most curious case; a nice point, indeed, for l'Abbé Gauthier to solve. Would the Abbé take responsibility of uniting them in holy wedlock? How would he go about it? Would he request Gretchen to love, honour and obey one half of the Romano duet? Mightn't the Abbé make a mistake and pronounce indissoluble marriage for the wrong one? Would Demetru be a competent witness to the wedding of his uxorious brother? How would they walk down to the altar together? Like the prophet Ezekiel's vision? Didn't such a union actually invite the very devil as a wedding guest?

Thorne shrugged his shoulders. Let his reverence worry about the canonical problems. As for himself, he was content to take out his notebook and jot down: July 9, Received 12 gold coins; *In re Petru Romano et al.*

III

When the tavern-loungers of the *Crystal Palace*, intrigued by the sound of loud quarreling upon the second floor, and the sudden ominous silence that followed thereafter, rushed up the narrow staircase of the boarding house, and broke down the door of the room, they were repelled by the gruesome sight before them. Upon the dusty and worn carpet there lay the outstretched form of a short buxom girl, of ample features, her eyes staring intensely at the ceiling, her face scratched and of a livid colour, and her throat showing the indelible imprint of fingers. Her lips were blue, and her hands seemed to be frantically clutching at nothingness.

On the side opposite the chiffonier, the door leading to the fire-escape was open.

Five men testified before the coroner. They had stood in front of 261 Rue St. Jacques, smoking and talking politics. They heard sounds of an angry and vociferous *chicane* issuing out of the fatal room. They couldn't make out the words. The blind of the window was down, and all they could see were silhouettes. The silhouettes seemed to struggle. At first they thought it was a kissing party; then they were alarmed by the silence, the disappearance of one silhouette, and the statuesque stance of the remaining outline of two men standing back to back, as if petrified. They heard the two men shouting at each other. Then the double silhouette vanished.

Even the coroner was fascinated by their testimony – grotesque, horrifying, macabre.

When the tzigane twins were brought to the office of M. Hirondelle, *Procureur de la Couronne*, the gypsies completely denied all knowledge of the murder. Petru identified the corpse as that of Gretchen Metzinger, and wept. Demetru was silent, stolid, uncommunicative. Occasionally, in outlandish monosyllables, he sought to console his brother.

Petru declared that earlier in the day they had gone to the *presbytère* to see the priest about his marriage to his bride, now dead. The priest was out, and so they had escorted Gretchen to her boarding-house and had gone back to the circus. They never saw her alive, again. All the dark melancholy of his native Hungarian forests issued plaintively from his words.

'So it was two other fellows!' M. Hirondelle chirped. With his pointed beak, his small head, his pecking manner, the Crown Prosecutor resembled nothing like the sparrow whose name he bore.

'How do you explain the scratches on your faces, Messrs. Romano?'

'We have no statement to make. We are innocent. Bring us Mr. Thorne.'

M. Hirondelle had had some unhappy experiences with rejected confessions. He still remembered the subtle castigation he had recently received at the hands of the Appeal Court. He desisted.

There was no doubt in his mind but that one of these gypsy foreigners had perpetrated this murder. There was motive aplenty for either of them to desire the hastened demise of this unwelcome complement to their domestic triangle. Demetru was annoyed; it wasn't difficult to see his point of view. Opposed to the complicated *liaison*, to him it would have been a *mariage de méconvenance*. Petru, on the other hand, realizing the hopelessness of his courtship, and the unlikelihood that it would end in sanctified consummation, may have allowed his unpedigreed blood to get the better of him, impetuously to do away with the unattainable Gretchen, rather than behold her the spouse of another. It was likely, too, that he may have quarreled with her, or that, harbouring the insinuations of his brother, had suspected unworthy motives for his darling's passion.

It was that matter of identification, however, which puzzled even the acute M. Hirondelle. Three of the saloon salamanders identified Demetru as the half of the silhouette which was hugging or strangling the late Gretchen Metzinger; two positively swore it was Petru. By the very nature of the motives, it was clear that if the one was guilty the other was innocent. The Prosecutor, convinced that Demetru had a more plausible motivation, more scars, and a majority of votes, decided to draw up an indictment of murder against Demetru Romano for that he did, on the ninth day of July, in the county of Hochelaga, in the Province of Quebec, unlawfully kill one Gretchen Metzinger.

IV

Mtre. Hirondelle was gloating over the easy victory which was to be his. An open and shut case; a conviction depending but little upon circumstantial evidence; a murder under supervision; a slaying before an audience. What a fine speech he would be able to address to the jury! How he would dramatize the great wrath which the accused held towards his brother's beloved! How he would picture with revealing adjective and apocalyptic epithet the scene of the slaughter of the silhouette. With erudite and scholarly definition, he would ingratiate himself with the judge, and before the avenging twelve he would play up the shocking and unnatural character of the creature which stood accused in the dock. Then in a peroration that would be long remembered in the history of forensic eloquence, he would ask, in the name of the dead girl, in the name of society, in the name of Justice itself, a verdict of guilty, *and* the extreme penalty. He would pronounce his very last word in three distinct, well-articulated, fatal syllables, falling like dread thunderbolts in the tense hush and silence about him.

The glorious tableau of triumph which Mtre. Hirondelle had conjured up before himself was suddenly marred by the intrusion of the burly figure of Robitaille, bailiff. Handing him a document, the corpulent Mercury of Justice mopped his brow, emitted an oraculur snort, and said, 'Young Thorne is learning the game, isn't he?'

Mtre. Hirondelle glanced at the legal sheets. He scanned the paragraphs, at first cursorily, then eagerly, his nose running over the script. He read:

That your petitioner, Petru Romano, against his will and without his consent, there being against him no civil or criminal suit motivating such detention, is being held and detained in one of the cells of the jail of the County of Hochelaga, and by such detention is unjustly deprived of his liberty.

His eyes leaped to the conclusion. The gall of the fellow! The Petitioner requested the jailer to bring the said Petru Romano into court before one of its honourable judges, and show cause why the prisoner should be so held in durance vile, or words to that effect. Not a word about Demetru Romano; all the modest Thorne wanted was liberty for Petru. That's all. Merely insisting on his inalienable rights. The colossal nerve! A Habeas Corpus asking for the production of the moiety, and no more, of the tzigane twins!

V

When Thorne and Hirondelle appeared before Judge Guillemette to plead on the petition for Habeas Corpus, Mtre. Hirondelle, his countenance full of the menace of case-law, called to young Thorne. A smirk on the defence attorney's face indicated that he was mentally rubbing his hands at the prosecutor's dilemma. He was happy to approach him; he would enjoy baiting him.

'Listen, Thorne, you think you are a wise one. Justinian come to life again. Well, I hope for your sake that you are getting a double fee. You ought to, lawyer in the wholesale trade. But I want to tell you a secret. You've made a mistake.'

Thorne was cock-sure. 'You wouldn't seek to mislead me? After all, I must cede before age, experience, and a Queen's Counsel.'

'There's another ten minutes before old Guillemette will come on the bench. He's probably busy polishing off some juicy sentences right now, and won't be down until he gets just the right smack and sting into them. Now unless you agree to my suggestion it will be all the worse for your clients.'

'So you're not only a Crown Prosecutor. Handing out clemency, too?'

'If you persist in your petition for Habeas Corpus, this is what I am going to do.' Was the man bluffing? 'I'll draw up indictments against your precious Petru for being party to an offence, for being an aider and abettor, for giving comfort and help to criminals, for being an accessory during and after the fact, and for any other felonies that I can possibly rake up out of the code. Even if I have to dig up all the archaic and obsolete statutes now feeding worms in the archives, to hold on to this David – and – Jonathan, I'll do it. He's bound to be nipped on one.'

Thorne was learning to be a dissembler. Agitated though he was by this threat of jeopardy to his client, he was, for the nonce, whimsical.

'If ever anybody had his back turned on crime, it was Petru.'

'I've given you enough rope,' said Mtre. Hirondelle, 'you know what to do with it.'

When the crier had finished his raucous *Oyez! Oyez!* and Judge Guillemette had taken his seat on the bench, Thorne, counsel for the defence, rose and begged permission of the court to withdraw his petition. Granted.

VI

The courthouse was jammed with spectators. The townsfolk who had found it so expensive to frequent the circus in weeks gone by, now all attended upon the sessions of the court, where the relict of the departed caravanserai, the tzigane twins, were seated in the dock upon a bench especially builded so as to conform to their peculiar sedentary habit.

Mtre. Hirondelle, like a factotum of the law, was hurrying hither and thither, his brief-case under his arm, his gown flowing in sweeping outline behind him, a genial smile upon his avian countenance. Upon the bench, there sat Judge Guillemette, solemn, long-faced and thin-lipped. He was known as a justiciary who seldom gave the accused any undue advantage; he considered himself the ordained instrument of the law-abiding citizenry, and the only benefit criminals ever wangled out of him was the benefit of the doubt.

Thorne sat inconspicuously in a chair reserved for counsel for the defence. Beardless minion that he was, he looked like a very tyro before the officious and goateed Hirondelle. The court officials first regarded him, habited in black, like an undertaker, with his gown hanging upon him as if worn for the first time, and his *rabat* askew at a most unsartorial angle, and then cast their sympathetic looks in the direction of the accused; the twins might as well put in their order then and there for a double coffin.

A jury was enrolled. Thorne exercised no challenges. The indictment was read; the accused pleaded not guilty.

His beak pertly lifted, the Crown Prosecutor pecked out his

evidence from the five witnesses, who to-day were unanimous in identifying Demetru Romano as the murderous strangler. They reiterated, to all intents, the story which they had told the coroner.

'You didn't observe any faces, did you?' Mr. Thorne was cross-examining the witness.

'I saw their whole bodies, down to the waist.' The witness was being very careful; he suspected pitfalls; he eschewed snares.

'It was a silhouette you saw?'

'No.'

'You didn't see a silhouette?' Thorne was wondering; this was too easy. It was.

'You can't catch me. I saw two silhouettes, melted.'

There was a titter through the courtroom. The witness was a poet.

'Could you tell' – Thorne was deliberate – 'one silhouette from the other?'

The witness did not answer.

'Could you?'

The witness picked up courage, 'I did, didn't I?'

'How did you recognize the silhouette of Demetru from that of Petru?'

'Because one was on the right and the other was on the left.'

Thorne requested the accused to stand up. 'Change your positions on the bench,' he ordered.

'Now,' he turned to the witness, 'who was the man you saw doing the choking?'

No answer. Thorne did not press him. No answer was the best answer.

'Tell the Court, sir, where were you standing at the time of the altercation?'

'In front of 261 Rue St. Jacques.'

'How did you come to be there?'

'I came out of 261 to get cool.'

'Admit it – isn't 261 Rue St. Jacques the Crystal Palace Tavern, and didn't you take some good shots to get so warmed up?'

'A bottle of beer or two.'

'Couldn't it be possible, sir, that you may have seen two silhouettes where only one was? You needn't answer. The jury will do that for you.'

There was a laugh behind palms in the courtroom, but the twelve good men and true seemed in no wise impressed and the judge positively frowned.

Thorne repeated the same line of cross-examination with respect to all of the five witnesses, and succeeded, insofar as the court-spectators were concerned, in damaging their evidence with insinuation, innuendo, and ridicule.

It was when the prosecutor, with an executioner's gleam in his eye, adduced expert evidence to prove that the flesh under the fingernail of the deceased Gretchen Metzinger was from the face of Demetru Romano, that the prospect of the accused began to look sepulchral indeed. The judge and the grave both yawned before them.

'Is it not possible, Doctor, that the accused should have marks on his face, the deceased flesh under her fingernail, and that still there should be no relationship between these facts?'

It was a feeble attempt, but it had to be thrown out for what it was worth.

The jury looked at the expert. 'It is possible,' he answered in a tone which indubitably added 'but very unlikely.' He should never, Thorne reflected as he sat down, have asked that question; the jurymen looked glum, as if they too had thrown the suggestion out for what it was worth.

It was then that with gloating self-satisfaction Mtre. Hirondelle announced that he had one more witness. There was in his voice an intimation that this was to be the *coup de grâce*.

'Call Petru Romano!'

There was a hush throughout the courtroom. Everyone was expectant, tense. The Crown was plucking a witness out of the very dock.

In a moment, Thorne was on his feet. 'I object, my Lord;

Petru Romano cannot possibly give any testimony except hearsay. It is obvious that he never was in a position to be a witness. It is a waste of the time of the Court.'

Judge Guillemette for one would waste no time. 'Objection overruled!' he said.

Thorne was not to be sat upon, not at any rate, without making it uncomfortable for the sitter.

'I object to Petru Romano giving testimony on the ground that no man can be compelled to testify against himself. Petru and Demetru Romano, it must have been clear to the Court long ere this, are one and the same personality. The Crown, by its own actions, has adopted that view, and a little consistency I submit, might lubricate the wheels of Justice. The Crown, in fact, has imprisoned both of them without bail, though, to use the terminology of my learned friend, charges were preferred only against one. Also, they were confined to one and not to two cells. They were given a single and not a duplicate dossier. In every way and in every respect they were treated as if they were one and indivisible. And one and indivisible they must be considered by this Court.

'In ordinary life, too, and the Courts are always guided by the good solid common sense of the inspired average, they have always been regarded as a unit. The bills for their clothes, for their rent, for their food, were always and everywhere addressed to the tzigane twins, and collection was made from one of them, and acquittance given to both. I herewith produce these bills as exhibits. On their travels, too, they have always paid only single fare.

'To consider them as two individuals, would lead to the absurdest of conclusions. Would anyone dare to maintain that one unfortunate enough to be born with four arms, should be considered a personality and a half? Then why should duplication of all limbs be considered a duplication of identities?'

Judge Guillemette seemed amused. 'This is very entertaining, Mr. Thorne,' he said, 'but where is the legal text in support of your contention?'

There was subdued merriment among the lawyers in the courtroom. Thorne would have to put through some hurried legislation to create such a text.

But the counsel for the defence seemed to have foreseen almost every turn of the proceedings. He was certainly not nonplussed.

'Section 2, subsection 13 of the Criminal Code,' he announced, and there was the rustle of pages in the courtroom as lawyers hurried to find the legal eldorado, 'defines a person as including Her Majesty, and all public bodies, and bodies corporate. Bodies corporate! What, my Lord, could be more aptly termed a body corporate than the tzigane twins?'

Mtre. Hirondelle was hopping about before the bench, trying to catch the judge's eye.

'This objection,' he spluttered, 'is ridiculous on the face of it. It was my learned friend himself who sought to take out Habeas Corpus proceedings asking for the production of Petru. He did, then, when it suited his purposes, accord him a separate personality.'

'But unlike others,' Thorne was smiling, 'I realized my ignorance. I withdrew my petition.'

'The next thing counsel will be saying is that the tzigane twins, being twenty-six years old, each is thirteen and therefore unindictable unless we prove that they knew right from wrong.'

'If it is prophecy and hypothesis that we are exercising ourselves upon, I would venture to say that it would not be beyond the Crown to read to tzigane triplets, if there are any, the Riot Act every time they bawl for milk on the ground that an unlawful assembly is one of three or more persons which causes persons in the neighborhood to fear that the peace will be disturbed tumultuously.'

'Persiflage!' Judge Guillemette was always terse. 'Objection overruled.'

There was a look of inscrutable cunning, of inexplicable confidence on the face of Petru Romano, when with his brother behind him, he stood in the witness box.

'I hope, Mr. Thorne, that you will waive your client's privilege of standing in the dock.'

The evidence of Petru, delivered with disarming and unfathomable frankness was a corroboration of the case of the Crown. He told the story of his brother's opposition to his marriage, the manner in which, despite his own resistance and the resistance of Gretchen, Demetru had strangled his wife-to-be, and of how, having realized that the girl was dead, they had both hurried away through the fire escape, taken a *calèche*, and prepared alibis at the circus.

Was the man crazy? Or had he caught his lunacy by contagion from Thorne, who smiled genially, 'No cross-examination'? He could have perjured himself with impunity; instead, he seemed happy to spin out a yarn that the Crown would certainly convert into rope.

There was no defence. When Mtre. Hirondelle stood before the jury, like a blackbird set before a dozen kings, the whole courtroom knew that he was going to indulge in one of those deformed-in-body-and-in-mind speeches. It worked like hypnotism. Without leaving their seats, the jury brought in a verdict of guilty against Demetru Romano.

Judge Guillemette, however, did not don his black gloves and cap to pronounce the dread sentence. He adjourned the court *sine die*.

VII

'It's alright, Demetru, you're not dead yet,' Thorne was proffering cold solatium to his convicted client. 'You observed, didn't you, that the Judge foresaw his dilemma, and postponed sentence. He can't hang you, because if you hanged, Petru here also would have to kick the bucket, and he's innocent. That's why I thought that there was no great danger in him giving his testimony. Two heads, you see, are better than one.'

Demetru was weeping. The tears ran down his swarthy countenance, and every sob that broke from his throat was full of a poignant self-pity.

'But what if they perform an operation on us, and divide us off, and tell Petru to go his way, and me to go mine.' He blubbered at the pendulous prospect.

'No danger of that. They wouldn't take the chance, even if the law allowed it, and the law doesn't. No person can be compelled to submit to a surgical operation if he doesn't want it, and besides, to slice you apart would be inflicting a kind of penalty upon you, and only the penalties mentioned in the code are legal. That's as old as the Magna Carta.'

'In the meantime?'

'In the meantime, let them worry. It's their problem, not yours.'

Demetru was lugubrious; no sense of fun.

'Cheer up, Demetru, you're creating jurisprudence.' Thorne was already on the other side of the cell. 'You're better off than many a convicted man. You've got a real gambling chance, two or nothing.'

That day Petru Romano received from the Crown Prosecutor's office a communication – verbal – saying that if he, Petru, were willing to become a government employee, to wit, a jail-guard, at the regular salary, his brother, Demetru, who would be his sole and only charge would get off with a sentence of life imprisonment. It was a permanent job, too.

VIII

Upon the advice and counsel of Mr. Thorne, Petru Romano spurned and rejected the offer of the Crown. He would never, he said, barter and sell his liberty for a paltry pittance of a wage. If punishment was to be meted out, he was ready to take the consequences. He sought neither favours nor privileges; willing though he was to receive his just deserts, he insisted nevertheless upon his unquestionable rights, not the least of which was his right to liberty.

Judge Guillemette, having announced a time for appearance of the accused Demetru Romanu, sentenced him to be hanged by the neck until he be dead, upon a day and at a place later to be appointed, and forwarded a report to the Secretary of State, for the information of the Governor-General, and therein indicated the non-decision of a point of law reserved in the case.

For weeks, thereafter, Thorne circulated petitions to be presented before the Governor-General. The petition spoke in glowing terms of the past history of British justice, of the sanctified principle of freedom of the subject, of the immortal dicta of the Magna Carta, and of international relations with the tzigani. It quoted from eminent authority to the general effect that it is a much lesser evil that the guilty sometimes escape than that the innocent be sometimes punished, and concluded, requesting that a pardon be granted to Demetru Romano, not for his own sake, but for the sake of his brother, Petru, who was innocent.

Even to this day no person can explain it. Early in September of that year, Mr. Thorne received on behalf of his client, Demetru Romano, by warrant under the hand and seal-at-arms of the Governor-General, a discharge out of custody, and a pardon extending the royal mercy to the said Demetru Romano on condition that within thirty days from the day of the receipt of the said pardon, the said Demetru Romano forsake and leave the Queen's domains, and never set foot therein thereafter.

IX

The tzigane twins were settling their account with Mr. Thorne. It was the fattest fee he had ever received, and well justified the recent growing of the professional mustache whose meagre herbiage he was so meditatively caressing as Petru counted out the bills.

'Justice is not blind,' Petru was saying, as he threw down the last dollar of a many-dollared wad.

'No, only slightly squinted,' antiphonically interjected Demetru.

Against the window-pane, a fly, a late September fly, kept up its insistent and unconcerned buzzing.

'We are very grateful to you, Mr. Thorne,' Petru had his hat in his hand. 'Capital punishment, you know – –'

'Should properly result,' Thorne concluded, as he filed an ambiguous smile on his lips, 'in a suspended sentence. Which it did. You escaped by the skin of your teeth.'

'By the skin of our spine, Mr. Thorne.'

Now that the case was finished, and the fee paid, Thorne thought it polite to evince some casual interest in the plans of his erstwhile clients.

'What do you intend to do now, gentlemen, – now that Her Majesty's men-at-arms are prodding you on your way?'

'Going back to Hungary. But before we do that, we go to Montreal for an operation. You see, we are not really Siamese twins, not inseparable anyway, or so at least we've been told – –.'

It appeared from Petru's narrative, told with much gesturing and cynical gloating, that Petru and Demetru were indeed born twins, but neither Siamese, nor indivisible; that their mother, the good dame, had been abandoned by Romano senior, a bear-tamer, who had departed, preferring the ursine to the feminine; that Mrs. Romano, left to her own resources, with a couple of bambinoes as like as two pennies, had gone to a Budapest doctor, and had converted them into an inseparable monstrosity, and that thereafter exhibiting her wondrous progeny in the towns and hamlets of Hungary, she had been able to eke out, from the gaping peasantry, a comfortable livelihood, until the boys, grown to man's estate, had themselves joined a circus.

'Well, I don't think that Demetru and myself want to continue as we are. For many reasons. We feel, too, that what one doctor could do, another could undo. Of course, we are taking a chance. After all, we heard only from strangers about this operation which our mother had performed on us. It may not be true. We may be indivisible. However, nothing ventured, nothing gained.'

'I wish you the best of luck, gentlemen. I would rather have two clients than one. But tell me, why didn't you inform me about this before the trial?'

'We thought it would embarrass you.'

'Yes, and somewhat inconvenience you, too.'

Mr. Thorne never spoke to his clients again. But he did see

them. A call from a private hospital informed him that two patients, having died on their surgical table, had left some documents for him. When he arrived there, Thorne found Petru and Demetru laid out symmetrically on a marble slab. A dead fly lay crushed beneath the arm of Demetru.

The twins, evidently, had gone to the operating table with some misgivings, for they had wisely made their will immediately before they went under the anaesthetic. Nor had they forgotten any post-mortem details. Mr. Timothy P. Thorne, content in the knowledge that a client once satisfied comes back, even as a ghost, for more, looked after the obsequies most punctiliously, even to the extent of having erected upon the grave of the immortal tzigane twins, a splendid tombstone upon which was engraved, in letters long since effaced by wind and rain, the requested epitaph: *And in their death they were not divided.*

Yclept a Pip

The Exec comes up to me one day and says: 'Cal, we have an important job for you. The boss just signed up a crackerjack, a writer and no ham neither, a guy by the name of Shakespeare, who's gone over big in England, and is plenty important. And' he says, and takes time off for a little gurgle, which tells me there's a crack coming, 'he's great shakes with royalty. Get it? Now, here's where you come in. We are promoting you at a raise,' he says, 'to be his bodyguard. You are going to be with him twenty-four hours a day, if not longer, and it's going to be your job to follow him around like you was his b.o., and phone in to us – keep this under your hat – daily reports on his activities.'

'Oh,' I say, 'a stool pigeon? Is he a public enemy, and 'I say, 'if so, what number? Because I don't mind being the guy's escort round and about Hollywood, but Alcatraz, that's going too far.'

'Skip it' says the Exec, and his face takes on that oil-upon-the-waters look. 'He's no racketeer, only we don't want that which happens last year to happen again. You remember that shyster playwright we ship from Broadway and sign up at a fat salary to sell us his ideas? Well, whenever a brainstorm strikes him, what does the wise guy do but ups and phones the b-g-b outfit and, for a price he arranges previous, lets them have the whole layout, and when – after he's been floating around for six months doing a strange interlude, we, mere acquaintances of course, have the gall to ask for results, he hands us the old-gold alibi. Hollywood, he says, stops the fountains of inspiration. Fountains of Inspiration! So we told him about the leakage in the plumbing and let him loose.'

'Well,' I say, 'if all I got to do is shadow a muck-a-muck bloke at a Hollywood salary, it's okay by me.' So he gives me a photo with the guy's mug on it, and tells me to go meet the Twentieth Century.

When I get there, I look around, and it don't take me long to spy him. That guy stands out in a million, anywhere. Get me straight, he don't grow six foot two in his socks, but his is a map you don't find its twin in a contest for strange faces. A convention of travelling salesmen, and a bunch of sound citizens get off that train, but he has that edge over them like a thoroughbred in a stableful of nags. Small nose, brainy eyes, and a forehead that goes testing the stratosphere – it don't take no judge of human nature to see that he's it. He sports a little mattress on his chin which don't counterfeit his age, thirty, add or take away. And it relieves me greatly to note that this Englishman wears no monocle.

I tell him who I am, and who sent me.

'Sirrah!' he says, 'a liege-man for my retinue!' Right away I know he has class. The fake Romanoffs, and eau de Cologne dukes that hang around the studios have nothing on him, not by a long shot. We get to talking in the taxi, and this Mr. Shakespeare keeps me laughing my ribs shaky with all kinds of gags, in every form and shape. He slings that lingo of his like nobody's business, words a yard long, and little juicy words too, that he brings over without declaring, and wisecracks enough to give you acute appendicitis. A bear on the high-class stuff with all the dressings. Somebody evidently has given him the lowdown on some Hollywood stars, so his cracks are coming fast and furious, not just cheap vaudeville stuff, but real college humor, and I ain't ashamed to admit that some of them don't make my concrete. Of course, I have some trouble with his wordage until I get wise to the fact that he pronounces introduction intro-duc-ti-ion, and things like that. But once I'm up on his errors, he's a howl. I mention that certain curvy actress who is making a hit, and what do you think he pipes up with? 'Look on beauty,' he says casual-like into his beard, 'and you shall see 'tis purchased by the weight.' But this is a tame one compared to others, which I'd have to give my tongue a physical culture course to repeat.

Furthermore, he is not just one of these four-flushing hail-fellow-well-met wisecrackers. I open my flaps and hear more common sense from him in that half hour taxi ride than I pick up in a lifetime of hanging around with the big shots and even you journalist guys with the gab, for there is one thing for which you have to hand it to him, this guy can not only size up people, but can see right through them like as if they were made of cellophane.

Well, we get quite thick, and pretty soon he's calling me Caliban, after one of the characters of a play he's writing which I consider quite a compliment. All the time I am giving the boss reports which say practically nothing since this fellow is square and above-board, and there is nothing phony about him at all.

And it don't take long before the town feels as I do, and everybody is talking about the Englishman, naming fedoras after him, shaking up drinks and calling them Stratford Specials – Stratford is the guy's hometown – and a pickled tongue company even advertises their stuff as 'The Tongue that Shakespeare Eats.'

Round and about the studio he gets along swell, everybody from the sweepers up thinks him one nice guy, and it's a cinch he's no snob catching raindrops in his nose. I see him myself join in a crap game with the boys just for the fun of it and the way he speaks to those dice would make any bones stand up and take notice. Indeed, he has a spiel all his own and it's the real McCoy. 'Aroint thee,' he says, 'Aroint thee ill-starred crap; come seven, come eleven; my doxy wants a golden quoif, roll dice and say "'tis given" I shake you hot, I shake you cold, I shake you till you are well rolled, Ducdame, ducdame, ducdame.' Personally, I never cash in when I give my imitation of this hocus-pocus, but I figure it's because of lousy diction.

It is only with the real big shots that Mr. Shakespeare seems not to get along so good. First of all somebody hints to him that the reason why he is brought over at this particular time, is because a guy by the name of Will Shakespeare is doing wonders as an All American, and the moguls want to cash in on the local boy's publicity. This isn't exactly flattery, and naturally when he hears this he's plenty burned up. And he looks so disgusted anybody can tell that as soon as his contract is up, he's going to pack in the whole shebang, and scram. In the second place, after an all night session at a night club when just to be one of the boys he acts as m.c. and where he first introduces that heigh-nonny-no stuff, which later livens up the hot spots in the land, he writes a scenario called Hamlet, Prince of Denmark. This scenario is put through the mill with a lot of criticism, especially the title. In fact the Danish Consul calls up as soon as he reads the news release, and raises such a row at the idea of slandering the Danish people in general, and the royal family in particular, that the big shots suffer for weeks from the yumping yitters. So that is cut out and the scene is laid in Danatania. Then the executives hold a mass meeting and after a huddle decide that Hamlet has too many double meanings, and is even funny, and they say it won't be long before Mickey Mouse is shooting a takeoff. So it is put down in the minutes that pending changes the company is working on a million dollar production to be released under the name of His Mother's Sin, by William Shakespeare. When he hears this, he begins tearing his hair and it looks like a case of premature baldness for him, but he suddenly stops and walks off talking to himself, and I think I hear him say 'for sufferance is the badge of all us scribes.'

After this, Shakespeare don't say much but sits down and writes a letter to the boss in which he tells him that in view of the fact that his title and his scenes are being messed up he wishes at least to give the members of his cast some pointers on how this stuff should be acted, and he don't wait for no answer. In fact, he puts down on paper what he thinks are the big hints on the Art of acting and tells me to hand them out to the cast, which of course I don't, but instead bring it to the boss, and it reads as follows: –

Speak your speech, I pray you, trippingly on the tongue; but if you mouth it as many do, I'd as lief the town-crier spoke my lines. Nor do not saw the air too much but use all gently, for in the very torrent, tempest, and (as I may say) whirlwind of your passions you must acquire and beget a temperance that may give smoothness. For it offends the soul to hear a robustious periwig-pated fellow tear a passion to tatters, to very rags, to split the ear of the groundlings who for the most part are capable of nothing but inexplicable dumb show and noise.

There's a lot more of that stuff, and it's as well that I don't hand it out to them cuties in the cast, seeing that they'd probably make as much out of it as I do, which is no score.

Well, when the boss reads that, he goes red in the face and there is all the symptoms that he's going to throw a fit from here to Addis Ababa, but he controls himself and dictates an interdepartmental memo in which he tells Shakespeare to kindly keep his nose out of the director's territory, and to please remember that his act is to write the stuff, and that he hopes and trusts he will bear that in mind.

When Shakespeare sees the attitude they are taking and guesses that they are telling him off, I expect to see him explode. Instead he just laughs into his beaver, and shoves the memo into a file marked *Dead*, and says to me 'I void my rheum upon them' and I reply 'You don't say,' dumb like.

After that I can't make him out for he sits in his office and scribbles verses hours at a time, lyrics and things like that, he makes his own tunes for them, and hums them all over the place, and let me tell you, they're knockouts. Only what is a most surprising feature is that he don't get paid for putting out the stuff which he calls 'dulcet and harmonious breath.'

Sometimes, when he's bored stiff, he steps out to the local eating joints and becomes pally with the actresses, who all fall for him, and nothing pleases him more than to hand out ideas for publicity stunts. Take the case of Marylin Sonnenscheidt. 'Were it not better' he says to her 'because that you are more than common tall that you did suit you all points like a man, and bear a swashing and a martial outside.' Next day I see her tripping down the avenue wearing pants, and sporting a turtle neck sweater, and a crew of reporters, falling all over her, wanting to know what's what, and you can bet your portable that that gag was worth a million in publicity-value.

Only I don't seem to see him much at society affairs, instead there's a couple of little nifty extras that he seems to be on the make for, and as for his job, he's not playing up to it at all. So I can't figure him out, until it strikes me all of a sudden, and especially when I park my lamps on a copy of a letter he types to a pal in London, called Benny Jonson, which reads as follows:

O good my Ben:

I rest here in Hollywood, amass fond shekels of the tested gold, live i' the sun, and do have but little to irk me in mine estate, saving that my masters (call them masters) in the high flush and insolence of their pelf presume to teach me my hand. But 'tis a small thing, and no matter. I go my way, and upon them fie, and foh! It marvels me only that they live and breathe, for time was that when the brains were out the man was dead. Now, even now, they are engaged in dismembering, disemboweling, quartering, and indeed generally encompassing the destruction of my prince Hamlet, which it fears me greatly will presently appear sans life, sans taste, sans proportion, and sans sense.

But sit down, sorrow. There be things that do console the troubled breast, and of these I count none greater than a child of grand mother Eve, a female, or for thy more sweet understanding, a woman, a maid, by name Anne Hathaway, by disposition and temper, most sweet and commendable, and by appearance so beauteous and fair to look upon she is indeed yclept a pip, which in this high and palmy state is the compliment supreme.

In sooth, I did offer her the benison of Hymen's bands, which she fain would accept, but quoth she: 'I love you, Bill, but — no wedding-bells yet. I have my career.' On this, I trust, there will be more anon.

In the interim, I have set myself to a conning of the tongue that is here spoken, and upon my troth, 'tis a so delectable, fresh, and subtil speech by the commonalty uttered, a poet would dote on't. An if you believe me not, what say you to a sonnet to my lady's hand, which beginneth thus:

The gorgeous sparklers on her cutex'd mitt. —

Eke this, of robbers discomfited in their arsenal'd dens:

Come, take it on the lam; we're on the spot!
I see the shadow of a fingerman.

It is my plan and purpose to commence a history and play in this tongue and to this end I hold lengthy discourse with my Anne.

Farewell, now, and in my absence despite, clink a canakin at the Mermaid.

Ah, I say, churches la femmy and it don't take me long and I get the dope on this Anne Hathaway. In fact, I see her, and she is indeed without exaggeration a honey. The swellest looking dame I see around the place in many a day, and it surprises and shocks me how I missed her, with eyes as blue as a St. Louis song, a little mouth like a maraschino, and a swell pair of shafts and I don't blame Mr. Shakespeare in the least bit.

Only he's in a tough spot. Not only she's not finished with her career, but she aint even begun, since she's peddling her act from studio to studio, trying to get a look-in at the cameras, and it's tough breaks all around. Shakespeare figures if he puts on the pressure he can land her the job, but then what's the percentage for him if she's a success, and he's left out in the cold with his cottage-for-two proposition. Anyway, he decides to take a chance, and its my personal belief he thinks more of her as a wife than a flicker star. Fortunately, at this time, the dame that's playing Ophelia in Her Mother's Sin, a Swede who scratches everybody's eyes out trying to get the part, suddenly goes temperamental and decides to quit the show because she gets lonesome and wants to go home. The director goes in a panic but Shakespeare steps in at the crucial moment and says she is no good anyway, especially in the scene where she is supposed to drown, because she can't sink on account of her big feet paddling her over the river, and further-more, he says, he's got the dame that can take the part perfect, and moreover, seeing that all his other ideas are scrapped, it ain't nothing but right that they should take his suggestion once, which they do, and Anne Hathaway makes it.

She's on location, and Shakespeare comes around from time to time to see how things are moving, and although he don't say a word, and he lets on that everything's jake with the show, I can see that his stomach's turning like a cement grinder. He tells me on the q.t. that the director's a zany who speaks an infinite deal of nothing – there's a sample for you, classy even when he's insulting – and takes me into his confidence to show me each and every creaking joint. He hardly sees straight when he lo and beholds a bevy of hoofers kick their heels in the air as Ophelia is drowning and singing old-fashioned songs, or when he pipes what's supposed to be the ghost of Hamlet's father all rigged up like a son of Frankenstein by Queen Kong, with electricity shooting off him in all directions, or two characters, Guildenstern and Rosencrantz, supposed to be princes or something, dressed up like a couple of stooges in the cloak-and-suit trade, and he positively gets a hemorrhage when Hamlet makes a speech about kicking the bucket, at the same time as he's shaking a cocktail, and when the finger is put on the king and queen, not by a play, but by a Walt Disney cartoon, he is within an inch of passing out. But he don't file no complaint, and indeed he gives the director a big hand.

Then one day, he offs and goes to a nearby college-town where he arranges to get himself invited to talk on This Thing, The Play, but I don't attend because I figure that aint part of my contract. When he comes back he sees his Anne, and they have a little party celebrating finishing of the picture, and she promises him that if she's a flop, wedding bells will ring.

Next thing I see the picture is released, and Mr. Shakespeare is gone for a much-needed rest to a place he calls the still vexed Bermuthes, leaving no forwarding address, and Miss Hathaway too hotfoots it, and I don't know where.

Well, speaking of much-needed rest, I feel that I am in for a little vacation myself, and so I go off on a binge. I don't know how long I am away, or how many tables I sleep under, but when I wake up, I feel like a medicine bottle, shaked up before using. I drink many coffees, and finally I catch on that Shakespeare is in town, has been for a day, and is on the go again, and I ought to go meet him at the train.

I am a little bit too early, and so I buy me a paper, and notice that His Mother's Sin is one big box office hit, rating a skyful of stars, and that it is packing them in especially in the hick movie houses, and I'm kind of glad for Hathaway, but feel low for Shakespeare and his crush.

Well, imagine my surprise when coming on the train who do I see but la Hathaway, hanging on to the arm of Shakespeare, and flashing, on her wedding-finger, a sparkler stronger than a klieg light.

'Say, what's this?' I say.

'There are more things than one dreamed of in your philosophy, my Caliban,' he says.

'When did it happen?' I ask, and turn my spotlights from one to the other, and Shakespeare catches on that I know a thing or two; especially when he sees my paper turned on the movie news.

'The brain may devise laws for the blood' he says, 'but a hot temper leaps over a cold decree.'

'There is plenty in that,' I readily agree 'but,' and here I let the cat out of the bag, 'Miss Hath – I mean Mrs. Shakespeare is a success.' When I wise up to what I say, is my face red?

They both laugh hearty, and then he shoots the works, and I gather that the day the flicker was finished, they all go out to a hick town to put on a preview and size up the reactions and they choose none other but the place where Shakespeare gives his spiel on the movie business. All the college students are there. They wait for a cue from Shakespeare, and right away they begin the razz. They razz the show so loud and funny, with special attention for Miss Hathaway, that all the big shots and the whole cast, scram, believing the flicker don't rate a twinkle, let alone the five stars in its build-up.

Naturally, Anne is very much put out, 'like Niobe, all tears,' says Shakespeare, and without losing no time, they wake a minister and he does the until-death-do-you-part act, and goes back to sleep.

Mr. and Mrs. Shakespeare are laughing, and the happiness market is cornered.

'Are you coming back to Hollywood?' I say.

'No,' says Mrs. Shakespeare, 'we have only just begun our

honeymoon. This is a stop-over. Cook's Tour around the world and back to England, to Bill's folks, and then he's going to write the great American play.'

The train is pulling out. Mrs. Shakespeare throws me a kiss, and I certainly don't fumble it.

'Farewell!' I shout, 'a long farewell!'

'So long, Cal,' and I see Shakespeare's hat waving good-bye.

No Traveller Returns ...

I stepped into my roadster, and began swallowing miles. The car agglutinated strip after strip of ribboned road. The engine throbbed like the heart of a dissected frog.

Yesterday I had said: I will carry my nostrils away from the smell of fried flesh. I will escape the ratty whisper in the ear. I will avoid the apothecary taste upon the tongue.

And now I was swallowing miles. Into a long highwayed vista, flanked by overhanging elms, I shot, like one motoring through a framed picture. Now and again, I crossed a wooden bridge whose broken boards rattled under the wheels, a rustic xylophone. I clung to the side of mountains; I leaped into the valleys. The car sped like an electric current.

Suddenly I came upon a stretch of road, with clovered meadowland on either side. It was a scented Paisley shawl before my eyes. But the odour always and ever became the odour of ether, and the noise of the machine was the noise of pestle in mortar.

Then I stepped on the gas. I seemed to feel a traffic cop behind me. A ghost on a motorcycle. I looked into the mirror. It was not Dr. Constantine Nekrovivos. I saw nothing, nothing except scenery.

Yesterday the doctor was alive. Then at twelve o'clock of the night they sat him down on a seat. Professor Constantine Nekrovivos, holding the chair of electro-dynamics. Then they pulled a switch. The power of eight hundred ordinary sized electric bulbs raced through his Greek body. Professor emeritus. A doctor pronounced the doctor dead.

But I knew better. Himself he told me that he knew the formulae for life. He could mix poisons for death; and he could brew a broth of eternal wakefulness.

When they sat him down upon the seat, he surely hated me.

It was not my fault. They said, Your name is Armstrong, and you are a press-agent. I said yes. They said, You also used to insure your friends. I said yes. They said, You had many friends. I said yes. They said, Then your friends would fall sick, and Dr. Nekrovivos would come, always Dr. Nekrovivos, and he would prepare a prescription, and your friends would die, and you would travel to a new city where you had more friends, and you would insure them, and the doctor would come, always Dr. Nekrovivos, and the friends would die. I said, Yes, yes, yes, yes.

Then they let me go.

At the trial, the prosecutor made me repeat what he said. Then Constantine's lawyer got up and called me a rat. He lifted his hand in the air, between finger and thumb dangled something and shouted, His own sweet hide. Twenty-four nostrils curled and seemed to snort squealer. Twenty-four eyes looked sorry that I had been given the protection of the Court.

When they led the doctor away, he stuck out his tongue, made with his fingers as if scissoring it, and then pointed at me.

So I didn't want to be around the place any longer; and on the following morning set out to put as many miles as possible between myself and the professor, his potions, and his upholstered seat.

The sun was a hot brasier. Clouds hung in the sky like an ad for featherbeds. On hill and valley, the grass was verdant with the varying shades of green. Now and again, a wind sallied forth from nowhere, and thither disappeared. It was a beautiful day. I sped along, only occasionally hearing the crackle of voltaged copper, only occasionally smelling a nostalgic grain of poison.

Suddenly the sky went dark. Black clouds rolled in the

heavens, like barrels. The wind stevedored them one against the other, making thunderous noise. Their metal bands snapped lightning. Rain poured down, a million broken casks.

I flew along in my motorized shell. But the storm was so wild, I had to stop. I noticed that I was near a railway station. I looked at the name. Once, on an envelope, I had seen it before. Then I remembered that the doctor's brother sold banana-splits in this town.

The unspigoted barrels continued to drench the world. Thunders roared in their cages. Lightnings shot across the sky like erratic lines on a blueprint chart. I crawled along the road. A half-a-mile away, a stranger, issuing from the woods, hailed me. I said, Hop in.

We drove on. Through the corner of my eye, I regarded him. He had a crescent-shaped scar upon his forehead. He moved in his clothes as if they were too big for him. When he spoke, his voice was anaemic. His fingers looked earthy, like roots recently torn from the ground. He smelled as if he had slept with worms.

He told me that he was a herbalist. He always went out to the woods before a storm. That was the best time to pluck out roots, mysterious roots which he called by a Greek name. And shriek like mandrakes torn out of the earth, he said, and smiled with totally black teeth. The corners of his mouth curled, like the fretwork of a violin. It seemed to me that I once knew a white smile like that.

The thunder was rolling over on its belly. Soon the storm would be dead. The crescent-scarred stranger talked much, using botanical terms. Once he leaned over from his side of the seat, and whispered in my ear ... I am about to make a great discovery. That whisper was familiar; it was the shadow of an echo of a voice that I had heard a long time ago, I thought.

We became very friendly. I will confide in you, he said. I trust you. You look like one who wouldn't spill a secret. I have unearthed, unearthed great wisdom. I have found the formula for life. Somewhere someone had said that to me. I looked again at the crescent-scarred stranger. It was not Dr. Constantine Nekrovivos.

He caught my look, and said: *Similes similibus curant.* Poison fought with poison; bane with bane battled; electricity shocked by electricity. He smiled his sable smile.

I drove into the courtyard of an inn. I invited the stranger. He opened his mouth so that I expected *Yes, only too pleased, certainly,* to issue forth, curtseying; but instead, he closed his mouth slowly, as if retracting a yawn, and said nothing.

At the table I noticed that he wore neither tie nor collar. I don't dress formal to go out into a storm, he said. I am much too preoccupied with herbs to worry about a cravat.

He spoke unremittingly. I did not notice that he touched no food. I have peeped through a knot-hole in the fence around hell, he said. Then he spoke about the fine furnishings in the inn. I have clutched, he said, roots; and I have heard the gossip of the worms. Herbs, he said, there are many miracles that happen underground.

Where do you live, I asked. I hoped incidentally that he would tell me who he was, precisely.

I live in a place in the woods where nobody can find me, he said. Then he went on to talk about plants, and their souls, especially carnivorous plants. Hylozoic, he said with his anaemic voice. Even a man, lying six fathoms deep beneath the sod, was a plant. A creeper, he said. His mouth was a humorous slit.

Then he bent over the table, his scarred forehead almost touching mine, and said, In fact I am interested also in the herbs which grow downwards from the sky. Such as lightning. He began to tell me about a most refreshing massage which he had once enjoyed from a lighting bolt, when a wet voice was heard in the courtyard.

The innkeeper was greeting a friend. What's this new style, he was saying. Evidently the man was naked, except for shorts. In staccato gasps, the friend was telling, like a courier returned from hot pursuit, of how a man, dressed only in winter underwear, had rushed out of the woods, in the rain, and had ordered him to undress, and had robbed him of his coat and trousers.

I turned to my guest at the table to make some comment upon

these strange doings. He had melted away, as if swallowed by some carnivorous invisibility.

Upon the menu-card before me was written, with the waiter's pencil I later discovered, as part of the dessert: *I will be back to pay the bill.*

Then I realized who he was. The handwriting was familiar. I had seen it on prescriptions, and now I saw it on my menu. The voice was a recognizable echo. Even the face was a clay mask of a face I had known. Only it had had no crescent-shaped scar on its forehead.

I stepped into the roadster, and sped back to the city. The car vomited forth all the miles it had so hastily swallowed. I rushed into the warden's well-appointed cell.

He is after me, I said. Who, he said. The doctor, Dr. Constantine Nekrovivos, I said.

The warden laughed a routine laugh. Calm yourself, he said. The doctor passed away last night at seven minutes after midnight. His brother, the confectionery man, called for his body early this morning. He wanted to bury it in the family plot. We dressed it in winter underwear, – tuxedoes are not included in the service here – and I sent it along with some guards. I presume he was buried this afternoon. He's dead, as dead as if he had taken his own prescriptions.

I saw him this afternoon, I said. I saw him, I spoke to him this afternoon.

The warden looked at me, measuring me for a straitjacket.

Do me a favour, I said. Phone the local sexton and ask him to go to the cemetery. Please, I said, he's after me.

Alright, the warden said.

When he put the receiver down he said, The sexton says he was covering the coffin with earth, when the storm broke, and he left the grave temporarily unfilled. He's going back now. He will phone again.

What will I do, I said. Where can I run away?

Travel, the warden said. Europe.

Greece, maybe, I said.

We both waited for the telephone ring to shred the air.

He said he would be back to pay the bill, I said.

You've got the jitters, the warden said. If you wish, I could give you accommodation here.

He was humouring me. A giggle jangled in the warden's throat, like keys.

Then the telephone rang. The warden stepped into an adjacent room. He came back. Looked as if he had spent a week in the hole. That's strange, he said.

What did he say, I said. What did he say.

Lightning struck the coffin, the warden said, went right through the coffin lid, and the coffin is empty.

I told you, I said. He's going to get me. Then my voice choked.

Portrait of an Executioner

I couldn't reach him by phone; his name is not in the telephone book. I couldn't go to his house; his address is not listed in the city directory, neither under name nor under occupation. A man of mystery, with no fixed domicile, he moves from province to province, bearing the pale innocuous name of Ellis – Arthur Ellis. But to over five hundred departed gallows birds he has been The Man with the Rope, The Gentleman at Dawn, Mister Death.

I had a rendezvous with Mister Death. I had written to him to his post-office box, the number of which he had confided to me, asking him to drop in at the office. As soon as I had heard from him – it *is* a curious sensation to lift the receiver and hear at the other end of the line the voice of the hangman – I had instructed my secretary to cancel all appointments. I didn't want my criminal clientèle to encounter the high executioner of Canada, even in only a social way. Such proleptic introductions, I felt, were demoralizing to the accused.

Mr. Ellis is one who for twenty-five years has been in the business of keeping important dates. Punctually at the trysting hour arrived a cheery effervescent little man, with two lines travelling down his nose to the corners of his mouth, like brackets, the result of continual smiling. I realized then why he was referred to by his intimates as Uncle Arthur; his was the most jovial avuncular manner I have ever beheld. There was nothing, I reflected, like meeting the unseen with a cheer.

He wore a felt hat, horn-rimmed glasses, – the better to see you, my dear, – a hard collar, and a dark suit sporting a white handkerchief in his lapel pocket. By his appearance he might have been the member of any one of a number of callings – certainly not the choice of a scaffold for a walk of life. When he stopped at the threshold of my door, he, playful fellow, adopted a miliary stance and saluted with a mock military gesture. He stood there, a firm solid parcel of a man, somewhat graying at the temples, somewhat wrinkled, and somewhat florid, but vigorous, broadshouldered, and apparently untouched by his gruesome labours. We exchanged greetings, but didn't discuss the recession.

I told him that I desired to immortalize him and asked him to talk about himself. He did; but all he seemed to say was that one couldn't make a living out of hanging. I got the drift. I drew up a contract. He read, and after looking at me through his spectacles with a hard shrewd glint, he signed it. Did he think that I would be one of the few in Canada to cheat the hangman, or did his profession teach him on principle to mistrust mankind?

He spoke. As if compensating for the dozens whom he had shoved into the Great Silence, he is loquacity itself, – yet an interesting conversationalist. His subject-matter, of course, militates in that direction; his very profession piques curiosity, and lubricates talk. Nor is Ellis unaware of the fascination which he, as the skeleton in the closet of the Dominion, exercises. Witty, experienced, dramatic in his utterance, his most commonplace remarks are made to sound like the profoundest of philosophy. A man who has looked upon Death, who has escorted hundreds to the grave, who has caught in his ear the last articulation of the unfortunate doomed, must return from his duties either with his soul hardened and calloused, or with a perspective upon life greater and more sensitive than that to which the average man is privy. Ellis, despite his firmly set jaw, has not been dehumanized by his calling. In fact, he is, as the biographers say, a great laugher, an uproarious human laugher. Indeed it is precisely his jolly manner coupled with the awareness of his macabre profession which creates about him an atmosphere of the uncanny.

I was surprised to learn that he had already achieved his three-score less three. He looked still vigorous, and, upon his own assurance, quite capable of coping with the hazards of his fearsome calling. Did he ever, I asked, encounter violence in a condemned man about to be executed?

'Seldom,' he smiled. 'Indeed only once. Usually they are quite docile and prayerful, resigned, the guts knocked out of them, dragging themselves to the gallows, or walking with an air of assumed bravado. But once I had a tough customer, a husky fellow, who swore he would break me in two when I came. When I came, he started something. There were some guards near the cell, and when they heard the hullabaloo the four of them ran towards us, looked – and ran downstairs for more guards. But I wasn't lightweight champion in the army for nothing.'

He puffed at his pipe. 'However,' he said with the air of a man politely offering a service of courtesy, 'usually it is no trouble at all. The danger, if any, is from infuriated mobs. There was a time, for example, when a crowd assembled about a jail in Alberta – in 1916 I think it was, to wreak mob vengeance upon M. Gervais, a graduate of the eastern university, condemned to death for murdering the deputy-sheriff of Prince Albert. That was the nearest, to my mind, that we ever came to a lynching in Canada. It easily might have resulted in a jail-delivery, but I expedited my work quickly, and there was no lynching, – only an execution.

'Or that other time in Ontario in 1919 when I was about to execute Frank McCullough, a returned soldier, for the murder of a detective. Many people felt that McCullough ought not to have been hanged, because his partner in crime who escaped really fired the shot that killed the officer. But they didn't understand the law. At any rate, hundreds of people congregated about the Don Jail, shouting: We want Ellis. We want Ellis. This was a case where the mob wanted to free the condemned man. The reserves had to be called out to quell that mob; and I, who had stood guard all night didn't get away until the next morning, when I was taken out of the jail after the execution in a patrol-wagon which bore a number of prisoners to court for their trials. That was a very exciting day. Yes, a very exciting day.' He paused. 'We want Ellis,' he parodied.

Mr. Ellis shook his head, dolefully, a gesture which seemed to be his commentary upon the mob's foolhardiness. 'Don't you sometimes fear revenge?' I asked, hoping to elicit from the recesses of his mind some Dostoyevskyan pathia.

'I fear nobody. I do my duty. I publish my picture and my name in the papers. I walk the streets daily. Every morning sees me at the Montreal post office. I fulfill the orders of justice and only a lunatic would hold me personally responsible for that; and from attacks by lunatics nobody is immune. The secrecy that I maintain concerning my identity and residence is for the purpose of protecting my family from cranks and nuisances.'

I asked him how he came to take up hanging as a profession. He tried to remember, and then supposed that he just drifted into it. Having served in the British Army with the Northumberland Fusiliers in India, Egypt, and South Africa he came to Canada in 1907 and acted for a time as an understudy to Mr. Ratcliffe, whom he succeeded in 1911 as the quasi-official executioner for Canada. There is, it must be understood, no official executioner. All executions are by law, supposed to be carried out by the sheriff of the district in which they take place, but sheriffs, being a squeamish tribe, usually delegate the commission to Mr. Ellis, who receives one hundred and fifty dollars (plus expenses) per head. Expensive social medicine, I thought to dole out to victims – one hundred and fifty dollars a drop. Even if reprieved? 'Yes' he replied, 'I am entitled to my fee as soon as I receive a telegram from the sheriff requesting that I reserve a certain date for a certain execution. I reserve that date, and then get paid regardless as to whether the execution takes place or not. It's my retainer. So it is wrong to picture me gnashing my teeth like a villain in a play as I read of a commutation of sentence.'

To rural districts where executions are to take place, Mr. Ellis transports by freight his paraphernalia which consists of a collapsible scaffold, black hood, kneestraps, and a brand-new rope. His scaffold is a most interesting working tool. It is held together, Mr Ellis will tell you with pride of a violinist talking of his Stradivarius, entirely by screws; there is not a nail in it. It is all painted red, a choice of colour whose motivation it is easy to comprehend, especially when one remembers what happened in the Sarao hanging, of which more anon. Part of the wood for the scaffold, Mr. Ellis boasts, comes from the original scaffold used to hang the Patriots of 1837. Now, in the city of Montreal, there stands a statue erected to the memory of these patriots.

After every execution, Ellis burns the fatal rope. And thereby hangs a tale. It appears that his predecessor Ratcliffe was dismissed on account of drunkenness, and also because he was converting a sacred office into an ignoble racket. The morbid and the curious, it seems, would buy his rope at a dollar an inch. Ratcliffe was fired when the sheriff of Victoria, B.C. met him in a hardware store whither Ratcliffe had repaired to buy his third length of rope that day.

No such indecorous deviations from formality appeal to the meticulous Ellis. He is one who is extremely finicky about the proprieties. Tradition he must follow; instance the fact that he will perform his justice-ordained task only if properly attired for the occasion. The appointed hour of the appointed day (in Quebec executions, for some obscure reason probably grounded in religion, take place only on Fridays) invariably sees him dressed in silk hat, cut-away morning coat, black vest piped with white, dark grey-striped trousers, winged collar, impeccable four-in-hand tie and black shoes. As Ellis says: 'I believe in decorum. I'm going to carry out a very very sacred duty. Why not be equal to the dignity of the law?' Who shall say him nay?

'I know that some of my enemies, and particularly those who are jealous of my job' – there are numerous applications for the position of executioner in the hands of Canadian sheriffs – 'have caused a rumour to be spread that I am a booze-artist. That's positively untrue, false. I never touch a drop of it for forty-eight hours before an execution. I stand on the gallows as sober as the judge whose sentence I am fulfilling. Yes, I do, on occasion, administer a stimulant to the condemned, but this only if and when I am medically advised to do so. In the Province of Quebec, by the way, this is not permitted. The Roman Catholic Church wants the condemned one to meet his Maker, bright and clear-eyed, and not befogged by drink or opiates.'

Ellis's indignation at his detractors had subsided. His pipe was in his mouth. In reply to my question he took it out again.

'Nauseated? Me? Of course it is not a pleasant job. Any man who says that seeing a fellow-man go to meet God Almighty does not affect him, is a liar. It's the greatest and most terrible spectacle that man can confront. But in five hundred executions I have never faltered. It is in the line of duty; somebody must do it, and surely it is you yourself and the citizens of this country who put me where I am. If the judge is the arm of the law, I am its fingertips.'

In 1914 Ellis was married. His wife, he assured me, knew at the time of how he made a living, but did not object. They have no children. 'I did not want my children to be born under a cloud of ostracism, I chose to be an executioner. But the son of an executioner has no choice.'

Observe that Ellis never refers to himself as the hangman. He likes decorum, he uses the word 'executioner.'

I pointed out to him that hangings were rare and far between. How did he spend his spare time? From his reply it appeared that he acts as a private investigator, and is also indirectly connected with the R.C.M.P. During the World War he made fourteen trips across the Atlantic on behalf of the British Secret Service. On one occasion he acted as political organizer for the late Sire Lomer Gouin, onetime premier of the Province of Quebec. But his avocations are few. He doesn't gamble, he can't play cards, he never saw a horse-race, he never bet a shilling, occasionally he goes to a movie, but not often – 'this jumping jack stuff and mockery' is not for him. I was left with the impression that no more moral man ever ascended a scaffold.

Mr. Ellis never attends murder trials. 'Supposing,' he said, 'you were defending a man for murder. You are addressing the jury with all the eloquence at your command. Suddenly, hat in hand, I tiptoe into the courtroom and take my seat on an obscure and withdrawn bench. But out of the corner of your eye, you have spied me. You drop the papers in your hands; you drop the subject on your mind; and with a dramatic finger, you turn around and shout to the jury; "There he is, the vulture come for his prey: There he is, the ghoul awaiting his victim." No, I give learned counsel for defence no such opportunity. I wait, and if the accused deserves it, they bring him to me ...'

When they are brought to him, ninety percent, according to the man who knows, even with their dying breath proclaim their innocence. Only rarely does a culprit confess his guilt on the scaffold. In many cases, maintains Ellis, the condemned men actually believe in their innocence. They have so faithfully and attentively absorbed their lawyer's eloquent alibi-ing that eventually, guilty as sin though they be, they have listened themselves into snow-white innocence.

Nor are women any better. In his career as collector of the law's penalties, Hangman Ellis has exacted the extreme one from more than half-a-dozen murderesses. Indeed, it is only the section in the Criminal Code on Murder that provides Ellis with all his customers, for although rape, treason, and piracy are also capital offences, no sentence of death has been inflicted in Canada during the twentieth century for these felonies. Of murderesses Ellis says: 'I do not agree that female murder should be extended special mercy simply on the grounds of sex. Misplaced sentiment, that's what it is. I know that some of the most vicious and heartless murders ever perpetrated in this country have been by women. I have studied their crimes and their methods, and I fail to find any traces of the *weaker* sex.'

In the hanging of Madame Sarao in 1935, Ellis had a grim experience, even for a hangman. Tomasina Sarao, together with two accomplices, had been condemned to death for the insurance murder of her husband Nicolo, an Italian street-cleaner. It was a most sordid affair, a coldly premeditated slaughter; in evidence it was brought out that Madame Sarao had in turn planned to shoot her spouse, push him into a street-car, or poison him, – eeny, meeny, miny, mo – and had finally, after several councils of war with her accomplices, decided to lure him outside the city in the hope of getting some extra street-cleaning work in a suburb, and there to bash his head with a rock. This was done, and Nicolo's beaten body was placed upon railroad tracks running through Dorval so that a train passing over the body might so multilate it as to destroy forever the traces of the true manner in which poor Nicolo had met his death. There he lay upon the tracks, but no train whistled into sight. The thing did not, as it were, come off according to schedule. No train had passed over these tracks for years. After the necessary judicial preliminaries Madame Sarao was entrusted to the good offices of Mr. Ellis.

Now hanging, that is, a good hanging, contrary to popular notions, causes death not by suffocation, but, to use the proper scientific jargon, by fracturing or dislocating the first three cervical vertebrae and so damaging the vital centres of the spinal cord that death immediately ensues. The knot of the noose is expertly tied behind the ear; and a drop of from six to eight feet, depending on the victim's weight, is allowed. In the Sarao case, the two men accomplices came first, Leone Gagliardi and Angelo Donofrio. They were tied back to back and dropped from two nooses through the same trap.

But when Madame Sarao was sprung, she dropped to the ground, her head completely torn off, the decapitated corpse a geyser of blood.

Reporters spoke of a bungled job. Letters were written to editors. Lawyers appealed to the Minister of Justice for what purpose it is not understood, not, I imagine, to ask for a new trial; and Ellis offered me his explanation.

'The length of the drop' – Ellis adopted a school-master's manner – 'is determined by the weight of the condemned person. The jail authorities give me a slip of paper indicating the weight of the unfortunate prisoner, and I make my calculations accordingly. Here,' he took a much fingered piece of paper from his breast-pocket – 'is the slip pertaining to Madame Sarao.' It indicated an average avoirdupois. 'Naturally I allowed for a greater drop. But in fact she weighed one hundred and eighty pounds. The law of gravity tore her head off. And mind you the authorities at Bordeaux jail are not at fault – they had no scales, and so they merely guessed her weight. A million-dollar institution without a twenty-dollar pair of scales.

'Anyway, after the execution, a reverend father of the Franciscan Order told me in the presence of officials that her death was more humane than that of her husband. So that's that.'

'I know murders and murderesses as nobody else does, and tell you that the death penalty is highly necessary, – no, not to provide me with a livelihood – but as a deterrent against crime. I have met them, these faddists, and so-called humanitarians who by their maudlin sentimentality work to defeat the ends of justice.' He spoke like a letter to the editor, and indeed he was quoting one of his own, 'What right have they to consider themselves a higher court of authority than that of our judges, and juries, and our department of justice? No doubt they are well-meaning, but if they had their way, British justice would become a mockery indeed.'

But this he would concede: hanging is not the best method of execution. It belonged to a past age, and electrocution, he felt was much better in every way. He criticized the inadequate equipment usually supplied by the county authorities in small centres, citing an execution in Woodstock, Ontario, which he understood was carried out in a woodshed. But capital punishment of some kind was absolutely necessary. That viewpoint he could not change.

What execution, if any, was he most reluctant to perform? Ellis did not stop to weigh and ponder.

'That of Louis Morel,' he replied. 'You remember the Hochelaga Bank hold-up and the murder of Henri Cleroux, the bank messenger. Louis Morel, an ex-detective was one of the six who paid for that crime. A fine fellow. I knew him well. We used to wrestle and play soccer together' – and then, sententious, 'he lived a fool, and died a man.

'Well, the day before the execution, I came into his cell. "Arthur" he said, "that underworld grapevine was trying to make me believe that you would not be here for my execution, but I am glad to see that you came."

"I am sorry I had to come," I said. "Why are you glad?"

"Because I want to ask you a favour."

"Anything, Louis, that doesn't interfere with my duty. Anything".' He is sincere about that duty line; he hands it out evidently, even to his best friends.

' "Well, Arthur, if ever you have made a quick job, do it for me to-morrow."

'And by God, that was the quickest job I ever did in my life.' He rose to go. One last question.

Did he ever compare notes with other executioners?

He did not. I regretted, as he left the office, that he had never met Diebler, le Monsieur de Paris whose avocation was gardening, or the Polish executioner who attempted suicide by hanging and bungled the job. What a triumvirate they would have made!

He put his hat on his head and said 'See you again,' and I said, 'In my office.'

The Tale of the Marvellous Parrot

Who has not heard of the rebbe of Berditchev?

The rumour of his sanctity has travelled beyond the farthest steppes; his piety is as a proverb even on the isles of the sea. Indeed, in the remotest hamlets of the Exile, they still say: as holy as the rebbe of Berditchev.

Beautiful was he to behold! When he walked through the streets of the village, so handsome was he, and so saintly, that little children were told: There goes the Angel Gabriel's brother, with his wings wrapped inside his sleeves!

Than the rebbe of Berditchev's chassidim, no happier crew in piety frolicked. They danced for the glory of God, but their feet were never sore; they clapped their hands to the tempo of their song, but never were they wearied. At twilight on the Sabbath at the Third Feast, when they ate at the rebbe's table his white bread and his herring, white bread was heavenly food, and herring a foretaste of leviathan!

When the rebbe smiled, the *shekinah* settled on his face.

When the rebbe smiled, such brilliance encompassed his presence that all the chassidim recited the benediction prescribed for the beholding of a rainbow!

And the rebbe smiled often. Was not the world full of pleasant things, God's face mirrored in it as in a pool of quiet waters? Were not his chassidim'lach, garbed and caftan'd in holiness, the chosen of the chosen? And was not the rebbe's spouse, Naomi, daughter of the rebbe of Zamosz, to be prized above rubies?

O, she was a treasure in the rebbe's house! When upon Sabbath afternoons she read from book devotional, the rebbe would sit and listen, thinking: If my good deeds, such as they are, and the good deeds of my chassidim fail to pry open the door of heaven, surely my Naomi will pray us into a portion of paradise.

Who could say as she blessed the candles of a Friday night whether indeed it was she who blessed *them*, or whether they, flickering and whispering, did not utter the blessing over her, pillar of purity and light?

But alas, alas, – from every house in Israel may the Lord forfend it – no child was born unto the rebbe of Berditchev.

The chassidim whispered among themselves: Let us search our hearts; perhaps for some unknown sin, the *Rebono shel Olam* has visited this punishment upon us that our rebbe should hear no *Kaddish*.

Once, as the rebbe sat at his table, telling wonderful tales touching the patriarchs, and was in the midst of the tale of Father Abraham and the Three Angels, a chassid, bolder than the rest, made mention of their secret thought.

No, my chassidim'lach, the rebbe said, you are blameless.

Thereafter for many days the rebbe fasted. He grew spare and lean so that when ecstasy took hold of him during prayers, he was seen almost to float from off the ground. But his prayers seemed unanswered.

The rebbe called together all the beggars of Berditchev, and gave them alms. This availed not.

Conning every sacred word, weighing it like a nugget, the chassidim sat all day long in the synagogue, reciting psalms. They hoped thus to storm the gates of heaven for the rebbe's name. In vain.

Then the rebbe said: It is written: Prayer, fasting and alms annul the severity of God's decree. I have prayed; I have fasted; I have given alms. Now a greater penitence is required of me. I must take upon myself the yoke of exile.

When the rebbe, with staff and knapsack, set out upon his journeying, not knowing whither, the chassidim wept and were downcast in spirit. Gone. Departed from our midst! they cried, breaking their fingers backwards.

Unknown, and in beggar's raiment, the rebbe journeyed from place to place. Folk beheld, and noticed the glow of godliness shining above his rags. One of the thirty-six! they said, a *lamed-vov'nik*!

For many months the chassidim heard no news of their Master. The sweet Naomi was very sad. In the court of the rebbe there was silence and sorrow as if *mithnagdim* had taken possession of it.

Then one day there came a courier from a distant land, bringing tidings. He had seen the rebbe in the East, debating with heathen philosophers, and confounding the infidel. It was also rumoured that he was steeping himself in the lore of the Cabbala, learning the mysteries of creation, and was already in spirit approaching the seventh altitude of wisdom. Men said that he could understand the language of bird and beast.

Whither is he going from the lands of the East, the chassidim asked.

To Jerusalem, the holy, the courier replied, there where the atmosphere of the land renders one wise to snatch the veil from off the face of the secret. Then he will come back to his chassidim.

And indeed, on a sunny morning there walked into town, barefoot, and in tatters, the rebbe of Berditchev, a staff in his right hand, and on his wrist – a parrot! A many-coloured parakeet! Green and blue and red and yellow, a rainbow shone upon its throat!

After the chassidim had welcomed their teacher, and had banqueted, and had sung joyous songs, and danced ecstatic dances, the rebbe retired into his chamber of meditation, taking his parrot along with him.

The rebbe understands the language of birds, the chassidim whispered, he is seeking to snatch out of the parrot's beak some ancient hoary secrets.

Many years passed, and still the rebbe had no heir.

Throughout all this time, the rebbe did but occasionally show himself to his disciples. Rather he preferred the company of the parrot, would spend hours with it closeted in his study, and the *gabbai* who stood guard at the rebbe's door, reported that sometimes he would hear strange voices beyond the threshold.

Darken that day, and blot it out from memory: The rebbe passed to his eternal rest!

The chassidim mourned. Naomi was all tears, crying with one breath: *The Lord giveth and the Lord taketh away, blessed be the name of the Lord forever,* and with another, Woe is me, that I have lived to see this day.

The chassidim approached the coffin to the synagogue, threw open the doors of the Ark of the Covenant, and the cantor began his prayer, when suddenly, out of the rebbe's chamber of meditation, adjacent to the Beth Ha-Midrash, there issued, fluttering, its throat green and blue and yellow, a flying rainbow, the rebbe's parrot, and settled upon one of the posts of the almemar, and it cried:

Yisgadal v'yiskadash shmai raba!

Bitter was the weeping at the rebbe's passing, but bitterer still that a parrot uttered his *Kaddish*.

Memoirs of a Campaigner

Some day, when my friend and master, Alter Chodosh, will at long last cease from trouble to retire on the mythical pension list of superannuated Zionist campaigners, he will no doubt take a year off from the then useless years which remain for him to compile a text-book on the art of campaigning. He will probably, if I judge his Hibernian Hebraisms aright, title it: *A Treatise on the Strategy of Withdrawing Contributions from Reluctant and Stiff-necked Hebrews, or, The Voluntary Tax, and How to Make Them Pay It*. He has a special aptitude for such a work; if he is not exactly the King of Schnorrers, a princeling in that realm he most certainly is. For if all the thresholds which he crossed, seeking to beard the lion in his den, were laid end to end, the resultant would assuredly suffice for a bridge from exile to Eretz Israel; and if all the elevators, which he rode in search of lofty contributors, were to add up their vertical mileage, Alter Chodosh would find himself plumb at the door of heaven.

In the meantime, swearing allegiance only to the Funds, Chodosh has no time for literary endeavours. Memoirs, he says, are written by those who have nothing further to do in this world except to remember. And Alter Chodosh still has some fat Jeshuruns to canvass.

'I was born to be a canvasser. Even my name is etymological cousin to *Altneuland*. For the sake of Zion, I cannot keep my peace.'

As a disturber of the peace of the smug of Israel, Chodosh has organized his tactics into a science. For every Jew, a different approach. *Quot Judaei, tot sententiae.*

'The vast majority of our people,' says he, 'are the most notoriously lavish givers upon the face of the earth. *Rachmonim bnai rachmonim*, compassionate children of the compassionate, you have but to utter the mildest sort of whimper, the meekest kind of *weh*, and they will forthwith tent their pocketbooks over you, like a refuge in the desert. Sometimes, indeed, they are too munificent; they don't practise generosity; they perpetrate it. They give without discrimination. As it is written: You ask a contribution for the Ark of the Covenant, they give; a contribution for the Calf of Gold, again they give!

'But some there are, alas and alack-a-day! Paralysis sits upon their fists, like a glove. Their uncovered palm is like the tomb of Moses: no man has seen it. *Lakchonim bnai rachmonim*, they have learned only half of the game of give-and-take.

'No, may the Lord forfend, I am not speaking ill of my people. The non-givers are not the wicked ones; they are merely sick ones. Physical wrecks, they suffer either from such pressure on the brain that their eyes are affected, and they can't see their own future, or they suffer from constriction of the heart. Constriction of the heart is a very contagious disease; it spreads immediately to the cheque-book in the bosom-pocket. These men, I must note, don't live long as Jews; they lose at least one month a year. For he who has a wide *lev*, alas, too frequently, has a narrow *kis* and vice versa. All in all, at the end of the year's accounting you find yourself minus Kislev.

'I mustn't forget the sufferers from intellectual diabetes. The world is so sweet for them, they can't understand their brothers' bitterness.

'The worst prospects are the laconics. You come in to see him, and like the fellow in the melodrama, he won't talk. As far as he is concerned, you are thousands of miles away – in Palestine. His conversation consists of long stretches of silence interrupted by looks at his wristwatch. Like the penurious photographer, he won't even give you a negative. Sometimes, however, he relents;

he opens wide the floodgates of his speech and says NO. He is like the Jew with the tuft of beard; of whom my father, may he rest in peace, told me to beware. My father would say: A Jew with a long beard, *nishkoshe*, you ask him for a donation or a loan, he takes hold of his beard, strokes it, and says *I will consider*. A Jew with no beard scratches his shave, and says the same. But a Jew with a short beard, he lays hold of it, and with an impetuous *tzip*, ejaculates; *Nein, ich gib nisht!*

'Such an one I goad into speech. I taunt him, I bait him. I speak about his arrival on the Mayflower, tourist class. I compliment him on the fact that some of his best friends are Jews. Only when I am driven into a corner by his persistent silence, full of pity for my U.P.A. card which has grown pale with blankness, do I point out to him that he cannot separate himself from the congregation, that he is not a nation by himself, and that even if he does flirt with assimilation, there still is a drop of his grandmother's, if not his grandfather's blood in him, and that, quoting Sokolow: If you won't follow the straight line of the law of Moses, you will have to follow the curved one of your noses ...

'I hate to hook an argument onto a nose. But tradition compels me. According to ancient lore, a child, prior to its birth, knows the entire Torah. At birth, an angel arrives and fillips him upon the nose, whereupon he forgets his prenatal erudition, and all of life becomes a process of recollecting the forgotten. I, therefore, practise homeopathy. What a fillip on the nose can undo, another fillip can do. The angel fillips Jewry to forget; and Alter Chodosh fillips them to remember.

'By contrast to the tight-lipped contributor, there is the loquacious one, the bridge-table diplomat, the café statesman. "What?" he says, "I should give money, and Jews are being killed in Palestine." Believe me, he doesn't mean it as crudely as that; he is merely looking for a peg for conversation. He knows the answers to his ejaculations as well as you do; he knows the profound difference between the recorded number of lives lost in the building of a nation's future, and the number of lives (unrecorded) which are breathed out upon the fetid air in the miasmic corners of Eastern ghettoes, lives lost to no purpose, vain and futile sacrifices; he knows, – as who does not? – the essential difference between creative sacrifice in the Homeland and chaotic disintegration in the Diaspora. Indeed, he probably has his cheque in his desk-drawer, signed and stamped. But he wants his money's worth, – a talk on international politics, a *shmoos* about England. Take him into your confidence; tell him what Weizmann is planning. For his contribution he wants to be a Cabinet Minister.

'My nemesis, however, is the charity-Jew. Somewhere, sometime, he learned a slogan: Charity begins at home; and on each occasion that I cross his door, bringing him regards from the homeland, he lies in wait for me, and hits me over the head with this literary shillelagh. As if I was a mortal enemy of the local orphan and widow! As if I had come to steal a crumb out of the mouths of the needy! But soon my wrath turns to pity. This man doesn't want a reprimand; he lacks an education. He doesn't even begin to understand the rudiments of Zionism. Zionism is not charity; it is statecraft. Thirty years ago, Nordau began teaching his generation his *aleph beth* and still there are Jews who haven't advanced beyond the *kometz-aleph-o*. Nordau said: The philanthropist, good soul though he be, addresses the enemies of Israel, saying: "You beat our Jews, we will send them aid; again you beat them, again we will send them aid. We will see who gets tired first!"

'Well, Zionism is not an endurance contest. Jewry is in pain; we don't want merely to alleviate it with charity; we want to cure it with a Homeland. Too long has our sole boast, uttered out of agony and despair, been: We have outlived the Pharaohs, we have outlived the Hamans, we will outlive this present tyrant too. We have been a people of outlivers. Now, on our own soil, we want merely to live!

'There are other types of *achainu bnai Yisrael*. God knows that a canvasser's work is utterly thankless; as compensation, He gives him variety in the Jews he has to call upon. Amongst these, I mustn't forget the patriot. That is the man who doesn't sleep nights because he is afraid that he will be suspected of double allegiance. As a result, he is a greater monarchist than the king, and more Canadian than the Iroquois. This man is not a scholar in Zionism; but in Canadianism he is a veritable ignoramus. He forgets that very English piece of advice which Shakespeare measured off for him in pentametre: *To thine own self be true, it follows then, as the night the day, thou canst not be untrue to any man.* But even if he doesn't recall his Shakespeare, I shall probably issue forth with this contribution, because, you see, we are very fortunate that Palestine is a British mandate. What will I do, however, when the patriot will move out to his son-in-law in New York? Teach him Shakespeare all over again?

'And now, my friend, you will pardon me. I have another important card to canvass. This is a Jew who told me that Palestine was just like his wife. On Monday she asks him for five dollars, on Tuesday for ten, on Wednesday again, and so on throughout the week. "What," I asked, "does she do with all that money?" "I don't know," he answered. "I never give it to her."

'Well, now I must hurry to tell him some interesting news. His boarder ran off with his wife. And I want to remind him that Palestine, which he so endearingly dubs his wife, and treats accordingly, also has an Arab boarder who is acquisitively and romantically inclined.'

Detective Story, or A Likely Story

The prospect of what he was about to do exhilarated him. Merely to think upon it was achievement. Never before, he knew, had anyone dared conceive of such a project and on such a scale, conceive let alone execute. Here it was – the perfect crime, the crime unprecedented in its ravages and perfect in its accomplishments.

With ironic pleasure, he already lingered over the details of the grand unparallelled plan he had devised. From no one, he reflected with pride, had he copied it; no one had inspired a single one of its beauties. Sinister flash of his imagination, fully-clothed had it sprung into being. It was nonpareil; for generations men would marvel at the boldness of the scheme, at the impressive scope of its devastation, at the subtle finesse with which it would be carried out.

It couldn't be otherwise. Had they ever before beheld or even heard of a crime of this kind, so harrowing in its extent, so breath-taking – apt word! – in its impeccably aesthetic consummation. He considered its novelties.

In the first place, it would be a crime without a motive. Search, pry, investigate, theorize as one would, one would never be able to discover the intent, the purpose behind the perpetration. One might perhaps suspect malice, but one would never be able to fathom motive. At last – it was inevitable – the detectives, the lawyers, the psychologists would be compelled to conceal their frustration in that poor substitute for a motive – the crime for crime's sake. A pitiable begging of the question.

And this, – afflatus thrilled him – was already an achievement of the first order. How could one ever begin to set the wheels of justice in motion against the unspeakable – and, if you please, inexplicable – iniquity, when one could not begin to give a reasonable explanation, yes a plausible excuse for the doing of the fell deed? They were stumped right at the outset, baffled and foiled even before they began.

This surely was a victory. Yet – his fastidious standards drove him onward – to conceal the crime completely and without trace, to cover the act in utter darkness, in short, to deprive his opponents of even a fighting chance, would be, after all, for him not much of a victory. Not for him. No, – he knew now that this was a *sine qua non* – purposely he would leave numberless clues in the wake of his criminal act, the overt act, clues everywhere, footprints here, fingerprints there, some lint from his clothing, some dust from his garments. The plan, in fact, would be full of clues. The crime, indeed, would be all of clues compact. And yet – of this he was convinced – helpless would they be to deduce their meaning, to read his signature, to establish his identity!

Nor would he resort to the cheap panic-born tricks of the excited bungler who wished to conceal the *corpus delicti*, in a weighted sack in water, in a lime-pit, in a furnace. The victim of the crime would remain, there for all to see; in fact, there would be more than one victim, more than one *corpus delicti*, – tens, hundreds. That, for the sake of his reputation, was essential. It was true that the encompassing of such a result might take time; but it was worth it.

Nor would all his victims, he determined, perish at the same moment. After all, he was not a pogrom-artist, a mere butcher. Properly spaced would they be, the fates which awaited his victims; each would behold his fellow dying, smugly feel himself safe, and then, without notice or warning, he, too, would be snatched away from life. Certainly that was the only method for an artist to adopt; it was a procedure which had style, effectiveness, and duration. It indicated, first of all, the existence of a system, an inscrutable system, but system nonetheless; furthermore, it afforded the artist an aesthetic satisfaction which was not, like these satisfactions usually were, rapturous and short, but controlled and indefinite; and finally, it enhanced that satisfaction by adding to the pleasure of perfectly accomplished crime the additional delight of actually and repeatedly witnessing the terrors of its anticipation.

Yet, as a matter of blueprint fact, at no time would the victims really suspect that a snare was being set for them, that their doom was sealed, that he, at last, had come around to them. The survivors, perhaps, might at moments entertain the suspicion that there was something not quite right about the manner of their passing, but it would rarely be more than that. Indeed, the survivors would in all probability – such was the very nature of the scheme he had laid out – be divided into two categories: those who suspected murder but possessed, despite ubiquitous clues, omnipresent *corpora delictorum*, and irresistible intuition no positive proof to substantiate their suspicions; and those – this he thought a noteworthy refinement – those who even applauded his workmanship.

In his mind's eye he saw it all, right from the very first move he was to make down to the last tentative attempts which would be everywhere undertaken to discover his identity. In anticipation he rejoiced at the consternation and confusion his acts would cause, at first the terror, then the frantic attempts at self-preservation, then the many and complicated ventures presumably intended to appease him, but really designed to draw him out into the open. He smiled at the prospect. How enraged, how mortified – that was the word – mortified they would be, knowing of every one of the enormities he had perpetrated, but not knowing, never knowing, who had perpetrated them. He even foresaw, with an amused pride, the report recording his achievements: it would detail the incidents of his career, tabulate the steps in his *modus operandi*; its opening sentence – he was sure – would read: In the beginning He created the heaven and the earth.

We Who Are About to Be Born: A Parable

At last the day had come. From eternity through all the millennial ages, as one after another the populations of babes left their celestial homes, always had he known that the day would come when he, too, like those multitudes which had pre-birthed him, would have to make his appearance in that unspeakable place. It seemed to be one of the rules of heaven – a rule established from of yore – that every year a certain number had to go. There was plenty of wailing among the chosen bambinos; but it availed nothing; you could not, at this stage, expect to stay on forever. The earth had to be peopled, too; and often it happened that even the most venerable of cherubim, cherubim who, peeping through the stars, had been witnesses at creation, were chosen to undergo their earthly existence. On them it was especially hard because they invariably felt as if they enjoyed certain acquired rights to remain in the place, a certain title, by prescription, to non-birth. But even these had to submit to the Law.

Now Raphael the wise cherub, most adult in intelligence, and in demeanour of course talcum-fresh and baby-like, stood before the implacable Commissioners. There were two of them, and they never divided in opinion. They never even varied their joint opinion. It was always one and the same, eon after eon, millennium after millennium: You *must be born*. You *must be born*, like the ticking of a watch, like the murmur of an ocean, like the monotonous whisper of all the sands of the earth. And now he who century after century had heard with a continuous sense of reprieve the four hastening syllables push the wailing generations into life, himself stood before the heralds, accouchant, proclaiming his doom. He would have to be born!

He didn't want to be born. He was quite happy and certainly contented in his present milieu. What with the fleecy clouds, what with the music, thrilling because it always seemed new, as if reaching some untouched spot in the ear, satisfying because always so familiar, and what with the great variety of incidents that kept happening, he couldn't think of a better place to be, nor of a better – a sad thought it was – pre-nativity to have. Already he had lived here, time out of mind, and was still, in innocence, in untouched wholeness, the complete babe. But nine months earlier – it seemed like but a song ago – he had protested with all his callow might when he had been informed that the arrangements had been made, his passport obtained, his visa initialled, and that soon, soon he would have to undertake his voyage into the unknown.

'How can you be so cruel,' he had asked, 'so cruel as to send me, with all the memories of this pleasant place into that dark valley of the shadow? For I have seen them, my predecessors, seen them returning from this wonderful voyage, full of scars and wrinkles, broken, the marks of a terrible experience upon them. And now from these heights –'

'You need not worry,' the Commissioner had said, 'here we think of everything. The angel Gabriel will attend to you; he will give you, as is the custom, a fillip on the nose, and in that moment you will forget everything you ever experienced here.'

'So I won't even have memories; them you will take away from me, too, not even a past, with which to greet the unseen.'

'You will have new memories. There you will begin accumulating new memories. Moreover, the memory of your stay here will never really be forgotten; you will have no clear recollection of your hitherto days, of course, but always you will have a fractional intuition, a sort of dim remembrance, a haunting confusion. You will know you have been somewhere, but where, precisely, you will not know. Our home will breathe in you; but you will have lost the map.'

And now, the day before birth, he was making his last appeal.

'Why can't somebody else go? Why must it be me? There are billions of cherubim still uninitiated. Why must I be the one to be un-heaven'd?'

'Because' – the Commissioner was most pontifical – 'if it weren't you, it would be another; and that other, too, would have the right to make the same expostulations as you. With the same result. None. For it is decreed.'

'Well,' the celestial embryo decided to take a new line. 'Well, I don't like the father you picked for me. I remember him when he was here as a bambino – a nasty fellow, no one could get along with him, and everybody was happy when he was born. Now, he is to be my father, which is on earth. At least, give me another, preferably –'

'Yes, preferably one that has not yet been born, no doubt. Sorry, young fellow, you are altogether too smart – but not too smart to live.' And the one Commissioner turned to the other, and as if by a signal, they both laughed. Also, after a while, at the very same instant, they both stopped laughing.

The little one about-to-be-born, the tiny gerund of life knew now that it was hopeless. His judges were calloused by their profession, they had seen so many go through the same frantic reluctancies, so many pass into the lesser Beyond that another infant setting out upon the trodden path touched them not at all. Nonetheless, the cherub wouldn't surrender. In a last fit of desperation, he pleaded with the Heavenly Midwives – there is no sex in heaven, though there should be, and we don't know whether midwives is the just word, but doubtlessly maieutic was their function – pleaded that his little bones were too soft to suffer the ordeal of life; that he knew beforehand that the climate would not agree with him; that even though he wasn't very enthusiastic about his appointed father, he still didn't care to add another burden to his father's already heavy load of living; that he would be content to remain in heaven, even without any of its privileges; that the whole business was not very sensible inasmuch as it would be much wiser to transport all of the earth's inhabitants back to their first home and re-establish things as they were in the good old days; that he really wasn't strong enough – he was repeating himself – and would no doubt come back in a very short time, so why send him at all; and that in any event the fear, the fear of being born had already been so vividly experienced that the Commissioners might just as well regard him as one of those who already had the necessary Past.

There was another one of those joint pre-ordained laughs; the which completed, the cherub was led away by a couple of cherubic smug survivors. He was led away, shouting and weeping, offering to have his wings clipped, never again to indulge in song, to stay in solitary confinement on a cloud, to live only on manna and nectar, to turn stool-cherub and help the Commissioners discover others fit to be born, to do anything, anything, if only they would let him Not Be. At the end, he was shockingly incoherent, calling a Mother, again and again.

On the following day, he ate a hearty breakfast. When asked for a last wish, he suggested an abortion. He appeared to be in high spirits, but when the Angel Gabriel, attired in rubber gloves and white coat, came to give him the final send-off he went hysterical again. Unable to walk to his destiny, he was carried; the last thing he remembered was the fillip of forgetfulness.

And, as it must to all, birth came to the heavenly cherub, now of the earth, earthy.

One More Utopia

Was thinking about a world of universal love when suddenly there walked into my mind – without knocking and without me even having heard his approaching footsteps – a man with a most compelling manner. It was his manner which was the noticeable thing about him, for his face was the least distinguished, most ordinary countenance I had ever beheld. Eyes, ears, nose, mouth – each in its proper place, and each of average dimensions. The kind of face you saw and immediately forgot, remembering only that you had seen a face, the man was not headless, he had a face. Interrupting my dialogue with self, he told me that he, too, had given thought to utopia, had experimented with various forms of it, and had at last succeeded, not only in devising, but in establishing the perfect, the ideal social community. Would I like to visit it?

Across a long stretch of indistinct and unidentified thought he led me until we stood, in a moonlit haze, on wide rolling grounds fronting a skyscraper. Incongruous, I thought, this metropolitan architecture midst country scenery; I was about to make some comment, but my guide showed so proud an expression on his face that I kept my opinions to myself, following him meekly as he strode up the walk toward the dimly-lit entrance of the great edifice. As we mounted floor after floor in the automatic elevator, a mingled odour of chloroform, ether, and carbolic was wafted on the air; it grew stronger and stronger with every burst of green which flashed its number on the floor-board. At last, the elevator stopped, and we entered a long whitewashed corridor. The drafts which rushed around its corners were definitely antiseptic.

A hospital, I said.

My utopia, he answered.

Oh, I said, the common misery of pain.

I couldn't conceal the sneer in my voice. I had expected an epigram and after having been dragged over God knows what distance, had been rewarded with a *cliché*!

No, no, no, not that, he said, though the democracy of disease is not to be despised. My experiment is built on firmer foundations. Of the solidarity of the sick, it is like this: cured the illness, gone the solidarity. But my work lasts, lasts, my friend, beyond the fevers and the chills.

A doctor? I asked.

After a fashion, but primarily a sculptor. Can't show you my complete studio now but I'll let you have a glimpse.

He approached a door, and mounting a ladder which stood near it, he pushed a little wooden panel set over the lintel.

Here, he said, have a look at the Kingdom of Heaven.

Through the opening I peered onto a very long room, obviously not a studio, there was motion everywhere, a dormitory I surmised. Its lights were shaded, I couldn't distinguish very much, but I could at least see that it held about a hundred persons. They all seemed to be engaged in conversation, naturally I couldn't make out what they were saying. Quite an ordinary scene, I thought, yet all the time, I felt, without being able to say why, that there was something unusual, something actually queer about the attitude, the gestures, the action, the whole atmosphere which filled the room.

See what I mean, said my guide.

I didn't answer, I knew there was meaning, but I had not yet identified the peculiarity which seemed to approach and then to recede from my understanding. I saw a man bring a glass of water to another; another man fix a pillow for his neighbor, others engaged in what seemed to be very sincere conversation; a man reading to his friend. Then I realized it all at once: there wasn't a single occupant who was not in one way or another doing something for his fellow-occupant; and all of them, the obligers and the obliged, appeared to be patients! No nurses! No orderlies!

Very economical, anyway, I said.

What economy, my guide asked.

Very economical – this grand cooperative effort in mutual hospitalization. Isn't it?

That's a view of it, he said, but not the whole view. I see that you don't quite grasp the social basis of my policy. Better stay until morning, and I will introduce you to my citizens – the only completely equal, totally happy and supremely religious community on the face of the earth. Tomorrow?

Tomorrow, I said, and it was tomorrow and I was looking at 'the citizens' again, only this time I was inside the dormitory. Again I was impressed by that spirit of friendliness, of an overwhelming amiability, a meticulous and exemplary considerateness which pervaded the room. It was as if everybody were playing a game: illustrate the Golden Rule. It was as if the milk of human kindness was being poured from fifty jugs into fifty glasses, all at the same time, and as if the glasses were being poured back into the jugs, and the operation repeated and repeated, in an infinity of variations. It was as if I was standing in a ward where one treated those touched by a lunacy called kindness. Altogether too much kindness.

Then I made the discovery which I had failed to make the night before when I looked through the glimmering dusk of the peep-hole. Startled, I said to my host, said without turning my face to him, so transfixed was I by the revelations,

But where did you get them all?

That you should have asked yesterday. Why do you ask?

I could hear him smiling.

All of them look exactly alike! But exactly! Peas in a pod! All of one face, every blessed man of them looking like the other's double! It must have taken you years to round them up!

We were now standing in the very midst of a group of citizens. I turned to my host for his answer. But which was my host? Everyone about me looked like everyone else, including the man – I had not heard him move, I had just heard him speak – who had brought me here.

He made himself known. You better not lose me, he said.

I won't, positively.

I grabbed his arm, and we walked away. The dormitory with its hundred heads kept staring at me, kept looking at my face, *my* face. I hastened my step, hurrying my host along with me.

It did take me quite a while – I heard him saying behind me – to collect my raw material. And it was raw. You should have seen it. But I managed, I fixed them all right.

We were not out of the dormitory. I looked at him inquiringly.

With my own little chisel, that's how I did it. Plastic surgery, the divine sculpture. All of these people, of course, were originally patients. War casualties. Faces burned, faces scarred, faces distorted. I was to make them look like human beings again. That I did. I built up a nose here, I grafted a cheek there; they came here faceless, and after a while they got themselves faces, each according to his wounds, his burns, his bone structure. For months I went along the routine of my work, a geographer and engineer of the human countenance. The results were surgically speaking good; but not really what I was after. The patients went out into society again, were received among people without shudders or disgust; everything seemed alright but there was something missing. To me, anyway. The landscaping of these faces was right, but the climate was wrong. There was something missing.

I could see that he wanted me to interrupt him.

What? I asked.

The face behind the face. They didn't match. Not subject to surgery. The human personality – the soul, if you prefer that unscientific term – is not subject to plastic surgery. The scars which their experiences had left upon their minds remained, the memory of the ordeals which they had suffered could not be banished. Not by sutures and graftings. Something more was needed, but what, what? Yet I was stupid not to realize it before, it was so simple: The reason for the misery of my patients was due to the fact that although they had been made to look more or less like other people do, they *knew* their experience had been different. No surgery could correct that knowledge, all surgery could do was make them just not look like freaks, but beneath the skin – well, there they were still scarred. Even their improved faces, altered, surgically perfect, were constant reminders. I decided, therefore to do things differently, like you see.

You mean everybody with the same face?

Everybody with the same face, all in my own image, and all kept together. I thus operated not only on their bodies, I operated on their world. Even the doctor was not an intruder, but one of them. And let me tell you, it worked. The ego which looked at its own face and saw that it was the face of its fellows, lost its personal insistence. Citizen No. 1 merged his personality with citizen No. 2. He looked at his neighbor and it was as if he was looking at a mirror. All about him he saw Self; his own face met him everywhere. Naturally, all the egos were soon fused, and naturally egotism soon became altruism, altruism egotism. I had achieved the first premise for utopia!

Neat, but how, if I may make so bold to ask, how is it that you, doctor, remain unaffected. Your ego, if you'll pardon my saying so, has managed somehow to escape fusion?

True, he said, but my face, please note, is really my own. No plastic surgeon gave it to me. When I look at myself I recognize somebody I knew from the first dawning of consciousness, but my citizens, my citizens with their brand-new faces, they were just born, their old selves have died, and their new self now appears for the first time and in duplicate, in triplicate, in centuplicate. An important difference.

I'll say, I said.

Then he vanished from my side, and I think I remained in that utopia for quite a long time, watching the great experiment in human relations, the collaboration of the carbon copies. Everything was going fine, according to premise, harmony and peace and goodwill, love reigning supreme as they say, until one day I encountered my host in the dormitory, or studio or polity, whatever you want to call it, and I noticed that he had changed. He had changed. I could recognize him from his 'citizens.' His citizens still remained an indistinguishable company, but him I could recognize.

What's the matter, I said.

How did you know?

Know what? I said. Is there anything to know? I just mean you're looking bad. You look worried. Lines on your face. They weren't there before. Do you know I can now tell you from your patients?

It really shows, doesn't it? he said. You have no idea what I've lived through. It's not going good at all. They're running out on me.

Their faces stand up all right, don't they?

Not that, he said. Suicide. They write little letters and then slit their throats. Can't stand the environment, they say. Just don't want to live any more. The monotony must have got them. Now I have to employ guards. Guards, guards in utopia! It's falling apart, the world I built is falling apart.

At this moment, as if it really was the end of the world, we heard a loud screaming, an unbroken and hysterical screaming. A citizen was doing the screaming. He was held by two guards, and was struggling to make himself free. Let me out of here, he was shouting, I can't stand it any more! Day in, day out, the same face, wherever you look the same face, it's driving me crazy. And the face, the face of an outsider, our enemy. Give me back, please give me back – he was blubbering now – my own face, the one with the scars, the burns, it's my own face, my own face.

He covered it with his hands.

Yes doctor, ain't love wonderful, all day long loving your own image, kind to your own double, and a hundred of them, caressing yourself, petting yourself – it's obscene, that's what it is, disgustingly obscene. Let me out of here. Please, I want to be human again; different, even if revolting. I want to be myself again; my real self, not one per cent of a composite nothing.

He had managed to struggle himself up to the doctor.

You killed me, he said. Murderer!

They dragged him away. It's spreading, the doctor said.

We went back into the doctor's office. He sat down in his chair, as if exhausted. This has become a house of hate, he said.

Then it happened. Along the corridors we could hear a rushing noise, a great turbulence, a sound of marching feet and clamorous voices. The sounds came closer and closer. They were purposeful, they were threatening. They're coming said the doctor, hear them?

The high heavens could hear them. Give us back ourselves, they were shouting. I opened the door and looked down the moving passageway. In I don't know how many blurred versions, the Face was approaching. You thought you'd make us all one, a voice was shouting, well, here we are, all one! After all, cried another, if we kill the doctor, it's only suicide!

The Trail of 'Clupea Harengus'
The Scientific Detective Story and How She Is
Writ for Summer Reading

Hilary Lance returned from his walk in the park, whither he had ventured forth to meditate upon Aristotle's anthropophagi. God-like, he regarded the sun-drenched afternoon, and saw that it was good. On earth there was peace, and towards men goodwill; a whole morning had elapsed and no murder had as yet been drawn to his attention. Mounting the stairs of his home, he whistled that popular tune – his very own composition, words and music – the *Blue Clues Blues*, and upon reaching the door, he opened it, by force of habit, with a skeleton-key.

With the help of his valet, he got into his smoking-jacket, upon which was woven, in code, the thirty-six plots of Gozzi, an habiliment which the renowned detective considered conducive towards the easy unravelling of those intricate criminological puzzles with which he was daily faced. It was thus, he boasted, that he could pull out, as it were, solutions, otherwise elusive, from his oracular sleeve, and thus it was, he averred, that he could wear his brain upon his cuff. Jervis kneeled before him to slip upon Hilary's feet those pneumatic-soled slippers, which gave him a cat-like tread. Then the great psychologist lit his pipe and his cigarette, and with both in his mouth, lost himself in a brown study, a study ornamented with smoke-rings which he blew into a linked chain, the better thus to observe the distinction between the two kinds of fumes. Lance always puffed away at his pipe and cigarette simultaneously, the pipe for intuition, and the cigarette for finesse, so that while the one side of his face – the pipe side –

seemed always inspired, the other retained an air of indubitable nonchalance.

Hardly had Lance settled himself in his comfortable chair, when Jervis somewhat hesitantly intruded to inform his master, that a nautical gentleman had called some while earlier and had left a parcel, saying that he would return anon.

Upon his desk Lance found the mysterious packet. He hesitated before he unwrapped it, for his activities in those *affaires*, as the French have it, since become famous as *The Case of the Mauve Chemise*, *The Run of the Blue Stocking*, *The Mystery of the Pink Tea*, *The Sign of the White Feather*, had brought him many enemies. It was not beyond the realm of possibility, therefore, that an attempt might be made upon his far-too-ratiocinating existence. Lance sniffed at the parcel, smelled smoke, and then carefully and with typical prudence, untied the string and noted the peculiar knots. As he opened it, there was revealed before his eyes, lying in state, exuding a smoky smell, redolent of the briny sea – a fish!

'Ah,' said Lance, 'an exercise in ichthyology! Cast your bread upon the waters, and after many days, Jervis, you will be in the dough. Bring me, bring me my *Compleat Angler*. Perhaps old Izaak Walton will help us fathom this mystery. We are in the Zodiac under the sign of Piscator.'

Lance hastily thumbed the pages of Izaak, but found, in that masterpiece of omniscience, nothing relevant, save: *And this will be no wonder to any that have travelled Egypt; when 'tis known the famous river Nilus does not only breed fishes that yet want names, but by the overflowing of that river and the help of the sun's heat on the fat slime which that river leaves on the banks when it falls back into its natural channel, such strange fish and beasts are also bred, that no men can give a name to, as Grotius, in his Sophom, and others, have observed.*

'Pointless,' sighed Lance, 'it's pointless. Walton corroborates our ignorance. We are up a maritime blind alley. Only detailed examination will identify the fish. So take down, Jervis, the following notes: In the dorsal fin 18 rays; in the anal fin, 17 rays; 55 scales in the lateral line, and 55 vertebrae in the vertebral column; a smooth gill-cover; an ovate patch of very small teeth in the vomer. Noted? Good. Now from the top shelf on the right hand side in the library pull down these books: Belon, *De aquatilibus libri duo*; Salviani, *Aquatilium animalium historia*; Ray and Willoughby, *Historia Piscium*, and Lacepede, *Histoire des Poissons*. If it's not mentioned there, then our fish is an impostor.'

When the heavy volumes were brought to him, Lance busied himself with the indices. At first he seemed puzzled, then as he scented the fish's trail through the labyrinth of the cross references, thick as seaweed in the oceanic paragraphs, he began to work with a feverish haste, and finally he cried:

'I've got it! I've got it! *Clupea harengus*! That's what it is! *Clupea harengus*!

'But, sir, this is a herring, a red herring,' interrupted Jervis, who was not a scientist. It must be remarked here that although Jervis was by vocation a valet, his master – so democratic is mystery which levels all things – frequently – the better to obtain the layman's point of view – invited his cooperation.

'Precisely, *clupea harengus*, termed in the vernacular a herring. But it is red, sanguine. That could have been caused only by paint or by blood. Paint it can not be, for such would have long ere this been washed away by the water. Therefore fee-fi-fo-fum, it must be blood. Blood on the exterior of a fish is not fish-blood; it must be human blood. Jervis, a murder has somewhere been committed. Why, who, or wherefore, I do not as yet know, but a foul deed done – that certainly has come to light.'

'But, sir, would not water have washed away the blood, too?'

'You forget, or you never quite grasped, the workings of that principle known as osmosis, Jervis, os-mos-is. However, be that as it may, let us examine the specimen more thoroughly. Do you observe the bulging eyes of the fish? Who knows what horrible scenes, what fatal combats this herring witnessed before he gasped his last? Who can guess what dire catastrophe these terror-smitten eyes beheld? If only fish could talk! But alas, having no lungs, they have no voices. Besides, this one is dead. But' – Lance held the fish by its caudal extremity. 'It could a tale unfold that would harrow up thy soul.'

Jervis passed his hand over the ridge of the herring. It was cold and clammy. 'It must have died in a cold sweat,' he opined commiseratingly.

'Fish do not perspire. They are cold-blooded creatures. Cold-blooded creatures!' – Lance was reasoning with himself – 'Then, these protruding eyes do not indicate horror and alarm. It must be biliousness. We will perform an autopsy, Jervis.'

The obliging Jervis was about to go for his instruments when Lance called him back.

'Hold a minute. Perhaps there are some clues still concealed upon this silent witness. These' – he pointed at the integuments of the herring – 'these may yet be the scales of justice. *Imprimis*: I have no doubt in my mind that the dastardly deed was perpetrated upon the high seas, else how could this fish not amphibious, have been in such close proximity to it. *Secundo*! The author of the yet unspecified crime is unquestionably a mastermind, one who was fishing or who had fish in his cargo, fish – the brain-food *par excellence*.'

'I suppose,' ventured Jervis, 'that that is how the Bismarck herring gets its name.'

'That,' replied Lance, somewhat peeved at this irrelevant interruption in his logical sorites, 'is neither here nor there, neither hither nor yon, nor ebb nor flow. A mastermind, a diabolical super-intelligence has somehow or other disposed of a human life. But who? That is the question. What was the motive? And who is the skeleton in Davy Jones' locker?'

Both were lost in thought for a long while, each regarding the fish from his own point of view – Jervis, touching and caressing it, as if he were *its* valet, and Lance, with a far-away look in his eyes, contemplating maritime vistas.

Suddenly Jervis stopped his examination, and drawing the attention of his master, pointed:

'Look, sir; these marks upon the herring – they are not natural. A herring is not born with such indentations in its body.'

'Correct, Jervis – not born with them. Like greatness, they have been thrust upon it. These were made by the packing wire, in which this herring was boxed. Now, there is only one firm that boxes its catch in this manner – The International Sucker, Carp and Herring Incorporated, and they ship weekly from Southampton via the fleet of Froth and Foam Ltd. By this evening's paper, I note that a cargo of fish left last week.'

'On what boat?' Jervis was hot on the quarry.

'The S.S. Dan Vine. Upon that ship our culprit is to be found. You will observe, Jervis, that the twine drawn through the herring's nostrils – if nostrils these can be called – is knotted with unmistakeable nautical knots.'

Jervis was alert to the implications. 'Then it must be a sailor.'

'No – absolutely not. These were very clumsily made; very. No tar worthy of the name would ever make a job like this.'

'But it must be a sailor. On freighters there are only sailors.'

'You miss the point. This knot was made by none other than the captain, the captain of the S.S. Dan Vine. Only the master of a ship, who had not touched the ropes for years, who was so erudite in the theory of navigations that he was ignorant of the rudiments of seamanship, who, in short, had forgotten the practice of his early apprenticeship, only such a one would in tying a knot, tie a sailor's knot, and yet do so with an appalling gaucherie.'

This speech issued from Lance's lips with the air of an irrefutable pronunciamento. There was nothing like deductive reasoning, bolstered by a grain of intuition. It was not fingerprints and doublecrossers that the criminal had to fear – but syllogisms, battalions of syllogisms mustered in formidable array. One could perhaps silence an eyewitness, but psychological insight and logical clairvoyance – these one could not outwit.

'Shall we now perform our autopsy?' asked Jervis. Always called in for the manual operations, Ariel's Caliban was eager to accomplish his part in tracking down the menace of waters.

'Yes. Take our *clupea harengus*; perhaps we will discover as in oysters, pearls; in herrings, clues.'

After photographing the fish, and after going through the necessary fin-printing, Jervis set to cutting it up. As he busied himself with the piscatorial inquest, Lance walked up and down the study, reciting verses from the Bible, of which Jervis caught here and there a phrase, such as: '*Canst thou put a hook into his nose? Or bore his jaw through with a thorn? Will he make supplications unto thee? Will he speak soft words unto thee?*' And later, as Jervis was examining the cranium by flashlight, '*By his neesings a light doth shine ... out of his nostrils goeth smoke.*' These muttered recitations of Lance went on throughout the entire autopsy; and Jervis, be it said, was not averse to this procedure; his pious soul saw in it a proof that science and religion were not incompatible.

Before long Jervis struck something metallic with his knife. He knew that it could not be the herring's voice, for Lance had assured him the herring had no voice. He pursued his labors with an excited zeal. In the gizzard of the fish, he found a coin, dated – 1935!

Lance was elated, jubilant. The inspirational half of his face twitched with the intimations of apocalypse.

'Jervis,' he said 'this coin is a gold mine for the prosecuting attorney. You will see that it is not rusty. By its appearance you may judge that it has been in water for perhaps no more than a day. The effigy of King George is comparatively untarnished. The Bible, my good man, repeats itself – The House of Windsor in the herring's belly. Assuming that the fish was caught last Thursday, the murder must have taken place on Wednesday. The penny, however, was not conducive to its health; internal complications arose; you recall the sickly hypochondriac herring before the autopsy. The captain of the S.S. Dan Vine, who, in an attempt to keep on nurturing his master-mindedness, had been pilfering the brain-food entrusted to him, went angling for fish to replace those he had voraciously embezzled. The resistance of our herring was undermined by the copper which lay heavy in its stomach; it fell an easy victim to the captain's machinations. Dead, it was strung together with the other captives, and boxed in his cargo.'

'But the motive. The motive, sir, of the murder.' Jervis queried impatiently. He was ready, at any moment, to gape in wonder at his master's marvellous revelations.

'That too, is now eminently clear. A numismatician's quarrel; evidently some coin-collector had stowed away on board the ship, to watch, and, perhaps if the opportunity arrived, to steal this priceless, this invaluable coin. A struggle ensued, in which the captain attempted to retain his treasure. In the combat the coin fell overboard, and was snatched up by our gourmet of a herring. It was somewhile thereafter, as I have explained, that the herring itself was taken.'

'But a 1935 penny is not valuable.' Jervis was frequently smitten with these interludes of stupidity.

'Yes, but in a hundred years from now – what a price it will command!'

Jervis stood before his master, petrified wonder. Thus out of a mere red herring, and without a word from a single soul, even without viewing the scene of the murder, the whole affair had been revealed in its compelling and simple conviction. The man was a wizard.

'This herring,' Lance resumed with an air of self-satisfaction, yet touched with modesty, 'this herring is worth its salt. Without it, a man would have gone down to a watery grave, and the world would not have been the wiser. Providence brought this silent witness, brought it out of the depths, to testify and to condemn. It is as the great Rupert Brooke once said:

> One may not doubt that somehow good
> Shall come of Water and of Mud;
> And sure the reverent eye must see
> A purpose in Liquidity.

'Now, Jervis, prepare a report in this case.'
When, sometime later, Jervis returned to Lance's study, he

was quivering like a tuning-fork. His face was pale; alarm was writ all over it.

'What's wrong?' asked Lance.

'Sir, I can't find it! It's lost! It's disappeared! The exhibit! The herring!'

Frantically, master and valet set to looking for the vanished fish. Under the table, in the book-case, in the liquor cabinet – they sniffed everywhere. Suddenly, Jervis, his nostrils quivering, jerked his head in the air, as if on the scent. He seized Hilary by the lapels of his smoking-jacket, exclaimed: 'Here it is! Here are the remains!'

Upon the smoking-jacket of Hilary Lance, flecking the mysterious plots of Gozzi, there appeared morsels of herring. Jervis looked at his master – his master looked at him.

'I must have nibbled away at it' Lance said, shamefacedly. 'It was very tasty, indeed, now that I recall. Too bad! Too bad! You may go, Jervis.'

Jervis went. His face was illuminated with the glow of admiration. His whole form took on a new lightness, as if he had just been initiated into grave secrets. At the door, he muttered to himself, like one repeating a code, 'Fish! The brain-food *par excellence! Par excellence!*'

Kapusitchka

I don't want a cent. I don't want a nickel. I want my cat. In the yard he is lying with his front feet stretched forward, and his mouth wide open, and his lips pulled down below his teeth. Like that. Flies are buzzing around him.

I'll stop crying. If you make him alive again, I'll stop crying.

He was such a beautiful cat. All black. With green eyes. In the dark they shone like marbles, no, like allees. And he had so much fun in our house. In the summer, he would sleep on the window-sill in the sun, all curled up. When he woke up, he would stretch himself, and would seem so long, and he would yawn, and his nice red tongue would show. His teeth would stick out, too, but not like they do now. At me he always smiled.

We always played together. We were friends, me and Kapusitchka. I would make a piece of cord twirl like a snake on the floor, and he would try and catch it. He would try and hit it down with his paws. It's a lie when they say he scratched. He never did. His paws had no nails. Whenever I took his paw in my hand, it was soft, like the green, green grass that grows on stones. He was a good cat. He ate up all the rats, but he never ran after birds on the roof, like other cats do.

If he was so terrible, why was he such friends with Grandma? She doesn't like bad things. She is always praying; she goes to see holy men who come from Europe. She wears a perruque. Always, in winter, when Grandma sits near the stove and knits socks – in winter Grandma knits socks – Kapusitchka would lie at her feet.

He would sleep, with one eye open. Just a little bit open, like looking through a keyhole. Sometimes he would play with the ball of wool, but when Grandma said, Kapusitchka! like that, he would always go to sleep again.

She used to bring him his milk in a special plate, and he would lap it up with his tongue, his tongue making a nice, licking noise, and the plate would be all clean. He never spilled the milk, like I did once.

He and Grandma were friends, also. Whenever he would be left outside, and be jumping at the door-knob to be let in, Grandma, even though she is a little deaf, would hear him, or she would see the door shaking, and let him in. At night, she would kitzu-kitzu him into the shed, and spread out empty coal-sacks for him to lie on, and close the door. She said it was never dark for a cat. In the morning when Grandma would get up the first, Kapusitchka would hear her, and begin to meow.

Always when I went to table, Grandma would say that you have to feed the cat first, because there is nobody to look after cats, they have no father and no mother.

Grandma liked the cat, because he always gave her news about guests coming to the house. Whenever Kapusitchka would lie in a corner, and begin to lick himself, wetting his paw, and with his paw wiping his sides, his head, and his ears, Grandma would say: The cat is washing himself; we are going to have guests.

Kapusitchka had whiskers like the French doctor on the square. When he began to stroke these with his paw, licking his tongue this way and that, we knew for sure that we were going to have guests.

How he knew, nobody told me, even though I asked. But it always came true. Before our cousin came from Russia, the one who brought pollyseeds for all the children, and wore her hair, that was golden, shooting in and out in braids on her head, like a Sabbath bread, Kapusitchka washed himself. Before the old rabbi, who stayed at our house for a long time, and used to ask me all kinds of questions from the Bible, came from Palestine, the cat washed himself. Before my uncle, the one my father called a good-for-nothing when he went away, came from New York with his violin, the cat washed himself.

Sometimes the cat washed himself, and we waited and waited, and looked at the door for somebody to come with baggage, and nobody came. But always when somebody came, the cat washed himself before.

At the beginning of summer, when the baseball games begin on the field, Kapusitchka washed himself, and after that, a guest came. A baby: I don't know where it came from. Everybody tells me lies. Father says a bird dropped it down the chimney, mother says she bought it in the fifteen cent store. Grandma says God gave it to us. Becky – my sister – says she heard them talking – it came from the belly.

Anyway, everybody was having a lot of fun, laughing and everything, making a fuss about him. What a nice baby, they said. And a boy, too, they said. Such big blue eyes, they said.

And all the time the baby bawled, and made a lot of noise, and everybody fussed about it, and rocked it, and called it baby names. They even made a big party for it, when a lot of men with beards came, and they sang, and drank ginger ale and beer, and ate peanuts. Everybody forgot about me, and I played with Kapusitchka, and both of us watched and nobody said anything to me, except one man who said: Such a big boy to play with a cat. Shame. You'll forget everything that you learn if you play with cats. Then that man gave me some peanuts, and a glass of beer, and said, Drink, drink. It was bitter, and I went away from the party to the yard, and Kapusitchka followed me, and rubbed himself against my stockings.

After that, uncles and aunties, and cousins and friends were bringing presents for the baby, blue sweaters, and blue covers for the carriage, and little shirts, and tiny shoes, and a lot of things like that. And everybody hugged the baby, carefully, and then asked me how I liked my new little brother. I didn't answer, because I didn't know what to say, and then everybody laughed, and said I was jealous. I am not jealous. I hate him.

All the time Kapusitchka watched them hugging the baby, and didn't know who it was.

Then one day my mother went away to the market to buy a chicken for Saturday. The baby was alone with Becky, and then Becky went out on the gallery because a friend was calling to her to show off how clean she looked in her Saturday dress after a bath.

Then Kapusitchka jumped up on the bed, and began hugging the baby, and playing with it, like all the other people.

When my mother came back, the baby was bawling its head off, and there was blood on his face and neck. My mother made a whole fuss, and began to scream on everybody, but especially on Becky.

Kapusitchka ran away in a corner, and was sleeping with one eye open.

Then when my father came from work, my mother told him all about it, how Becky was minding the baby, and she went away, and how when my mother came back, the baby was crying, and there was blood on him, and she said, Me for his little head. She blamed it all on the cat, because he was playing with the baby. Then my father got good and sore, and began to shout, Where is that cat? And when he found Kapusitchka he took it into the yard, and with a piece of wood he hit him, and now Kapusitchka is lying there with his mouth wide open.

Grandma was not around, because she went out to talk to another Grandma up the street, and I was crying, but my father said for me to shut up. Then he went and killed Kapusitchka.

Now he is lying there in the sun, with his teeth showing, and flies buzzing all around him.

I hate my brother. I hate my father. I only want my Kapusitchka.

Make him alive again, and I'll stop crying. Only make him alive again.

... And It Shall Come to Pass

'Now dreams. You've had dreams. Tell me about your dreams.'

The young man who sat before the spectacled psychiatrist, his hands sweating palmprint and fingerprint upon the arms of the chair, had been a difficult, a stubborn patient. It was very evident that he did not believe in psychiatry and that his appointments were kept as faithfully as they were only the better and the oftener to demonstrate that disbelief. It was only after the most gradual of persuasions that he had finally been led to communicate a bare outline of his life; of his fears and compulsions he had spoken with reticence, an accused's reticence; and when, on occasion, he had broken down enough to offer a meagre instalment of confession, he had each time repented of this volubility and, as the now familiar haze gathered about his eyes, had retreated once again into the oblivious introversion which was his usual state.

But to-day he spoke freely, almost garrulously. Long suppression distorted his speech into a hectic, excited incoherence, – he would never be able to follow the course he had set himself, he was bewildered, the war had ruined him, he was insufficient, all the doctors of the world would not be able to bring him back to his former healthy self.

His image gaped grotesquely from the doctor's thick lenses.

His patient having come upon a talkative day, the doctor was not one to miss his opportunity. Certainly he was not going to let him recede again behind that cloudy mother-of-pearl shell of his.

'Tell me,' he said, 'about your dreams.'

At every mention of dreams, the young man, as if he

recognized in the word the beginning of a malicious palpation, had bristled with hostility.

'I told you – there are no dreams!'

'But you complain of a disturbed sleep. What is it that disturbs your sleep? Is it not some dream?'

The patient looked at the doctor quizzically: could one eavesdrop on a dream?

'Well, it *is* that, doctor. Many dreams, one dream. Again and again it comes, tearing my sleep apart. A night passes dreamless, and I think I've escaped it, I'm done with it, and then, the next night, there it is again; buzzing and buzzing and buzzing, the motors gasping, the motors – '

The recollection of his dream shook the patient to his very being; he shuddered back into silence.

'Don't you want to tell me about it?'

It was a great effort that the young man was making. 'Yes! Yes! I've got to tell you about it! I can't stand it any more for even when I'm miles and hours away from it, it follows me, the sound of that motor, that last motor in the world ... You've got to help me, doctor.'

'That's what I'm here for.'

The young man paused. It was as if he was girding himself for some great leap.

'It doesn't always start at the same place. But always it ends at the same place. Sometimes it's more mixed up than others, but it's the same dream, every time the same horrible dream ... I am in a plane, my old bomber. Somebody has declared war against us, and I have been given the honour of undertaking the first mission against the enemy. All I carry is one bomb, but it's a bomb to end bombs, if I place it properly this will be my last mission, too. The One Bomb War; that's what it's going to be. We are so certain of success that our plane carries in addition to the usual personnel also a foreign correspondent. In every dream, I see him, his mouth at the mouthpiece, shooting his talk down to the tower below where it is broadcast to all the households of the land. He gives a minute-by-minute report of our course, of the beauty of the stars, of the excitement of the men, of the loved ones waiting our return, of the war that is to be settled, like the wars of old, by the courage of individual champions. He has even brought a Bible along, and reads from the story of David and Goliath. The dream blurs through dials, clouds, faces, whirling propellers, flashes of the moon, and the correspondent's teeth ... Then below us a city, a great city with towers and crisscross streets running in exact conformity to our map.'

Over his face there came a look of elation – and terror.

'O here it is, here it is, that dream changes to nightmare!'

'Not any more.' The doctor was at his soothingest. 'Not here, in this room.'

The young man extracted a handkerchief from his hip pocket, and wiped his hands. 'The bomb is dropped! Is it possible, doctor, that in the dead silence of a dream there should be heard thunder, thunder as if all the storms of all the centuries had gathered again for one grand final burst? That is the sound that in these dreams my brain must muffle and hold.

'The force of the bomb-burst thrusts the plane higher and higher in the sky. I feel as if I'm riding a splinter. Finally we descend, we steady, and I am making for home ... Now the newspaper correspondent really goes to town. He all but cries, "Hello, mom, we made it!" Right, he says, has triumphed. The enemy is wiped out. The world is safe again. Teeth, teeth, teeth!' The young man's irony was heavy and bitter. 'The smile of victory ... '

'But what is there in such a dream to frighten you? It's just a recall of your war-experiences.'

Uncomprehending, the patient stared at his doctor. Finally he spoke: 'Because we never make home! Because the dials all go crazy, and the plane descends and descends and we never seem to come anywhere near to ground. Large masses, rocks, meteors, I don't know what, whirl wildly in space, the biggest flak you ever saw! No matter how much we call to our guiding station, we get no answer. No where any light – only the cold pinpoint constellations, and that grinning taunting moon. And space. And space ...

Do you know what happened, doctor – we bombed the earth away from under us!'

'And that's when the dream breaks?'

'Usually – with us going in circles, lost all bearings, looking for a landing, the gasoline going lower and lower ... O, to crash would be happiness! ... And yesterday it was even worse. The foreign correspondent ended the dream for me. He took to his Bible again. The last thing I remember are his words trailing away into a quiet, reconciled panic.'

'Do you remember his words?'

'Yes. *In the beginning God created the heaven and the earth. And the earth was without form, and void, and darkness was upon the face of the deep. And the Spirit of God ...* '

Over the eyes of the patient there gathered again the familiar far-away haze.

And the Mome Raths Outgrabe

The Conference of whose proceedings I intend here to give an account is still in session; my report may perhaps strike you as premature. That it well may be; by the time this letter reaches you, the whole tenor and direction of The Conference may have changed; a new luridness by then may have been thrown upon the actors and their relationship to each other; the manic perhaps may have given way to the depressive; but I doubt whether the aura of general madness which surrounds us all here will ever completely pass away. And when I say *ever* I mean it in the merciless metaphysical sense. For originally The Conference was to have lasted three days, already a week has passed, and as yet nowhere among the delegates is there the slightest indication of the imminence of departure. My report, then, is an interim report, but its content, I cannot help but think, is proleptic and already shows in the part the pattern of the whole. Myself I write as from cauchemar, write so as to establish contact with something real – or is it with something fictitious but convalescive? – something, at any rate, which is different from the ambience about me the true nature of which I am frankly unable to assert.

I did not believe when I first repaired to this small town to attend the mysterious Conference at which 'cis-and ultra-Atlantic delegates' were to be present, that I would witness so strange, so fantastic a *dénouement* – a continuing *dénouement* – to a convention which began, and for a while proceeded, according to the usual rules for conventions made and provided. As I write – and I am writing in the very midst of the most hectic (up to now) session of The Conference – the atmosphere is thick with hate, curdled with sneers; it has not yet come to violence – I don't think it will, – these people, despite their passion, are too deeply conscious of the vatic role they are expected to play, – but it is enough that, scholars and gentlemen, they have forsaken their usual diplomacies, have turned their introversions inside out, and are now insulting each other with quotations, with innuendoes, and even with mimicked inflections.

It wasn't that way four days ago. When the delegates first met at a reception given for us by some local personality whose name I now forget, it was something to watch their shynesses curtseying to each other. I don't know how many times that evening these bright phrase-makers commented upon the fine weather we were having, or tried to remember, remembered, and inquired after mutual friends; they were certainly on their best behavior. The next day the social life warmed up even more, the delegates went to some small informal parties, were gay, caught themselves praising each other's work and there were even cases of harmless practical jokes. Of political activity – the corridor cabals that mark the opening days of a convention – of this there was neither sign nor susurrus. The townsfolk, too, thought the visitors right guys. Main street had as yet no inkling as to what kind of a Conference it was harbouring.

Nor was there anything in the first business sessions of The Conference which might have portended the turn which things did eventually take. There was, to begin with, a speech of welcome, macaronic of literary allusion; and then a symposium upon the relations between a man and his critic (in which two of each participated); this was full of coy exchanges, banter, and hunched delight; and on the following morning, as most of the delegates overslept – for foresight and considerateness you have to hand it to our Committee on Arrangements – a paper on *The Bane of Existentialism*. The afternoon – a trade-discussion, led by an eager young man who spoke on *The Economics of our Profession*. He was very businesslike, very disillusioned, very realistic; the effort with which he spurned metaphor and embraced statistics would have sparkled a glass eye. And then in the evening The Conference broke up into smaller seminars devoted to subjects recondite; this for the professors was decidedly the violet hour.

But as yet – no sign of the coming storm. The purpose of The Conference – the setting of standards – was being pursued unobtrusively, playfully, almost with diffidence, as became so urbane and temperate an assembly. It may have been, of course, that this attitude was due to the fact that the delegates realized that up to this moment they had been dealing with the mere trivia of their vocation, matter with which they disdained to involve their true, their real personalities. Whatever the cause – planned abstention or habit of mind – it was upon the social aspects of The Conference that they concentrated. They skipped sessions and organized private drinking parties, there were poker games, and one delegate spoke to me of a crap-game. The historicity of the game I doubt, I think my informant made it up so as to provide background for his picture of the poet in a fine frenzy rolling; but the very invention of the anecdote is typical of the mood of The Conference. The Conference was something to be got through, as pleasantly as possible; ended, everybody would go home, the local delegates with a new set of *bons mots* and a new list of correspondents, and the foreign visitors with material for the book on the state of the American economy.

Then it happened, although when it happened, it didn't declare itself for the monstrous thing it was to be. No session had been called for the morning of the third day; instead – a luncheon meeting. Here the ultra-Atlantic delegates were given the opportunity of bringing greetings from Europe-in-process-of-becoming. They were very moving, these greetings, the most moving I have ever listened to; the full extent of the tragedy which agitated the minds of the speakers was evidenced by the fact that not a one – with the possible exception of the Russian delegate who desisted for reasons diplomatic – not a one did so much as suggest what he meant by Europe-in-process-of-becoming. Becoming what? The question which disturbed the minds of all, save the pedants familiar with the phrase in its transcendental associations, remained unanswered. Instead, as the luncheon ululated to a close, the chairman rose to announce a change in the agenda for the afternoon. The nineteenth century Nobel Prize winner who was to have addressed the Convention had not arrived; a wire from him expressed, pathetically, but economically, his regret; and the afternoon session, therefore, would be taken up with a discussion of Carroll's *Jabberwocky*. As he ended, copies of *The Jabberwocky* were distributed to the delegates by the waiters.

The delegates received this announcement with mixed feelings. *The Jabberwock* after the description of the plight of Europe seemed particularly insensitive a sequence. The circulation of the text of the poem, too, was deemed supererogatory and insulting. (For the sake of total impression, however, I here reproduce the text; it is consigned – insult alleviated – to a footnote.)* On the other hand, *The Jabberwock* in lieu of the Nobel Prize Winner was a substitution which had much to recommend it. The delegates did not really mind. The item, after all, was in harmony with the

*Twas brillig, and the slithy toves
　　Did gyre and gimble in the wabe:
All mimsy were the borogoves,
　　And the mome raths outgrabe.

'Beware the Jabberwock, my son!
　　The jaws that bite, the claws that catch!
Beware the Jubjub bird, and shun
　　The frumious Bandersnatch!'

He took his vorpal sword in hand:
　　Long time the manxome foe he sought –
So rested he by the Tumtum tree,
　　And stood awhile in thought.

And, as in uffish thought he stood,
　　The Jabberwock, with eyes of flame,

mood which had been created during the past three days – slight, frivolous, of no real consequence. The fun was going to continue.

Thus is it shown how rarely men are wont to recognize the auguries of their own doom. The Townsfolk were much shrewder, for it was precisely at this juncture – the waiters had apparently done some extra-curricular circulation of the outlandish text – that there began to be heard the rumour that The Conference was an assembly discoursing in code.

But of this, or of the profounder more mystical perils which lay ahead, the delegates were happily oblivious. Singly, in groups, gaily, as if to a picnic, the delegates strolled into the convention hall for the afternoon session.

Perhaps it was the Chairman's opening remarks which really effected the change in attitude and induced that nightmarish unreality which is *the* event of this Conference. Believing that thus he maintained the impartiality expected of his function, the Chairman (the Chairmanship here is a rotating one) felt it his duty

---

Came whiffling through the tulgey wood,
   And burbled as it came!

One, two, One, two! And through and through
   The vorpal blade went snicker-snack!
He left it dead, and with its head
   He went galumphing back.

'And hast thou slain the Jabberwock?
   Come to my arms, my beamish boy!
O frabjous day! Callooh, Callay!'
   He chortled in his joy.

Twas brillig and the slithy toves
   Did gyre and gimble in the wabe:
All mimsy were the borogoves,
   And the mome raths outgrabe.

to thrust *The Jabberwock* onto the convention floor in the nakedest of terms. Yet had he done only this, it would not have been so bad; non-committal as were his preliminary remarks, they were nonetheless accompanied by a sly exegetical use of the eyebrows, a pantomime I think which was responsible, as much as anything else, for the sultry hostility which began to be felt in the hall. For one thing, the ambiguous nature of his impartiality annoyed everyone, for it made the striking of a counter-attitude very difficult; for another – and this was probably the basic motive – the Chairman's tone was considered in extremely bad taste; it was all very well to treat serious subjects flippantly as had been done during the past three days, that was a mark of culture, but to treat a light subject flippantly – this was a breaking of the rules and this they would not tolerate.

It may seem to you, removed as you are from the tense atmosphere which here converts every undertone into Sinaitic thunder, that the attitude of the Chairman was innocent enough. Consider, then, what he did, and what he said. Having, not without inflectional insinuations, elocuted the poem, he swung into an appreciation. Good! But what was the nature of his appreciation? It was a poem, he said, of a rare and engaging forthrightness. (*This was like a slap in the face.*) Taken for its lean literal self– its interpretations allegorical, moral, and anagogical held for the moment on the thither side, it was with a rippling muscled energy that it communicated its simple truisms. (*Simple truisms!*) Because its sentences were whittled and of a fine syntactality, because its drama was exclamative, and its idiom green and fresh, it succeeded immediately in winning (*business of the eyebrows*) that suspension of disbelief without which all poetry must stillborn die. Even from the unsuspending (*coyness*), its statements taunted refutation. Indeed, as one moved from stanza to declarative stanza (*smile*), returning in the end to the same utterance which constituted its exordium and first mood (*pause*), one was left with the conviction, singular in our time, that here was a poem (*benignity and embonpoint*) that meant exactly what it said. And he sat down.

Did I say that what the delegates resented was that the trivial was being cavalierly dismissed? That was not it at all. It was that a *serious* theme was being thus handled that shocked them. *The Jabberwock* was serious; upon this every speaker insisted. (A Sunday-supplement book-reviewer did venture to suggest that perhaps the thing was written in fun; the Committee on Credentials is now re-examining his documents.)

Now whether this universally shared serious view of the poem was adopted by way of reaction to the Chairman's speech, or whether it was with the delegates a constant conviction and the frivolous reception given to it at the luncheon was a pose designed to cover up their real sensitivity to something fundamental, or whether, again, this change of attitude was the result of some insidious barometric influence, or, indeed, a pentecostal visitation, I have no way of knowing; I know only that *The Jabberwock* here is being treated as if it was some halidom, some hieratic document which holds in it the substantive secrets of the craft, and indeed the meaning of life itself.

Hence the fanatic partisanship. Its intensity is incommunicable. A summary of the debate which has been going on these last three days – is it three? It may be four, or five, or six, – time here is merged into one undistinguished continuum – may in some measure suggest that intensity, but only suggest, and only in some measure. The comradeship which prevailed during the opening days of The Conference has vanished. Even the forms of address with which the delegates recognized each other have changed. Where formerly it was Mr. Ewen, or the genial Mr. Ewen, or just Al who was referred to as having said this or that, to-day, now, all such quotations are breathlessly attributed to AE, diphthongally pronounced. Is this because the delegates feel themselves driven by some overwhelming urgency? Or because, now at last concerned with the real, the essential, they would affect the idiom of the executive? Is this the infection of the conspiratorial? Whatever the cause, the result is one: differing upon a cardinal matter, the delegates have become alienated one from the other, there is no orthodoxy, there is no heterodoxy, it is all schism, and the sole nexus between them is the alphabet.

First to speak was CB whose history of English literature is distinguished for its attempt to deduce all poetry to paradox. Those familiar with his writings know that CB esteems in a poet the same double-jointedness which he esteems in an acrobat – and that where this is lacking he must either discover some chatoyant irony, or condemn the work as sheer hysteria. CB held that far from just meaning simply what it said – fatuous was the mind which so concluded – the poem was chock-full of connotations, implications, associations, and *double-ententes.* Its very vocabulary replete with portmanteau words showed that this poet intended two meanings where the limited versifier would have been content with but one. CB did not wish to labour the obvious point which would be made out of the key words of the fifth stanza: *One, two! One, two!* He contented himself with citing the single instance: the vorpal sword, – that is to say, a sword at once verbal and horrible. And one did not know – here the equivocal was injected into the composite – whether it was the second because of, or in spite of, the first. It was a cerebral poem: in the body of the poem itself Carroll had taken care to stress this fact; when the hero stood, he stood in thought, in uffish thought. The turning point was reached in the word *snicker-snack;* the battle was a battle in the old tradition, chivalrous and strange, after the manner of Malory; but the description of the battle included its own ironic comment. The weapons not only snacked, they snickered, – even as at a later date, Eliot's footman was to snicker. 'The jaws that bite! The claws that catch!' One of the most startling paradoxes in our literature!

In a poem of this kind, by definition topsy-turvy, in construction hysteron-proteron, one naturally expected the words to imply the opposite of what they meant. Carroll scorned such facile somersaults. 'You expect,' Carroll seemed to say, 'the jaws not to bite? They do! The claws not to catch? They catch!' CB was at a loss to recall a single instance in the whole of European literature where such technical subtlety was excelled, or even equalled.

Of the same opinion – but with a difference! – was EW who scoffed both at the chairman's simplicity and at CB's attempt to reduce poetry to philology and rhetoric. Profounder elements, deeper factors entered into the making of a work of art. In such labour the soul, too, was engaged, and nothing illustrated this truth better than *The Jabberwock*, a poem which revealed in its structure, in its approach, in its mood and manner, the sure indicia of internal trauma. Carroll had been a man torn by conflicting appetencies, a split personality; he would say it boldly – a schizophrenic. For Carroll had been not only Carroll, but also Dodgson, the reverend Dodgson with a fondness for little girls; had been not only Carroll the fantasist, but also Dodgson the mathematician, first of his generation to look on Euclid bare. It was not difficult to imagine the damage which these two diametrically opposed pulls would cause to the Cardod-Rolgson psyche. Mathematician, count thyselves! The task before Carroll, then, was to make one of what was twain, to bring together the writer of verse and the author of the *Treatise on Determinants*. The contest which provided the central action of the poem was a contest which had really taken place in the tulgey sacred wood of the poet's personality. It was to the eternal glory of this broken soul that he had found his healing through art. *The Jabberwocky*, with its enigmatic sequences, its dream-settings, its composite words – which were to ordinary language what algebra was to arithmetic – had provided the poet his own therapeutic psychiatry. The poem was not, as the chairman had so lightly judged, a simple equation; the poem was more than the quadratic equation CB had claimed it to be; it was the record of the diagnosis, treatment, and cure of a great and terrible wound.

I cannot describe to you the uproar which ensued when the delegate who announced himself as a Freudian, apparently encouraged by EW's audacities, launched upon his own thesis and read, and, as he read, converted into a selection of *graffiti* the second stanza of the classic poem. Of course he didn't agree with EW; EW had come to the right house but had entered the wrong room. What adult had any doubt, he asked, about the identity of the vorpal sword? Who was at a loss to see, behind the tum-tum baby-talk, the true terminus of the protagonist's search? Was he indeed a *man* who equated uffish thought with high contemplation? I don't think I need transcribe the other of his rhetorical questions; those I have already cited must give you, I believe, an idea of what he was up to; through the remaining stanzas, you (adults and men) may very well make your way on your own.

To him and to EW and to CB, it was the poet X (really k.s.; you may judge of the tempo discussion had by this time reached from the fact that these initials were to such abbreviation hissed) who made reply. He has quite a style, this X. CB, he said, was an exegete who doted on the explication of an ambivalence; an ambiguity resolved, he said, set the day for CB; a shrewd but esoteric homily made its high noon, and nothing sent him happier to a moonlit bed than the pillowed recollection of some alchemical ingenuity which had hardened the aura that circles about a good poem to metal minted and milled, a ring of gold, palpable, precious. But it was fool's gold. Poetry began where language ended. The word in the line of poetry could not even properly be called a word and should perhaps be designated otherwise. He did not wish to be guilty of introducing a new critical term and was content to refer to this other entity as a not-word. In using the word prosody he had first to broaden the common definition to include not only the science of poetical form, metre and metrical composition, not only the melodic pattern and visual design but also the sense-beyond-sense of the not-words of the poem; and having defined prosody, *The Jabberwocky*, he submitted, provided the norm, model, and exemplar of the art.

The Abbé B. agreed with X. Not for X's reasons. The Abbé, great authority on *la poésie pure,* is an excitable Frenchman, never speaks but he eloquizes, never eloquizes – jubilates. 'Here, here at last,' he cried, fluttering his copy of *The Jabberwock,* 'is literature untrammelled by definition, poetry unshackled by semantics! How scrupulously M. Carroll, a mathematician, yes, a mathematician seeking in poetry the effects of pure music – *l'art le plus mathématique* – how scrupulously he has avoided the gross irrelevancies of meaning! How he has eschewed the ubiquitous pitfalls that trip and catch and send the unwary poet staggering to earth and to the dictionary! Vibrating in the serene unlexicon'd empyrean, moving with the incommunicable music of the spheres, like music unparaphraseable, intraductible, ineffable, this is truly a poem *in excelsis.*' And so on, and so on. He really might have reached a high pitch of eloquence had he not been so frequently interrupted.

In fact all of the speakers were being interrupted all of the time. It is this aspect of the proceedings, I note as I reread the above paragraphs, which fails to emerge from the meagre quotes through which I have sought to summarize their speeches; but I am myself too much involved in the turmoil to take stenographic notes. Hecklings and interruptions are the rule; delegates keep jumping up on their chairs; the chairman is continually rapping for order; private and personal controversy is being indulged in everywhere. A *PMLA* contributor rises to shout that borogoves is a *hapax legomenon*. A man at the back of the hall keeps singing: *Not-words! Not-poems! Not-poems! Not-words!* and he in turn is drowned out by another who calls, and calls again for H.D., that is, Humpty-Dumpty, who, he says, has the key to the poem. There is whistling, there is outgribing, there is bellowing. Delegates walk out of the hall, demonstratively; soon they return, and this too, they do as if they were asserting a principle. Nobody stays away for long. Only the Russian delegate Djz has, ever since the issue took debatable form, continuously absented himself. It is rumoured that he is in cable-communication with the secretary of the PEN club whose delegate he is.

But here he comes! He is followed by his two assistants. They carry papers. Somehow he has got the floor. He is speaking, no, he is reading. He pauses to give a sign to his assistants. They begin distributing the papers. A mimeographed text of his speech. Djz waits until everybody has a copy.

As his voice climbs up and down his sentences, the delegates follow him on the papers before them.

'The method of the poem is dialectical throughout.' He pronounces the e's like a's, and breaks the sentence into halves. ' ... dialectical throughout. The very technique of its neologisms, composites in which two words come to embrace on the page only to sever and do battle in the mind, follows admirably the Hegelian formula which provided Carroll's great contemporary the pattern for his own insights. Already in the opening lines – in the gyring and the gimbling – is the pattern explicitly announced. The poem as a whole, too, progresses schematically: its opening stanza – thesis; the following – violent antithesis; its final stanza – reversion on a higher level, certainly, to the original static thetic condition.' As he warms to his subject his articulation and syntax become even more markedly Slavonic. 'Once realized the principle of unity behind the poem, many of its merely verbal difficulties disappear. It is seen immediately that we have before us a parable, a Krylov fable of the revolutionary struggle, uttered, it is true, in code – Carroll knew the sensitivities of his Victorian audience – but in a code whose key is not far to seek. The key is – the society. The method is – that of his *Symbolic Logic*. Published in 1865, it follows, it is to be noticed, by seventeen years the issuance of *The Communist Manifesto* and precedes by two – *Das Kapital*! One must not ignore, also, Carroll's trip to Tzarist Russia where he had plenty opportunity to see the evils of the system intensified to the nth degree. What Carroll is really composing, therefore, is not some ditty for the nurseries of the exploiting military and financial castes, as would have us believe the intellectual lackeys of capitalism, but the first Marxist poem in English literature!'

After a pause the accent of the Volga continues.

'The opening lines describe the nature and plight of the proletariat under capitalism. Appropriately its members are characterized *toves*; thus, in a single dialectical word allusion is made both to the inherent toughness of the working class, that is to say, its potential strength, and to its dove-like meekness beneath oppression, that is to say, its actual condition at the present moment in history. Positively is recognized in the *borogoves* the hidden anagram of the *bourgeoisie*, a class which the great poet describes as *mimsy*, which he explains means *miserable* and *flimsy* – a precise description of both the unstable status and the subservient condition of this parasitic-symbiotic groupment. As for the *mome raths* – here Carroll, with true dialectical dexterity, has reversed his usual technique; here, instead of making a single amalgam of two words, he has split the one word in two, and has written for momeraths – mome raths. But what *is* the momerath? Who knows the morphology of philology will recognize at once; it is but another name for the proletariat. If the proletariat is, by etymology, the class which proliferates, the momerath is the class which for the time being is dumb, numb, mum. But now it *outgrabes*; *outgrabing*, says Carroll through the mouth of Humpty-Dumpty, the ideal dragoman of capitalism – the royalist men and the royalist cavalry cannot put him together again – *outgrabing* is something between a whistling and a bellowing.' The method of the bellowing is now relentlessly exposed.

'The Jabberwock, voracious and prehensile, is very easily identified. Finance-capital has never been more realistically pictured. In the wake of the Jabberwock, moreover, there appear the usual valets – the kept Jubjub bird, Art, and the furious fanatic incense-fuming kidnapper of souls, the Bandersnatch. Between these two categories, the Jabberwock and his satellites on the one hand, the momerath on the other, there can be no peace; conflict must ensue.

'Now the inherent contradictions begin to resolve themselves. How? Through struggle; the sword, at first verbal, later (according to bourgeois notions of morality) horrible, the vorpal sword is taken in hand. Unfortunately, the initial stages of class struggle are always bedevilled by hesitations, doubts, failures to identify the real enemy. In his moralist trappings, this enemy conceals the true exploiting character of his role. He is, like the manx-cat, uncatchable; he has no tail; he is also handsome. The hero looks for the manxome foe; the foe – at the very moment of search – is sitting on his back. Temporarily, he abandons the struggle, content with the concessions his threats have wrested from the enemy, concessions symbolized by the tum-tum tree, a sort of bread-fruit which supplies enough for two meals per day – tum-tum – instead of one. But not as yet, three.

'From its original objective the course of the revolution is side-tracked away. In place of energetic conflict, the working-class falls prey to consolatory ideologies, evangelistic slogans, catch-words, otherworldliness – in a word, uffish thought. The paralysis of the proletariat is the opportunity of the capitalist. To recapture the meagre concessions it has granted, The Jabberwock – by no means weakened – sotted and sated, it gurgles and burps, it *burbles* – comes whiffling through the tulgey wood. Now the proletariat must fight defensively: and numbers must make up for lack of vision. *One, two! One, two! And through and through the vorpal blade goes snicker-snack!* Quantity becomes quality. The Jabberwock meets its superior, and is slain. Then, and then only, is conjured up the last stanza, reproducing the same images as occurred in the first. But with what a change! Quality has been spread to quantity. The outgrabing of the momerath this time, one may be sure, is more like a whistle than a bellowing.'

Throughout his reading Djz was interrupted not even once. Both his remarks and his intonation seemed to have fascinated, consternated, the delegates into silence. But it is not for long that the delegates remain dumbstruck. Now, as if by some sudden common impulse, they are shouting all at the same time.

Some are tearing the mimeographed sheets into shreds.

Others have rushed out from their seats into the aisles.

One of the delegates, a young man, has elbowed himself up to the platform, has mounted, and, striking a handstand, is thus trying to address the audience.

He is ignored.

The Chairman is calling upon M to speak; but the Chairman is now only a gesturing figure.

All over the hall the uproar is deafening; about M, as a matter of fact, fist are flying. The Chairman has left the platform. Now only the hand-stander occupies it. At the rear of the hall, another fistfight! Several fistfights!

But look! – a sudden paralysis must have possessed the brawlers. The delegate Z, I observe, abandons his fight in the middle of a left hook. Others grimace, break off their arguments, and look for doors. Everywhere there is a drive toward the exits.

Now the reason has reached me. Somewhere in the hall somebody has dropped one (or several) of those bombs. The hall is cleared.

I doubt whether The Conference will ever catch its breath again.

Letter from Afar

The unnegateable negation! ... I write from its very centre and vacuum. For miles and miles about this miserable hut which, though unbarred, is still a prison, the wind whistles its shuddering arctic vowels. They are sounds – these echoes of non-existence – suited to the annihilating nothingness to which I have been condemned. Cold they are, the antonyms of life and its heat; and vowelled, like cries from a throat to which no face is attached.

Three years have passed since I was first *reprieved* to this village in the snow – how innocent then appeared this snow that now is not the least of my punishment: its implacable whiteness, the hypocritical smile of its crystals, its relentless and undialectical persistence! – and this is the third time that I set down (upon snow?) the apologia for my confession. Perhaps this time it will at last reach beyond the snowdrifts and the frontiers; perhaps my earlier communications have already been brought; I do not know; here we are cordon'd and coffined against everything but the world's gathering winds.

I do not even know whether this village bears a name on the map; in all likelihood it is known to its founder by a number, the number is probably Zero. By compact, by judicial decision, by the morality of our revolutionary code I am supposed not to be, to have ceased, to have been negated. Nobody. Nowhere. On the other side of the world the necrologists have no doubt marked me down as 'liquidated'; when this document is revealed, if ever, it will almost certainly be pronounced a forgery. But I take my chances, both with friend and foe.

I take my chances because this letter, sent at greatest risk, I owe to History. (How the letter issues I need not tell here; I do not care to satisfy the curiosity of the interceptors; if, however, it is brought to its destination, the circumstances of its bringing will naturally reveal themselves.) I owe it also, though to a much lesser extent to my brave and gallant friend, Captain Lansing. He took his chances for me. It seems many many years ago, but I have not forgotten that it was he and his company of daring men who sought, as I stood in the very midst of my confessions in the courtroom of the capital of that pendant-state, to snatch me out of the hands of my prosecutors. It may be that he undertook this picaresque sally because he desired the glory of a derring-do *coup de la personne*, an ideological kidnapping; I think, however, – am I succumbing to the bourgeois frailties? – that there was not a little in his act of the friendship which had flourished between us during my exilic sojourn in Pennsylvania.

Had he succeeded in his project the world would have known by now the manner and the method of the extorted confession; unfortunately, there was, as always, a traitor among my friend's agents, and though his well-armed plane duly arrived, and though his men did manage to shoot their way into the courtroom, the soldiery of my captors – in more than sufficient numbers – were waiting for them, and I failed to be rescued. I am told that Captain Lansing and his comrades, after leaving casualties behind, barely accomplished their escape from the precincts of the Hall of Justice. They got lost, it appears, in the busy thoroughfares, and finally vanished in one of the side-streets of the metropolis. I hope they were able to make their way safely to the frontier whence they had so quixotically issued. I hope also that Captain Lansing has forgiven me for the vile epithets which during the subsequent course of my confession I heaped upon him and his masters.

His masters for their part, seemed very much concerned about me. Much speculation, I recall, went on in the reactionary press about the motives for my confessions, confessions through which I was allegedly currying favour with my judges. How was it possible, the journalists asked, that a man like Jan Czernik whose revolutionary career had filled a dossier in almost every European country (a plutocrat insult) and whose wilfulness was notorious (a plutocrat compliment) should now abjectly admit to, indeed insist upon, crimes which nullified his entire *curriculum vitae*?

It was a question which, though primarily designed to taunt my oppressors, hurt me, hurt my vanity. But it is not for the sake of my own little footnote in the textbooks of the future that I write this letter. It is, I repeat, for the sake of History itself that I must explain what actually happened. To the men of my generation and my kind, Marxists whose métier was the manufacture of incidents, History was God. We held it to be, like God, eternal, ubiquitous, omnipotent. A false confession, then, constituted towards History the same offense that blasphemy constitutes toward Religion. The impression of having committed that offense I now wish to destroy, wish to make clear for my sake, perhaps also for the sake of Captain Lansing, but above all for the sake of the Historic Record, what it was that made me shout my guilt to all the air-waves of the world.

The press – my accommodating jailers, naturally for purposes of their own, kept bringing me the pertinent clippings – the press was very verbose, through 'reliable sources' very informed about the motives for my confession. It was fear, the correspondents said, which prompted it. Fear of what? Death? Didn't the so-called reliable sources know, as I knew, that even the most slavish confessions were rewarded with the capital sentence, that pleas for clemency, both those in which the accused joined and those in which he feigned not to join, were almost always rejected, and that on the day following a verdict the sentence was invariably executed?

Confronted with these objections, objections so elementary they rose of themselves, the speculators exclaimed: Torture! The accused has been tortured into confession! An absurder hypothesis is inconceivable. My trial, and the trials before mine, all were public; that was why they were held at all – for their publicity; privately these matters could have been expedited much more cheaply and with much less trouble; – and all could see that these men bore no marks of ill-treatment upon them. Unmarked I was, well-fed, and in full enjoyment – this word, perhaps, is not exact – of life and limb. Is this to say that I knew of no tortures taking place? Not at all. But the tortured were never invited upon the stage. Whatever the impresarios of the trial lacked, they did not lack a sense of the relationship between means and ends.

These conjectures, however, did not exhaust the ingenuity of the journalists. They had other theories. My confession – now we were in the realm of psychology where everything was profound and fundamental – my confession was a manifestation of the peculiarities of the national soul. That soul, they explained, loved self-abasement; it did not sense itself fulfilled unless it smote itself *Peccavi* again and again; it longed to wallow in guilt. And my trial provided the trough. I can only say that I am doubtful of the existence of an individual soul, let alone a national one. The soul they spoke of, in any event, was not of my nature. Yet I confessed. Believe me, the soul had very little to do with my outpourings.

I read of yet another hypothesis: here it was the dialectic which was blamed. I confessed, it was contended, because I was persuaded through the compulsion of my own dialectic to proclaim myself to be the opposite of what I really was. It was because I was so Hegelian that I invented in my own person and for the sake of diagrammatic symmetry my own antithesis. This suggestion, though I have in baldly stating it sought to ridicule it, has more than an inkling of truth; but as a sweeping simplification it is, of course, a distortion of the dialectic, not an illustration of it.

It was also stated, in explanation of my confession, that I was the victim of drugs and Svengalis. I was hypnotized, I was narcoticized. Those who advanced this theory did not seem at all troubled by the fact that the superior science of their own countries has somehow been unable to duplicate these mysterious drugs, nor its mesmerizers able to achieve the same forensic triumphs. The West ought not to feel embarrassed. It was neither through gesticulation nor yet through potions that the confession was obtained.

My arrest came to me as a shattering shock. Except for the military representative from abroad, I was, in my own principal-ity, top man. It was an eminence, I feel, that I had truly earned. My association with the Movement dated back to my early semesters at the university from which subsequently I was expelled for radical activity. In the initiating period of our struggle, it had been I who had organized and led our underground work. My record, moreover, boasted also its prison-sentences, two years at one time, five at another, and finally a death sentence later commuted. The commutation itself had been an accolade in my career, my comrades abroad had arranged it through some reciprocal deal. I was a member, an honoured member of our International; I knew the makers of the revolution, all except one, by their first names, and was similarly addressed by them. In recent times, it had been I who had led the action that brought my country within its new orbit, and when at length I was recognized officially as my country's leader, no one questioned the appointment. I had earned it.

And now I was being escorted for interrogation at headquarters by my own police!

My prosecutors, I flatter myself, at first underestimated me. Malenkov, the burly uniformed bureaucrat who sat behind his desk as the lamp over his head shot its glare at me, apparently expected a ready surrender. He read, with indignation, a long document of charges: I was a deviationist; I had once been friendly with the traitor recently liquidated in Mexico; I had spent time in Pennsylvania where I had laid the groundwork for my role as *agent-provocateur*; I had made deals with my reactionary jailers; I was sabotaging the new regime; I had a criminal knowledge of English; I was in reality a nationalist and not an internationalist; my whole career had been marked by but a feigned loyalty to the cause, a dissimulation of thirty years acted out only so that I could win myself that key position through which I could most effectively betray the revolution ... In this vein he continued for some time, going through my criminal exploits in their many variations. Then he handed me the document so that I might sign it and attest to the truth of any or all of its accusations.

I flung it back to him across the desk. I had not yet been tamed by interrogation and still felt that I had both in friends and achievements resources to draw upon. What did he think this was, I asked, a practical joke? Did he know whom he was addressing in this fashion? Wasn't he fearful of his own position the moment I got out and was able to report him to his superiors? Who had fabricated this list of charges? Whose nightmare was it? What foreign agent had planted this notion in the minds of our stupid police? Was this the reward of a lifetime of self-sacrifice?

– But the charges are true, aren't they? Partially true, perhaps? You cannot deny your contacts with the West, can you?

– Contacts!

– Don't interrupt! Nor the record of your association with the Mexican. Nor the fact that in all of your recent public addresses you have catered to the petty-nationalist aspirations of your compatriots. Nor the fact that the reactionaries, for some reason or other – with whose head did you pay for it? – extended to you their mercy. Can you? ... But you are tired. Perhaps tomorrow you will realize that we know more about you than you imagined. Or the day after to-morrow. Or the day after.

There were many to-morrows, and many days after. Night after night I was brought from my cell to that desk and that lamp to have the cauchemar repeated. My interlocutor was working upon what he considered a safe principle – everyone sometimes deviates, the flesh is weak, and weaker still the mind, convictions become enfeebled, and in all careers, even the most dedicated, there must come moments of hesitation and doubt. He assumed that mine somewhere had known the typical frailty. If only he would probe long enough, I would give in, I would succumb before his assumed omniscience.

But I had nothing to confess.

Then one evening it was with a special cordiality that he greeted me as I was brought into his office. To-night, he said, there are not going to be any questions to mar our friendship. We are going to a movie.

He led me down the long prison corridor and at the end of it into a small room built and furnished like a theatre. He motioned for me to sit down on one of the seats facing the screen, while he took up a position at a table in the orchestra pit. He gave the signal to the operator at the back of the theatre to set his machine in motion. He faced me. It was obvious that he had seen the film before.

It was a silent film. On the screen there flashed a picture of the room in which I had recently indulged in so much conversation. Or one similar to it. In a moment there was pushed into it a person whom I recognized as having seen at the earlier congresses of our movement – the engineer Rasminsky. This person glowered at his examiner, his examiner grimaced back at him; they were both gesticulating at one another. There was, I could not but realize, something comic about the whole scene, so reminiscent was it of the archaic staccato movies of several decades ago.

But soon the comedy and the silence ended. The film was really a talkie. It made noises. It was now from another room that the noises were issuing. I descried Rasminsky again.

I have no doubt but that our age will go down in history as an age of progress. In almost all fields of human endeavour the world has progressed toward undreamed-of objectives. We have perfected the sciences; we have improved the arts; and we have refined the disciplines, including that of torture. With our contemporary knowledge of the workings of the human body and with our numerous mechanical devices for testing them, we are able to-day to draw a graph of human endurance, indicating with precision the point where pleasure is converted into pain, suffering's point of saturation, the point penultimate to unconsciousness. The reactions of agony require no further empirical tests for their discovery; they are known, catalogued, equated, to the last unit of torment. The professors of torture who moved energetic through the film knew well these equations and managed expertly their best devices. The body of Rasminsky, moreover, reacted with expected sensitivity.

All this time, Malenkov was scrutinizing me from the darkness beneath the screen.

I found myself watching the film with a scientific impartiality. That Rasminsky's body should writhe and twist in its ordeal seemed to me to be natural; what I wondered at was the wide scope he managed within the tightened stricture of the vice-like contraption in which he was held. It was, however, his voice which shot knives of compassion through my whole being. He had not been gagged; the professors, too, had to have their reward. He had not been gagged, and soon, under the pressure of his suffering his voice lost its humanity, he screamed like something antediluvian, he made sounds which seemed to travel up to his throat from navelcords which ended somewhere in a pre-evolutionary forest.

At last, after a fade-out showing a number and a date, the film ended.

– Let's go.

Malenkov walked me back to his office. Not with a single word did he refer to the film; on the contrary, once in his office, he designed a conversation of the utmost casualness and at length – do not imagine that people who are heavily-built are necessarily heavy-minded – he obliquely led me to believe that bygones were bygones and now he was ready to take me into his confidence. He admitted that the charges which he had levelled against me were perhaps not *personally* justified; they were, however, easily justifiable *historically*. Here he launched upon a detailed analysis of the political and economic situation in my country, with particular reference to the two powerful philosophies which were contending for its support. I had done a very good job, he conceded, in persuading the elite away from the poisonous attractions of the West, but the masses, the cattle of habit, they were still hungering for the old mangers. Only a great catharsis could shatter them out of their illusion, and that catharsis would come only if one who had led them, one whom they idolized had been shown to have feet of clay. Then, and then only would ensue that distrust and revulsion which was the true prophylaxis against the disease of the West.

He didn't have to be more explicit. – Do you take me, I cried out, for mad? My whole life I have devoted to the proletarian cause, and you suggest now that at the end I should consent to have myself pictured as an agent of reactionaries, a spy, a renegade, a traitor?

– You have made admirable sacrifices for the cause. This would be the most admirable. *We* would know the truth.

– And in the meantime, for the record, I besmirch and befoul my career!

– Observe, it is not I who treat you as a *careerist*. You choose that designation. Indeed, I am beginning to wonder whether a fighter who places such value on the concept of 'reputation' is, or ever was, the man to understand our materialism. Is it your vanity that you seek to protect, protect at the expense of the living toiling masses?

I have to admit that out of this encounter my opponent emerged victor. That night, as I tossed through nightmare after nightmare, he was victor again and again. The scene in the theatre which at its performance I had steeled myself to look at dispassionately, objectively, now began crowding into my dreams. Rasminsky, – I was Rasminsky. More than once throughout the night I found myself roused from my hectic slumbers by long animal cries struggling knotted and frantic from my own throat. I was happy when at length came day, or at least wakefulness – in that constantly illuminated place it was difficult to tell day from night – to release me from the professors and their experiments.

I knew then that I was approaching a decision. Rasminsky's ordeal I would never suffer; there was always suicide, – even under the eyes of the most vigilant jailers there was always suicide which could save me both from the disgrace of confession and those units of torment. But here there intruded the true, the fundamental dialectic – the dialectic of life and death. I was, my examiner's jibes to the contrary notwithstanding, indeed a materialist; I certainly did not believe in any Hereafter; the supreme reality to me was – matter; and the highest form of matter, since all matter through it was known, was my own living body. This I must preserve. At all costs. Malenkov was right, reputation was nothing, it was an artifact, it could be made, unmade, and made again. The important thing was – to survive.

But – argument here ran into walls as unyielding as those of my cell – but the confession was but a prelude, a swansong of the courtroom; invariably the verdict was followed by the terse announcement: Sentence duly executed. Here the pendulum of my argument dropped, and swung no more.

At the next interview I again refused to make myself party to a judicial travesty, myself at once fictitious prosecutor and real scapegoat.

– Not even after our talk of yesterday? Not even after the movie?

– Not even … What have I got to lose, I blurted out, my life? I lose that anyway. I won't confess, there's no incentive.

– So that's what's bothering you?

– A trifle, I admit. But it's my own precious trifle.

– But why, dear comrade, didn't you say so? That can be arranged. Your life will be spared. You do your part, and your life will be spared.

– What if you don't? I complain to you?

– Allow me to explain your position to you. We don't have to make deals with you. If we wished it, we could rid ourselves of you forthwith, and an end! If we felt like handing you over to the professors, we could do that, too. But that we do only to real criminals, to the saboteurs, to the Rasminskys. You we are offering a privilege – the privilege of doing a last service to the cause you say you hold so dear. It's a hard service – that's why we have had to have these many talks. I am glad to see that you have come around to our way of thinking. Your natural life-expectancy? That, as I said, can be arranged.

– But I have to trust you?

– Yes, you have to trust us.

He waited for me to insult him. I did not. My silence, however, did not strike him as a sealing of our compact.

– Tomorrow, Comrade Czernik, he said, I will show you that we are to be trusted.

Malenkov's attitude toward me altered overnight. My regimen was changed, I was allowed privileges, I was given better food. And I was told that I was about to go on a journey. To my friends abroad.

So I was really as important as I thought I was. It couldn't be otherwise, the record of a lifetime of revolutionary devotion does not go for naught. When in the custody of Malenkov I left the prison to board a plane that was to take both of us to our destination, I was, so I felt, only technically a prisoner. We had come to almost an understanding. Only a detail – my somatic continuance – remained to be worked out.

The trip was uneventful. We landed at the airport of the central capital. Instead, however, of motoring into the city to visit the scenes which but a few years earlier I had left to take up my duties in my own country, Malenkov directed me toward another plane which stood waiting at the far end of the field.

– We have, he said, somewhat farther to travel.

– Farther? But it is here we see our friends.

– They will be friends whom you are going to see there … He made a gesture indicating remote distance.

The crew of this second plane, I observed as I stood in the terminal building, were everywhere the recipients of a special respect verging on servility. They seemed to be more than mere airmen. I thought, in fact, that the attitude taken towards them all, from Malenkov down, contained in it not a little of fear. The crewmen, for their part, carried themselves as if they were members of an elite. We entered the plane.

We travelled most of the night. I do not know in what direction we flew, or whether in a straight line, or, as I several times suspected, in confusing circles; but at dawn, as we again broke below the clouds, there extended before us a vast plateau, with here and there idyllic wooded interludes, an expanse over which in the distance there frowned a range of lofty mountains. It seemed an empty land. I looked down and sought in vain to descry the well-known miniatures of human habitation. Not anywhere was there a sign of shelter or of smoke. There was not even a railway line to be seen; faint parallel shadows below did suggest a road made up of two ruts, but even this may have been but a topographical illusion.

Then suddenly as we banked and then flew a space, and the motors changed their time, I noticed for the first time an air field, and not far from the field a cluster of houses, a solitary hamlet dropped in that illimitable space.

The sun was out, the day was warm, and as we walked across the field toward the largest of the houses, Malenkov made conversation praising the weather, the landscape, and this pleasant land. I could not but agree. But it was not the weather which filled my mind at that moment; it was impatience at the prospect that soon, soon the purpose of our journey would be revealed, soon I would know why I had been taken this great distance into unknown and unidentified territory, soon I would meet the men who would decide whether I live or die!

I met them. In the large barnlike structure which apparently served as a sort of club – the walls were placarded with slogans and with blown-up photographs of the Hero of the Revolution, – I saw again the men who had so greatly influenced my thinking, who a decade ago were my comrades and mentors at the capital and at various European conferences. I did not, it is true, immediately recognize them. They had aged, aged more than was accountable to the ten years which had elapsed. Their old revolutionary vigor, I thought, had waned considerably. These were not the firebrands of yore. The decisive gesture, the incisive look – they were missing. But I recognized my friends.

There, as we entered the building, there he stood, his face marked with the passing years, his head still cocked on a side, as was his habit when I knew him, the first Chairman of the International, in his Swiss exile Lenin's most intimate collaborator, the organizer of sabotage and strikes, one of the principal Architects of the Revolution, the incomparable, the peerless Gregory Zinoviev! Beside him that other, his beard now white, his eyes behind his spectacles dimmed, but noble his stance as when in the old Czarist Duma he launched his Bolshevik thunder, Lenin's deputy, Lenin's editor – Leon Kamenev! And Smirnov, organizer of Siberian victory, the brave, the indomitable Ivan Nikitich! And Bakayev! And Mrachkovsky! And Ter-Vaganian!

They had not been killed! I saw them, I saw them move, I heard their voices, they were alive! The sentence of August 24, 1936 had been a hoax, an ingenious tour de force of propaganda, a means toward the consolidation of the worker's state, a duping of the enemies abroad. The report of the rejecting by the Praesidium of the appeal of The Sixteen had been a great wonderful lie, perhaps the most useful lie of our century. The announcement: 'The verdict has been carried out' – fiction, a piece of political fiction! The Sixteen, they, and members of their families were alive, alive and resting upon the laurels of their last sacrifice for the cause.

I saw it all clearly. The announcements of executions, it now came to me, always emanated from some impersonal agency. No reporter, no third person, no named individual had ever reported *seeing* the accused executed. The firing squads had existed merely in a news release. Shadows had been flung upon the screen of History, simulating death; but the actors had walked off to their retirement, to the reward for final immolation, not of themselves, but of their names. And even these names, these glorious names now suffering temporary eclipse, would one day be resurrected, would one day, when the struggle would have come to an end with the inevitable victory, be reinstated into their rightful places, this tale of their last and greatest self-sacrifice crowning the record. They were alive! Waiting in the antechamber of History, they were alive!

The Malenkovs kept their word.

Our return back to the capital, and then to my prison – I now felt that 'my prison' meant the prison I possessed, not the prison that possessed me, – was, save for one remark of Malenkov's, altogether pleasant. He took the trouble to point out to me that now that I had seen what I had seen I was committed, that I could never move in the area of conflict again, and that if I should so much as breathe a word of what I knew, I would suffer an end like

Rasminsky's. For the rest he was jovial, gloating with me over our shared secret. I, too, felt that I had ceased to be an accused and had become a collaborator; it was as if I was being born anew out of the chrysalis of one Jan Czernik; henceforth I was to be a new person, or rather a new impersonality using the reputation of that stranger called Czernik to advance the Cause which now remained my only tie to natural existence.

We spent during the following weeks much time together, Comrade Malenkov and I, making a coherent whole out of the evidence which was to be presented at the projected trial. In this task, I must admit, I was not of much help; most of the facts were unknown to me, it was upon Malenkov's intelligence service that I had to rely for allegedly corroborative detail. Even to the end I was doubtful of our concoction; so much depended upon my naked say-so, that I had misgivings whether our production would carry that persuasiveness without which the whole thing was doomed to failure.

Then – on the third day of my trial as I was growing more and more sceptical of our procedure – the prosecutor suggested, I affirmed, confirmed, and re-affirmed – it was Captain Lansing who came to my aid. But not in the way he intended. His purpose was frustrated. His attempt, however, we exploited to the full.

The making of testimony during the following days was very easy sailing. Against me no charge of treason was conceivable, but it must be believed, – didn't Captain Lansing risk his life to save me? No emphasis of my value to the West would be made but it carried conviction; – didn't the West send its banditti to rescue me? Hadn't the court seen to what lengths the enemy would go to prevent me from confessing the truths which now, in the light of my proletarian conscience, I was at last making public?

The verdict was reached, the sentence was uttered, and the report of my execution duly released.

For about five months thereafter I lived in the community of The Sixteen. Assured as I was in my own mind of the greatness of the deed which I had done, this period of approbative self-contemplation was most satisfying to the ego which I projected forward into the twenty-first century. I flattered myself that mine had been an act of the highest heroism, heroism – since it lived upon itself and not upon an audience – heroism in the absolute sense. I, too, during these months, lived within myself, and did not notice the true nature of my surroundings, nor the changed character of The Sixteen. Then one day, over some trivial thing, we quarrelled. I think, fundamentally, it began over a difference in speech; my accent, since I was from an outpost, was not exactly of a metropolitan perfection; the Old Guard, I sensed, was poking secret fun at the intruder, treating him, if not as yokel, then as dilettante. We quarrelled.

Our altercation opened my eyes. I began to see my heroes in a light I had never seen them before. I began to make a study of them, noting their own peculiarities both of speech *and* of thought, their relationship to each other, their hopes, their ambitions. The result was that when I did not pity them I despised them. Also, because they had been the bait which had led me into my plight, I began to hate them.

For though they were alive – that was true – they were not really living. They were merely – present. They were vegetating. The days had meaning for them only in terms of its meals and its comforts – a materialist approach, yes, but not such as should have recommended itself to the titan leaders of our Revolution. Giants they may once have been, now they had dwindled to dwarfs, to little homunculi of an intolerable pettiness. In contemporary world affairs they showed absolutely no interest; it was their *boast* that they were apolitical. They lived; that is to say, they ate, they drank, they slept; but they had really ceased *to be*. The intellectual Kamenev, the subtle Zinoviev, Smirnov the strategist – they were now no more than peasants – no, that is a reactionary characterization, I have known peasants of the most revolutionary mettle – they were no more than a peasant's cattle.

How did they pass their days? As I said, with a time-table of natural functions. Their talk was small talk. For excitement, they feuded with one another, organizing schisms, inventing local heterodoxies, effecting gala reconciliations. Their conversational amusement – that stemmed largely from a series of parochial allusions, a communal folk-lore which had grown up during the past ten years and which was understandable only to the members of the community. I felt myself excluded.

I, in turn, kept my mind amused through the invention of a game I secretly played – the game of the kaleidoscope. The object was to find out under how many different aspects my contemporaries could be viewed. Thus I saw them as a harem of eunuchs, emasculated of their former vigour, performing a role essentially auxiliary ... I saw them as a menagerie, a zoo of once noble animals, now unclawed and edentate, kept only against the case when they should have to be shown to some prospective newcomer ... I saw them as the patients of an asylum-ward, the worst of the wards, the one in which the poor things, cataleptic, maintained all day long, like human plants, the attitude in which they had been placed by their keepers ...

It is difficult to live in a limbo. I feared that I, too, would eventually become as they were, simple, senile, sputtering and mumbling away my days in gossip and small rancors.

I decided to rescue myself from this yawning vacuum. I toyed with the idea of escape. It seemed impossible, so remote and severed were we from the whole wide world. I thought that perhaps one of the airmen ... one could never tell. I became reconciled with my companions, and began a series of probing conversations. Desperation does make one naive. I deceived myself into believing that by couching my inquiries as hypothetical problems, I disguised my thoughts. It was stupid, but I didn't care. I was prepared for the alternatives – either to hold on to life, real life, even if only by a conspirative thread, or to drop altogether into the abyss.

The temerity of my imaginings was not long in receiving its reward. One, or some, or all of my comrades reported my questions to the elite airmen. On their next trip to our village, they invited me into their plane.

I expected liquidation. There was no reason now why faith should be kept with me, I had broken the contract first. Nonetheless, I was spared, reprieved to this my northern exile. Perhaps I may yet get the bullet behind the ear, or worse, the Rasminsky treatment; to me, (hopeful?) it looks as if I am being preserved here so that when necessity arises I may be taken back to The Sixteen there to be shown to some new accused whose Zinoviev I would be. It is really of little consequence. I have already ceased to be. Only one ambition – the result of conscience or of indoctrination, I know not which – now motivates me: to render my last service to History.

It will also unmask the Usurper.

And it will mean, too, the end of The Sixteen. Do you think that the Usurper will allow them, these ideal puppets for a counter-revolution, to remain after my disclosure long alive? Thus will the decoys be decoyed; thus in the cold satisfaction which is mine in making these impersonal revelations there will glow also the warmth of personal revenge. The static breaks its mould. The contradictions come to grips, the enduring struggle begins anew ... Let the world's winds rage.

A Fable

The warfare among the beasts of the forest, unceasing and bloody, was taking its toll. One day it was a hare that fell prey to superior guile, the next day a fox that fell victim to superior force. The wolf was beaten by the bear, the bear was mauled by the tiger, the tiger devoured by the lion.

Nobody felt safe. And everywhere the complaint was the same – the inequalities of combat. The denizens of the forest were not evenly matched. In most conflicts, the outcome was a foregone conclusion. It was not only not sporting, it was fatal.

And indeed, was the porcupine with his puny quills a match for the pachydermatose monster who laid him low? Could the elephant with his ferocious tusks be dared by the small, furred, toothlesss midgets? Of what avail the majestic antlers of the stag against the fang and claws of the brigand wolf? And how could one cope with the lion, supple and daring, mighty of paw, carnivorous?

Meanwhile, as these questions – snorted, howled, roared, bellowed – were rhetorically advanced, contention continued. The population of the forest was being systematically decimated.

'And by ourselves!' said the fox.

Making use of his natural persuasiveness – something about united rations – the fox convoked, under a declaration of temporary truce, a general assembly of all the beasts of the domain. As the lion stood by, sullen and suspicious, the fox presided over the meeting and began by explaining its purpose.

It was not that anyone entertained any thought of outlawing war; that – in a jungle – was unthinkable. (Sighs of relief. Roars of applause. Groans of despair.) Not he would ever be the one to move for the degeneration of the noble animal species. The qualities of resourcefulness, bravery, self-sacrifice, engendered by war, ought ever to be kept alive in the race – even if it did mean the death of some individual members of that race. These would not have died in vain. (Belches.) But things had come to such a pass that war was no longer a true test of courage. Why? Because the combatants were not equal!

Could it be said that the struggle between his humble self and, let us say, meaning no offense, a tiger – was a fair fight? A fair fight was one in which both champions went forward to the fray similarly and equally armed. Was it just to oppose the feeble horns of the goat against the crushing, tearing, overwhelming ponderosity – the example was random – of a bear?

No; the truth of this fact everyone, at one time or another, had felt, either in his own person or through his kith and kin. What was now needed was an inter-animal convention, a supra-bestial agreement laying down the rules of war, a pact which would outlaw –

Dozens of ears stood cocked. Now, at last, a solution!

' – which would outlaw,' the fox continued deliberately 'the use of paws, claws, horns, antlers, tusks – '

Here the fox was interrupted by a squirrel gesturing towards a skunk and shouting: 'Chemical warfare, too?'

'Everything, except one thing, one weapon.' He paused for effect. 'Intelligence.'

The din which greeted this announcement was surely not intended as applause. 'A wise guy!' … 'A smart aleck.' … 'Everybody's weapon – but his own!' … 'How foxy can you get!'

'Ask him how and with what he ate that chicken last night? … Intelligence!'

But the assembled delegates did not wait for answers to their jarring questions. 'Give up my claws!' cried the wolf with indignation. 'I'll give it up alright! Right into the deer's throat!'

'Without tusks!' snorted the elephant. 'Good. How about this? Is this legal?' And he squashed with his foot a bear that was raising its paw to strike down a jackal that was going for a field-mouse.

The fox, however, was a born parliamentarian. Rowdy audiences disturbed him not at all. 'All those in favour of my motion,' he said, 'please signify by raising the right hand' ...

At this, so menacing a forest of paws, claws, tusks, even fangs – all moving forward towards the chair – bristled in the air that the fox forthwith climbed a tree and asked for a leave of absence.

But the meeting did not disperse. It was now converted into a melee, a free-for-all. Everybody was howling at the same time; above the noise the lion's roar could be heard.

Then – suddenly – a shot was heard!

A great silence fell upon all the beasts. They knew what this meant – something more powerful than anything they had was approaching. Those two-legged things were in the vicinity. They were as if paralyzed.

Descending from his tree-limb, the fox again took the chair. 'I have,' he said, 'a new motion to put forward. Did you hear that noise? Do you know what it is? It's a bomb, an at-him bomb, and the him is us! I tell you it is a weapon the most shameful, the most uncivilized, the most anti-jungle, ever yet invented! I call for a formal vote against it. Better, I ask our friend, the bear, to pass around the peace petition.'

Oh, what a scratching and a scrawling was there, with claw and tusk and tooth!

The meeting then adjourned, the delegates withdrawing each to his own pursuit, the wolf to claw at the two-legged one's lamb, the fox to steal his chickens, and the bear to raid his honey.

The Bells of Sobor Spasitula

The city of Paris is the most beautiful city in the world. A truth. But a patriot's truth, a tourist's truth, glib on the lips of those who come there – and depart. To the émigré, though grateful for asylum, Paris is no more than his postcard *pied-à-terre*, a milieu of silhouette and montage; the essential dimension, the dimension we Russians designate *podushi*, alongside-the-soul, this, for *us* at any rate, is always lacking.

The broad boulevards and the cafés with the gaily-striped shadow-lettered awnings; chateaux, and gardens and palaces; the Seine making acute accents against the piers of its bridges; the zigzag mansards and the aspiring gothic, Eiffel's gigantic circumflex – they are but pictures in an album. They are somebody else's environment.

But an album is no habitat, and upon the page of Paris itself we émigrés are only marginalia – in cyrillic print. The text is not ours, and cannot be. Except through indirection. Because every one of the graces and prodigies of Paris serves only to remind the exile of something similar, or even contrasting, but always longed-for, that he left behind in his homeland.

His homeland to a banished man – what is it? A memory. A dream dissipated. A sickness of the heart. For once one has crossed the frontier, that line where the world changes its face, one's native land becomes suddenly metaphysical, a blurred concept, a series of interrupted conjurations, something out of time and out of geography that must henceforth have its being only in the mind.

And there not always. There, too, it suffers its deaths and disinterments. It dies, and something else dominates, the need for a residence permit, the struggle for livelihood, and then, abruptly, some trifle will evoke it once again: a brass samovar descried in the window of some antique shop; a compatriot's heirloom table-cloth, with rooster hemstitched upon it, staccato and criss-cross, in green and red; a cap seen in a crowd of hats and berets; a certain smell of the snowfall – and all the Russias ache and throb in the memory!

Then is the Russian firmament, that vaster steppe with its far-flung fires, spread over me again, and I imagine myself at last returned from exile, at home, safe, – until, startled by the nightmare in the dream itself, shocked, I observe that the so welcome sky is still presided over by a moon of a bloated Tartar cast, a Malenkov of a moon, cold, unsmiling, inhospitable. The spell is broken, the stones of my exile rise up again, and I find myself still before the masonry of Paris, fulfilling the expatriot's routine.

Every day as I go from the limbo of my flat to the dingy fourth-floor office of *Istina* (Truth), where, in a private inferno, I daily, like Sisyphus, heave up upon the eighty-four stairs the same boulder-heavy hopelessness that to-morrow must again be hoisted up that height, and the day after to-morrow, and the day after, it is amidst the grandeur and in the sunshine of the *Champs Elysées* that I promenade to Tartarus. Is this a device for obtaining some assuagement for a spirit oppressed? Is. But the relief proves only temporary.

For soon, even here, relief itself becomes allusive, and the marvellous avenue, bursting, at the Arch of Triumph, into a glorious twelve-pointed star, flashes recollection of the imperial épopée, Napoleon and his campaigns; I walk on, musing on how the descendants of the invaders of my country now shelter me; and then, finding myself standing under the curvetting Marly horses – that cavalcade of uplifted furious foreleg and snorting nostril and wide wild eye, all fixed motionless in a last eternal charge against the trembling air – I think, not without gratification, of the zeros of my native clime, and of Napoleon's mounts, no vapour from their nostrils, stiff and frozen in the deep, white drifts of Russia.

Then, though the boulevard is murmurous with its many noises, though loud the brekekex of the klaxons of the taxis, though *le dernier cri* is 1955, in my heart it is 1812, through my head there resounds the triumph of Tschaikovsky's *Overture*, and, full of pride, full of nostalgia, I seem to hear the strains of the *Marseillaise* as they wrestle with, contest against, succumb to, and finally fade before the clangorous, festival, jubilant churchbells of Moscow!

O forty times forty churches of Moscow, burgeoning with turrets and belfries – stamens of the ghostly pollen! – germinant with your cones of divine balsam, fructuous with domes! O cupolas in quincunx, silvered, gilded, gala with green of the apple-leaf, red of the cherry, the hyacinth's blue – you are still my horizon! You are still my hope, ovoids of resurrection, bright-hued and Easter, rainbow of a second covenant! With the uplifted proffer of your domes – pursed flowers of homage, ananas of a sweet savour – with your oblate bulbs and holy tubers, O forty times forty churches of Moscow, join an exile's name! With your bouquet byzantine, first-fruits tendered to heaven, remember me!

For an aging man – O campanile of Ivan Veliky, bells of Pokrovsky! – an aged man a continent out of earshot, still hears, or thinks he hears, the reverberant echoes of your carillon! He remembers you, ye nineteen spires of the Kremlin, now turned cold pikes in Christus's side! And you, *Sobor Spasitula*, Cathedral of the Saviour, sacred memorial of thanksgiving for the going-away of Napoleon, you still rise before me, church of the swordless Victor, – me alien in the Paris sunlight – you rise an exaltation to a heart that never was and is not émigré!

Yes, even though I know that beside the waters of the Moskva, where once five-domed you rose, now one will vainly seek your site!

For in 1931, The Cathedral of the Saviour, for a decade sequestrated and sealed against worship, was finally razed to the ground, and the ground given over to some bureaucrat erection, some rookery for the soviets. Myself, having escaped The Terror in 1922, I learned of the fate of The Cathedral only from report, I was spared that spectacle, and that is why The Cathedral for me still continues – indestructible are the cadasters of the mind! – as part of that cherished skyline, to be remembered with veneration, with affection. And with bitterness. Bitterness not only over the sacrilege which levelled down that shrine, but bitterness because always its recollection evokes recollection of the last days of my friend and life-mentor, the composer Vladimir Sergeivich Terpetoff, one of the early martyrs of The Revolution.

Though the person Terpetoff and the memory *Sobor Spasitula* for me blend together into a single reminiscence, it is not to be inferred that Terpetoff was a saint, or of clergy, or even pious. There is a metropolitan of our church who still reproves Terpetoff's last act as that of a blasphemer – but the reverend scholar has indeed to stretch and subtilize the canon law to produce even the slightest measure of conviction, and then only in his own mind, and there only for a while. The poor prelate! It isn't that he is pharisaic; but he too is in exile in France unorthodox, and must try very hard to find a theme over which to canonize.

Most certainly Terpetoff was not a saint. This is conceded. He lived too much through his five precious senses to qualify for the aureole. Still, his religious predilections were not to be denied. His body and his soul, he took them as special donatives from God, and if he sought to enjoy the one and to probe the other, both to the full, his was a self-indulgence with quasi-sacred undertones, a kind of human *Amen!* gratefully uttered in response to God's *Fiat!*

It was when I was first initiated, being a medical student who toyed also with *belles lettres*, into the *cénacle* of Kiosk that I met Terpetoff. Fifteen years my senior and just returned from the Austrian front with the medal of St. George and a bullet-fractured knee-cap, he reigned here arbiter in matters musical. His reign was mild. Unlike Krasnovitch, our literary editor from whose sanctum only categorical imperatives issued, Terpetoff was to us, *les jeunes*, tolerant and indulgent.

I was surprised, therefore, when after our first meeting I learned that he had served with the army. One had only to spend an hour in the company of Terpetoff, musician-aesthete – mystic, to realize that here was one man, surely, who had neither the temper of steel, nor its hunger. There were, moreover, a number of exemptions from military service that he might well have invoked; he did not invoke them. It was the Army that invoked them, asserting, principally, that the morale that Terpetoff's music might build up on the home front among civilians would far outweigh – begging his pardon – the consternation his presence might cast upon the enemy on the field of battle ...

This argument Terpetoff especially resented, not because it seemed to asperse his soldierly virtue, but because he held his music to be a thing apart, *au dessus de la bataille*; he persisted therefore, brought influence to bear, pressed, and at length was reluctantly inducted, duly trained an officer, and ultimately sent to the front. An Austrian's bad aim – it was Terpetoff's third day out, he was standing in a sector not yet technically under fire – effectively demobilized him.

All this that I say about his ineptness for soldiering must not conjure up a picture of some frail, anaemic dilettante, stunted by long years in a conservatorium. Terpetoff was a broad-shouldered man, though lean, – well-built, strong-limbed; he filled his uniform to a neat unwrinkled mould, and, when inspected up to the epaulettes, must have seemed not unformidable. It was only when one met his gaze that the full gentleness of his temperament shone forth, demilitarizing his garb; and when he smiled his smile, – why, had he across the front that smile smiled, – he would have rendered himself – the devil take it! – subject to court-martial for fraternization!

That smile and twinkle of his first shone for me when one evening somebody in our circle drew to his attention my first venture into musical criticism. It was no more than an impressionistic feuilleton about an exceptionally mediocre performance of ballet. I had slanted it for publication in our vanguard magazine; its tone may be surmised when it is grasped that this was the sort of magazine that publishes a new literary manifesto with every issue. So the review, naturally, was omniscient, forward, and full of youth's clumsy ironies. It was the cold winter of 1916 and, calling upon current event to frost up my verdicts, I gallantly assumed that the choreographer had been arthritic and the ballerina defeatist while the composer I exonerated by supposing a myopic copyist to have betrayed his score into dissonance. Perhaps these strictures were just, – but callow, as I look at them now, they certainly were.

But in Terpetoff's eyes the little pasquinade found favour – with reservations. On behalf of the choreographer and the corps he made ingenious excuses and seemed almost to reprimand my rudeness and cruelty, not to mention my clumsiness; but as to my censure of the composer he had nothing but praise. Going home that night, I walked on air. It is true that a certain *esprit de l'escalier* troubled me, true that it flashed on me that it might have been the animus of competition that had prompted Terpetoff, not only to commend with such warmth my unkindnesses towards the unfortunate composer, but also to add sarcasms of his own, more biting because at once more knowing and more subdued than mine, true that this gave me to pause in my elation; but I soon banished all doubts. I was but twenty, and was it not the renowned Vladimir Terpetoff who had applauded me?

For Terpetoff was then one of our leading composers. He had the patronage of the Court and the ear of the elite. Symphonies, tone poems, concertos, ballets, even simple lyrics, hopped onto the five branches of his staff notation, and throbbed there, semibreve and quaver, like so many plump small bosoms of singing birds. Critics hailed him, – despite his indifference to programmatic music which he held to be too literary but which, for its usefulness as a discipline, he did not altogether scorn – hailed him the melodic continuator of the tradition of Borodin, Cui, and Rimsky-Korsakoff. One of the rare surrenders he made to purely descriptive music, *The Ballet of the Baba Yaga*, was a sensation in its day; cultured Moscow, and even the coachmen on their troikas and the maids in the pantries, could not stop humming the tunes to which the toothless hag, in a mortar propelled by its pestle, flew through the air: a harpy at first innocuous, a granny at the hearth, in her tantrums not to be boorishly spat upon, but to be humoured, and smilingly caressed, and, like last year's snow, ignored. For a time the musical phrase which accompanied the witch's last subsiding *entrechats* served, in polite society, in lieu of a retort, and was sounded jocularly to rebuff improper suggestion.

These successes, of course, pleased Terpetoff, but they were not the design of his art. Though he was fated always to have the critics verbalize his music – even I, whom he tried to persuade to the beauty of pure sound, never quite disembarrassed myself of the habit of translating, as he called it, harmony into grammar – it was melody that was his major musical pursuit, melody and cadence, the invisible pattern of sound-waves, hieratic and unalloyed, – I am quoting, – the wordless calligraphy of the soul inscribed forever on the air.

Sometimes I thought that he was making an ethic out of music, as if its notes were those shining constellations that Kant converted into conscience. Certainly he seemed to hold music an absolute. 'Do lawyers annotate the imperial ukases for their euphony!' he would exclaim. 'No more should the listening to music be made a basis for annotation … One doesn't look at a great painting to deduce the moral of an anecdote; one looks at it to establish contact with the eternal principles of harmony and beauty. So too music. To listen to it is not merely to participate in an act of communication; it is to perform a rite of communion.'

'Only the very subtle,' I said, aware of my own deficiencies, 'can reach such a degree of appreciation. My ears not only want to listen, but my mind wants to understand, and I can't understand unless through words. Isn't that the way it is with everyone?'

'Yes, yes, of course, but "the heart has reasons, Reason does not have." The deepest understanding – that comes only from feeling. It is the emotions that bind us not only one to the other, but all of us to our earliest ancestors. A wordless cry of anguish – is it not understood the world over? Ah-h-h … Oh-h-h … not words, ejaculations – has Zamenhoff invented a clearer esperanto? ... Five thousand years ago some Slavic girl in some far-away *stanitza*, because her spirit was joyful, or was troubled, sang a song. Herself, she has been dead and gone these many centuries. But that song, while she was alive, made vibrations on the Russian air, and those vibrations, Arkady Mikailovich, they have not stopped.'

I suggested that they were hard to hear, being so old.

'*Are* hard to hear. But they are there.' Like a scientist reporting on the results of his experiments, he proceeded to enunciate his law of the conservation of sound. 'It's never lost! It's somewhat transformed, perhaps, the turning world stirs it up a bit, like sugar in a glass of tea, but the sweetness is still there! Only we're dull and deaf ... Don't hear ... O how I wish God had made me keen enough' – and he laughed abruptly, an absurdity recognized – 'to catch the scream of the labour-pain of the amoeba!'

'To be reproduced,' I ventured, encouraged by his laugh, 'on the trombones?'

'Pizzicati on the most tautened strings!' Terpetoff, though a serious man, was not a starched one and had not minded my brashness. 'But,' he continued, 'since such finical drolleries are beyond our grasp, we must reach out for what is within it – to-day's resonance, made up not only of what has been sounded to-day but also of what from long ago is still audible, still trembles on the air. For that is the real task of the composer: to eavesdrop on the vibrations still extant, and to catch the wind in the act of talking human. I do not say divine; human is enough. For in the composite of these sounds is the oversoul of mankind. To overhear the Oversoul! Ah-h-h ...'

He fell silent, as if meditating the unattainability of all things greatly desired.

'Even then,' I joined his thought, 'even when the musician traps the re-re-re- reverberant vibrations, all he gets is an echo.'

'An echo? That is much. Echo is the very manner in which sound observes its Golden Rule. Let the composer catch those echoes, the diapason of the human heart, and then –' He made a sweeping gesture.

And then, what? For some weeks now I had felt that Terpetoff, despite the few years that divided us, really belonged to a past generation, that he was of the school of those Russian utopians, Tolstoyans, who thought that they could goodwill the world into brotherhood. Didn't he realize that most people were motivated – did one have to say this? – by interests other than music? Why must we Russians always be either nihilists or universalists? Out of a stifled impatience, therefore, I demonstratively changed the subject and began talking about my experiences that very afternoon among the invalids and the cadavers in the hospital. I dwelt in detail upon the human body as I found it in the wards, too frequently pus and putrescence, and upon the human soul, as I heard it when unrestrained, all terror and appetite.

'So you're taking me to task, Arkady Mikailovitch, for being too high and heady! You take me to the depths to show me a world, you think, I do not know. But you have misunderstood. All my altitudes have no meaning without those depths. It is just because of the depths that the altitudes are high.'

'But who lives in that thin air? Angels?'

'Angels I know only by definition, and by definition they are the least worthy of God's creatures. They do not crawl, they need not climb, they only fly. But man can know both, both depth and height. He must know the depths, that's the way he's born, but height is not inaccessible. And the height has meaning only because of the depth, the ethereal only in relation to the palpable. Indeed, evil itself often gives good its significance.'

On Terpetoff's lips, the Terpetoff that I had known, it is true from only a half dozen meetings, this was new and strange. I had thought that day that my coarse imposition of the lessons of anatomy upon his exalted musical evangelism would be resented, would result in mutual alienation. I did not care; I had grown fond of him as a person, and could not tolerate the notion that he was so different from myself. He wasn't, except in degree. He continued:

'Not only does everything have its opposite, but it is their very opposition that endows each of the opposites with force and meaning. Imagine how unbearable life would be if everything about us was always good, always beautiful! Imagine if one woke every morning to the odour of the rose, breakfasted and dined on its petals, went clothed in the fragrance of its leaves, used its thorns for *clefs-à-dents*, its pollen for snuff, breathed its attar all day long, and at night upon a bed of roses reposed, imagine – what a stink life would be! ... No, stench and perfume, the world must have both. The search is for the ratio. Which brings us back, since ratio is one of its deciding principles, to music; of which we have already had enough ...'

I never again, even in the midst of his most didactic discourses – I do them an injustice by so describing them, for they were never sermonizing, nor smug, but always replete with parable, ingratiating with trivia – I never again entertained misgiving about Terpetoff being a full man; that 'stink of roses' had humanized him for me, then so convinced, as a physician-in-training, that I knew the cloth that man was cut from; and always when he launched forth upon an exposition of his ideas, I took them, not as preachments intended for others, but as rules of which he himself secretly hoped to be worthy.

It was from that day, too, that I date the sealing of our friendship, for that was the day when he confided to me, much to my embarrassment and greatly to his satisfaction, that the composer whom I had so wantonly attacked – and upon whom he himself had heaped further ridicule! – was one Vladimir Sergeivich Terpetoff! ... He had been tempted to co-operate in a ballet war-benefit, it really wasn't his métier, but once undertaken he had hurried with it so as the sooner to put it behind him, and that he had done by way of *nom de guerre*.

As our friendship grew – on my part it was still a discipleship – I learned, of course, much about music, but it was Terpetoff's personality, really, which was the true Stradivarius. To me, a youth standing on the threshold of a new world, the world of art, literature, music, Terpetoff's ideas were novel and challenging. Moreover, my friend, unlike most musicians, was not limited as to his expression only to brassbound wind and stretched catgut. He had conversation. It may be that I was especially susceptible to his themes, that alternation between the real, so attractive to the boy who considers himself a man, and the ideal, so attractive to the man who hopes it possible to be more; whatever the cause of my interest, I found his talk of an unflagging fascination.

Why he, for his part, favoured me with his friendship I do not know. I took it, naturally, as a tribute to my precocity; but it did not fail to occur to me also that it was perhaps the malleability of my youth which he found so rewarding. It might have been, too, because I played, in fact, was, a good listener, a good listener and a timely interrupter; for they were my interruptions, I noted, which not rarely stimulated him to his most provocative paradoxes and audacities.

I must confess that I appropriated as my own such of his dicta as best suited my interest and temperament. No doubt this is one of the secretly operative reasons – how sage our Pavlov was – for my long remembrance of Terpetoff: unknown to himself, his ideas played a not insignificant part in my first love-affairs. Again and again, in the tentative courtships of young manhood, I found myself advancing as my own Terpetoff's notions, even phrases, both garbled to my purpose.

It was with Natasha that I insisted, posing as the man of the world that I thought Terpetoff was, that life ought to be lived not only to the full octave, but in several octaves: 'Let us touch all the keys of the spinet world,' I urged her ... all we struck, Natasha and I, were a few tuning-up notes. Natasha had stage-fright. It was the same with Manya, although with her I was almost successful. When I told her that life (young lovers never deal in less than Life!) – that life should be like a rainbow, running in its emotions all the way from ultra-violet to infra-red (Terpetoff *verbatim*) Manya, who was not only a university student with scientific curiosity but was also romantic by nature, did in fact proceed to investigate the spectrum with me, but at the last moment re-adjusted herself, asserting, alas, that she preferred the purity of white. White was, she said, a composite of all the colours, – did I not know?

It became obvious to me after several such frustrations that not only had I done my friend an injustice by excerpting from our conversations only one aspect of his thought, but that I had done myself an injustice, too, by failing to understand that an attitude, especially in the relationship of love, was best expressed *without* words – just as Terpetoff had indicated. When, after these failures, I began to suppress the analects of Terpetoff that suggested themselves for each occasion, and did confine myself to small talk and sighs, I was, in fact, luckier. Even then I could not help thinking of whatever epigram or parable it was that my friend would have considered pertinent to my sallies.

I do not know, of course, how Terpetoff proceeded in his affairs of the heart. At the age of thirty-five he was still unmarried, but not because celibacy appealed to him. Now and again I would meet him at the Hotel Metropole, where his friend Strynenko led the orchestra, and would find him there in the company of some flower-stalk-fragile dancer, and I would think, How right it is, how typical, that he should be infatuated by the phthisic beauty of ballerinas! But I was in error, for the next time, at the *café-chantant* in the Petrovsky Park, it would be some red-cheeked girl, with two golden braided plaits, all health, teeth, and laughter, who would be his companion; and another time still it was the sophisticated Madame Leontov, with her pince-nez worn like a pectoral, and her sables, loose on her shoulder. Between her and Terpetoff the relationship, I believe, was platonic, if not – to judge by their conversations, she was a shrewd and clever woman, – almost socratic. A man, Terpetoff would say in justification of platonic relationships, was not complete unless he suffered from some sexual peculiarity ...

But even the few talks we did have about the passions always tended very soon to leave the boudoir for the philosophic grove. In a general way and without a naming of names he would tell me of the beatitudes and comminations of love, and of love's great moments he would speak as of some high blue oblivion, a paradoxical state where all was nothing, and this nothing – everything. This I had already learned to understand and thus far I followed him. But then he would go on to say that true civilization would not take place until a man or woman were able to achieve this self-effacing all-embracing condition by a simple act of will, and this with regard to any other whomsoever, and this without the intervention of flesh ... I said that this, love humanitarian that had the potency of love sexual, would be a wonderful thing, I had found no reference to it in any of the textbooks on obstetrics, and that I would like to be there when it happened.

'It's no use,' sighed Terpetoff, 'you doctors are always fettered by anatomy.'

This was at dinner, and it was later that evening that he invited me to hear a rehearsal of his Opus No. 13. We went to his apartment on the Tverskaia, where a number of his fellow-musicians, let in by the maid, were already strumming on their violins and dehydrating their wind-instruments. Madame Leontov, too, was there, humming passages from the score. Though Terpetoff had designated his work by a mere number (again his predilection for the abstract), the melodies of which it was composed were so identifiable, so pregnant with association, that their sequence alone did in fact seem to tell a story, – so much so that Strynenko ventured, amidst the non-committal silence of the composer, to suggest a more descriptive title. He would call it, he said, and indeed so marked it on his score, *Prelude to the Dormition of the Little Mother*. It was, I thought as I followed the performance, a most apt title.

Began the music quietly, almost in the style of a lullaby, soothingly. The Mother of God – not the beautiful young Bride of the Roman cult, but the small, aged, venerable Matouchka figured in the art of the Greek Orthodox Church – in a calm and tranquil sleep on her couch lies. Form a holy guard about her bed the eleven apostles.

The labour of our Blessed Little Mother Marya is accomplished. She has brought the Saviour into the world, and the Saviour has drawn the world towards the Kingdom of Heaven. Here the melodies of the Eastern liturgy, at first slow and mysterious, then rising crescendo, then pacing forward seraphical-

serene, in turn proclaim Annunciation, Ascension, Assumption. And so divinely sweet this music is, one feels, one knows, it cannot last!

Suddenly, indeed, there is a change. Suddenly is heard an excited agitation, a ruffled synod of six little themes – these were, Strynenko had interpreted, five pairs of apostles, frightened, murmuring, and St. John the Evangelist, fearless, minatory. There is trouble in the world. The trouble is Judas.

With sounds deep and sinister, as if he would pogromize the saints, with sounds wheedling and falsetto, a silvery tinkling, as if he would corrupt them, he intrudes upon their frantic councils, heightens their alarm, and at last, so dominant are his strains, overwhelms them. One longs for the first motif, the lullaby. It is not heard. Sleeps the Mother of God.

Sweeps instead through the composition a great and bitter melancholy. The heart of the world is breaking, breaking into two unequal parts, one aching under oppression, the other aching with regret and remorse! Like rain in autumn, sad and slow, notes fall … Gusts of sighing drive them off-tone and aslant … They are so hurt they cry not with their own voices … A sobbing, as if mankind would retract its breath … Because all that injurious breath, it wasn't really meant … So poignant-human is this music, one prays, one hopes, it soon will cease! …

Rumble of menace! Thunder! Cymbals and clashing, again and again! The apostles have summoned the heavens to their aid! Persist, however, the strains of sadness still, persist, but altered now, transfigured, and at last the theme that has not been sounded since the beginning floats into the rolling tempest, hushes it. It is the theme of the Blessed Mother of God, now roused from her sleep. It is as if a lullaby woke itself.

Now the beatific presence has returned to the composition, but the finale, though choral in style, is not religious. Secular it is, even modern, a harmonious correlation of recognized melody, snatches from the song of peasant in the field, humming of artisan at his bench, woodsman's hollo and bargeman's shanty, all *of* the world, concordant, yes, and pious, too, the carpenter with his hammer doing honour to St. Joseph, the stable-boy at the manger serving Him, and over all maternal Blessed Marya – the pitch and summit of all music, The Holy Family, The Human Family!

How shall he who has experienced an immersion in music communicate that experience to him who has not? Madame Leontov was so enthusiastic that she took with her a transcription of the score. But scoreless and unplayed, how may its essence be communicated? The best that one may do is to array in their order the verbal associations that the music evoked. It is this that Strynenko did when he gave Opus 13 its name. Whether the same verbal associations had run also through the composer's mind, Terpetoff would not say. Since Terpetoff did not compose in language but in rhythms, alternations, patterns, it did not matter, for they were either these very associations, or others akin to them that whispered behind his ear-drums. Whatever they were specifically, they were in general pattern an amalgam of the earthy and the heavenly and opened for me yet another window onto my friend's temperament.

They gave me also that understanding which I was often to invoke as I tried to gloss over what I then considered Terpetoff's gravest weakness. He drank. He drank rarely, but when he drank, he drank too much. Even as he lifted to his lips his first glass of vodka, he already knew how the bout would end. He would try to make a joke of it and would say that the first drink was to wet the palate, the second to whet the appetite, the third to wash the first two down, and the fourth surely was allowed for thirst ... But he would proceed to a fifth and a sixth, until, his tongue turning slowly on its hinges, his speech became thick and ambiguous.

My friend, I then said, is, though superfine, not a prig. Was not music, too, a kind of alcohol, distillate of sound? And look, I said, what happens when he drinks! The very core of his true nature emerges, and he's even kinder and more loveable than ever ... even to the point of tears ... tears that suddenly sprinkle his face like the notes of some little intimate descant of the conscience! ... I would sit there, then, and for sociability's sake slowly sip at my drink, and then, after a while, get up to leave. His formal words of parting, then, *'Prosti! Ne pominay lihom!'* – the conventional goodbye of our language, how it would take on a new and deeper meaning! 'Forgive me! Don't remember me by the wrong I have done you!' For, certainly, he never had done me any wrong, only good. Throughout all the years of our friendship, no reproach, no grievance ever came between us. Except one.

Nor was even that a real grievance but rather a protégé's sensitivity. Since Terpetoff stayed in Moscow for most of the year I met him practically every week, either at his home, or at the opera, or at Madame Leontov's. I looked forward to these meetings with Terpetoff; they were, at that time, the events of my life.

And then one day I called at his door and discovered that Terpetoff had left Moscow, had gone to some country place. I was surprised, he had said nothing to me about it. When would he be back? The maid did not know, probably – and she ventured a guess, or, as I thought, delivered an instructed vagueness. My friend, of course, owed me no accounting as to his comings and goings, but somehow, since every heart desires another's heart to be its mirror, I felt what is for a Russian, and I suppose for others, a special distress, *ne-otzvchivy*, unresponded-to.

This happened not once but often.

When he returned, sometimes after a fortnight, sometimes after a month, and we would meet, he would not so much as mention his trip. I had to lead up to it. 'I hear you were out in the wilderness, Vladimir Sergeivich. Did you have a nice rest?' His drawn expression, his tired look, of course provided my answer, but Terpetoff skirted the question. 'Most exciting!' he said. 'Exciting – away from Moscow?' 'Collecting peasant melodies – very exciting! And this week I heard one – ' he pursed his lips and shook his cigarette, held between forefinger and thumb, in the air – 'a siskin of a song! But the song of a siskin cursed with humanity ... Listen.' And, apologizing for the inadequacy of his voice, he proceeded to sing it, and it was, in fact, a song full of beauty and anguish.

Finishing it, he smiled, shook his head, as much as to say: The treasure-trove these moujiks have! and was off on a rhapsody about our Russian country-side … the log cabins with their pale-blue window-frames and thatched roofs, like so many Slav faces, blond-haired and blue-eyed … the ikons over the hearth … the grove of slender-branched birches, a mirage of pencilled whiteness … the paysage … the customs … and the people! O, these peasants, he was in love with their simplicity, earthiness, naiveté, even their heavy-handed cunning! The bright gala of their dress, – the women proud under their kakouchkos, their diadems, beaded with false pearls; the full-cheeked high-coloured children, bubbles iridescent in the sun, and the peasants, descendants of serfs, walking about their menial tasks, in their accordion boots, with the dignity of boyars – that, that was true Rus! … And he would hum his tune again. 'You should hear them, my young friend! Live with them!'

I did not answer. Not once had he invited me to go along with him. I nursed my resentment in silence, contenting myself with an automatic nodding of the head. I had no claim upon him.

But Terpetoff, appearing not to notice my resentment, continued with his monologue. Having disposed of the charms of the peasantry, he was expatiating now upon the virtues of the proletariat. New winds were blowing through Russia, the war was going badly, the s.r.'s, the Mensheviks, the Bolsheviks, all were coquetting with the peasants and workers, and I was not over-surprised to hear these eulogies upon his lips. I did feel that he was honest in his sentiments; he had arrived at them, I knew, not through some doctrinaire syllogism, but emotionally, through his experience, his personality. Nonetheless I found his remarks unpalatable. My own family, my father's modest factory, were being threatened by these radical movements; I was not, therefore, a proper audience for such talk. As for Terpetoff, he had achieved his position and fame under the old economy; therefore he, I thought, was not the proper advocate for these heterodox notions. When he spoke about love for the masses I could not restrain myself further, and burst out:

'The mass! I hate the word! It's the mammoth mob, no more, no less, stampeding over everything that's delicate and different!

O that ivory-pure narod! – mastodon with the tusks of envy! Ivan, Stepan, Bulvan, I can love them, each of them, in the measure of his nature! But the masses – the amorphous monster whose heart is as petty as its body is huge – can you truly say you love that?'

'You discard, *golobchik*, my dear pigeon, Arkady, you of the Pravoslavonic faith, love of humanity?'

'Love of humanity, if possible, yes! ... But it's possible only by way of simple arithmetic ... adding one to one, another to another, – and not by the symbolic way of algebra! ... Given z as standing for the masses, is it possible to fall in love with z? The answer is as obvious as the question is absurd! The love for z – that's not love, not even affection, it's just a kind of indifferent benignity towards the anonymous! ... The masses, I fear them! And I hate them! ...'

That was not true, of course, or only partially true. To hate the masses is as impossible as to love them, and for the same reasons. But my resentment over Terpetoff's private rustications, the flaw in our friendship which these unshared journeys of his represented, having to manifest itself some way, I suppose, had expressed itself in this presumably violent ideological difference.

'Too bad! Too bad!' Terpetoff said, mockingly, but now, seeing that I seemed so upset, mocking at himself, 'I shall not be able to rely upon you to help bring about my perfectionist world, the world where everybody, though in cold blood, will love everybody else with an eugenic ardour! ... ' He pointed a whimsical finger. 'You are sabotaging utopia!'

The gesture, though I considered it only a strategic and simulated retreat, did pacify me. 'I hope it never happens, because if it did happen that one could get the same pleasure out of altruism and continence as out of egotism and passion, why, then there would be an end to marriage and giving in marriage ... Wouldn't be worth the trouble ... My dear Vladimir Sergeivich, you, you are endangering the future of the race!'

Like a tolerant older brother, he had received my outburst good-humouredly, and we parted that night on our usual friendly terms. After that, in spite of the recurrence of his sudden decampings, our relationship continued as before. Some small consolation I eked out of the thought that, even if he had invited me, I could not have gone with him (still, still he should have given me the privilege of expressing regret!) for now I was busy not only with my curriculum of studies but also with an interneship at one of the convents lately converted into a military hospital.

Here our Russian destiny was being brought in from the front … piecemeal … on stretchers … Like a series of disheartening communiqués, all reporting retreat, the casualties were filed in their beds … Nightly the delirium of the wounded swirled about a single vortex, the Slavic and its mutations … it eddied sometimes into ringing cries of *slava*! glory! glory! … but oftener, muffled and subdued, it slid *slabost* into whispers of surrender … until, inarticulate and gurgling, it was finally towed down under the tossing sweat-floods of fever … Every word offered a political diagnosis.

But the pious reigning circles, in the tradition of the Blessed Vassily, seemed to feign the idiot. Had it really been noticed that the calendar said 1917! and that it had already bled out six of its months? … Benevolently surveying the results of his recently-assumed commandership-in-chief, the Czar continued to walk the wards of the hospitals. His admirals, as if sagely meditating a tactic of divided waters, continued to stroke their flaring beards; and his generals, proudly smoothing out the ribbons on their chests, continued to predict victory, victory upon all the fronts over all the embattled legions of all their antagonists.

One legion, however, all the strategists forgot – the revolutionary veterans of the Siberian camps, a force which they themselves had brought into being, which even now was stirring from its long penal hibernation, which even now was making its way, by various routes and in joint action with similar forces from abroad, toward the defeatists in the garrisons, the soldiers in the trenches, the mobs in the slums …

Then, unexpectedly, in the midst of some routine negotiations between the contending political parties, exploded the first attack. At our convent-hospital, I remember, this attack was facetiously characterized – the chancelleries were no wiser – as a mild onset of the Petrograd falling-sickness. How wrong, how fatally wrong we were! For it was no mere social migraine that had dizzied the metropolis. It was the beginning of The Russian Epilepsy!

It showed all the symptoms. There was the premonitory aura of the dazzling slogans (flash! *brotherhood* ... flash! *justice* ... flash! *equality* ...), and there was the terrible horrific fulminative scream: Revolution!

Swooned the mighty head of Russia ... Was it to be wondered at? What abscesses they were that pressed beneath that skull! The world knows it now for what it was, our noble leadership, with its champagne-soaked brain of caviar ... with its arachnoid merchant-class, webbed meningitic in greed and rapacity ... and that large soft lesion, its intelligentsia ... But then it saw only that the Russian body had fallen to the ground, convulsed and thrashing. The quivering bulk, the whirling extremities – were they not signs of vitality?

Paroxysm. Legs jerked and kicked – the puttee'd legs of soldiers deserting their posts, voting – the scrutineer was Lenin – voting for peace in a ballet of raised legs ... jerked and kicked the felt-bound legs of peasants, jactitating, like some primeval mille-pede, over the vast provinces ... As for the arms, they gyrated in a frenzy of seizure ... fingers clutching and closing ... over handfuls of air ...

Woe to him who stepped into the radii of those robot flailing limbs!

Meanwhile the eyes of Russia, dilated, immobile, stared forth unseeing from that swooned head. Only at the mouth, as, between grinding teeth, each Bolshevik *prikaz* was newly sputtered out, was there a foaming or bloody saliva ...

From October to the following March, the body of my country, torn by inner cramps, the clonic spasms of intraparty conflict, turned and twisted and rolled in its convulsions. Then, after a while, these, too, ceased. The first violence was over.

There followed the raucous stertor of tyranny.

Upon me its effects were almost immediate. My father had once dared to resist a factory strike and now found himself a special target of the workers' animosity. Though he made concessions, though he compromised, it was all to no avail. When the porter at our door presided one day over a meeting of his soviet, at my father's board-table, using his whiskbroom for gavel, my father decided that the time was come to leave Moscow. Taking with us only cash, or whatever could be turned into roubles, (this, too, was destined to dwindle under the inflation), we made our way, disguised as our own employees, toward the still unerupted South. Our factory, our home, they fell into other hands. My medical studies, interrupted, were never to be resumed again.

In spite of his proletarian sympathies Terpetoff, too, found himself among the déclassés. His successes under imperial patronage did not at all recommend themselves to the new occupants of the Kremlin. Accordingly I invited my friend to come along with us. He smiled wryly at the invitation, thinking, no doubt, of his own lack of hospitality with regard to journeys out of Moscow, thanked us, and said he would stay. He still had some money and until things settled down again, which, of course, they must – this was the universal delusion! – he would remain in Moscow, or, perhaps, make some new excursions into the country in search of folk-music. I did not try further to persuade him, it seemed hopeless. The land is on fire, and Terpetoff, he cups his ear for melodies!... That was the first time I felt older than my friend, and indeed I never again felt younger than him.

We remained in the southern provinces for almost two years, waiting, as did hundreds of others, for 'the return to sanity.' We moved first to Kiev, to Odessa, to Rostov, to the villages of the plains, and it was all like the flashing of the scenes of some incredible fantastic dream: Czarist officers at dinner brilliantly deploying their cutlery across the table ... Baron Wrangel, gazing at himself in a mirror, studying his long Hapsburg countenance ... among the cornflowers self-banished Social Revolutionaries planning agrarian reform ... stolid peasants ... singing no songs ... But real and not part of a dream was the growing depletion of our savings. We kept wondering about Moscow and who was now muddying the carpets in our home. Perhaps what we were getting was just White propaganda, perhaps things had come back to normal, there were rumours of a New Economic Policy that Lenin was about to inaugurate – it was decided that while my parents and my sister stayed on, I should return to the capital.

It was a long, and now a dangerous, way, and after many adventures, of which it is not necessary to tell here – this is Terpetoff's story – I left behind me the gibbets on which the Whites hanged the Reds and the trees on which the Reds hanged the Whites, and finally that winter reached 'stone-built Moscow.' It was a changed city; the old landmarks were still there, there had been no shelling here as in Petrograd; and except for broken windows and boarded-up doors, the great buildings stood as before. But it was not the Moscow I had known. The luxury stores on the Kusnetsky-Most were shut down; the traffic was melancholy and drab; there were queues for rationing; now and again a government sleigh would appear in the square, unload its cordage of wood, and the shivering Muscovites, snatching up their logs, would hurry home with the revolutionary bonus ... It didn't look like the stability my parents were hoping for.

At the end of my first day, moreover, as I lay on my bed in the boarding-house room that I had rented, I became aware of another change in the Muscovite atmosphere. I realized that all day long I had heard no church-bells. The churches had been expropriated, closed; some that I had passed during the day I saw to have been gutted, defenestrated. Most of their bells had been removed, melted down for cannon. Only here and there had I noticed, in some isolated belfry, the familiar recurring outline.

The next day, making discreet inquiries, I discovered that our factory was now a co-operative, that is to say, that it had been pillaged not by one but by all in common. Our home? Well, the carpets were not being muddied .. they were no longer there. The present tenants, habitual expectorators, had found them a great inconvenience ... and had disposed of them. My heart was heavy within me. How would my father, my mother, my sister, accept this dashing of their hopes? For all, all now belonged to an irrevocable past ... with our governesses under their parasols ... with the featherbeds of my childhood ...

Tired of the subterfuges and dissemblings which these inquiries had forced on me, hungry for some honest talk, I wondered whether my friend was in Moscow. I doubted whether he would still be living in the same apartment; after all, two uprooting years had passed; nonetheless, I went there. Terpetoff? They knew nobody by that name. I wandered about the streets.

Thus at random surveying my expropriated city I had spent practically the entire afternoon when, attracted by a poster on an easel in front of the Korsh Theatre, I stopped to read it and was convinced, for the first time, that there was something, something actually operative, in my friend's theory of the echo. For my lonesomeness was receiving its reply: there, among the items of a programme of music to be performed that very evening, the bright red letters spelled it out – VLADIMIR TERPETOFF! ... I now had, if not an address, at least a place of rendezvous. I was in luck.

In luck? As I read on, doubts assailed me. For the performance, it said, was to be given by The People's Orchestra. So ... so my friend had made 'adjustments' ... Worse, he had completely capitulated, for the piece of his which was to be played was titled *Overture Proletarian!* ... Should I, then, see him at all? How could one know, how could one tell, since everything had been stood on end, upside-down and wrong side up, where Terpetoff's loyalties lay now? ... Was I not, perhaps, running the risk of denunciation? ... Could not be! Our past relationship! ... My fears were ridiculous, it was shameful that I should entertain them ... Of course I would attend the performance ... Still ... might I not be inviting disaster? ... The possibility was not altogether to be excluded, and I determined that I would be cautious, circumspect, and, if necessary, would pretend that I had broken with my reactionary family and had seen the new dawn's red revolutionary light ... O, the ruptures between friends, the hypocrisies, the distortions of self, that Terror imposes and compels!

I arrived early at the theatre but in vain watched at the door to catch Terpetoff coming in. Inside, among the seated audience, too, I could not find him. Planning after the performance to look for him among the musicians, I settled down to listen to the *Overture Proletarian*.

The theatre was unheated, the audience wore its overcoat, and when, at the conclusion of the Terpetoff composition, the last on the program, the people burst into applause, I could not be sure, because of what I knew of the special quality of Terpetoff's music, whether they clapped in appreciation, or just to keep warm ... As they hurried out of the theatre, I made my way, against the grain, towards the orchestra.

I recognized Strynenko. A proletarian! ... But even more surprising was the presence there of Madame Leontov, this time without sables. She looked drawn and haggard. She was, I gathered from their attitudes, questioning Strynenko about some passages in the score. I greeted them both.

'Wonderful music, Terpetoff's, wasn't it?' said Strynenko, turning to me, blandly grinning.

I understood the grin, but ignored it. 'Wonderful – and wonderfully played ... Is Terpetoff here? ... I would like to congratulate him.'

Strynenko looked surprised at the question.

'Have you forgotten that our friend avoids first nights? He's never there on opening night.'

That was true. It was a golden saying of the French, Terpetoff would explain, that it was *la deuxième nuit qui était de la première classe*.

'Where is he living now?'

Strynenko shrugged his shoulders. 'Haven't seen him much lately.'

'Didn't he come to rehearsals?'

'No. He knows us,' – this with a sweeping gesture towards the musicians, packing up their instruments, 'and he has faith ... And justifiable faith, I think ... Wait till you read the review in the *Nowa Gazeta* to-morrow morning ... You'll see ... '

'I'll look for it. It should prove very interesting.'

'Very,' Strynenko said. 'Terpetoff, you know, has had bad times. Wouldn't co-operate ... But to-night's performance, I'm sure, should mean a change, a change for the better.'

'If you really want to find him,' Madame Leontov interposed, 'there's a tavern about six blocks from here where, I believe, he spends his afternoons ... Myself I haven't seen him for quite a while ... He's much too intransigent for me.'

'Intransigent – and writes proletarian overtures?'

'Well, that's recent, that's new.' She looked significantly at Strynenko. 'But a change is coming, I'm sure.'

'I hope so, for his sake, comrades, and for ours. We can't afford to lose such talents ... '

The next morning I hurried to get the *Nowa Gazeta*. Strynenko was right. Its music-critic was more than enthusiastic, he was panegyrical. Since copies of that journal are no longer available, and since the review presented a novel interpretation of Terpetoff's music, it is worthwhile, I think, here to interpolate his remarks.

'Our revolution' he wrote, 'the social *zukunftsmusik* of which up to now we have heard only the exordium, has found its first musical dragoman! He is the composer Vladimir Terpetoff, whose *Overture Proletarian*, acclaimed last night at the Korsh Theatre, may be taken, not only as a model of the kind of melody which reaches, without benefit of program notes, right into the heart of the people, but also as a *tour de force*, an illustration of how the technique of Marxian dialectics may be applied to composition itself.

'The work begins with a delicately lilting melody, sweet, uncomplicated, of a primitive innocence. In tone it is Russian pastoral, and one cannot but evoke, as gently one is transported by it, our early communal villages, still free from landlordism, still rocked in the cradle of a benevolent Nature. There are no clashes here, no discords. All is pure harmony ... Thesis! ...

'But soon an insidious intrusion is felt ... its notes creep stealthily upon the introductory theme ... there is something familiar in these motifs, one has heard them before ... but not like this ... and then, under the ironic distortions, the mocking parody, they are recognized! The peasants and soldiers in the theatre recognized them, recognized them and smiled. Once they would have frowned, once they would have trembled, there was a time, even, when they would have fallen to their knees ... now they smiled. For the composer Terpetoff, so as to indicate the break-up of early society into oppressed and oppressing classes has here made play with – the monkish canticles once heard by this very audience in the three churches of the Romanoffs ... has here juggled and toyed with the liturgic music customary to the celebration of the baptisms, nuptials, anointings – and sepultures – of the Czars!

'At first these sacerdotal statements emerge *laskovy*, caressively, as if to recall the unctuousness of the long-robed bearded patriarchs standing sponsors about the "Little Father", kind paterfamilias of all the Russias ... But this is but a temporary, a festival trait ... Before one has even noticed the transition, the ferial has returned, and there have intervened a half-dozen duplicate themes, none of them caressive ... Is it too far-fetched to consider these themes as musically representative of the notorious hyphens of reaction? ... Certainly as one listened to these themes, hurrying and scurrying about, here whispering in secret confabulations, there expostulative, exclamatory, one could not but count them on the fingers ... the Romanoff-Rasputin catechism ... the clerical-feudal antiphony ... the feeble tremolos of Menshevist reformism joined to the somewhat slack *baraban* of White bravado ... the Gutchkov-Miliukov duet ... These musical phrases, at times of a castrato melos, at times of a berserk rhythm, but always interruptive one of the other, are finally identified, a cabal in counterpoint ... identified ... and then ousted, dominated by a new theme which had been skulking, as it were, behind the *coulisses*, and now has made bold to proclaim itself. This theme is heard on the high notes of the clarinets, suave and ingratiating, and on the cellos, pompous, abdominal, ominous ... Not Slavonic its idiom, but unambiguous it still is, and before it the lackey locutions that had hitherto made such a to-do, subside ... fade off ... in little rattlings of audacity return ... subside again. It is the charivari of imperialist capitalism that the orchestra is playing. Antithesis!

'At this point the cellos, though still masters of the score, cede to the violins ... Intolerable sadness ... The bows linger over the strings as if they would curl and embrace them ... would comfort one another ... But at these contacts only threnodies throb ... Dirges ... they never end. Why? Because it is not of a final death that they speak, but of Capitalism's protracted, lingering, endless moribundities ...

'It is as if the music, through its very tentativeness, were saying: "Clay, ashes, dust – these are clean words: sand sprinkled to dry and finalize life's signature ... But the sociological death which Capitalism brings in its wake – O that is not as ashes clean, as definable as dust, as earthy-pure as clay! That death is but putrefaction, viscid, unabating, a rank and seething decomposition, death quick with its own charnel-house quickness; a rutting rot it is, at once cadaverine and spermatical ... " All this, in its painful temporizings, in its endless versions of life-in-death and death-in-life, all this the music seems to say. Seems; for like the sobbings of great loss, the notes gasp contradictions. When they would breathe in, something happens and they become panting exhalations ... When they would breathe out, some sudden reflex sucks them back ... The conflicts, the contradictions are unendurable, stifling, and must be resolved.

'And here it is that Terpetoff achieves his splendid peroration, yes, synthesis! ... From the drums, thunder ... and from the trumpets, bright sharp lightnings! ... O days of October! ... The paunchy cellos try to intervene, but they are deflated, punctured, overcome by clear clarion revolutionary strains. A modernistic effect is heard, a twanging, a harsh cello vibrativeness supplemented by a long screeching note on the violin, then a pause – the cello strings have burst! They will be heard no more ... The firm, martial formalisms of the revolutionary music now abate, wither, wither and give way to the pastoral sweetness which initiated the composition, but now played in a new tempo and with even softer variations ...

'Clear, unsophisticated, happy harmony! Because of its very ease and fluency, Terpetoff here has excelled himself. For such inspired passages, let it be boldly said, are born not out of the mere tic of talent; they are of the composure of genius. Translucent, serene, this is a *finale* that is unclouded *aubade*, a conclusion that is really a beginning ... a cradle of concord ... pure melody ... as sober as the fresh of dawn, as sane as sunshine ... '

The article was subscribed K., and from its last line, which I remembered as an hexameter in one of Krasnovitch's unpublished poems, I assumed his authorship of it. So he, too, Krasnovitch, the implacable editor, had made his accommodations! It had to be conceded to his credit however, that he was being kind to an old friend. But had he really known? ...

For the composition which I had heard that night was not the one which Krasnovitch had so glowingly described. True, the composition was now titled *Overture Proletarian*, true the score had been changed from that which I had once read and listened to, there were now certain satirical alterations in the tempo, slight shifts in the sequence of passages, but the composition was still, even under its new name, Opus No. 13, *The Prelude to the Dormition of the Little Mother*!

How could Terpetoff have done such a thing? Was he that desperate now for bread, for vodka? To re-name an unpublished composition, inspired by sentiments quite different from those which the new name implied, and to offer it as an oblation to hated Authority, – the Terpetoff I knew just wasn't capable of such counterfeit! But there it was, nonetheless ... This it had been which had brought the grin to Strynenko's lips. Mdme. Leontov, re-examining her score, even her it had puzzled. Was it, then, a hoax? If so, a stupid, a dangerous hoax. Terpetoff was not stupid. How long could one expect the nature of a piece of music, which had been rehearsed by an entire orchestra, to remain undiscovered? Then, perhaps, Terpetoff had actually explained everything, made a clean breast of it, confided to the proper authority that what he had done was to revise an unproduced composition so as to put it to new use, and that Authority had agreed to the deception! A dialectic change, as it were; the score's old quantities changed to make the score's new quality ... But then would Krasnovitch, who was close to the musical arbiters, if not a principal arbiter himself, would he have made himself ridiculous in the eyes of his comrades with that absurd review ... thesis ... antithesis ... about what was after all nothing more than a rehashed, synthesized *Ave Maria*!

I found the tavern about which Mdme. Leontov had spoken, and in it, at a table, his bottle, his glass, and a newspaper before him, alone, Terpetoff. We embraced. He was almost maudlin in his greetings. The bottle – was it his first? his second? – was more than half empty, and spoke from within him with ceaseless indignation. He had had a bad time of it these past two years. It had been better had the commissars been afflicted with deafness, or, failing that, had been smitten dumb, but, being neither deaf nor dumb, they had not been slow to express their dissatisfaction with his reactionary music. They wanted music for the people, revolutionary marching songs, sentimental ballads. His piano concertos? They were not left-handed enough!

Music and the class struggle! He just could not understand it. The poor Russian nightingale! It had better itself emigrate abroad – before it were banished for conspiring through melody counter-revolution! Only the parrot was now safe in Holy Russia, only the parrot could accommodate itself to the new dispensations. It hooted, it cackled, it chirped, it clucked; it had all the talents. 'On whose hay-wagon do you ride?' asks the peasant, and advises: 'For him sing the song!' It was a compromise he could not and would not make.

How, then, had he earned his living? A fiddler at weddings! He had stayed away from the cliques and the bureaucrats and had contented himself with picking up a few roubles here, a few roubles there. He had not fed on sterlets and chaud-froid partridge, as in the good old days, but he had not gone hungry either. If only they would let him alone … God, God, he lifted his eyes in prayer, it's enough the pig is a pig: don't endow him also with butting horns!

I pointed to the paper which lay before him.

Yes, Terpetoff sighed, that's where the horns are beginning to grow! That's the special favour Strynenko did me. Write for your country, he says to me, compose for the people, and renown and affluence will again be yours. But that would be a kind of prostitution, I say, and even if I wanted it, I can't do it, it just doesn't write itself that way, I'm better off not writing at all. So he showed me! Took my old Opus 13, revised it, and presented me with a *fait accompli*! … Now wait until Krasnovitch finds out that he has been duped!

It was not long to wait. One of the members of the orchestra saw to it that Krasnovitch soon discovered what manner of music it was that he had so unreservedly eulogized. Krasnovitch was mortified. He thought all Moscow was laughing at him, and thirsted for revenge. Despite the explanations which were proffered to him by the musicians, he held Terpetoff personally responsible for the deception.

Soon he set the wheels in motion to extract from the composer an honourable amends. Such irresponsibility, he argued before the Commissar of Culture, could not be tolerated! To let it pass would be to encourage further defiance of the cultural standards and discipline upon which the regime was based! What good was it to command the loyalty of the workers and the farmers when, in the more influential domains of action, the objectives of the Government were either passively frustrated or intentionally sabotaged by the intellectuals? Terpetoff had wantonly mocked the proletariat and its aspirations; and before the precedent which he had dared to establish grew to epidemic proportions, an example ought to be made of him. No, he would not be too severe, but the situation, he felt, did call for, first, an apology, a public recantation, a sort of penitential manifesto outlining the duties which an artist owed to the state, and, second, a truly proletarian composition, honest in intent and, of course, original in conception.

The Commissar was only too eager to exercise his authority, strike a blow for the State. He had his ablest sleuths investigate Terpetoff's antecedents, and, the full dossier before him, he summoned the composer to his office. Krasnovitch, too, was there, and would not tire, in the months ahead, in describing his sweet revenge.

'But it wasn't I,' Terpetoff expostulated, 'who author'd the offending composition! It was Strynenko who tampered with an old work of mine.'

'Yes, a clerico-reactionary work! Strynenko sought at least to improve it ... But you miss the point. It doesn't matter who wrote the piece, it is credited to you, and therefore upon you falls the duty of rendering this particular service to your country.'

'What service?'

'To explain, using your own experience as object lesson, what are the rules which govern the creation of proletarian art.'

'But I recognize only art – '

'Then your eyes should be further opened so that they may learn to descry distinctions!'

'Is this, then, your idea of cultural freedom?' Terpetoff was losing his temper. 'Do you think it compatible with civilized notions concerning the dignity of art that the composer should be compelled to recant his staff-notation – and not even his own staff-notation – simply because a politician wants to listen to music politically? You are trying to reduce us to less than persons! As for writing music to order, the very humiliation of that circumstance makes it impossible! I can't do it! I won't!'

'Too proud, eh?' The Commissar was toying with his dossier. 'Your sense of your own dignity won't permit it, eh! Imagine – making oneself subservient to the needs of Russia's millions! But you weren't always that haughty, M. Terpetoff!' He waved the dossier in the air. 'Weren't too proud to humble yourself before the peasant woman, Evdokia, of the *stanitza*? Oh, no! Not there!

Ate her nice big de-li-cate cucumbers, didn't you? Swilled up her borsht, drinking from the samovar, like a real *moujik*? Cleaned the plate with chunks of rough black bread! Fastidious, weren't you? Dignified! ... But, of course, that was for your personal pleasure, for self-expression, so to say, mortification of the spirit, and this, this is only for the future, for the culture of your people! Terpetoff, we can't compel you to write our kind of music, the régime of the knout, you know, is over, but ... '

But Terpetoff wasn't listening any more. The production of the dossier had effected a sudden and complete change in him. He flushed a deep scarlet, and seemed even to disdain to deny, to protest, to explain. Silent he sat there, shamed, as if suddenly callow and naked in the presence of his mockers. His secret was known. It was blackmail, the blackmail of this four-kennelled son of a dog, that he had to contend with now; argument was irrelevant. Slowly he raised himself from his chair:

'Yes,' he said, 'I shall do as you say. You shall have it, a composition from my own hand, composed expressly for the people. I shall try to make it memorable.'

I never saw Terpetoff again. But I heard him. Two days later, as he kept his promise to the Commissar for Culture, I heard him. All Moscow heard him. And it *was* memorable.

The old Dmitri, resident watchman of the Cathedral of the Saviour, later reported what took place. 'The devil take it, it is an ordinary Thursday, and I hear this hammering on the barred door of the church. Who can it be? ... I unbar the door and it's no long-haired priest like I had expected, it's this young man, excited, wild-looking, this intellectual pushing me out of his way. "You can't come in here," I say, "this place is sequestrated ... for the purposes of the Revolution ... peoples' property. So kindly go away ... You want to pray? Go home and pray!" But does he listen to me? Before I know it he's running through the nave, and me with my old feet after him, and he's at the foot of the staircase leading to the belfry, when he turns around, pulls out a hammer from his pocket – Holy Carpenter Joseph, they come with a hammer to do you honour! – and he's threatening me with it.

"Ho, ho, my little choirboy," I say, "that's the way it is, then we'll see who's clever, the old Dmitri or you!" And I run outside and I lock the door from the outside. "Pray, young man, pray for the Second Coming!" And I run across to the office of the Commissar for Religious Property, and return with the Commissar himself ... Five minutes it took, no more than five ten minutes, but when I open the church, nothing, he's not there! I can't see him! Is he hiding? ... Did he escape? ... But suddenly the bells ring out! Once, twice, three times! The bells – they haven't been rung for years! "Scan-dal-ous!" the Commissar cries out, "he's alerting a counter-revolution!"'

Wildly, furiously, in random peals, in clangorous alarum, the bells rang out. People stopped in the streets to make the sign of the cross; windows were flung open; all eyes turned toward the domes of the Cathedral of the Saviour. But from the circular boulevards which run like the rings of some great and ancient oak about Moscow's central core, the Kreml Spaskiya, only the swinging outline of the bells was to be descried. It was about the church itself that the true ovation to Terpetoff's last concert was given.

For there, an armed soldiery summoned by the Commissar to emergency duty, had surrounded the cathedral. Their rifles aimed upward at the clamorous helmet of anger, they loosed volley after volley. To no effect. The ringing persisted. Terpetoff was composing an *opus*, not a mere exercise in tintinnabulation. Again the rifles sent forth their leaden notes; still the peals resounded. Terpetoff was not to be silenced. Music for the people? He was composing music for the people!

At last a bullet struck its mark. Both arms flung outward – for an instant a living ikon poised against the spires! – Terpetoff hurtled headlong forward, his body slamming and somersaulting and sliding down the slope of the roof detaching in its fall a shower of loose stones and broken tiles. The body, shattered, lay motionless on the ground. Slowly the bells jangled to a stop.

That was the last time I heard the bells of Moscow. Thousands heard them with me, but one will search in vain, in the files of contemporary newspapers, or in the records of Marxist history, for a report of Terpetoff's fatal demonstration. To-day I cannot hear bells anywhere without recalling my friend's defiant last gesture. It is well that there should be at least such recollection, for in his homeland Terpetoff has remained wilfully unremembered these past three decades, The Cathedral of the Saviour is no more, and as for the score of Terpetoff's concluding composition, it exists to-day, if it exists at all, only in the small cicatrice produced by a piece of falling stone, which a certain former Commissar of Religious Property still bears, the shape and size of a minim, upon his forehead.

Textual Notes and Emendations

This collection of thirty-five stories is the second in a series of volumes of A. M. Klein's writings projected by the Klein Research and Publication Committee. It contains all the completed short works of fiction, many hitherto unpublished. There are a number of incomplete works of fiction in the Klein Papers in the Public Archives of Canada – chapters of novels and fragments of stories – many of them substantial and important. These will appear in a subsequent volume. Of the thirty-five stories in this book, two or three may be considered marginal additions, eg 'Epistle Theological,' 'Portrait of an Executioner,' and 'Memoirs of a Campaigner,' in that either the narrative or the fictional element is slight, but even these stories sufficiently reflect Klein's interests and ideas, and his qualities of imagination and style, to warrant their publication. This volume seemed the only appropriate place for their inclusion.

One of the basic intentions in this collection of A. M. Klein's stories was to establish, from the published and unpublished versions that existed, the most accurate text. To do so, I tried to keep to Klein's text as closely as possible, ignoring occasional lapses in grammar, such as unaccountable shifts in tense, or departures from standard practice in punctuation. Where errors affecting the clarity or accuracy of a passage occurred, I made the needed changes and noted them in the list below. Some of the changes from the published text are based on what seems a more accurate version in the manuscript, and some on Klein's own alterations written on the tear-sheet of the published version. In general, misspellings and errors deemed to be purely mechanical were emended silently. Klein used italics for a variety of purposes: to indicate quotations and foreign words, and for emphasis, but he is inconsistent, sometimes even within the same story. The practice of italicizing foreign words and quotations is standardized in this volume, but Hebrew words which are names of holidays or people or places – for example, Yom Kippur, Baal Shem Tov, Erez Israel – are not italicized.

For several stories in this volume, there exist two or three drafts or published texts. I used the last version, so that in the present edition Klein's latest changes are incorporated. Where the changes from an earlier version, however, are slight, as for example in 'The Seventh Scroll' and 'No Traveller Returns … ,' I placed the story in the chronological sequence at the earlier date and recorded this fact in the textual notes below.

EPISTLE THEOLOGICAL – *The Reflex* (January 1929)
'attribute … to lack of initiative and executive ability, and the
divine will': 'attribute … to lack of initiative, executive
ability, and the divine will.' In Klein's handwriting the am-
persand and a comma are often indistinguishable. p 12, l 6

PROPHET IN OUR MIDST – *The Judaean* III, 7 (April 1930). By Ben
Kalonymos
Klein was fond of using pseudonyms, and he used them
frequently for his fiction. Ben Kalonymus was an early
fourteenth-century Jewish scholar in Provence, a translator
into Latin, and a didactic but witty satirist.

BY THE PROFIT OF A BEARD – *The Judaean* III, 9 (June 1930). By
Ben Kalonymos

THE LOST TWINS – *The Judaean* IV, 1 (October 1930). By Ben
Kalonymus
plain: plan p 24, l 14

THE TRIUMPH OF ZALMAN TIKTINER – *The Judaean* IV, 2 (November 1930). By Ben Kalonymos
transpired in Palestine and a compelling nostalgia: transpired in Palestine, a compelling nostalgia p 30, l 24

THE PARLIAMENT OF FOWLES – *The McGilliad* II, 1 (November 1930)

THE CHANUKAH DREIDEL – *The Judaean* IV, 3 (December 1930). By Ben Kalonymos
This story was reprinted in *The Canadian Jewish Chronicle*, 23 December 1936, under the pseudonym Ben Kalonymus.

THE MEED OF THE MINNESINGER: A VIVID SHORT STORY BASED ON THE LIFE OF A GREAT THIRTEENTH-CENTURY POET – *The Jewish Tribune* (5 December 1930). This story was reprinted in *The Jewish Standard*, 30 March 1934.
In the original version the story was not divided into two sections.

MASTER OF THE HORN – *The Canadian Jewish Chronicle* (30 September 1932)
This story was written several years earlier. A typescript dating from the 1927–30 period is in the Public Archives of Canada, Klein Papers 3376–83.
The major break before the final section beginning 'The High Holydays approached' was omitted in *The Canadian Jewish Chronicle* version, but is indicated in Klein's typescript. The published version has at least five seeming breaks in the narrative, probably introduced by the typesetter for reasons of spacing. p 65, l 34

THE PARROT AND THE GOAT – *The Judaean* IV, 6 (March 1931). By Ben Kalonymus

THE BALD-HEADED MONARCH – *The Judaean* IV, 8 (May 1931). By Ben Kalonymus

TOO MANY PRINCES – *The Judaean* v, 2 (November 1931). By Ben Kalonymus

ONCE UPON A TIME ... – *The Judaean* v, 7 (April 1932). By Ben Kalonymus
 To set off clearly authorial interpolations in the story, I have added the quotation marks at the beginning and end of speeches, and parentheses in the president's speech.
a wild stampede of donkeys, braying: a wild stampede of donkey's hooves, braying p 88, l 18

SHMELKA – typescript dating from 1930–3
 A later typescript (1934–7), which contains a few minor revisions, is the version used here; Public Archives of Canada, Klein Papers 3699–3714.

THE SEVENTH SCROLL – *The Jewish Standard* (22 September 1933); typescript (1934); Public Archives of Canada, Klein Papers 3680–98; *The Canadian Jewish Chronicle* (12 September 1947). Klein's final version is the one used here, but because the typescript version of 1934 is very close in date to the first published version and contains nearly all the revisions by Klein that appear in the 1947 published version, the story is placed at this point in the chronological sequence.
drawing: in the *Chronicle* version this word is italicized, but not in the typescript or *Jewish Standard* version. p 107, l 2

BLOOD AND IRON: A SATIRE ON MODERN GERMAN IDEOLOGY – *The Jewish Standard* (January 1936)
 This story was reprinted, under the title 'The Biography of a Dictator' with the subtitle 'A Fable for Our Times,' in *The Canadian Jewish Chronicle*, 4 August 1944, the year that Klein published his satiric poem *The Hitleriad*.
music: musical p 113, l 14

FRIENDS, ROMANS, HUNGRYMEN – *New Frontier* I, 1 (April 1936)

BEGGARS I HAVE KNOWN – *The Canadian Forum* XVI (June 1936)

A MYRIAD-MINDED MAN – typescript dating from 1934–7, Public
Archives of Canada, Klein Papers 3384–3415
faker: fakir p 126, l 1. The same word appears later on p 153, l 5
agglutinition of involutionary: agglutition of onvolution-
ary p 135, l 25
phenomenon: phenomena p 136, l 34
waved: possibly 'saved' p 137, l 36
masterpieces: masterpiece p 148, l 15

WHOM GOD HATH JOINED – typescript dating from 1934–7, Public
Archives of Canada, Klein Papers 4480–4504
ample features: apple features p 160, l 35
A jury was enrolled: In a marginal note Klein added: 'A
jury of his peers?' p 165, l 33
testify against himself: In a marginal note Klein added:
'Besides can't put one in witness box without other.' p 168,
l 9

YCLEPT A PIP – typescript dating from 1934–7, Public Archives
of Canada, Klein Papers 4505–16. By Marco Kirkham

NO TRAVELLER RETURNS ... – typescript titled 'From Whose
Bourne ... ' dating from 1934–7, Public Archives of
Canada, Klein Papers 2973–80
This story, with a change of title and only a few other minor
changes, was published in *The Canadian Jewish Chronicle*,
30 June 1944. For the typescript Klein used the pseudonym Marco Kirkham; for the printed story he changed the
pseudonym to Arthur Haktani, a play on his own name
(Haktani in Hebrew means 'the little one' or in German and
Yiddish 'klein'). In the Klein Papers 2981–5 there is an
incomplete and undated typescript of this story with a number of variations. Klein's final version (1944) is presented
here, but because the changes are minor, the story is placed

at the more appropriate earlier date in the chronological sequence.

corners: corner. In both typescripts Klein uses the plural. p 187, l 23

PORTRAIT OF AN EXECUTIONER – typescript headed Rouyn, Quebec, where Klein spent the year 1937–8 practising law; Public Archives of Canada, Klein Papers 3441–53. By Marco Kirkham

This story is a somewhat fictionalized treatment of an interview that Klein had with Arthur Ellis, Canada's official hangman, in 1936, at which time Klein obtained the rights to Ellis's memoirs. Klein also wrote a poem 'In Memoriam: Arthur Ellis,' Public Archives of Canada, Klein Papers 2101.

THE TALE OF THE MARVELLOUS PARROT – *The Canadian Zionist* IV, 10 (March 1937); reprinted in *The Canadian Jewish Chronicle* (11 April 1941)

MEMOIRS OF A CAMPAIGNER – *The Canadian Zionist* V, 2 (May 1937)

DETECTIVE STORY OR A LIKELY STORY – undated manuscript, probably 1943, Public Archives of Canada, Klein Papers 3582–4. 'Detective Story' appears as a story within chapter 2 of Klein's projected novel 'The Golem'; see Public Archives of Canada, Klein Papers 3323–7.

WE WHO ARE ABOUT TO BE BORN – *The Canadian Jewish Chronicle* (2 June 1944)

The version used here is the published version as amended by Klein on his tear-sheet. Klein may have intended this tale to be a story within a story. On the proof-sheet of this story Klein added the following marginal note: 'Shall this story be attributed to a mediaeval author read by Rabbi Loew, and prompting the creation of the golem?' Klein is here referring to a projected novel, of which he completed two chapters. Also in the Klein Papers is a page headed *A Documentary*, with commentary, in which Klein lists 64 items, many autobiographical; number 11 reads 'Story of We who are about to be born,' while number 12 lists 'Story of Utopia,' probably a reference to his story 'One More Utopia.'

which is on earth: 'on earth' is an approximate reading of two quite indecipherable words in Klein's handwriting p 215, l 13

ONE MORE UTOPIA – *The Canadian Jewish Chronicle* (7 September 1945)
This story was produced by Rupert Caplan as a radio play in the CBC series 'Play of the Week.' It was adapted for radio by Aaron Harvey. A copy of the script is in the Public Archives of Canada, Klein Papers 3426–40. See note above for 'We Who Are About to Be Born.'

THE TRAIL OF 'CLUPEA HARENGUS': THE SCIENTIFIC DETECTIVE STORY AND HOW SHE IS WRIT FOR SUMMER READING – *The Canadian Jewish Chronicle* (28 June 1946)

KAPUSITCHKA – *The Canadian Jewish Chronicle* (15 October 1948)
Although there is no record of an earlier publication and no manuscript is available, this story, or a version of it, was probably written much earlier. A letter from Leo Kennedy to Klein in 1936 contains a reference to it. The 1948 date is kept here, however, in the chronological listing as there is no way of knowing what changes, if any, Klein made in the story between 1936 and 1948; in fact, we cannot even be certain that a complete earlier version existed.

wore her hair, that was golden: wore her hair that were golden p 233, ll 32–3

... AND IT SHALL COME TO PASS – *The Canadian Jewish Chronicle* (29 October 1948)

AND THE MOME RATHS OUTGRABE – *Here and Now* (June 1949)
In this story Klein uses various forms of the title for the
Lewis Carroll poem: *The Jabberwocky, The Jabberwock,*
and *Jabberwocky.* In three draft typescripts, Public Archives
of Canada, Klein Papers 2751–2801, Klein does not begin
new paragraphs at the following places: p 244: 'But of this,
or of the profounder ... '; p 246: 'Now whether this universally shared ... '; and p 247: 'In a poem of this kind ... '
double-ententes: Klein has *double-entendres* in his typescripts
p 247, l 9
Symbolic Logic: symbolic logic p 251, l 16
The method of the bellowing ... : The typescript version reads
'The mathod of the ballowing is now relantlessly exposed'
and Klein seems to suggest there that the sentence be set
off in a separate paragraph. p 252, l 13

LETTER FROM AFAR – typescript, probable date 1949, Public
Archives of Canada, Klein Papers 3333–52
Klein was intrigued by the puzzling behaviour of the defend-
ants in the Soviet show trials, their seemingly willing, even
eager, confessions. His recurring interest is evidenced in a
number of statements. In one note (Klein Papers 3332) he
explored the question: 'Why do they confess? What is it
that makes these hardened revolutionaries, these tough
political-minded apaches suddenly turn soft like putty
beneath a prosecutor's gaze? ... ' In a letter to his literary
agent, dated 15 December 1949, which accompanied this
story, he wrote:

Dear Miss McKee
'How are the notorious Russian confessions extorted?'
This has been a question which has agitated the pub-
lic mind since 1936, date of the first Trial of the Sixteen.
Enclosed please find a short story – 4500 words –
advancing an entirely new hypothesis concerning the man-

ner and method of these confessions. Not torture, not drugs, not hypnotism.

The title you will no doubt recognize as that of Lenin's famous communication from his exile in the British Museum to his disciples in Russia ...

A few months later, in an editorial entitled 'The Confessions,' he returned to the subject (*The Canadian Jewish Chronicle*, 24 February 1950).

A FABLE – *The Canadian Jewish Chronicle* (8 August 1952)
This animal tale was published as an editorial in *The Canadian Jewish Chronicle*.
not only not sporting: not only sporting p 272, l 9
united rations: possibly should read 'united nations' p 272, l 21

THE BELLS OF SOBOR SPASITULA – typescript, probable date 1955, Public Archives of Canada, Klein Papers 2827–2972

Notes

Cheshbon Hanefesh: spiritual self-examination and self-appraisal

fainéantism: idleness, sluggishness

prophet ... fed by ravens: Elijah, 1 Kings 17:6

Laudas divitias, sequeris inertiam: You praise riches, you follow laziness.

Litvacks: Lithuanian Jews, often regarded as hair-splitting pedants

Sambation: legendary river across which part of the ten 'lost tribes' were exiled by the Assyrians

artistocrat: probably a Klein coinage, a compounding of 'artist' and 'aristocrat,' though possibly it is a typographical error

Catullus: Roman lyric poet of the 1st century BC

Lewisohn: Ludwig Lewisohn (1882–1955), American writer whose autobiography *Up Stream* (1922) recounts his experience with anti-semitism at US universities

Hillel, who declared: Hillel, outstanding rabbinic authority in the 1st century BC; Pirke Avoth (Ethics of the Fathers) 1: 13

Rabbi Zadok ... enjoined: Pirke Avoth IV:7

poet royal: David. See Psalms 7:15

pilpul: a method of Talmudic study involving sharp dialectical argumentation, 'logic-chopping'

Shemayah ... bade: Shemayah and Avtalyon, two leading rabbinic scholars in 1st century BC, teachers of Hillel; Pirke Avoth 1:10

mon frère et mon semblable: my brother and my likeness. Klein echoes Baudelaire's 'Au lecteur' in *Les Fleurs du Mal* 'Hypocrite lecteur, – mon semblable – mon frère!'

upper Pamalyah: Heavenly court

six hundred and thirteen injunctions: the number of obliga-
tions, positive and negative, incumbent on the Jew

St Augustine: while studying law in Carthage, St Augustine
(354–430) led a sensual life and abandoned his Christianity.
After returning to his faith, he became one of the most
influential medieval Christian theologians.

Kashruth: Jewish dietary laws

shealith (sing. shalah): legal questions addressed to a rabbi

phylacteries of Rashi and Rabbenu Tam: reference to a dispute
between Rashi, the great biblical exegete (1040–1105),
and his son-in-law, Rabbenu Tam, regarding the proper
placing of the biblical passages in the phylacteries

Mikvah: ritual bath

Nidah: Talmudic tractate dealing with ritual uncleanness

minyan: a congregation of at least ten adult Jewish males needed
for communal prayer

Malthus: the Rev. Thomas Malthus (1766–1834), British
political economist noted for his theory of population growth

executioner of fowls: a 'shochet,' a religious Jew trained to practise kosher slaughtering

Mohel: a Jew qualified by piety and training to perform ritual
circumcisions

Hagar: Abraham's servant and concubine, mother of Ishmael;
Genesis 21:15–21

Midrashic quotations: Midrash, commentaries on the Bible, from
c400–1200 AD

Purim: a festival celebrating the saving of the Jewish people from
massacre in Persia (see Book of Esther); a time for giving of
gifts

Chometz: food not permitted for use on Passover, which has to
be disposed of just prior to the fesival

Kaddish: a kind of 'magnificat' in Jewish liturgy, of which one
form, the 'mourners'' kaddish, is recited by the nearest male
kin of the deceased

Rabbi Joshua the son of Levi: 3rd century AD, renowned authority on Jewish religious law

Rabbi Akiva: c50–135 AD, probably the foremost scholar of his age. He exercised a decisive influence on the development of 'halacha,' the code of Jewish religious laws.

am ha'araz: a simple or an uneducated man

like Aaron: according to Jewish tradition, the High Priest Aaron, brother of Moses, loved peace and pursued it. See Pirke Avoth 1:12.

mitzvah: commandment or religious duty; good deed

It is good: Genesis 1

greater things than are dreamed of: Shakespeare, *Hamlet* 1:5

PROPHET IN OUR MIDST: A STORY FOR PASSOVER

Haggadah: narrative of exodus from Egypt, supplemented by prayer and song, recited Passover eve

Cheder: Jewish elementary religious school

Four Questions: the reading of the Haggadah is introduced by someone, usually the youngest person present, asking four set questions regarding the festival

Jeshurun grew fat: Deuteronomy 32:15

matzoh: unleavened bread eaten during Passover week

Mizraim: Egypt

Seder: 'order' (of service); the term is applied to the reciting of the Haggadah and the Passover meal

Shagitz: young non-Jew, impious person

Elijah Hanavi: Elijah the prophet

Afikomen: the morsel of matzoh with which one ends the Passover feast

BY THE PROFIT OF A BEARD

Chassidic: pertaining to religious sects that emphasize worship through joyful song and dance as well as through set prayers and study

Zaddik: an exceptionally good and righteous person, a holy man

Shechinah: the Divine Presence or Immanence

Torah: the Holy Scriptures, and by extension all learning related to the Scriptures

goyim (sing. goy): non-Jew

Kaddish: a kind of 'magnificat' in Jewish liturgy, of which one
form, the 'mourners'' kaddish, is recited by the nearest male
kin of the deceased

Krias Shma: recital of biblical passages (Deuteronomy 6:4–9,
11:13–21, Numbers 15:37–41) in morning and evening
prayers and at bedtime, affirming faith in One God

Gabriel: the high-ranking archangel who serves as messenger
of Divine Comfort

how do you like something America: Klein occasionally trans-
lates a Yiddish idiom very literally.

taki: truly

Haggai: supervisor of the king's female household in the Book of
Esther

goyishe-kepp: non-Jewish mentality, dullards

leviathan: fabulous sea-creature, according to Jewish legend
the food for the righteous in the eternal afterlife

THE LOST TWINS

Yom Kippur: Day of Atonement, the most important of the
High Holydays

Kaporah: sacrificial animal, scapegoat

traifa: unkosher, ritually unclean

shalah: legal question addressed to a rabbi

Kol Nidre: melodious prayer chanted at opening service for Day
of Atonement

Chala: egg-bread, usually braided, baked for the Sabbath and
holidays

matzah: unleavened bread eaten during the week of Passover

Leviathan: fabulous sea-creature, according to legend the food
for the righteous in the eternal afterlife

Mogen Dovid: six-pointed Star of David, conventional Jewish
symbol

Mazuzah: parchment scroll affixed to doorposts of Jewish homes
affirming the principle of monotheism and faith; Deuteronomy 6:9

Shaddai: one of the names by which God is known, expressing
     attribute of might
Og, king of Bashan: giant king defeated by the Israelites led by
     Moses; Numbers 21:33–5
Shabbos Goy: a non-Jew who performs tasks for Jews forbid-
     den to them on the Sabbath, eg, lighting a fire
Kol Yisroel: all Israel

THE TRIUMPH OF ZALMAN TIKTINER
Titus: Roman general who captured Jerusalem and destroyed
     the Temple in 70 AD
Erez Israel: land of Israel
Yeshivah: Talmudic academy
Herzl: Theodore Herzl (1860–1904), father of modern Zionism
Chassidim: fervently pious Jews; members of religious sect who
     stress joy in worship as well as set prayers and study
mit leiten gleich: like everyone else
Seder-service: the service at the Passover feast
psiyas ha-derech: miraculous shortening of a journey
maskel: enlightened one, emancipated person
parnassah: livelihood
Allenby: Edmund Allenby (1861–1936), British commander
     in the Middle East during World War I; liberated Palestine
     from the Turks
Jabotinsky: Vladimir Jabotinsky (1880–1940), militant Zionist
     leader, founder of the Revisionist Movement
Chalutzim: pioneers, early Jewish settlers in Palestine

THE PARLIAMENT OF FOWLES: A SHORT STORY
Behold his bed: Song of Songs (Song of Solomon) 3:7
Hiram: supplied cedars of Lebanon to King David for his palace,
     and later to Solomon for the building of the Temple
Queen of Sheba: a royal visitor who, according to tradition, came
     to test Solomon's reputed wisdom
cripple ... Mizraim: probably Pasebkhanu II, Solomon's Egyptian
     father-in-law

Mizraim: Egypt

Shunamite: probably should be Shulamite, Solomon's beloved, celebrated in Song of Songs; Shunamite refers to Abishag, the lovely young woman chosen as nurse-companion to King David in his old age and final illness; possibly both Shunamite and Shulamite refer to the same person

biped moulted birds of the Greek philosopher: men. In response to Plato's definition of man as a biped animal without feathers, Diogenes the Cynic sent him, by way of comment, a plucked fowl. See Diogenes Laertius, *Lives of the Philosophers*, ch. 15.

parody of a well-known author: Robert Browning's 'Song' from *Pippa Passes*

benediction upon hearing: the first of a sequence of benedictions at the outset of the morning prayer service

footstool of the Lord: Isaiah 66:1

C'est mon métier: that's my line

Sang the nightingale: the nightingale's speech is in sonnet form without rhyme

The flowers appear on the earth: Song of Songs 2:12

THE CHANUKAH DREIDEL

The symbol (K) indicates Klein's translation of the term, provided by him at the end of the story.

Chanukah: festival celebrating the victory of the Maccabees over the Syrian king Antiochus Epiphanes, and the subsequent rededication of the Temple in 164 BC

dreidel: a spinning top

Chassidic: pertaining to religious sects that emphasize worship through joyful song and dance as well as through set prayers and study

tzitzith: a fringe of threads worn by pious Jews on the four corners of a garment or prayer shawl; Deuteronomy 22:12

afikomen: the morsel of matzoh eaten at the conclusion of the Passover feast

caftan: long cloak worn by Chassidim (K)

Zaddik: a saintly person; a title sometimes bestowed on the
    leader of a Chassidic sect
Baal Shem: Israel Baal Shem Tov (c1700–60), literally 'Master
    of the Good Name'; founder of Chassidism
Pamalyah Shel Ma'ola: Celestial Tribunal (K)
zmiros: Hebrew for 'Songs' usually the songs sung after meals
    (K)
roast Leviathan: according to Jewish legend, the leviathan will be
    food for the righteous in the afterlife
Tosfoth: literally 'additions,' meaning additional commentaries
    to the Talmud (K)
Mattathias: the mover of the revolt against Antiochus and the
    father of Judah Maccabee
shtreimel: the fur cap worn by Chassidim (K)
latke: Yiddish for 'pancake,' favourite food on Chanukah (K)
gematria: mystical interpretations of the values of the Hebrew
    letters (K)
trendel: a spinning top
Shaddai: one of the names by which God is known, signifying
    might
Shofar: ram's horn, to be blown to announce the coming of the
    Messiah; also sounded on the High Holydays
Yomtov: holiday
yarmulkah: skull-cap
misnagdim: Jewish opponents of the Chassidim

THE MEED OF THE MINNESINGER
A VIVID SHORT STORY BASED ON THE LIFE OF
A GREAT THIRTEENTH-CENTURY POET

Susskind von Trimberg: a famed minnesinger in early 13th-
    century Germany who abandoned his role at the court of the
    nobility to share the plight of his fellow Jews
Edom: in biblical times a bitter enemy of Israel, described by
    Isaiah as an enemy who knew neither righteousness nor
    pity in its dealings with Israel
Covenant of Abraham: the rite of circumcision

Mizraim: Egypt
peccavi: I have sinned
'By the rivers of Babylon': Psalms 137:1–4
goyim: gentiles
Chazanuth: cantorial singing
When Esau greeted his brother: Genesis 33:4
Halevi: Yehudah (Judah) Halevi (c1075–c1141), famed Hebrew
    poet and scholar, who was born in Spain and died on a
    pilgrimage to the Holy Land. See Klein's poem 'Yehuda Ha-
    Levi, His Pilgrimage.'
Maariv service: evening prayer service
Qui rejecit accipiat: He who has rejected will accept.
mezuzahs: parchment scrolls affixed to doorposts of Jewish homes
    affirming faith and the principle of monotheism; Deuteron-
    omy 6:9

MASTER OF THE HORN
Tsoros: troubles, misfortunes
minyan: a congregation of at least ten adult Jewish men needed
    for communal prayers
Kedusha: literally 'Holiness,' a prayer recited during congrega-
    tional service
Landsleit: fellow countrymen
Haggada: sections of the Talmud and Midrash containing homi-
    letic exposition, parables, stories, maxims, as distinct from
    the legal sections called 'halacha'
Anshe Volhynia: Fellowship of Volhynia. Klein, as an infant,
    came with his parents from the Russian province of Vol-
    hynia to Canada.
un Maudit Juif: a damned Jew
frask: slap
Covenant of Abraham: rite of circumcision
Frelichs: a merry tune
Ellul: Hebrew month in late summer just preceding Rosh
    Hashanah

Shofar: a ram's horn sounded once each morning, except on
  Sabbath, during the month of Ellul, and on the High Holy-
  days
Rosh Hashanah: the Jewish New Year's day
Gabbai: synagogue official
Tekiah: a note sounded on the shofar
Mizrach wall: eastern wall, reserved for honoured congregants
tallis: prayer-shawl
And cast us not aside: excerpt from a prayer recited frequently
  during the High Holyday services

THE PARROT AND THE GOAT
Chad Gadyah: 'one only kid,' opening line of the concluding
  song of the Passover feast
zuzim: an ancient Middle Eastern coin of small denomination
Abib: a month in the Jewish calendar corresponding to a period in
  March–April, the period during which the Passover festival occurs

ONCE UPON A TIME ...
Titania: Queen of Fairyland in Shakespeare's *A Midsummer
  Night's Dream*
Robin Goodfellow: the fairy Puck, a playful goblin
Peaseblossom ... Moth: fairies in Shakespeare's *A Midsummer
  Night's Dream*
von Hindenburg: commander of German army in World War I
  and President of Germany 1925–34
Elijah: according to Jewish legend, the prophet Elijah visits every
  Jewish home during the Passover feast and sips from a
  wine cup set aside in his honour.
last of the Mohicohens: a typical Kleinian pun alluding to
  James Fenimore Cooper's novel *The Last of the Mohicans*

SHMELKA
rebbe: teacher
shadchan: marriage broker

THE SEVENTH SCROLL

twenty-two seals of Deity: letters of the Hebrew alphabet

Shein ... Dalid: letters in the Hebrew alphabet; 'iota' refers to the Hebrew letter 'yud.' Later in the story Klein refers to the Hai and the Ches, two letters which closely resemble each other in sound and shape.

Shaddai: one of God's names, expressing the attribute of might

mezuzahs: parchment scrolls affixed to doorposts of Jewish homes affirming faith and the principle of monotheism; Deuteronomy 6:9

ben-Kamzar: Talmud, Tractate Yoma 38b

Yud-Hai-Vav-Hai: the tetragrammaton, letters forming God's name

Ezekiel's injunction: probably a reference to Ezekiel 44:7

twenty-four fast days: Talmud, Tractate Pessachim 50b

Chazak! Chazak!: At the end of the public reading of each of the Five Books of Moses during the Sabbath service, the congregants stand and in unison cry out 'Chazak! Chazak! V'nischazak!' ie, 'Be strong, be strong and be strengthened!'

Mishnaioth (sing. Mishna): the texts recording the oral law which is the basis of the Talmud

virtuous woman: Proverbs 31:10

tzitzith: a fringe of threads worn by pious Jews on the four corners of a garment or prayer-shawl; Deuteronomy 22:12

the great terror: Deuteronomy 34:12

cheder: Jewish primary religious school

Sefer Torah: the Torah scroll

Miriam-bath-Rachel: Miriam the daughter of Rachel

lulav: palm branch carried during Succoth, the Feast of the Tabernacles

Talmud Chacham: very learned Talmudic scholar

mensch: man, used here in the sense of man of stature or dignity

Male and female: Genesis 1:27

son of eighteen years: Talmud, Tractate Kiddushin 30a

fructify and multiply: Genesis 1:22 and 1:28

marry first and study afterwards: Talmud, Tractate Kiddushin
     29b
'You hang millstones': Talmud, Tractate Kiddushin 29b
mitzvah: commandment or religious duty; good deed
Tauna (tanna): rabbinic scholar in the period of the first and
     second centuries AD
wears a perruque: Jewish religious law requires married women
     to keep their hair covered.
kaddish: a 'magnificat,' in one form a mourner's prayer recited
     by the nearest male kin of the deceased, usually a son. By
     extension the term is applied to the offspring who has or will
     have the responsibility to recite it.
Chai v'kayom: literally means 'living and everlasting'; the phrase
     'go scream "chai v'kayom"' is a popular expression derived
     from the liturgy, uttered ironically to denote futility
golem: witless creature
make of the Torah either a crown: Pirke Avoth IV:7
give ear O ye heavens: Deuteronomy 32:1

BLOOD AND IRON: A SATIRE ON MODERN GERMAN
IDEOLOGY
Big Bertha: huge cannon built by Germans in World War I for
     firing across the English Channel from the French coast

FRIENDS, ROMANS, HUNGRYMEN
Ezekiel's chariot: Ezekiel 1
Friends, Romans ... tears: a play on Antony's speech in Shake-
     speare's *Julius Caesar* III:2
asked ... wait for an answer: an echoing of the opening lines in
     Francis Bacon's essay 'Of Truth'

A MYRIAD-MINDED MAN
Be fruitful and multiply: Genesis 1:28
nuit de noce: wedding night
mirabile visu: marvellous to see

Demostheneses: Demosthenes, famed Greek orator, 4th century BC

the Psalmist combined in one verse: Psalms 137

goy: gentile

Theocritus: Greek pastoral poet, 3rd century BC

Canticum Canticorum: Song of Songs (Song of Solomon)

shepherd ... En-gedi: probably David, who hid in the caves of En-gedi when fleeing from Saul; 1 Samuel 24

Mizraim: Egypt

Graetz: Heinrich Graetz (1817–91) Jewish historian

massacre of Kishineff: a particularly vicious pogrom in 1903 in the Russian province of Bessarabia

'O, Eli, Eli': 'O God, my God, why hast Thou forsaken me?'; Psalms 22:1

Judaei quorum cophinus faenumque supellex: Jews, whose furniture is basket and hay; Juvenal, *Satires* III:14

keepers of the vineyard: Song of Songs (Song of Solomon) 1:6

Mamaluge: cornmeal cake

kugel: pudding

lokshen kugel: noodle pudding

Sir Oliver Lodge and Conan Doyle: Lodge (1851–1940), British physicist and author; Doyle (1859–1920), famed writer of detective stories

orare est laborare: to pray is to work

physic ... to the dogs: Shakespeare, *Macbeth* v:3

Ahriman and Ormuzd: Zoroastrian supreme spirits of darkness (or evil) and of light

shaidim (sing. shaid): demons; for Rabbi Jochanan's assertion see Talmud, Tractate Gittin 68a

manner of Xerxes: Xerxes is supposed to have chastised the sea for destroying the bridges across the Hellespont which he had built in preparation for his invasion of Greece.

matzoh: unleavened bread eaten during the week of Passover

Fiat Lux: Let there be Light.

Shamas: sexton

Mincha and Maariv: afternoon and evening prayer services

batlanim: synagogue habitués; in current usage usually a pejorative term denoting idlers

Mikvah: ritual bath

shechita: kosher slaughtering

genizah: repository for damaged religious books and articles

shemoth: names, writings

Shulchan Aruch: code of Jewish laws compiled and systematized by Joseph Karo in the 16th century

funest: baneful, deadly

thanksgiving that the Lord saw fit: Jews are enjoined to voice a special blessing on beholding a strange or exotic creature or sight; Talmud, Tractate Berochoth 58a

fetor: stench

Hierosolyma est delenda: Jerusalem must be destroyed; cf. 'Carthago est delenda,' the slogan used by Cato the Elder to inspire the third Punic War and the destruction of Carthage

Chamberlain ... and Drumont: noted European anti-semitic writers in the late 19th and early 20th centuries

And from thine own loins: free rendering of Isaiah 49:17

Lo the poor Indian: Pope, *Essay on Man*, Epistle 1:99

sangre azul: blue blood

At the head of death: Talmud, Tractate Baba Bathra 58b

Trebitsch Lincoln: (1879–1943), Hungarian-born adventurer and spy

WHOM GOD HATH JOINED

Blackstone ... Coke: Sir William Blackstone (1723–80) and Sir Edward Coke (1552–1634) famed British jurists

la glorieuse incertitude de la loi: glorious incertitude of the law

obiter dictum: passing remark

Beelzebub: pagan deity, meaning 'Lord of the Flies'

tzigane: gypsy

Janus: Roman deity represented as having two faces looking in opposite directions

Omnibus has literas inspecturis salutem in Domino: Greetings
    in the Lord to all those who are examining these writings
    (credentials)
Ezekiel's vision: Ezekiel 1:4–28
chicane: quarrel
Procureur de la Couronne: Crown Prosecutor
mariage de méconvenance: marriage of inconvenience
Justinian: Byzantine emperor (483–565) in whose time the
    code of laws known as the Justinian Code was formulated
rabat: neck band worn by some judges and members of the
    legal and clerical professions
calèche: carriage
sine die: without any date specified
And in their death they were not divided: 2 Samuel 1:23

YCLEPT A PIP
In addition to the quotations and slight paraphrases from Shake-
    speare's plays listed below, there are many passing allusions
    and verbal echoes not listed.
b.o.: a widely advertised abbreviation for 'body odour'
'Look on beauty': *The Merchant of Venice* III:2
Will Shakespeare ... All American: (1912–74), triple threat half-
    back for Notre Dame University 1933–5
'for sufferance is the badge': *The Merchant of Venice* I:3
'Speak your speech': *Hamlet* III:2
'void my rheum': *The Merchant of Venice* I:3
'dulcet and harmonious breath': *A Midsummer-Night's Dream*
    II:1
Marylin Sonnenscheidt: probable reference to Marlene Diet-
    rich, movie star
'Were it not better ... martial outside': *As You Like It* I:3 –
    paraphrased
Benny Jonson: Ben Jonson (c1573–1637), famed playwright
    and poet, contemporary and friend of Shakespeare
Anne Hathaway: (1557–1623), wife of Shakespeare
a Swede: possibly a reference to Greta Garbo

'an infinite deal of nothing': *The Merchant of Venice* 1:1
'still vexed Bermuthes': *The Tempest* 1:2
'there are more things ... philosophy': *Hamlet* 1:5
'The brain may devise laws': *The Merchant of Venice* 1:2
'like Niobe, all tears': *Hamlet* 1:2

NO TRAVELLER RETURNS ...
Similes similibus curant: They cure similar things with similar
    things.

THE TALE OF THE MARVELLOUS PARROT
rebbe of Berditchev: Rabbi Levi Yitschok (1740–1809), Chassidic
    leader and scholar, known as 'the merciful one.' See Klein's
    poem 'Reb Levi Yitschok Talks to God.'
chassidim: literally 'the pious ones'; followers of a chassidic
    rebbe (rabbi). They emphasize fervour and joy in worship as
    well as scholarship and ritual observance (chassidim'lach:
    'little chassidim' – a term of endearment).
leviathan: fabulous sea-creature which, according to legend,
    will be food for the righteous in the afterlife
shekinah (shechinah): Divine Presence or Immanence
Rebono shel Olam: Master of the Universe
Kaddish: a 'magnificat,' one form of which is the mourner's
    prayer, recited by the nearest male kin, usually a son
Father Abraham and the Three Angels: Genesis 18:1–16
Prayer, fasting and alms ... decree: Midrash Rabba, Genesis 44:15
lamed-vovnik: one of the 36 anonymous righteous persons for
    whose sake the world is preserved
mithnagdim: Jewish opponents of chassidim
gabbai: synagogue official
'The Lord giveth': Job 1:21
Beth Ha-Midrash: House of Study
'Yisgadal v'yiskadash shmai raba!': 'Magnified and sanctified be
    His great name!' – the opening proclamation of the Kad-
    dish prayer

MEMOIRS OF A CAMPAIGNER

Alter Chodosh: a fictitious name meaning 'Old New'

King of Schnorrers: a novella (1894) by Israel Zangwill, British novelist; schnorrer – beggar, freeloader

Eretz Israel: Land of Israel

fat Jeshuruns: Deuteronomy 32:15

Altneuland: title of a Zionist novel (1902), 'Old New-Land' by Theodor Herzl, the father of modern political Zionism

Quot Judaei, tot sententiae: so many Jews, so many opinions

weh: woe

Lakchonim bnai rachmonim: takers, sons of compassionate men

lev: heart

kis: pocket, purse

Kislev: Hebrew month, about November-December

nishkoshe: all right, satisfactory, not bad

tzip: light tug

Nein, ich gib nisht: No, I don't give

U.P.A.: United Palestine Appeal

Sokolow: Nahum Sokolow (1860–1936), noted British Zionist leader

shmoos: chat

Weizmann: Chaim Weizmann (1874–1952), distinguished scientist and statesman, President of the World Zionist Organization (1920–30, 1935–46), first President of the State of Israel

Nordau: Max Nordau (1849–1923), European intellectual and critic, associated with Herzl in founding the World Zionist Organization

aleph bet: alphabet

kometz-aleph-o: traditionally a child's first lesson in reading Hebrew; the letter 'aleph' with the vowel sound 'kometz' beneath it produces the sound 'o'

achainu bnai Yisrael: our brother Jews

To thine own self: *Hamlet* I:3

THE TRAIL OF 'CLUPEA HARENGUS': THE SCIENTIFIC
DETECTIVE STORY AND HOW SHE IS WRIT FOR
SUMMER READING

Aristotle's anthropophagi: a reference to cannibals mentioned
in Aristotle's *Politics*, Bk 8, ch. 4, 1338b

the thirty-six plots of Gozzi: Gozzi, 16th-century Italian
dramatist

'And this will be no wonder to any': Izaak Walton, *The Compleat Angler*, ch. 19

It could a tale unfold: *Hamlet* 1:5

S.S. Dan Vine: play on the name of the well-known detective
story writer S.S. Van Dine (1888–1939), creator of the
detective-character Philo Vance

Ariel's Caliban: Ariel and Caliban, preternatural characters in
Shakespeare's *The Tempest*

'Canst thou put a hook': Job 41:2

'By his neesings a light': Job 41:18–20

'One may not doubt': Rupert Brooke, 'Heaven'

KAPUSITCHKA

allees: glass marbles with colour swirls inside

pollyseeds: sunflower seeds

You'll forget everything: reference to an old Jewish superstition

Me for his little head: literal translation of a Jewish saying which
means 'if harm is to befall, let it fall on me and not on
him'

AND IT SHALL COME TO PASS

'In the beginning God created': Genesis 1:1–2

AND THE MOME RATHS OUTGRABE

Some of the critics referred to in this story may be identified as
follows: C.B. – Cleanth Brooks; E.W. – Edmund Wilson;
the poet X (really k.s.) – Karl Shapiro.

cauchemar: nightmare

Malory: Sir Thomas Malory (c1394–1471), author of *Morte Darthur*, a medieval romance
Eliot's footman: see T.S. Eliot's poem 'The Love Song of J. Alfred Prufrock.'
PMLA: *Publications of the Modern Languages Association*, an important academic journal
hapaxlegomenon: a word used once only in any book or document
Krylov: famed Russian fabulist (1769–1844)

LETTER FROM AFAR
coup de la personne: personal coup
Peccavi: I have sinned
Svengalis: Svengali, a villainous hypnotist in George du Maurier's *Trilby* (1894)
traitor ... in Mexico: Leon Trotsky, denounced as a deviationist by Stalin, and assassinated in Mexico in 1940
cauchemar: nightmare
Zinoviev ... Ter-Vaganian: Soviet leaders who were convicted in a show trial in 1936 during a Stalinist purge of Trotskyists and other possible rivals to Stalin

THE BELLS OF SOBOR SPASITULA
Sobor Spasitula: Cathedral of the Saviour, one of the most beautiful of the Russian cathedrals, which was situated in what is now Red Square
pied-à-terre: temporary lodging
Malenkov of a moon: Malenkov was the rotund premier of Soviet Russia after the death of Stalin.
Tartarus: region in Hell reserved for punishment of the wicked
le dernier cri: the latest fashion
Ivan Veliky ... Pokrovsky: the bell-tower of Ivan the Great in the Pokrovsky cathedral, located in the Kremlin
cénacle: literary coterie

au dessus de la bataille: outside or beyond the battle

esprit de l'escalier: a witty retort that springs to mind after the occasion for it has passed

entrechats: ballet steps

shining constellations that Kant converted: a reference to the opening statement in the conclusion to Kant's *A Critique of Practical Reason*: 'Two things fill the mind with ever new and increasing wonder and awe ... the starry heavens above and the moral law within me.'

'The heart has reasons ... ': Pascal, *Pensées* 227

stanitza: large Cossack village

clefs-à-dents: possibly a slang expression, or in error for 'cure-dents' meaning 'tooth-picks'

nom-de-guerre: assumed name

Pavlov: Ivan Pavlov (1849–1936), Russian physiologist who developed the notion of conditioned reflexes

café-chantant: a café that provides entertainment

moujik: peasant, illiterate or coarse person

kakouchkos: decorative woman's headdress in Old Russia; Klein uses what is probably a corrupt form of 'kakouchnik'

boyars: circle of czarist courtiers

the S.R.'s: Social Revolutionaries, a political movement of agrarian reformers

narod: people, masses

slabost: a weakness

prikaz: regulation or order

Baron Wrangel: general in the counter-revolutionary White Army

la deuxième nuit ... classe: the second night that was first class

zukunftsmusik: music of the coming age

Romanoff-Rasputin: Romanoff, the family name of the Russian czars from 1613 until the abdication of Nicholas ii in 1917; Rasputin, a Russian 'monk' who exercised great influence over Czar Nicholas ii and the czarina

baraban: drum

Gutchkov-Miliukov duet: both Gutchkov and Miliukov were members of Kerensky's cabinet in the Russian Provisional government of 1917 and were later prominent in the counter-revolutionary movement.

coulisses: wings

aubade: morning serenade

chaud-froid: cold, jellied

This book
was designed by
WILLIAM RUETER
and was printed by
University of
Toronto
Press

DATE DUE
DATE DE RETOUR
